A NEST OF VIPERS

A NEST OF VIPERS

A Bangalore Detectives Club Mystery

HARINI NAGENDRA

PEGASUS CRIME

NEW YORK LONDON

A NEST OF VIPERS

Pegasus Crime is an imprint of
Pegasus Books, Ltd.
148 West 37th Street, 13th Floor
New York, NY 10018

Copyright © 2024 by Harini Nagendra

First Pegasus Books cloth edition May 2024

ISBN: 978-1-63936-614-9

10 9 8 7 6 5 4 3 2 1

Printed in the United States of America
Distributed by Simon & Schuster
www.pegasusbooks.com

For Venkatachalam Suri and
Dhwani Nagendra Suri, always

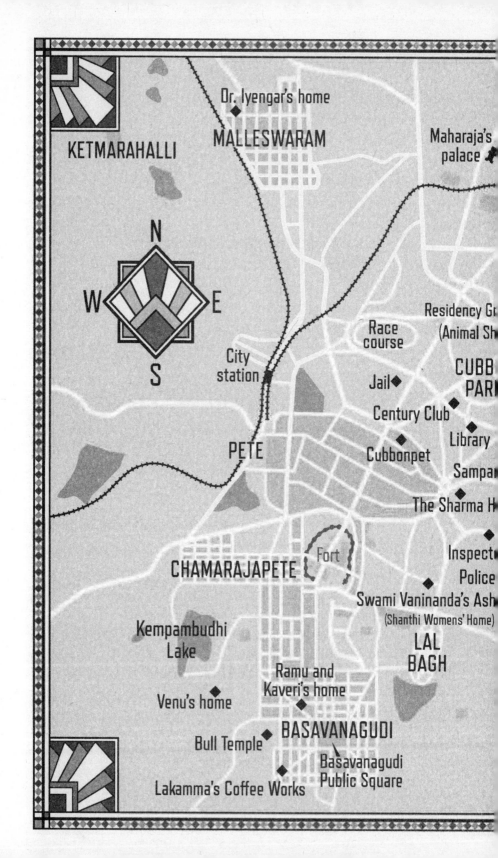

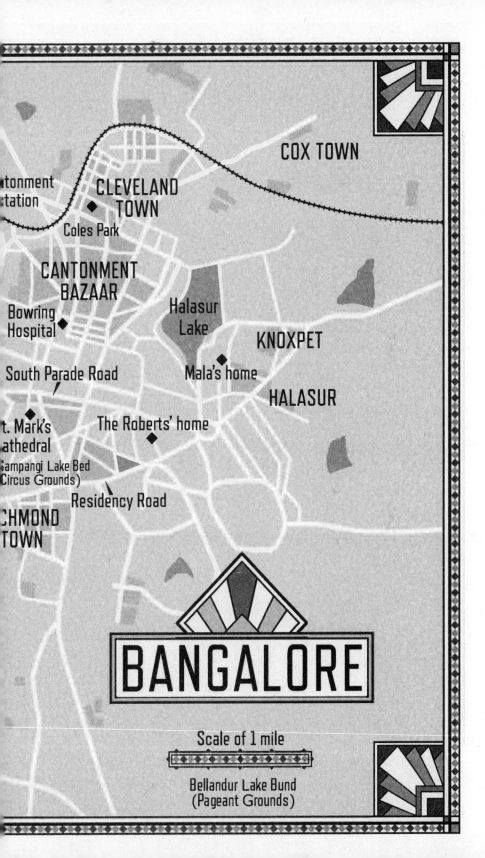

This story takes place in 1920s Bangalore, so a few of the words may be unfamiliar.

If you don't know them, **Kaveri's Dictionary** on page 324 will tell you what they mean and how to pronounce them. It also explains a bit about the geography and history behind this book.

And read onto Kaveri's Beauty Routine on page 327 for some fun tips.

1
Wrestling a Tiger

'Where did all the animals go?' asked Miss Roberts, poking Kaveri with a bony finger.

Kaveri gazed around the interior of the Maximilian Circus tent where they were seated, trying her best to ignore Dr Roberts' acerbic maiden sister. It *was* a good question, though. At least fifty feet high, the tent had space to seat over a thousand – people, not animals. Surely a circus of this size ought to have animals?

'I think they're in cages, at the side,' Anandi leaned over to respond. Miss Roberts' eyes narrowed, taking in the fact that a native 'servant maid' had had the effrontery to address her directly. With a haughty sniff, she looked away. *How rude*, Kaveri thought, glaring at her back. Anandi seemed unfazed. She pulled an exaggerated grimace at Kaveri, and then looked back at the stage, standing on her toes and trying to peep into a little gap in the middle, where the red velvet curtains had not completely closed.

'You know, Kaveri, I went to Calcutta with my brother last year to see the famous Royal Bengal Circus in the Maidan. That was held in a tent which was at least twice this height . . .' Miss Roberts rattled on. Kaveri blinked, losing the thread of the conversation as she tried to picture the size of that tent. She had seen a photograph of the grassy grounds of the Calcutta Maidan recently, in a picture book. How heavy would the poles need to be to hold up a tent that was double the size of this one? And how many people could the tent seat? Perhaps the new mathematics book she had checked out from the library would have some details on this. Kaveri smiled, thinking of her matriculation certificate that had arrived in the post this morning. She had got full marks, cent per cent in her Mathematics examination! In celebration she had danced around the table with Ramu as her mother-in-law Bhargavi looked on.

The evening at the circus was really the perfect end to a day like this, Kaveri thought, settling into her seat. Their first-class section had chairs of plush red velvet at the front, decorated with satin bows. How different they looked from the spartan wooden benches at the back of the tent. Her joy dimmed as she twisted in her seat, seeing how people jostled for space on the hard seats, noting how the rough jute sackcloth that was spread across the muddy floor had already become slushy, the women and men holding their plain cotton saris and *lungi*s high to keep them from getting stained.

Kaveri studied Anandi's beaming face. 'Doesn't it seem wrong to you?' she said. 'We get so much space, and sit in such luxury, while the others are crammed into those hard and uncomfortable benches.'

'They look like mangoes stuffed into a wooden crate for sale,' Anandi responded matter-of-factly. 'I'm glad

I'm not sitting there.' She leaned back in her seat, slipped off her chappals with a sigh of satisfaction and placed her feet on the red-carpeted floor.

Kaveri watched Anandi fondly. The slim young woman sat with her head held high, paying no attention to the glances of disdain that came her way from the 'high class' turbaned gentlemen in the front rows, or their wives clad in expensive silk and diamonds. Even though Kaveri missed her mother-in-law's presence – Bhargavi hadn't been able to join them at the circus because of an upset stomach – she was glad they could use the extra ticket to invite Anandi. It was a rare treat for her. When Kaveri and Ramu had first met Anandi, she had been timid and fearful, a battered wife fleeing from her abusive husband. After finding sanctuary with their friends Mala and Narsamma, and helping Kaveri capture a dangerous gang of thieves, she had transformed into a different person.

Anandi nudged her. 'Ramu *anna* has finally made it, along with Dr Roberts.'

Spotting her husband, Kaveri beamed with pleasure. They had been married for several months now, but her neighbour Uma aunty teased her that she still acted like a new bride whenever she saw him. She adjusted the mussed pleats of her new sari. Would Ramu appreciate the light orange chiffon with a brocade yellow blouse, or would he think it a touch too bright? All thoughts of her attire disappeared when she glanced up to find him next to her, giving her his crooked smile – the special one he reserved just for her. Her stomach gave a little flutter.

Ramu gently prodded her with his foot, reminding her that his boss Dr Roberts was next to him. Kaveri flushed, turning away from her husband to greet the English doctor, whom she admired and respected. How different he was from his sister – like mangoes and gooseberries!

Just as Dr Roberts took the seat next to his sister, and Ramu sat down next to Kaveri, a man dressed in red and yellow circus colours hurried up to Ramu, whispering in his ear.

Kaveri looked at him curiously, straining her ears to hear their conversation, but the hubbub of conversation in the tent filled her ears, drowning everything else out. The man stepped back, obviously waiting for a response, as Ramu turned to Kaveri, pulling her close and speaking loudly.

'We have been invited backstage, to meet their star attraction – the incomparable magician Mr Das. What do you say, Kaveri – shall we go?'

Backstage? Kaveri nodded, eager not to miss this chance, but her mind raced. She had never been to a circus *or* a magic show before, so it was hardly likely that she would pass up a chance to meet a master magician up close. But why were they being singled out? As they followed the man, she and Ramu speculated in whispers.

'Your fame as Bangalore's unparalleled lady detective must have spread to the circus world,' Ramu teased her, placing a warm hand on her back. Kaveri poked his arm, retorting, 'You forget, you are the upcoming doctor whose fame is growing . . . maybe they read about you in the newspaper last week, about the surgery you performed on the metal worker injured in the train accident, helping to save his arm.'

They followed the man to the other side of the stage, up a set of steps, and then behind the plush red curtains into a narrow corridor, lit by a lantern dangling precariously from on the wall. The air within was dank, and the smell of burning kerosene filled her nostrils. Kaveri sneezed, moving closer to Ramu, gripping his arm as they moved towards the red baize door at the end of the corridor.

Quickening their steps, they reached the door just as the man opened it wide, ushering them in. Kaveri blinked rapidly, her eyes readjusting to the brightly lit room, the mirrors on the wall sparkling as they reflected the light from wax candles lining the walls on tiered silver stands. Squinting past the glare, Kaveri focused her attention on a man standing at the end of the room. Could that really be the master magician, Das? How ordinary he looked. Short and stocky, clad in a simple white *kurta* and *pyjama*, he was bent almost double in front of one of the mirrors. Kaveri stared at him, watching in fascination as he outlined his eyes in black *kajal*, his breath leaving small clouds of moisture on the glass. He dipped a piece of cotton into a small pot of rouge, staining his cheeks and lips.

Meeting their eyes in the mirror, Das slowly straightened, turning away from the mirror to greet them. 'The lady detective and her husband!' he exclaimed, opening his arms in theatrical welcome. 'It is such a pleasure to meet you. My son Suman was very keen to meet you.' His hooked nose gave him the appearance of an elderly, statesmanlike eagle. Das's face was caked with powder, accentuating the lines carved onto his face. Yet he moved nimbly, belying his grey hair and wrinkles. If she had seen him from a distance, Kaveri thought, she would have believed him to be in his late forties.

'Forgive us for calling you backstage like this without warning.' A slender young man, clad in a bottle green kurta and pyjama, entered from a side room and came hurrying up to them. That must be Suman, Kaveri decided, noting how different he looked from his father – taller, slight of build, his smooth cheeks contrasting with Das's full beard. He seemed out of breath, almost as if he had run all the way. He turned to Kaveri, pressing the older man's arm hard, as though in warning. 'My mother was a keen fan of detective books. She would have been so excited to have met you.'

'Is she not here?' Ramu asked, looking between the two men.

A beat of silence echoed through the room. 'She is dead,' Suman replied shortly, his mouth twisting. He seemed like he wanted to say more, but just then a fusillade of knocks sounded on the door, and it was flung open. Turning in unison, they saw a burly man looming in the doorway. Another performer, Kaveri guessed, studying his over-sized purple satin shirt, shimmering with sequins, worn over equally loose-fitting navy blue velvet pants.

'The programme is beginning soon. Get your guests out of here,' he said in a loud voice, swaying slightly as though he were drunk. Kaveri looked at the bandage on his right temple, wondering if he was injured, and on medication.

Suman scowled at him, but Das gave his son a warning look as he responded to the burly man. 'We will be ready in just a few minutes. But come, Harish, meet my new friends.' He gestured to Kaveri and Ramu. 'The most intelligent lady detective in all of India, who has solved cases of murder, theft and embezzlement, Mrs Kaveri Murthy – and her husband, Rama Murthy, a brilliant doctor and surgeon who is fast making a name for himself. Pailwan Harish is a powerful strongman who can twist steel bars into knots with ease.'

Das seems to know a lot about us, Kaveri thought. Harish's massive fists clenched on the doorframe. Suman took a step forward, then stopped, as Das placed a restraining hand on his arm. Harish gave them one last glare and left, slamming the door violently. Ramu placed a protective hand on Kaveri's shoulder, drawing her close to him.

'Baba.' Suman's voice was stiff with tension, but he spoke quietly. 'We should let them go now, or else they will miss the start of the performance. We can meet them again later in the evening.' He gave Kaveri a sudden shy smile, his face lighting up. 'You will come back to see us again, after the show concludes, won't you?'

Suddenly, Das was all briskness, pumping Ramu's hand vigorously, leading them out of the room. Seeing Suman follow them, he turned to his son, saying, '*Accha, beta*, can you get my costume ready for me?'

Once Suman had gone back into the room, Das turned towards Kaveri. The larger-than-life persona he carried fell away from him, like a discarded robe. All at once he seemed older, more vulnerable. He reached for her hands, holding them tightly.

'My son admires you greatly,' Das said, his soft voice almost inaudible against the hiss of the kerosene lamps. Kaveri blinked, startled at seeing tears in his eyes. 'Your guidance will be important for him. I hope you can help him.'

'Baba!' Suman repeated, his voice now urgent.

Das pressed her hands once more, and then released her, clasping Ramu on the shoulder as he turned back into the room, closing the door on them with a gentle thud.

Ramu shook his head at Kaveri as they walked back down the corridor, pushing aside the heavy curtain that separated the stage from the steps that led to their seats. 'What was *that* about, Kaveri? I'm not sure what to make of the father and son duo.'

'Das was hinting at something. I wish I had some idea what it was.' Kaveri felt as bewildered as Ramu. 'I liked his son though. Das was putting on an act for us, but

Suman seemed straightforward, honest.' And very young, she thought, thinking back to the sweet smile he had given her, making him look like a vulnerable schoolboy.

But there was no more time for private conversation, the show was about to start. When they arrived at their seats, Kaveri took her place to the right of Miss Roberts while Ramu sat on her other side, sandwiched between her and Anandi. The air inside the tent was warm and stifling. It smelt of jasmine, roses and sandalwood incense, overlaying the mustiness that emanated from the stiff, wiry red jute carpet below them. She felt her nose twitch and hastily pulled out her handkerchief. It would be awful if she sneezed on the silk-and-brocade sari of the woman in front of her!

Kaveri jumped as Miss Roberts shouted into her ear. 'Look at all these native women, dressed to the nines in shining silk. A bit too bright, don't you think? Too vulgar for me.' The older Englishwoman patted the velvet fabric of her cream frock, looking with complacence at its lace fringe embroidered with red roses. 'You Indians have good taste in jewellery though, I admit it freely.'

Kaveri pressed her lips shut. It would be *very* inappropriate for her to be rude to the sister of Dr Roberts, the head of the Bowring Hospital, where Ramu worked. Miss Roberts was stuck-up and snobbish but, Kaveri tried to remind herself, she had a kind heart beneath the layers of prejudice.

She tuned the woman out, nodding on auto pilot as Miss Roberts droned on, her nasal voice buzzing in Kaveri's ear like the high-pitched drone of a mosquito. She poked Kaveri's arm for emphasis. 'I wanted to wear my rubies. They would have gone so well with my new dress, but my brother refused to let me take them out of the bank. He is worried about the recent thefts across the city. Two of our neighbours' homes were burgled last week when they came to the circus.'

Thefts? Kaveri leaned forward, trying to focus on what Miss Roberts was saying, tuning out the hubbub of conversation around her. 'What did they lose?'

But Miss Roberts was in full flow and could not be interrupted. 'I didn't even want to come, but my brother insisted we must see the magic show,' the older woman sniffed. 'Such charlatanry, manipulating the audience through tricks and illusions, separating fools from their hard-earned money.' She turned around to glare at the audience at the back, packed like sardines into elevated benches.

'Come now, m'dear,' her brother remonstrated mildly from the other side. 'They are adults, capable of deciding whether they want to pay a few annas for some entertainment. Tonight's events will be a spectacle – the likes of which they have never seen before, and never will again. The Maximilian Circus has been everywhere – Egypt, Turkey, Algeria, Spain.'

'Our tickets cost a pretty penny,' Miss Roberts grumbled.

'We didn't pay an *anna*.' Dr Roberts looked at Kaveri apologetically. He often had that expression on his face when she saw him with his sister. She was a good woman, who had come all the way to India to look after his children, as he often took the pains to explain to others. But there was no denying the fact that she was infuriating!

Kaveri turned her attention to Dr Roberts.

'We received free tickets from our good friend, Major Wilks,' he explained. 'He's in charge of security arrangements for today's event.' He waved to a uniformed man in scarlet and white, standing in a stiff military pose at the opening of the tent. The man looked at them as Miss Roberts called out in her high nasal voice, 'Yoohoo – over here. Major Wilks, halloo.' Wilks's face darkened as he nodded stiffly then looked away.

Miss Roberts twisted her body into a pretzel, looking around the room to see if she could find anyone else she considered prominent enough to be seen saying hello to. Dr Roberts went on hastily, 'Such generosity. These front-row tickets cost a fortune, you know.'

'Thank you for sharing your extra tickets with us . . .' Kaveri said, her voice petering out as Roberts gave her a surprised look. 'You didn't? Ramu found an envelope with three tickets on his table . . . he thought they came from you.'

Roberts' face cleared. 'That must have been Wilks. He said he had a few spare ones. I suspect he wanted to fill the row closest to the performers with reliable people. Nobody here seems like the kind to create a disturbance. Still, one can't be too careful I suppose, not with the Prince due to arrive in just a few days.' He gave Kaveri a meaningful glance.

She guessed at what he hesitated to put into words. The Prince of Wales was coming to the city in a few weeks. After his disastrous visits to Bombay and Calcutta a few months back, marked with riots and arson, the British were very keen to see that his time in Bangalore went smoothly. Ramu had told her that they were now monitoring all public events, keeping a keen lookout for what they classified as 'rabble rousers' – freedom fighters who used public performances like this as venues to spread the word to others about the independence move-ment. The jails were full to overflowing, with the police picking up anyone they thought was a troublemaker and locking them away.

A blood-curdling yowl cut off her thoughts, slicing through the buzz of conversation in the tent. Kaveri winced as Miss Roberts' hand shot out to grip her tightly, her nails digging into her arm. *Why can't she grip her brother's hand*, Kaveri thought crossly. She peered across Ramu to check on Anandi. The young woman's eyes were wide, startled in alarm, but Mrs Ismail – the wife of their good friend, Inspector Ismail – had occupied the empty seat next to her. She held Anandi's hand in hers, patting it reassuringly. That was odd. How had Mrs Ismail afforded a front-row seat? Police inspectors didn't get paid all that much – especially the native police.

Kaveri's eyes scanned the rows of velvet seating and found the bulky figure of Inspector Ismail. He was in uniform, patrolling the aisles. Of course. He was probably in charge of security arrangements and had wrangled a good seat for his wife. She waved at him, but he did not respond with his usual broad smile. His face was set in grim lines as he turned his back on her. Kaveri's jaw dropped open. Why would Ismail, one of her dearest friends in Bangalore, ignore her publicly?

Kaveri kicked her toes at the carpet. What an evening it was turning out to be! First, the strange visit backstage to see Das and Suman, with its mysterious undercurrents of tension. Then the discovery that thefts had been taking place in wealthy homes across the city. Now Inspector Ismail, cutting her dead in a crowd of people. She turned to Ramu for support, but he was deep in conversation with Anandi and had not noticed her interaction with Ismail. She started to tug at his arm, wanting to tell him what had happened, but Miss Roberts gave her no opportunity. As the angry yowl died away, leaving only a rasping sound lingering in the air, the Englishwoman leaned towards her again, speaking with a satisfied smirk. 'Tiger. I knew there would be animals! The previous circus I went to had horses, camels, elephants, even a zebra.' Her breath was hot and fetid, and Kaveri had to stop herself from wrinkling her nose, trying to move as far from her as her seat would allow.

Noticing her agitation, Ramu turned towards her, giving her a questioning look. 'Later,' she mouthed at him. The performances were beginning, and she would have to shout to be heard above the din. He interlaced his fingers with hers once more, rubbing her palm with his thumb. She took a steadying breath and felt herself relax. With her husband next to her, she could face anything – and this was just a circus performance, not a site of danger, she reminded herself.

2

Jadoo

As Kaveri struggled to rein in her worries, a blaze of trumpets sounded through the tent. A hush fell upon the audience, as the curtains rolled back slowly. They watched with avid fascination as a cage with a massive tiger was wheeled in. A heavily muscled man with a broken nose walked alongside the cage, carrying a long, wicked-looking whip with cat tails.

Naked except for a leopard-patterned skin tied around his waist, the man – introduced as the Incredible Rajamani, Master of Tigers – opened the door of the cage and pushed his head inside. He grappled with the tiger's ears before wrenching open its mouth and sticking his head into its massive jaws. The audience openly demonstrated their appreciation, the back benchers standing on the wooden seats and stamping their feet in chorus.

Kaveri pressed a hand to her forehead. The noise was too loud, and she could sense a headache starting. This close to the stage, they smelt the powerful stench coming from the tiger's mouth. She leaned across to Ramu, whispering 'How can he stand that stink?'

'He's probably drunk. And the tiger is certainly drugged. It wouldn't be so passive otherwise.' Ramu's voice was impassive, but she saw his pulse twitch at the side of his throat. She looked back at the stage just as the Incredible Rajamani walked into the cage and climbed onto the tiger's back, forcing it down to the floor. The tiger's growl rumbled through the tent.

Her husband pointed to the wings of the stage. 'A tiger this drugged would not roar, Kaveri. But you need the ferocious growl to add to the mystique. They record the tiger roaring and play it from a microphone. The audience is fooled into thinking that this man has the power to subdue an animal this ferocious.' Ramu's face pulled into hard lines and Kaveri touched his leg in silent sympathy. Only last week, she had seen Ramu treat the injuries of a kitten they had rescued from a tree, cleaning its wounds twice a day. She knew how much the mistreatment of the magnificent beast must hurt him.

While the audience erupted in cheers, Kaveri looked at Ramu, who had squeezed his eyes shut, shaking his head. She thought of the newspaper reports last week, hagiographic accounts of the Prince of Wales's exploits in the forests of Mysore, with centrespread photographs of the young monarch posing with a long rifle, his booted foot on the carcass of a massive tiger. This performance seemed very similar in intent. The British spoke endlessly of the virtues of 'fair play', but their hunts were not a fair fight – neither was this.

No one else seemed to have an issue with the act. Everyone in the room seemed entranced by Rajamani's demonstration of 'bravery', even the Roberts. Only Kaveri and Ramu seemed to be squirming in their seats, unable to stomach the travesty of such a performance. As the act drew to an end, Ramu got up, still looking shaken. 'I'll be back,' he mouthed, pointing towards the toilets.

Kaveri turned towards Anandi, wanting to ask her what she thought of the caged tiger, but stopped short as Anandi's eager face crumpled.

Kaveri whipped her face around to see what had spooked her friend so much. A stocky man stood in the wings of the stage, holding Anandi's gaze. His fleshy lips were pulled back in a predatory smile, exposing *paan*-stained teeth. As Kaveri watched, the man drew a finger across the red satin bandana tied around his neck, exaggeratedly miming a decapitation. Ashen-faced, Anandi shrank back into her seat.

Kaveri's hackles rose instantly. She leaned forward in her seat, glaring at him. Her eyes moved across him, automatically noting each detail, from his shiny velvet brown pants and satin yellow shirt to his fleshy face, observing the tattoo of a small snake on his right temple just above his ear. He took no notice of her, his focus intent on Anandi like an eagle watching a mouse.

'Who is that, Anandi?' Kaveri asked her. But the young woman had retreated into the seat, sitting so far back that her body seemed embedded in its velvet lining. 'Nobody,' she muttered, refusing to meet Kaveri's eyes.

'What do you mean, nobody?' Kaveri persisted, turning to point to the man. But there was no one there. She craned her neck, but could not spot him anywhere. The only time she had seen Anandi so frightened before was when she spoke of her husband, Pawan. But Pawan had fled Bangalore some months back, after piling up a series of gambling debts. Could he be back in the city?

Kaveri turned back to Anandi, who was stroking her fingers over her throat repeatedly. Seeing Anandi's stricken face, Kaveri's anger quickly turned to concern. *Should she exchange seats with Ramu and sit next to Anandi?* Miss Roberts might find that rude and complain to Dr Roberts. Even though she knew her husband's boss was fair, and would not take offence for silly reasons, Kaveri hesitated. She did not want to make things difficult for Ramu.

Kaveri settled back into her seat when she saw Mrs Ismail capture Anandi's restless hand, massaging her stiff fingers. She thought of a conversation she had had with Uma aunty a few days back, during one of the weekly meetings of the Bangalore Detectives Club. Uma aunty had wondered out loud about the contrast between the quick and clever-minded Inspector Ismail and his phlegmatic wife. 'She is so sleepy-eyed, always quiet. I don't know what keeps them together.'

'I think she observes much more than she lets on,' Kaveri had objected.

She felt even more sure of it today. Mrs Ismail might seem indolent, but Kaveri was sure she had noticed the man who had frightened Anandi. She would tell Ismail, who would then deal with it in his own way, keeping Anandi safe. After all, Ismail was as fond of Anandi as she was. A bit more reassured, she relaxed into the chair just as Ramu came in. She wanted to tell him what had happened, but a flourish of trumpets indicated the start of the next performance was beginning. It would have to wait.

Most visitors came to the circus especially to see the Maharaja of Magic – Das. His face was everywhere on the posters for the Maximilian Circus, his mesmerising eyes staring directly at the viewers, his hooked nose and hooded eyebrows compelling their attention. Das had looked much more ordinary when they met him backstage. She leaned forward, eager to see how he would seem on stage, fully made-up, in his performing *avataar*.

The audience murmured, restless in anticipation. Two stocky men strode onto the stage holding pearly white conch shells. They blew on the shells, signalling the arrival of the magician.

As Das appeared onstage, followed by Suman, Kaveri was taken aback. She had expected him to be wearing a flowing coat and top hat, as he did on the posters. But Das did not wear Western clothes. He and Suman were dressed identically – in a short Bengali kurta over loose pyjamas. Das wore a scarlet kurta in velvet, while Suman was dressed in the bottle green costume in which they had seen him earlier. Over their kurtas, they both wore waistcoats and turbans of dazzling blue. The brilliant colours of the peacock feathers embedded in their turbans were reflected in the strings of turquoise beads looped around their necks and arms.

'The boy's the warm-up act,' Dr Roberts said, glancing across to them. His sister had lost her air of petulance and now sat with a look of childlike excitement on her face. The audience around them clapped loudly. Even Anandi laughed in delight, the strain on her face gone.

Only Major Wilks, sitting ramrod straight at the edge of the row, and Inspector Ismail, standing at the end of the aisle, seemed uninterested in the performance. They stared away from the stage, their eyes scanning the audience. Had they been instructed to look for any signs of disturbance?

Ramu stroked the inside of her wrist lightly. 'Anything wrong?' he mouthed.

'Nothing,' Kaveri responded with a reassuring smile. She castigated herself internally. It was unfair of her to worry Ramu like this. After a hard day of work at the hospital, he deserved to be able to relax at the circus without wondering why his wife was on edge. Perhaps her mother-in-law was right. Bhargavi said that ever since she had become a detective, her mind worked overtime. She saw suspicious things everywhere, even in the most normal of situations. She shook her head vigorously, trying to rid herself of the uncomfortable thoughts crowding her mind.

Das bowed deep and low, fixing the audience with his compelling gaze. 'Ladies and gentlemen – sisters and brothers – you may wonder why I, the Maharaja of Magic, am not clad in the traditional attire you might expect from me – top hat and coat tails.' He gave them a brilliant smile. 'It is because I – I am not a mere magician. I am a *jadoogar*.' He paused, staring down at the audience. Kaveri looked around, seeing everyone's gaze was fixed intently on the stage – except for Mrs Ismail's, whose thick eyebrows were drawn together in a frown, and Ramu's, who returned Kaveri's gaze with a questioning look.

'Jadoo is an ancient Indian art – one that is handed down over generations,' Das continued. 'My family has trained in the art of jadoo for centuries, performing for kings and rulers across the world. What you see here is no trickery, my friends, but the result of generations of *riyaaz*, sacred practice, and our *bhakti*, devotion to the God and Goddess of Magic, Shiva and Parvati.' Anandi's mouth was hanging open, Kaveri noticed, and she was leaning forward on the edge of her seat, her thighs pressed close together as though she was prepared to leap off the chair and onto the stage.

'Many foreign magicians have tried to learn our secrets. They come to our shores, seeking to gain access to our knowledge, and use it to discredit us. Fools. We are blessed by the Gods.' As Das's sonorous voice boomed through the tent, Kaveri saw many of the turbaned heads in the front row nodding vigorously.

'Quite brave of him to say this to a mixed audience with British people,' Ramu breathed into her ear. 'Foolhardy even, to speak so when tensions run high.'

Das's words seemed to have found resonance with the people sitting in the back rows. They clapped and hooted, whistling and standing in their seats. Kaveri could see the few English people in the audience exchanging uneasy glances. Major Wilks got up from his seat and moved towards the side aisle of the tent, speaking to Ismail.

Das seemed unperturbed. With a mocking look at Major Wilks, he gave a dramatic bow to the audience, bending until his face was almost parallel with the stage. He snapped his fingers, and men hurried in, wheeling in gigantic petromax lanterns, lining them up along the sides of the stage. The lanterns hissed as they fired up, shining their dazzling light onto mirrors draped in sequined brocades and onto crystal lamps, illuminating the stage in iridescent colours.

It was magical, fantastical, endless. One impossible trick melded into another. Later, when the performance concluded, Kaveri could not tell how long she had been glued to her seat as Das subjected himself to danger after danger, escaping unscathed as the backbenchers cheered and hooted.

Mango trees were created from twigs. They grew, flowered and produced fruit. The young magician pulled a sharp knife out of his sleeve, sliced the mango and handed the pieces to a little girl in a frilled lace frock sitting on her grandfather's lap in the front row. As the child devoured the fruit, the sticky juice spilling onto her dress, her gaze remained focused on the stage.

Suman invited the little girl's grandfather to come up onto the stage. He opened his mouth to ask a question, and three rabbits hopped out of his mouth in succession. Suman waved his wand, and one of the rabbits turned into a plush velvet stuffed toy. He threw it down to the little girl, who caught it and hugged it, her eyes shining. The audience went wild, cheering and clapping. At the back, people stood up on the benches, whistling and calling his name. Kaveri couldn't believe her eyes – even Miss Roberts was on her feet applauding.

Ramu placed an arm around her shoulders. 'You look entranced.'

'I can't wait to go to the library and look for some books that can help me learn how he does these tricks. Especially the one where he dips his fingers in molten lead, drinks carbolic acid and dives into boiling water, coming out unharmed. I have heard of Houdini's tricks but couldn't imagine how spectacular they would look until now. Even though I know it's all a trick, he still manages to make it seem real.'

Suman bowed deep to the people seated in the rows below him. Das stretched his arms, cracking his knuckles. The audience clapped for a long time, and Das looked at his son with pride, placing an arm around his waist. Kaveri felt a lump form in her throat. She hadn't seen her father for months and missed him dearly. He had a habit of cracking his knuckles just like that.

Suman stepped back, handing over the stage to his father.

'We will now begin the main performance,' Das said. 'A recreation of the battles between Kamsa and Lord Krishna.' He smiled at the mixed audience. 'My compatriots here know the story. But for the benefit of our foreign guests, I will summarise it.'

Kaveri saw Ismail look at the stage with interest. His constables hung on Das's words. Only Major Wilks remained aloof, his eyes glittering with disdain as he tapped one large boot on the carpeted floor.

'Kamsa, the evil demon king, was so powerful that no one could defeat him. His subjects prayed to Lord Vishnu to save them. Vishnu agreed, reincarnating himself as Lord Krishna, Kamsa's nephew – who killed Kamsa. This story symbolises the triumph of good over evil, through the removal of the evil usurper, and the restoration of rightful rule.'

Kaveri followed Ramu's gaze, looking at Wilks. Standing erect against the side of the tent, near the stage, the man had taken a couple of steps forward, his intent gaze fixed on Das. Ismail stood stiffly, watching his constables as they muttered to each other.

'This show is a tribute to the Gods above, who see everything and know the innermost truth that lies in our hearts. It is so we can remind ourselves that truth triumphs over falsehood, and good is victorious over evil.'

'Das is skirting the edge of danger,' Ramu commented again, a note of admiration in his voice. His voice was pitched low, just for Kaveri's ears. 'A little further, and he could be arrested for sedition.'

Kaveri agreed. She had not known what to make of Das, especially after that strange meeting with him backstage. But her respect for his courage grew on listening to him speak so boldly onstage, in front of so many people. Das must know the dangers he courted, choosing such a theme for his performance. He had just transformed the theme of the religious epic familiar to his largely Indian audience into a powerful call for freedom.

As a thin man sitting in the pit began to play on a reed-like *bansuri*, the melodious sound of the bamboo flute filled the air. Das raised his wand, and with a hand flick, made a blue mask appear in mid-air, holding it high and turning it towards the people sitting in front of him. The mask was beautiful, decorated with glittering sequins, and adorned with an iridescently blue peacock feather at the tip. He tied the mask to his face, taking on the role of Lord Krishna.

With another flourish of his wand, he plucked a red mask, diabolic in appearance, from the air. Drumbeats filled the theatre as he announced, 'And now, meet Krishna's evil uncle, King Kamsa.' People stood up to cheer as Das fastened Kamsa's mask onto Suman's face.

Kaveri found herself sitting on the edge of her seat, leaning forward, mouth slightly open. She could taste the sense of anticipation, sharp and bittersweet.

Signalling for silence, Das paused, looking around at the audience. 'We need a volunteer. One lovely young lady to act as Putana, the evil demoness who was King Kamsa's sister.' The audience shifted in their seats, refusing to meet his eyes.

'It is only a small thing we will ask you to do,' he said, his voice soft and coaxing. 'You need to take this knife, here' – he pointed to a sharp dagger with a curved blade on a table – 'and try to kill Krishna.'

A collective gasp ran through the seats. Suman looked down into the seats, shielding his eyes from the bright lights that lit the stage. No one spoke now. A rustling sound came from the seats, as women shifted on the benches, their stiff silks brushing against the wood. The clock on the wall ticked loudly.

A small spring of tension wound tight in Kaveri's stomach, and she pressed her belly with both hands.

The clock ticked loudly, while the audience sat in silence. Das walked up and down on the raised platform in front of them, stopping in front of Kaveri. The magician's eyes bore into hers, transfixing her. She felt as though she was falling, falling hard, plummeting into the depths of his eyes. Involuntarily, she felt her hand rising. She felt Ramu place a hand on her arm in warning, but was unable to tear her eyes away from the magician.

She saw a tall figure move from the aisle. Ismail, who had been standing to the side, stepped in front of her, breaking her line of sight to the magician, shattering her connection to Das. Kaveri brought her hand down sharply.

Dimly, through the roar of noise filling her ears, she heard Ramu ask in a horrified voice, 'What *on earth* has come over you, Kaveri?'

'I don't know. I felt like he hypnotised me. Without my knowing it, my hand went up.' She shivered. 'I don't know what is going on, but I don't want to be a part of it.'

She turned to thank Ismail, but he had melted into the shadows once more.

Just then, she saw Anandi jump up. The young woman looked nervous, but her eyes held a glimmer of excitement.

A satisfied smile spread across Das's face. 'Please give us a big round of applause – for this beautiful young woman, who has bravely volunteered to play the part of Putana.'

As he pulled her up onto the stage and tied a green skull-shaped mask to Anandi's face, Anandi looked like she was regretting her impulse. Kaveri stretched one hand out, fruitlessly wishing she could pull Anandi back. What viper's nest was Anandi diving into?

3

Chained in Irons

Mrs Ismail's normally plump and cheerful face was carved in grave lines. She placed a hand on the empty seat next to her.

Still wearing Kamsa's mask, Suman shook his fists in the air, declaiming to the audience. 'I will never give up,' he roared. 'I will kill Krishna or die trying.'

The audience roared their approval. From her left, Kaveri saw Ismail step forward and whisper to one of his men. The man set off at a run, towards the back of the theatre. Major Wilks exchanged a significant look with Ismail, and Kaveri felt her neck prickle in warning.

Ramu had seen it too. 'For an officer who came to Bangalore to plan out the security for the Prince's visit, Wilks seems unnaturally interested in a circus performance,' her husband whispered softly, making sure that Miss Roberts would not hear. 'I wonder if he's come to keep an eye on someone specific. Rumours are rife in the city about what will happen when the Prince is here.'

Was this strangely compelling magician part of a secret plot against the visiting Prince? A man like Das would be able to go anywhere, fit into the tightest places, evade arrest and capture – the circus was the perfect place to house such a man, a place where he would not stand out or seem suspicious. Kaveri shook her head vigorously, trying to get the image of Das in chains, being led away by the police, out of her mind. Perhaps Bhargavi was right – she was becoming obsessed with looking for mysteries in perfectly normal settings.

The man with the flute got up from the wings, replaced by a violinist, who set up an ominous dirge. Das, still playing Krishna, held his arms behind his back, and his son, in the visage of the evil king Kamsa, handcuffed him, ostentatiously tossing the key into the bench seats at the back of the auditorium. The crowd, visibly on Krishna's side, shouted loud insults at 'Kamsa'. Anandi shrank back from the table, gnawing at her nails as Suman trussed up his father in a series of hefty chains, fastening them with five heavy padlocks and throwing the keys into the audience.

Contorted into such an uncomfortable-looking position, hands trussed behind his back, Das should have seemed helpless, diminished. But he appeared even more powerful, invincible even, as he looked out at the audience, seeming to search for someone. His eyes reflected the bright stage light, glittering like black diamonds as they fastened on Kaveri.

He seemed to be trying to communicate with her, moving his lips. The moment seemed to last for hours, as Das looked deep into her eyes. She felt like a butterfly trapped in a glass box, frantically trying to free itself. When Das finally looked away from Kaveri, she sucked in great gulps of air, feeling as though a tight lock placed on her chest had been lifted, leaving her free to breathe again.

No one else seemed to have noticed anything – not Ramu, who was still focused on the stage, nor Suman, who was still tugging at the chains, demonstrating that they were solid.

Two men ran in, wheeling a small metal cage. Suman placed a hand on Das's back, forcing him into the cage. The clang of metal on metal resounded through the tent as he slammed the door shut, locking it with a padlock and tossing this key too into the audience. The onlookers murmured, shifting in their seats uneasily. The cage looked tiny – barely enough to contain a dog, let alone a man.

Suman deposited a heavy-looking watermelon on a small table, placing it down with an audible thud on the centre of the stage. He reached towards Anandi and pulled her towards it, placing a sword with a wicked-looking curved blade in her hand. He held her hand in his, and guided the blade towards the melon, slicing through the thick skin with ease. The fruit thudded to the ground, splitting and scattering everywhere, its pink fleshy pulp looking like blood. Anandi placed her hand over her mouth, but Suman tugged her hand away, interlacing her fingers with his and raising their joined palms high as he roared at the crowd, holding the sword aloft in his other hand.

'See how sharp my sword is? Now let us see how Putana and Kamsa, together, annihilate Krishna.'

Releasing Anandi, Suman picked up a thin red silken cloth and threw it over the cage, obscuring Das from view. Peering to the side, Kaveri saw a man standing in the wings of the theatre place a disc into the gramophone. An eerie scream filled the theatre just as Anandi gingerly inserted the tip of the sword into the cloth. The elderly man sitting in front swiftly placed his hands over his granddaughter's eyes. She scrambled off his lap and held his legs tightly, keeping her back to the stage. The audience had fallen into a stunned silence.

Suman gripped Anandi's hands in his, guiding the blade as she stabbed into the cloth, piercing it and thrusting deep into the cage. Kaveri could see beads of sweat dripping from Anandi's forehead onto the stage. If Das was still in there, trussed up in chains – as he surely must be – the sword would have cut through his body. Kaveri's jaw clenched, and she forced herself to relax, repeating over and over to herself in her mind – *It's just an act. It's not real. It's just an act.*

Spots of dark and light began to dance in front of her eyes. Through the haze that filled her vision, she saw Anandi push Suman away with trembling hands, drop the sword on the floor and step back, shrinking against the side wall.

Suman watched her go, making no effort to restrain her. He gave her a small sympathetic smile and picked up the sword again. With one swift move, he raised it over his head, brandishing it high, and then brought it down swiftly, slicing through the bars of the cage. A crimson liquid immediately began to ooze from the box, seeping onto the floor. A woman shrieked from the back, as the people sitting in the benches turned to each other, worry written on their faces. The elderly man sitting in the central row in the front picked up the small girl, placing her on his lap and holding her close, soothing her tears as she clutched on to her mango seed. Kaveri's jaws clenched involuntarily again, and she bit her lip, tasting blood. *It's just an act. It's not real. It's just an act.* She forced herself to concentrate on the words as if they were a mantra, her eyes watching the stage.

Noting her distress, Ramu picked up her hand, placing it in his and holding it hard. She moved closer to him, leaning against his shoulder, shaking a little, repeating her mantra in her mind. She pressed even closer to her husband as two men came in from the wings, wheeling in a cart with a tall basket. Suman took off its lid. A coil of snakes became visible above the lip of the basket, seething and writhing. They hissed in warning as they rose higher, some spreading out their hoods.

'Cobras and vipers,' Kaveri breathed. 'There must be at least ten snakes in that basket.' *How could Das possibly survive their deadly bite?* She saw Anandi edging away from the stage, inching down the steps, away from the writhing basket.

Kaveri dug her nails into her palm. Once, when she had been very small, their gardener had been bitten by a carpet viper. He had been rushed to the hospital, and received treatment in time, but she could still remember how he had writhed in agony. For a while, they had thought he might lose his leg – and that was only one snake.

She held her breath, watching the snakes move through the air, lunging at each other, the basket shaking with the movement. Suman pulled off the silk cloth that covered the cage. Kaveri tried to see if Das was inside, but the bars were thick, obscuring her view. With one powerful thrust, Suman opened the door of the cage. He forced the basket of hissing snakes inside, slamming the door shut and covering the cage with the cloth again, just as a loud scream pierced the air. Suman shook the cage again and again. The sound of hissing cobras filled the room.

Miss Roberts screeched, and her brother shifted his chair closer to her, holding her hands in a tight grip. A baby began to wail, the sound taken up by other children across the room. Kaveri saw a few parents rush out, holding their crying children to their chests.

The walls of the circus tent, which had seemed large and welcoming just a few minutes back, had started to close in on her. *Silly goose*, she chided herself. Scattered thoughts chased each other, running through her brain like the headless chicken she had seen near the butcher's shop in Ulsoor last week.

Ramu felt her shudder and he put his arm around her. 'Are you alright? It's not like you to be so shaken.' He pointed to the gramophone that they could see at the side of the stage, playing what she knew must be a recording of the hissing of snakes, and the screams of agony that seemed to originate from the cage.

She took a deep breath, as her body shuddered. 'Even though I know it must be a well-staged trick, I get the sense that something is very wrong.' Kaveri pointed to Anandi, a small shrinking figure on the massive stage. 'If anything happens, we should make sure Anandi returns to us safely.'

Suman swept off the blanket with a triumphant look on his face, pointing to the cage. Trumpets blared out once again, as a bright light shone from the top of the ceiling, illuminating the interior of the metal cage.

People stood up, trying to peer into the cage. The bars were set fairly close to each other, close enough that no man could slip through. But for a pile of chains and locks, the entire cage was empty. No cobras, no blood – no magician.

There was a moment of silence, the stillness thick and stifling, like the hot air in the moist tent. Then one woman gasped audibly, the noise reverberating through the tent. That seemed to break the spell. The trumpets started to play again, picking up their pace, now accompanied by a pulsating drumbeat. A few people jumped up onto the benches and began to dance on the seats. Men started moving into the aisles as they danced to the beat. A small group of men, wearing masks, forced their way onto the stage, picking Suman up. They placed him on their shoulders, and carried him down the steps, parading him down the aisle to more whistles and cheers.

Only Kaveri noticed the expression on Suman's face. The mask of Kamsa, which he had taken off, now dangled from his fingers. The triumphant expression had faded from his face upon seeing the empty cage. He should have been beaming with pleasure on the successful completion of a dangerous act by his father, enjoying the appreciation of the onlookers. Instead, his eyes looked lost, confused – his expression dazed, as though someone had hit him on the head. His head turned from side to side, searching for someone as the people carrying him moved through the aisles.

Kaveri leaned closer, studying his lips as they moved. The drumming was deafening, and she could not hear what he spoke. She craned her neck, trying to read his lips.

Ramu, sitting closer to the aisle, looked in the direction of her gaze. 'He is repeating the word "Baba" over and over again,' he told her, his fingers drumming on the sides of the chair.

'Can you go closer to him, and ask what happened?'

Ramu nodded, weaving through the seats towards Suman. Kaveri saw Anandi, still standing uncertainly on the stage. Catching her eye, she gestured for her to come down. Anandi nodded, and carefully jumped down from the stage, making her way towards Kaveri.

The men with masks seemed to be everywhere now. *Where had they come from?* Kaveri craned her neck, unable to spot Ramu or Suman in the crowd. She watched with increasing worry as the men began to move menacingly towards the audience, thrusting their hips and gyrating at the women with lewd gestures. The well-dressed women in the front seats began to scream, clutching their menfolk.

Ismail's whistle pierced through the hubbub. The uniformed policemen standing at the side of the tent pushed their way through to the front of the tent, brandishing thick bamboo lathis.

'To the back, men, to the back,' Wilks roared through a megaphone. 'Protect the women and children.' She followed the direction of his arm, seeing a burly man with a mask accosting a young woman, trying to pull the sari off her shoulder. She gripped her *pallu* with both hands, kicking at his shins. Kaveri moved towards them, but the girl was too far away. She clenched her fingers into a fist, feeling powerless. Mrs Ismail pushed her way through, raising her steel bottle like a club and bringing it down on the man's head, looking far from sleepy or indolent now.

People had seen the man accost the young woman. An exodus began at the back of the tent as men stood up, hoisting children on their shoulders and shielding their women with their bodies, huddling close and hurrying out through the side exits.

Trapped by the exiting crowd, the audience in the first-class seats froze, unable to move. The men moved closer, grabbing hold of their chains and gesturing threateningly towards their wallets. An organised theft, Kaveri realised in shock. Using the chaos as cover, wearing masks to hide their faces, they were systematically looting the wealthy people sitting in front. Where was Ismail?

A few women began to wrap the folds of their saris and shawls around their necks and arms, trying to hide their jewellery. Others hurriedly removed their chains and bangles, stuffing them into their petticoats and hiding them inside their blouses. Kaveri looked around frantically, and saw Ramu, struggling to reach her, separated from her by the crowd. She called to him, but her voice was swallowed up by the noise around them. Near the entrance, Miss Roberts was safely sheltered in her brother's arms. As two of the men approached the row of seats where she stood, Kaveri clutched her reticule to her tightly, wishing it was small enough to wrap inside her clothes. It did not have jewels or money – but it held something far more precious to her, her notebook in which she had written down her case details.

'*Thaatha,* save me,' a small, thin voice called out in fear. The small girl with the mango seed struggled with a masked man who had picked her up and was grabbing at the chain around her neck. He pushed her grandfather aside, and the man stumbled, knocking into a chair. Kaveri's face contorted in anger. Stuffing her reticule into her blouse, she hiked up her sari, and climbed over the seats that separated them, moving towards the burly masked man. His back was to her, and he did not see her coming. She jumped down from the chair and grasped him below the shoulder, locking him in a tight hold. The movements that she had practised over and over with her *kalari* teacher came to her automatically, as she tripped him by placing her leg in front of his, pushing his knee down, making him collapse on the floor. She grunted in grim satisfaction, grabbing the chain from his open fist and restoring it to the weeping child. The girl gazed at her with shining eyes, leaning forward and throwing her sticky arms around Kaveri.

Ismail blew his whistle hard, signalling to the policemen to return to the front of the tent. The policemen ran towards the men, brandishing their sticks like clubs, laying about them right and left – and the hoodlums dropped their loot, running towards the exits. Mrs Ismail made her way to her husband, still brandishing her steel bottle like a club. She spoke to him briefly. She saw Ismail turn, looking at Kaveri standing over the man on the floor. He grabbed the nearest policeman by the arm, sending him running towards them.

Wilks shouldered his way into the fray, catching Inspector Ismail by the elbow and speaking into his ear. As the constable moved towards the hoodlum, carrying handcuffs in one hand, the man got up and ran away. Kaveri debated whether she should follow, but in an instant, he was at the exit, and beyond her grasp. Feeling helpless again, Kaveri handed the girl to the old man, watching as he limped away to the exit, carrying the child on his shoulders. She massaged her fingers, rotating her neck to relax her stiff shoulders, and then remembered – where was Anandi?

Ramu was still some distance away, but Kaveri spotted Anandi fighting her way through the throng. She had almost reached Kaveri's side when a stocky man appeared in front of her, blocking her path. Broad-shouldered and heavily muscled, with a red bandana around his neck, this was the same man who had frightened Anandi earlier. The man Kaveri suspected was her husband, Pawan.

Anandi drew herself to her full height, standing up to him and shouting something at him. Kaveri strained to hear what she was saying, but the hubbub was too loud, and she could not make out the words. The man moved closer to her, yelling back at her. He pulled a box out from his shirt, opening it to show her something inside.

'No, Pawan!' Anandi shouted, shaking her head in vigorous denial. Then she turned, running away from the man and towards the escaping crowd. The man turned to go after her, but stopped when he found Kaveri blocking his path. His eyes glittered with malice as he drew his finger across his throat.

Kaveri withdrew against the seats, watching him smirk as she shrank back. *Take the offence, not the defence,* her kalaripayattu teacher always said. When her teacher, an elderly lady, could fight off would-be assailants twice her size, what did Kaveri have to fear! She reversed direction, leaning towards the man instead of shrinking away. Blocking his arm with her elbow, she reached out to grab his neck, stiffening and extending her index and middle fingers together, reaching for the sensitive point at the base of his neck that could incapacitate him. After her last encounter with a dangerous drug smuggler, her teacher had made her practise this on a lifelike dummy over and over again until it came as naturally to her as breathing.

But just as her fingers brushed his collar, another policeman rushed up to them, shouting loudly. Startled, the man quickly stepped back and gave her one last glare before turning and running away. Desperate not to lose sight of him as she had the previous man, Kaveri hitched her sari up around her ankles, and chased after him. But he was too swift for her, disappearing through a side entrance just as she reached the aisle.

She stopped, placing a hand on the back of one of the first-class chairs, the other hand pressed to her stomach as she fought for breath. *I need to do more laps at the pool – I'm getting soft,* she thought. Hearing a soft moan, she focused her attention on her surroundings again. *Where was that sound coming from?* The hall was mostly empty now except for a crumpled heap of green clothes lying in the aisle.

The circus tent, so full of festive celebration just a few moments ago, had transformed into a scene of chaos. The men with masks had thrown stones at the lights, breaking many of them. The shadows seemed full of danger.

Ramu ran up to her, his face full of worry, pulling her into a hard embrace. She hugged him back quickly before taking his hand and hurrying past the empty seats to investigate the heap in the aisle.

'Suman!' Ramu sounded alarmed. He crouched down, placing a hand on the crumpled form and reaching for his arm to check his pulse.

'Still breathing, thank God,' he said, looking up at Kaveri. He ran his hands expertly across Suman's head and chest. 'No visible signs of injury, but he has a lump on his skull. Perhaps he fell and hit his head on a chair.'

'Or someone hit him,' Kaveri added. She heard the heavy tread of footsteps, and looked up, her face brightening when she saw Inspector Ismail approaching. Turning towards him, she spoke eagerly.

'We found Suman – why do you think—'

Before she could complete her sentence, he cut her off. 'Mrs Murthy, please stop right there. This is a job for the police. I must ask you to leave now.' His tone was stern, leaving no scope for demurral.

Kaveri reached out to steady herself, placing her hands on the chair behind her. Already reeling from shock and exertion, she could not bring herself to speak, to ask him what was wrong. Inspector Ismail had never behaved to her like this – regarding her with hard eyes, as though she was a stranger.

As she gaped at him, opening and closing her mouth, his wife appeared behind him.

'My dear, you ought to go home now,' she said, moving towards Kaveri and grasping her by the elbow. 'See how exhausted Anandi is.' She pointed to the entrance, where Anandi stood leaning against a wooden pole, looking on the edge of collapse. Kaveri saw Dr and Miss Roberts being escorted away from the theatre by a posse of middle-aged policemen. Wilks stood in the corner, deep in conversation with a lanky constable.

'Come, Kaveri,' Ramu said softly. 'The Inspector is right.' He took her other arm, steering her towards the exit where Anandi was standing, watching them. She tried to look back at Inspector Ismail, but he had turned his back on her once again.

Kaveri barely noticed Mrs Ismail bidding them farewell. She took in the tent with its awry carpet and broken wooden seats, the canvas frame torn by the crowd rushing towards the exit. Behind them, she saw two policemen carrying Suman on a makeshift stretcher, moving purposefully towards the gap. The frightened little girl must be safely home now with her grandfather.

The masked men seemed like a gang of organised thieves, appearing at a pre-planned time to loot the audience when their attention was captured by Das's disappearance. Thanks to the quick work of Wilks and Ismail, the men had not succeeded in their plan. Had the police been tipped off that something like this was going to happen? She would have asked Ismail, but the way he was behaving today, it was unlikely that she would get anything out of him.

Anandi's body trembled against her as Kaveri placed an arm around her waist, Ramu holding her shoulders as they half-carried the young woman towards the car. Pawan must have some hold on her still, Kaveri thought, making her so afraid that she had run, despite having Ismail, Kaveri *and* Ramu nearby for support.

Anandi looked down, refusing to meet her gaze. Ramu met her eyes, shaking his head slightly. This was not the time to interrogate Anandi. It would have to wait.

The ground outside the tent, so full of vehicles a short while back when they had entered the circus, was now empty and desolate except for a few policemen standing and talking in small groups. A light rain fell, soaking Kaveri's clothing, the wind cutting through her brocade blouse and chiffon sari with ease. The wet grass tickled the soles of her feet, wetting her flimsy chappals as she shivered with cold.

A series of disconnected images flashed through Kaveri's mind as she walked carefully on the muddy ground, slippery with wet fallen leaves. Iron chains, angry snakes and a tiny cage, from which no human being could have been able to get in or out. Except perhaps a magician. She patted the outline of her notebook against her hip, poking through her reticule. She had to write all of this down to make sense of it.

As Ramu moved around the bonnet of the car, reaching for the door on the driver's side, she saw a flash of red on the ground. Anandi let out a small scream, and they followed her gaze, seeing a crumpled figure lying next to the car. Kaveri's heart hammered in her chest. It was Pawan – the red silk bandana tied around his neck. He couldn't be alive – his neck was twisted into an impossible position.

Anandi turned to Kaveri, burying her face in her shoulders as Kaveri held her tightly, patting her back again and again as Anandi's body shook with the violence of her sobs. Over Anandi's head, Kaveri watched as Ramu crouched down to feel for Pawan's pulse. Anandi quivered in Kaveri's arms as seconds passed like minutes and hours. After a short while, Ramu shook his head. 'Dead,' he said to her, waving his hand in the air to signal a nearby constable, who came racing over.

The two men gripped Pawan's shoulders, carefully

turning him. Kaveri took a deep breath, steadying her nerves and forcing herself to look carefully at the dead man. His eyes were open, his face still distorted in pain. The front of his shirt was a bloody mess – the knife that had killed him still lay embedded in his breast. His face was puffy with fluid, distending the tattooed snake on the right side of his forehead, making it seem alive and writhing.

'He's dead . . .' Anandi said in a thin wail. She extricated herself from Kaveri's grasp, holding one hand over her mouth and one over her throat. Her eyes, huge and frightened, caught Kaveri's. Kaveri reached forward, trying to grab hold of Anandi again, but she slipped through her arms, collapsing to the ground.

4

A Door Slams Shut

Later next morning, Kaveri sat sipping strong filter
coffee from a steel tumbler, restlessly tapping her feet
against the red oxide floor. The sound of a horn had her
leaning forward to press her nose against the window before sitting back, deflated. It was just the neighbour's car.

'Not here yet?' her mother-in-law Bhargavi asked from
the doorway of the kitchen. 'You'll wear out the floor if
you continue pacing up and down like that. You remind
me of the lion we saw when we went to the Lal Bagh zoo
last month. Caged, waiting for freedom.'

They had returned home very late last night, after
dropping Anandi to the women's shelter where she lived
and worked. She had looked pale, but refused to allow
them to come in with her. Kaveri had wanted to go after
her, but Ramu had held her back. 'Let her get a good
night's rest,' he advised. 'She will be in a better condition
to speak to you once she sleeps. That goes for you too,
Kaveri. Tomorrow, when you are well rested, you can make
sense of what she says and everything that has happened.'

The horrific events at the circus had wrought her
nerves up, and the sleepless night that followed only
made things worse. Kaveri had found it difficult to keep
her eyes open this morning. The coffee helped, but now
she felt faintly nauseous.

Kaveri drained the tumbler in front of her, pouring it
down her throat in one swift gulp before responding to
her mother-in-law. 'I need the car to meet Anandi,' she
complained. 'It's strange to think that I had never driven
a car until I moved to Bangalore a few months back –
and I already miss it so much. Perhaps I should call the
garage again, and find out what's taking them so long.'
She tilted the glass, trying to lick the last remaining
drops of the coffee.

'No more for you,' Bhargavi said firmly as she took
the tumbler away. 'That's your third cup since you woke
up.' She looked at Kaveri with concern, noting the dark
shadows under her eyes. 'Something is bothering you.'

Kaveri stared unseeingly at the carved rosewood table
in front of her, rubbing her toes along its clawed feet.
'After Pawan threatened Anandi, she ran away from him.
Pawan followed her, and we lost sight of her for a few
minutes. When we saw her again, something had frightened her so badly that she was on the edge of collapse.
Did she witness his murder?'

Bhargavi's voice was grave. 'I know Inspector Ismail is
not like other policemen, but when an abusive husband is
murdered, the battered wife is the first person they suspect.'

'I am so afraid of that, that it has been eating me all
night,' Kaveri admitted. 'A constable was going to come
around to take our statement after lunch. What if they
take Anandi into custody?'

'Speak to Inspector Ismail instead,' Bhargavi advised.
'It will be easier to explain to him directly.'

Kaveri gave her an uncertain look. 'The Inspector behaved very strangely yesterday. Aloof, almost hostile. I don't know if speaking to him will help.'

'Nonsense, he is one of your biggest supporters,' Bhargavi said robustly, pushing the telephone closer to her.

Kaveri picked up the receiver, speaking to the operator. When Ismail came on the line, she paused, hearing his curt greeting. Her carefully constructed statement went flying out of her head, as she spilt out everything in an incoherent, stammering rush. She kicked herself as she wound down. This was not how she had wanted to break it to him!

The second hand on the wall clock ticked loudly as she waited for his response. Trying to keep calm, she struggled to focus on the creeping progress of a lizard crawling across the wall, a black fly in its beady focus.

A deep voice carried over the telephone barking out orders in a crisp British accent behind Ismail. Unable to bear the Inspector's silence, she blurted out again, 'You know Anandi hasn't got a violent bone in her body. She wouldn't do anything to Pawan.'

'Thank you for the statement, Mrs Murthy.' Ismail spoke with cold finality. 'We will follow up with Dr Rama Rao and Anandi, and only then decide on next steps.' He hung up abruptly. Kaveri shuddered, watching the lizard put out a long pink tongue, flicking the fly into his mouth.

'Major Wilks was at the police station. I heard his voice, issuing instructions,' she fretted, putting down the telephone receiver. 'I hope he's not in charge of the investigations. He seems like such a hard man.' She pulled at the curtain tassels, picking at a loose thread.

'I know you don't want to hear this, but I must ask you,' Bhargavi said gently. 'Are you sure that Anandi did not do something to him? I know how badly he treated her – Ramu told me she would have died of her wounds if Mala had not found her and brought her to his hospital. Could you blame her if she snapped and stabbed him?'

'I cannot believe it.' Kaveri shook her head fiercely, loyal to her friend. But in her mind, a treacherous voice whispered, 'What if she's right?' She squashed the thought, her mouth set in stubborn lines. 'If even you think she may have done it, what hope can we have from the police? I don't know if Anandi realises how much danger she is in. I must meet her immediately and get some answers from her. We have to find out who killed Pawan, otherwise she will always remain a suspect. I wish my car was here.' She looked towards the window again.

It had been weeks since she had last driven her beloved Ford. The garage had been working on major repairs to the car for quite a while now.

'That car saved you from a major accident just a few weeks back,' Bhargavi said, catching Kaveri's glance at the window. 'You have called them twice already this morning. Let them take the time they need to repair the car.'

But Kaveri paid little heed to her. Hearing the sound of a horn, she jumped up, opening the door eagerly. Her car had finally arrived.

Bidding her mother-in-law goodbye, Kaveri hastily washed her face clear of tear stains and picked up the keys from the garage's driver. She rushed to the back of the house, attaching a leash to Putta's collar and taking her dog with her. Anandi loved Putta – perhaps he would help lift her spirits today.

The wind from the open window blew on her cheeks, making her hair fly in the wind. As she drove, Kaveri felt her spirits lift, the depression that had engulfed her since the previous evening slowly dissipating with the wind. As one of the first women to drive in Bangalore, she had become used to seeing people gape at her in open admiration as she drove by. If she was being honest, she missed the attention, Kaveri admitted to herself ruefully. Was she becoming too vain?

She had a special fondness for Anandi. Ramu and Kaveri had nursed her back to health, sheltering her from Pawan, finding her a new job and a place to stay. Anandi had repaid them amply, helping Kaveri capture Shanthi's husband's murderer while risking her own life. But how could one talk of debts or of repayment, for friends who had together endured the desperate difficulties that they had?

She would not mourn Pawan's death, Kaveri decided fiercely. Though even a man like him deserved to have his murder investigated, the killer caught and punished. She moved the clutch to a higher gear and pressed on the accelerator, eager to get to the Women's Home as fast as possible.

'I won't desert Anandi when she is in difficulty, Putta.' Kaveri told the big dog, who whined in soft agreement from the back seat. 'She can keep repeating she is fine, but I know something is deeply wrong.'

Putta yipped in agreement. As Kaveri turned into the compound of the Women's Home, he sat up straight, ears erect. He was a favourite with the women who resided there, and loved the pampering and treats he received from them.

'Silly puppy. You will get spoiled if you go on like this,' Kaveri scolded him. He only panted in agreement, giving her a charming lopsided grin. Pulling up at her destination, she gave him a sideways glance. Even after all these months of having Putta, she still could not understand how he had received the Ugliest Dog of the Year prize. Yes, his face wasn't exactly symmetric, and he wouldn't have won an award for elegance, but he was the most beautiful dog she knew – inside *and* outside.

Kaveri parked outside the compound and threw her arms around Putta, kissing the top of his head. He licked her face, looking up at her worshipfully. Feeling her mood transform, she tugged at his leash, pulling him out of the car and opening the gate, admiring the neat line of brightly coloured chappals along the compound wall. The thoughts of the horrific experiences of the previous evening were beginning to fade, replaced by other memories. How different the building had looked and sounded a few months back, when the women inside had been drugged insensible. Now that Shanthi had taken over, converting it into a shelter for abandoned women in her husband's memory, the atmosphere had completely transformed. The once-silent compound was filled with chatter and hope.

A group of young women, their hair neatly tied into long plaits that swung from their backs, were breathless with laughter, following Anandi who led them through an exercise routine that involved shaking their arms and legs in the air, throwing their heads back and yelling at the tops of their voices. One of the women edged close to the mango tree. She stopped, letting out a tiny scream as she spotted a palm-sized insect covered in bristly hairs that lay close to her feet.

'Wait!' Anandi ordered, stepping forward. She bent down, using two dry leaves to pick up the bright green insect, carefully placing it on a large mango leaf. 'Don't touch it,' she warned. 'It's a Baron caterpillar. It feeds on mango leaves and turns into a lovely brown butterfly, but it's also intensely poisonous – if your skin comes in contact with it, you will be covered in rashes, scratching for days.'

The woman moved away from the tree, resuming her exercise routine. Kaveri exhaled, feeling several pounds lighter, her spirits lifting further as she watched them yell at the tops of their voices. Anandi had a book in her hand – the book that Kaveri had found for her in the library, a week back. Written by an American woman suffragist, the book extolled the virtues of exercise for young women, to build their physical and mental confidence. Women were trained to speak softly, be ladylike. Shouting, the writer claimed, would help them become more assertive, occupying space in the same manner men did, demanding to be treated as equals.

Rich and poor, old and young, the women in the shelter had never been exposed to such radical ideas. Some were child widows, others married women abandoned by their husbands, or battered wives fleeing abuse. Freedom, rights – for them these were alien words. With Shanthi and Anandi's gentle coaxing, they were beginning to come into their own as individuals – and to form strong bonds with each other, gaining confidence in leaps and bounds as they helped their sisters.

The fete to be held by the Anglo-Indian Women's Society next week, where Bhargavi and Shanthi were organising a stall, would showcase the craftwork of the women and help them earn their own money. For many, it would be the first time they were in charge of funds that they had generated themselves – not handouts from the men in their family, but cash that they could use as they wanted. To decide to spend, or save, as *they* saw fit. The wooden tables on the verandah were piled high with their work – crocheted lace doilies, appliqué bed sheets, embroidered cushion covers and knitted children's sweaters and booties.

Kaveri stayed where she was for a moment, one hand on the gate, watching the women as they completed a series of jumping jacks. When they lined up in pairs, picking up table tennis rackets and moving towards the tables in the verandah, Anandi turned away, leaving them to their practice. She had laughed and joked with the other young women, but now her shoulders slumped, her feet kicking up puffs of mud as she walked to the garden tap. Kaveri moved towards her, placing a hand on her shoulder as Anandi bent to wash her face,

Anandi turned. Her face fell.

'It's you, *akka*. What do you want now?'

First Ismail, now Anandi? What was happening to all her friends? Anandi had *never* spoken to her like this before, as though she was a complete stranger poking her nose into someone else's business. Kaveri felt a heaviness in her chest. In a rational corner of her brain, she reminded herself that she should not take it personally. Anandi had been through an immensely traumatic event, losing her husband just the previous night. He had treated her horrifically, but she must have loved him once.

'I only came . . . I just . . . I wanted . . .' Kaveri hesitated.

Anandi cut her off. '*Akka*, I will say this only once,' she burst out, speaking in a rush, as though she had memorised a speech and wanted to get it all out before she forgot it. The agony in her voice stopped Kaveri short. 'Please, let me finish.' Her voice was desperate, high pitched. A couple of women playing close to them stopped, turning to give them curious glances. A puff of dust from their fast-moving feet came into Kaveri's face, and she coughed, her eyes watering.

Anandi continued heedlessly. 'I know you mean well, *akka*. And you want to help me. But have you ever considered that perhaps I don't want to be helped? You can't save everyone in the world. Leave me to my fate. Maybe I deserve what is coming to me.'

She placed a hand over her mouth, looking horrified that those words had slipped out. Then she ran from the compound to her room, running so fast that Kaveri could not catch up with her. As Kaveri reached her door, panting for breath, Anandi slammed it in her face, bolting it from inside. Kaveri stopped, hearing the sound of furious weeping on the other side.

'Anandi, please – let me in,' Kaveri pleaded, feeling helpless. 'Let me know what is wrong. You don't have to handle this alone.'

There was no response. As Kaveri waited on the other side of the closed door, she heard a small 'Woof!' A cold nose pressed into her hand, and a small tongue softly licked it. Putta stood outside the door, one ear cocked to the sound of Anandi's sobs, quieter now.

The dog barked in response to her distress. His barks were not loud, but they were insistent. He kept barking, repeatedly, then threw his body against the door. Kaveri stepped back, watching the dog as he whined, an unmistakable sound that said, as clearly as if he had spoken, 'Let me in, woman.'

A hesitant, watery laugh came from the other side of the door. 'Silly dog,' Anandi muttered, but it was said with real affection. She opened the door slowly, her eyes red and her nose swollen from crying. Putta reared up in the doorway, placing his paws on her shoulders, and licking the tears from her cheeks. She buried her face in the loose folds of skin hanging around his neck.

Kaveri swiped at her cheeks, wiping away her own

tears. Putta, starved, abandoned and maltreated by his former master for being the 'Ugliest Dog', could so easily have become ill-tempered and ferocious himself, unwilling to trust people. So many such animals turned bitter – just like people did. But abuse seemed to have strengthened the ungainly pup's innate empathy and affection. He unhesitatingly sought out other wounded souls, comforting them without hesitation.

Anandi looked calmer now. When she stopped petting Putta, the dog jumped up on the bed, and turned around a couple of times, making himself a comfortable nest in the middle of her blankets. 'Woof!' he barked, looking up at Kaveri.

Anandi's room was neat as a pin, the bed parallel to the wall, cushions lined up at right angles. On the wall, she had displayed her latest masterpiece – a large appliqué work piece representing a forest full of butterflies. Kaveri sat down on the bed, picking up a stack of embroidered silk handkerchiefs with Anandi's signature element, butterflies – they were now one of the Home's bestselling pieces, thanks to which Anandi had built up a sizeable nest egg in the bank. Keeping a wary eye on Putta, Kaveri picked up the delicate kerchiefs and set them safely aside on the table.

'These are so beautiful, Anandi,' she said impulsively. Butterflies were Anandi's favourite creature – ever since she had read Kaveri's biology textbook, discovering an entire chapter on metamorphosis, she had been hooked, obsessed with caterpillars. On the floor, she saw that Anandi had placed a heavy book, *Insects of Surinam*, on a small rug. Ramu had gifted the book to Anandi, ordering it from London for her after Kaveri had told him of Anandi's interest. Anandi was fascinated by the rich illustrations of metamorphic insects, but even more fascinated by the fact that the woman who wrote it, Maria Sibylla Merian, had travelled across the world to document insects almost 250 years back. That was Anandi's dream, as she had confided in Kaveri once. To travel the world and study butterflies. That's what she was saving for.

Those dreams seemed far away now. Anandi sat down on the other side of the bed, ignoring her compliments. 'What do you want to ask me?' she said bluntly.

'Did you know Pawan was in town?'

'No!' Anandi shook her head so violently that the entire bed shook. Putta whined again, licking her foot. 'I swear to you, I didn't know. Until I saw him at the circus.'

'I believe you.' Kaveri put out a hand, assuring her. 'You seemed defiant at first, when you saw him, shouting at him to go away.'

Anandi eyed her warily, but did not say anything.

'Then something happened. He took something out of his pocket and showed it to you, frightening you. What was it?'

Anandi's eyes swivelled around the room. 'He told me that he would come to the Women's Home and take me away. I was scared that he would frighten the women here.' She spoke in a rush, her voice high and unconvincing.

Kaveri stared at her, and Anandi gave a rueful laugh, refusing to meet her eyes. 'I had forgotten what a bloodhound you are when on the trail of a murderer. You're not going to leave me alone, are you?'

Kaveri flinched. Why would Anandi not understand that she was only trying to help her?

Sensing the tension in the air, Putta whined, trying to lick Anandi. Anandi moved closer to him, putting an arm around him, and scratched his ears. 'He is saying he will stay with me, isn't he? Leave him here, *akka*.' Tears were flowing freely down her cheeks now. Her voice shook. 'I know what you want to ask me. But please, *please* don't press me. I can't tell you anything now, so soon after Pawan's death. I need to sort through a few things on my own first.' Anandi's hand gripped the iron bedframe, squeezing so tightly that Kaveri could see her fingers turning white. 'Ask me again in two days,' she beseeched.

5

Many Ways to Skin a Tiger

Out of sorts after returning home, Kaveri went to the one place that always calmed her – her shed, which stood in a corner of the compound. When she looked up at the painted sign for the Bangalore Detectives Club that hung outside, her tense shoulders relaxed. Her shed was her sanctuary.

She pulled out a small ladder, climbing up to pull out one of her favourite books from a high shelf – a volume by Henry Sinclair Hall and Samuel Ratcliffe Knight. *Solutions to the Examples in Higher Algebra* was just what she was looking for. Now that she had got her matriculation degree, she wanted to progress to the next stage, enrolling for an Intermediate examination. Yet, how could she, when none of the colleges in Bangalore or Mysore accepted women to study Mathematics and Science? In his last letter to her, Kaveri's father had sent her some exciting news. The Maharani of Mysore, who had founded the Maharani Girls' School where Kaveri had studied in Mysore, was trying to change these rules.

If they opened admission to women, she wanted to be prepared, ready to write the entrance examination at short notice.

Kaveri spent most of the morning in her shed, solving her way through page after page of problems. Gradually, her headache dissipated, along with the nausea that she had battled since those many cups of coffee earlier. Her stomach rumbled, reminding her that she had missed breakfast.

Her mother-in-law had told her she was going to be at Shanthi's home all day, and Ramu was coming home late, so she prepared a simple lunch for herself – coconut rice with toasted sesame seeds and fried curry leaves, along with a simple red pumpkin *raita*. Kaveri ate in the library, rifling through the typed manuscript in which she had recorded the details of her second case. The memory of the horrific scene that had started the investigation came back to her. The sight of Shanthi's husband, shot with a gun, slumped against a desk, blood dripping from his chest onto the floor. She pushed the plate away, squeezing her eyes, willing herself to forget that horrific scene. Using another technique that her *kalari* teacher had taught her to banish tension from the mind, she settled down on a straw *chaape* in a corner of the room to practise *pranayama*. Alternately breathing through her right and left nostrils, she focused her attention on her breath, calming slowly. Getting up to open the window, she tilted her face up, soaking in the sun and the sight of the yellow and lime green butterflies, greedily sucking nectar from her carefully tended rose garden. Bhargavi loved the butterflies – she had recently ordered a silk *Kanjeevaram* sari made up in the same colours from the weavers of Kanchi, which was due to arrive next week.

Kaveri went towards the table in the corner, removing the white silk cloth that protected her new Underwood

typewriter from dust. A gift from Ramu, on the successful conclusion of her second case, she prized it above
anything – well, anything except the magnifying glass
jewellery set that he had had designed for her, after her
first case, when she had solved the murder of Ponnuswamy
at the Century Club.

A small smile appeared on her face when she remembered how excited Bhargavi had been when the typewriter
had arrived at their home. She had even blessed Kaveri's
typewriter when it first arrived by performing an auspicious *puja* to Lord Ganesha, God of new beginnings.
Their investigations during the murder of Shanthi's
husband had brought Kaveri closer to her once-acerbic
mother-in-law, something Kaveri had once feared would
never happen. Bhargavi, who had at one time cavilled
at the thought of Kaveri being involved in anything as
unsavoury as solving murders, was now a wholehearted
supporter of hers.

That was definitely a good thing, as Kaveri seemed to
be stumbling upon murders all the time in Bangalore.
But she had to move quickly, even though Anandi had
asked for a couple of days – or the trail would grow cold.
Kaveri pulled out the mechanical pencil sharpener that
Ramu had ordered from a catalogue last week, tired of
seeing nicks and cuts on her hands. How easy this was –
even she, always clumsy with a blade, could use this easily.
Humming with satisfaction at the prospect of sorting out
her scrambled thoughts, she opened her trusty notebook,
scribbling down rough notes. There seemed to be at least
three events that merited further investigation: Das's mysterious disappearance from the cage, the gang of thieves
who had appeared in the audience, and Pawan's death.

She thought of Suman's bleak face, and his eyes, so
frantically searching for his father after he'd disappeared

from the cage. Had he expected that Das would return to the stage, bowing to the audience's applause, as magicians usually did at the end of shows like this? Kaveri had once read a book from the library on famous magicians. Harry Houdini, the American escape artist, could get out of water torture chambers and straitjackets, even staging an escape after being buried alive. Had Das been trying to emulate Houdini's escapades? For Suman's sake, she hoped that Das was alive and safe, and had returned to the circus later that night.

There was something very peculiar about the Maharaja of Magic. Remembering his hypnotic gaze on her, Kaveri felt an icy cold sensation at the base of her spine, as though someone was sliding an ice cube down her back. She suppressed a shudder. There was no need to let her imagination get the better of her. There must be a logical explanation for the 'magic' that Suman and Das had performed onstage – and for everything that had happened afterwards.

The gang of robbers had appeared as soon as Das's performance had ended. Pawan had arrived before the start of the performance, then reappeared at the same time as the masked men, also wearing a mask. It seemed too well timed to be a coincidence. Could Das have been in cahoots with the robbers – staging a dramatic disappearance, diverting the attention of the audience at the same time that the thieves spread across the room? And Pawan's death had occurred only a short while afterwards. Perhaps one of his fellow thieves had killed him after an argument.

Kaveri set aside her notebook and inserted a new sheet of paper in her typewriter, starting a new file where she could type in her scribbled notes. It seemed she had a new case on her hands! She felt a flutter of excitement, as she thought of the list of questions she wanted to ask. Married into a wealthy family, with enough money to hire an army of servants, and with a mother-in-law who shared the load of cooking and house management with her, she knew she was fortunate. Many of her friends, like Uma aunty who had to take care of her grandson at all odd hours of the day, or Mala, who had once had to work as a prostitute to feed herself, could not understand how she felt. How could she tell them that time hung heavy on her hands? When she was working on a case, she felt worthwhile, helping someone who needed assistance. When she had been studying for her matriculation, she had felt like she was making something of her life. But otherwise . . . there were days she just sat staring at the clock, willing it to move faster.

Only her *kalari* teacher understood how she felt. 'Kick harder,' the normally taciturn old woman had advised Kaveri one evening, pointing to a stuffed dummy hanging from a hook. 'The world is full of many things that women cannot change. Close your eyes, picture something that makes you angry, and transform it into this dummy in your mind. Then *kick*.'

Some days, Kaveri kicked until she was sore. It made her feel better – for a while. But nothing would replace the satisfaction of a new case, where she finally got to use her skills as a detective.

Deep in thought, fingers flying furiously, she jumped when she felt a hand on her shoulder. 'Kaveri?' She saw Shanthi, her mother-in-law's cousin, studying her curiously. 'I did not mean to startle you. Bhargavi *akka* and I are back home. She sent me to call you.'

Kaveri jumped up, hugging Shanthi with pleasure. Her eyes lingered on Shanthi's forehead, where her hair had started to turn silver. Her heart went out to the older woman. Shanthi been through so much since she was widowed, but bore her loss with quiet dignity.

Kaveri put away the typewriter, and made her way back to the main house with Shanthi. Bhargavi was already seated at the dining table, drinking a cup of steaming hot coffee, with the newspaper open in front of her. Skimming past advertisements for bromide enlargements of oil colours and outdoor photographs, she looked up at Shanthi and Kaveri, gesturing to the open page. 'Did you see this? The Prince of Wales shot and killed another tiger yesterday.'

Shanthi let out a snort of disgust. 'You know how this is done, don't you? The Maharaja asks his men to go into the forest and snare one of these poor beasts. One or two of the beaters and hunters may even die in the process – but what does that matter? They snare the defenceless beast, place it into a cage, and feed it with meat laced with tranquillisers. Then they bring the cage close to the location where the Prince and his team is taken to hunt, and release it – and, surprise, valorous Edward, Prince of Wales, demonstrates his peerless hunting skills again.'

'Shanthi. Keep your voice down.' Bhargavi shifted uncomfortably on her chair. 'If you talk so loudly, even the people walking on the road will hear you.'

'So what? I don't care,' Shanthi muttered. But she lowered her voice all the same. Her fingers drummed on the table restlessly. 'As it is, I watch my words all day. I can't speak freely at my home, or the factory – I never know what gossip the security guards or the factory workers might take back with them, and to whom. Even at the Women's Home I am very careful – if I am suspected or arrested, the Home might be closed down, and then what will become of the women? It is only at the meetings held by the Congress that I can speak freely.' Shanthi banged her fists on the table, sending her bangles clattering.

'You know I do not approve of your going to the meetings, Shanthi,' Bhargavi said, her gaze intent on her cousin. 'Especially now, when the police are noting down the names of everyone who attends these conversations about our independence.'

'Yes, yes, I know all that,' Shanthi interrupted abruptly. 'Ever since Prince Edward was greeted by crowds booing and jeering the British Empire in Bombay last November, the police are on high alert here. They want to make sure his visit to Bangalore two weeks from now goes smoothly. But I will not be scared away from these meetings just because of a foreign prince and his Indian defenders.' Shanthi's lips were compressed into a defiant line.

Bhargavi leaned across the table to take Shanthi's hand in hers, pressing Shanthi's palm against her check. 'Don't I know you better than anyone else?' She turned to Kaveri. 'See this stubborn face. Shanthi had the same look even when she was a child – if you told her not to do something, whether it was to climb a tree in her long skirt, or to go loitering on the road, she would do whatever she pleased.' Bhargavi patted Shanthi's cheek. 'At least you don't stick out your tongue at me now when I tell you something.'

This drew an unwilling laugh from her cousin.

'Bhargavi *akka*, I never could get the better of you in an argument. I will leave all this aside, and only return to it once the white warrior Prince leaves our homeland, carrying a few bales of tiger skin as tokens of many successful hunts.'

With a determined shake of her head, Shanthi drained her coffee in one gulp, setting the steel *dabra* and tumbler aside on the table, and picking up the newspaper.

'What else do we have here? Come, let's see what the Mysore Maharaja has planned for the visit of Prince Edward.'

As Kaveri and Shanthi turned the pages of the newspaper, Bhargavi stood up, turning to leave the room. They had purchased some new saris yesterday, and she had been keen to take them to the tailor to get matching blouses made. 'I will bring the blouse piece material for you, Shanthi – you can take it over for the girls to embroider,' she said.

Watching Bhargavi leave, Shanthi exhaled in relief. She turned to Kaveri, who was holding back a smile.

'Bhargavi *akka* looked after me like a mother when my *Amma* died many years ago. But she does not realise that I am a grown woman now, capable of taking care of myself.'

'It is only because she loves you.' Kaveri felt impelled to defend her mother-in-law. It had taken her a while to understand her, and get a sense of the soft, caring woman that existed under the prickly exterior she showed to the outside world. But she also understood how Shanthi felt. Once disapproving of Kaveri's alter ego as a detective, Bhargavi was now one of her biggest supporters, but there was still much that Kaveri needed to keep hidden from her – otherwise Bhargavi would try to forbid her from doing anything too risky. And how could one detect at all without taking risks?

Shanthi squeezed her eyes shut briefly. When she opened them, she seemed weary, a few years older. 'I did not want to tell Bhargavi *akka*, but the discussions in the pro-independence meetings have now taken an acrimonious turn. Even though most members of the Congress agreed to Gandhiji's proposal for a national civil disobedience movement, a small group is opposed.

They insist that the movement has achieved little in the past year, and the violence of the British Empire can only be countered with force.'

'What does Sarojini Naidu say?' Kaveri asked. She admired the poetess and freedom fighter, and she knew Shanthi thought a lot of her too – Mrs Naidu had introduced Shanthi to her late husband at one of the meetings.

'She agrees with Gandhiji. If we are violent, then we lose our claim to moral high ground. We need to drive out these invaders from our soil – but we cannot let the ends justify the means. The outside world is watching us, and we need to demonstrate that we are not like the British.'

Kaveri wrinkled her nose. 'We should greet the Prince with riots, or any form of protest that can lead to blood on our hands,' she said slowly, feeling her way through the complex argument she was struggling to articulate, even to herself.

Shanthi watched her curiously.

'But? There is a "but", am I right, Kaveri?'

'You told me once that Gandhiji was influenced by a passage from the New Testament which says, "To the one who strikes you on the cheek, turn the other cheek; to the one who takes your coat, give also your shirt." But how can *ahimsa*, non-violence, protect us from the brutality of the British? We are safe in Mysore, shielded by the protection of the Maharaja. But what of the hundreds of innocents who gathered to protest in Jallianwala Bagh, mowed down by General Dyer's bullets? Should we forgive Dyer, handing him another gun and turning the other cheek? That makes no sense.'

Kaveri's voice broke, as she continued, 'It's not just the protesters, I am thinking of women like Anandi too. If a woman is being abused by her husband, should she reason with him, try and make him see the error of his ways, and if he disagrees, return for more abuse? Even if she is pregnant, and he is kicking her swollen belly?'

'Like your former milkman Manju – Venu's brother?' Shanthi asked Kaveri.

Kaveri clenched her hands into fists. 'He beat Muniamma so brutally that she almost lost their baby. If I were married to such a man, I would have hit him back so hard that he would never have the courage to look askance at me, let alone raise his hand.'

Kaveri's shoulders remained stiff for a moment as she thought of all the abused women she had met in the past few months – Muniamma, Mala, and now Anandi. But when Shanthi came forward to hug her, she relaxed into her arms, returning the hug with a fierce embrace before she disengaged herself.

'Let us speak of other things for a while. You were typing furiously, Kaveri,' Shanthi said, deliberately changing the subject as she noted Kaveri's distress. 'You do that only when you have a new case. Did anything happen recently?'

'There is a lot I have to tell you,' Kaveri said, sitting down across from her. 'I thought the news of Pawan's death and Das's disappearance would be in the papers today. I suspect Inspector Ismail spoke to the reporters, asking them to keep it under wraps.'

'Pawan is dead?' Shanthi asked, head cocked. 'I assume Anandi knows. She seemed very upset when I saw her this morning. Oh, she tried to put a brave face on it, smiling whenever she found me watching her. She can't hide it from me though. I know her too well.'

'She was there when it happened,' Kaveri said. 'Pawan was at the circus yesterday. He threatened her. She seemed defiant at first, but he said something to her that made her so frightened that she collapsed. Then . . .'

Shanthi listened carefully, as Kaveri quickly told her everything that had happened the previous night.

'So, Pawan reached a sticky end. I always suspected he would. That man is bad news through and through,' Shanthi said. 'I learned very recently that he had returned to Bangalore. I feared that she would get a visit from him some day soon.'

'But Anandi told us months ago that Pawan had escaped from Bangalore.' Kaveri paced the room, her steps small and jerky. 'He owed so much money to local moneylenders that he fled, unable to repay them. How has he managed to return?'

6

Sliding Backwards and Forwards

'Let me talk to her,' Shanthi said. 'I'll see if she will confide anything in me.' But her voice was not very hopeful. 'She is not speaking to me as much these days.'

'Not speaking to *you*?' Kaveri could not believe it. 'Anandi seeks your advice for practically everything.'

Shanthi gave her a wry smile. 'Not any more, not since I counselled her to stop going to the independence meetings.'

'I didn't know you had started taking her along with you,' Kaveri said, her curiosity piqued.

'A couple of months back, she came with me for the first time. Perhaps it was a mistake. You know how passionate she is when she gets involved with anything. I told her that we should take a break from the meetings for a while, until the Prince's visit. There are rumours swirling everywhere. Some say that a group of protestors are slowly making their way to Bangalore, gathering from different parts of India – Bombay, Calcutta, Madras, even the smaller cities – Ahmedabad, Belgaum. They plan to do something big to disrupt the Prince's visit. It could be violent.'

Kaveri placed a hand on Shanthi's arm. 'I read in the newspapers that a small group of armed protestors stormed a police station in Chauri Chaura, setting it on fire.'

'That's exactly what I am worried about, Kaveri,' Shanthi responded soberly. 'Twenty-two policemen died that day. A horrific death. Locked into that police station, with no way of escape. They were our compatriots too, even if they worked for the British. Family men, who left behind parents, wives. Their children are now fatherless – and that is our moral responsibility.' Her eyes filled with tears. 'The Congress Party is very worried about the likelihood of violence spreading across the country. We cannot afford a repetition of the events of the 1857 mutiny – the British clamped down on us so harshly after that, in the aftermath of the terrible violence that engulfed the whole country. It set us back by decades.

'Anandi refused to see sense. When she insisted on going, we exchanged a few harsh words. I told her she was being irresponsible, that she had a duty to the women in the shelter which came first. She retorted that her primary duty was to the country – why could I not see that? I had to make her see reason. I threatened to fire her from her job.' Shanthi's eyes were sorrowful. 'It was an empty threat, of course. Firing Anandi would be like cutting off my right hand. She is so dear to me – like another younger sister. But this was the only way I could think of to get her to listen to me.'

'Did it work?' Kaveri asked.

'She seemed horrified, and said she would stop going to the meetings. I am not sure if she meant it, though. Relations between us have been strained ever since.

She only speaks to me when she needs to. Most of our communication is in monosyllables these days.' She heard Bhargavi's footsteps, and turned to see her coming down the stairs. 'Don't tell Bhargavi *akka*. She knows nothing of this. It will only alarm her further.'

Kaveri nodded in silent assent.

'What are the two of you discussing so intently?' Bhargavi approached them, her eyebrows bristling with curiosity.

'Nothing important,' Kaveri said, quickly pasting a smile on her face. Bhargavi's eyes narrowed on her, but she did not say anything more.

'Uma aunty sent this across the wall, with Rajamma, to fire up your brains.' Bhargavi opened the large steel *dabba* she carried. 'Thinly sliced *bendekaayi*, dipped in rice batter and fried.'

Kaveri's face lit up. 'My *ajji* fed it to me every day during my exams.' She put her hand into the dabba, taking out a large handful of the crisp, dark green slivers, admiring how they glistened in the sunlight. The women crunched on the crispy fried snack as they discussed their plans for the rest of the day.

'Bhargavi *akka* and I have to return to the Women's Home now. I promised the priest at St. John's Church that we would stock a stall at their January fair, in just a few days. Some of the women have created exquisite pieces, but they are only half complete and we need to help them to complete their work,' Shanthi said, before the two women went out to the car, carrying a bundle of fabric with them.

Kaveri walked out with the two women to see them off at the gate, discussing the beautiful crochet and embroidery collection she had seen at the Home that morning. She walked back slowly, her mind replaying the conversation with Shanthi as she crossed the verandah and headed towards the front door. She hated to keep anything from her mother-in-law, with whom she had now forged a close relationship. But she had given Shanthi her word. Kaveri sighed as she entered the house – relationships could be so complicated! People shared secrets with their loved ones – they also kept secrets from the same people because of love. She hoped she and Ramu would never keep anything from each other.

The days ahead were going to be long and lonely. Bhargavi had left with a small suitcase, going to spend the next few days in Shanthi's house, while they worked on the designs for the fete. Ramu was also busy at work preparing for a vaccination camp, and would return only much later at night.

Alone at home, she would go mad if she did not find something to do. And – as her favourite detective Sherlock Holmes said – it's much harder to find the murderer once the trail has gone cold. Evidence might disappear, while people's memories grew faint, overlaid with more recent events.

Normally, she would have headed straight to the police station, to ask Inspector Ismail for information. But Kaveri remembered his scowl, the distant and curt tone in which he had addressed her on the telephone. She felt strangely reluctant to walk into the police station. What if he sent her away?

Perhaps it was better to call. She picked up the telephone, and asked the operator to connect her to the Wilson Gardens police station.

'Inspector Ismail has not yet returned. It will take another three to four hours,' a young constable shouted down the phone line. Behind him, she could hear a lot of noise.

Three to four hours?

Kaveri needed something to do, else she would go mad. Getting into the car again, she drove out to her favourite spot in Bangalore, the Century Club swimming pool, taking one of her new silk swimming costumes. Mrs Green, the Anglo-Indian shopkeeper's wife on South Parade, had stitched it for her last week, but she had not had a chance to wear it yet.

The blue costume was bright and cheered up Kaveri's spirits, as did the sight of the spectacular tree-lined avenue of Cubbon Park, with the raintrees laden with fresh green leaves that hung over the car like green chandeliers, a green ceiling instead of a red carpet highlighting her way to the pool. She pushed aside all thoughts of the man she had seen standing on the road behind her, watching her drive away.

When she got out of the pool and went into the ladies' room to dry herself, she cut her finger on a sharp sliver of wood on the door. The wound was small but deep, and Kaveri watched the blood drip from her finger into her towel. The acrid smell reminded her of the metallic stench of blood and fear that had overwhelmed her when she had found Pawan lying dead, his eyes open, yet seeing nothing. Good mood ruined, she hastily put on her sari and fled from the pool.

Not knowing what to do with herself after she returned home, she moved to the table and opened up the newspaper again, planning to search for any mention of Das's disappearance or Pawan's death.

She flipped back through every page, then closed it with a sigh. Nothing! How had the police managed to keep the news of the previous night's events from the newspaper altogether? Behind her, their maid Rajamma entered the room. Broom in hand, she walked closer to

Kaveri, who was browsing through the photographs on the inside pages.

'What is this?' Rajamma poked the centrefold photograph – showing a large elephant in the forest, carrying a number of people sitting on an ornately decorated howdah.

'This is the British Queen's son, Prince Edward. He came to Bombay in November last year – and has been hunting in the forest.' Kaveri decided not to mention the widespread *bandhs* and *hartaals*, the protest strikes. Instead of loyal Indian subjects lining up in the streets to greet the Prince with applause, he had been greeted with empty cities – the bazaars shut, the trains blocked from moving, and the streets taken over by protestors.

'In two weeks, the Prince will be in Bangalore.' Kaveri turned the page, showing Rajamma photographs of Bellandur Lake, where a pageant was being set up to greet the Prince. Loyal to the British, the Mysore Maharaja was determined that the Prince's visit to Bangalore and Mysore would be very different. The local papers were full of praise for him. Even though he planned to visit for just a day, they had devoted an entire four-page section to the details of his visit.

As Kaveri flipped through the pages, describing the plans to Rajamma – who was an unabashed supporter of the 'white Queen' – she could not help wondering how the visit would play out. A 'city of the dead', the London *Times* had called Bombay. The furious police had packed tens of thousands of 'political prisoners' off to jail, but this had only sparked further unrest, spreading like wildfire to Calcutta and other cities.

'See, Rajamma, if you learned how to read, you could read this for yourself,' Kaveri coaxed. 'You should join the meetings of the Bangalore Detectives Club.'

Rajamma picked up her broom and started to sweep the room. 'When you are there, why do I need to read? You can read to me whenever I want to know something.'

Kaveri resisted the urge to stick her tongue out at her. Rajamma continued sweeping, pulling out the sofa to tackle the dusty corners and throwing open the wooden shutters to air the room. 'How can you sit and work here in such a musty room? You will fall sick like this.'

Kaveri prowled restlessly around the house whilst waiting for Ismail to return to the police station. When that became tedious, she helped Rajamma with her cleaning, wiping down the life-sized porcelain dog statue on the front verandah with soap and water. She took down the curtains in her shed and washed them, putting them out to dry on the clothes line at the back of the house. She went over every inch of the garden, pulling up weeds, removing the diseased yellow leaves from the hibiscus plant, and cutting off the dead heads from the rose bushes.

Then, still left with excess energy to work off, she climbed over the back wall, searching for her partner in crime, their motherly neighbour Uma aunty. But the house was locked, and no one responded to her knocks on the doors, back *or* front. Kaveri let out a small scream of frustration, climbing back over the wall and kicked her mango tree quite hard. She heard a stifled laugh behind her.

Only one person laughed like that. 'Venu,' she said, a little sheepish that she had been caught behaving so childishly.

'Yes, *akka*,' their young milk delivery boy grinned cheekily. Putta barked in agreement. 'I was at the Women's Home, delivering milk. Anandi *akka* asked me to bring Putta back with me. What did the tree do to you?'

'Nothing. But I was very frustrated. So I decided to kick it.'

'What does frus ... frus ... what does that word mean, *akka*?'

'Frustrated.' Kaveri repeated it slowly, elongating every syllable, and Venu repeated it alongside her. She was trying to teach him a few more complicated words of English now, and he had not heard this one before.

Her annoyance melted away, and she smiled down at his earnest face. 'It means that I am very annoyed with myself. I have a big puzzle I am trying to solve, and I am trying to move ahead, but keep getting stuck in one place.'

Venu bobbed his head up and down. 'I know what you mean, *akka*. Sometimes, I try to run with the milk in the morning, so that I can cover more houses quickly, but some of the lanes are very muddy, especially after it rains. My feet get stuck in the mud, and I end up slipping and sliding back a few feet, instead of forward. I am also very frus ... frusted.'

Kaveri reached across and ruffled his hair. 'Frus-TRA-ted.'

Venu repeated the word once more. Then his eyes widened. 'But what is the puzzle you are trying to solve? Is it a new murder? Can I help?'

Kaveri flinched. At Venu's age, she had been playing with dolls and swimming in the large pool at the Mysore Maharani Girls' School. In the short time that she had known Venu, he had already seen a number of murders.

Venu had witnessed so much hardship in his young life. He now managed a team of young urchins who were able to quickly fan across the city, spotting suspicious activity and informing Inspector Ismail's team. No one noticed small boys on the road, but Venu and his group knew everything that went on in the city. He was still a child, though. She felt protective towards him, fretting about his too-thin frame. She tried to feed him as much as she could, but he was always on the move these days, taking up as many jobs as he could to save up for a new roof for their leaky home.

'Let's stop all this talk of murder,' she said, trying to sound stern. 'And Venu, you should not get involved in these kinds of things now. Remember, I want you to sit the primary school exams in a year.'

Venu paid her remonstrations no attention. 'I know,' he announced. 'This must have something to do with yesterday's circus performance. The one where the old magician mysteriously disappeared.'

Kaveri looked at Venu. 'You know about the disappearance of the magician? What else have you learned?' She decided not to tell him about Pawan's murder yet.

'Very little, *akka*.' Venu flashed one of his characteristic sweet smiles at her, his grimy cheeks stretching wide from ear to ear. 'I saw the magician's son walking towards the police station though, and I was curious. So I climbed up the fig tree outside the window, and listened. Inspector Ismail was leaving, but he quickly dictated his report to the constable, and I overheard some of it. But why don't you ask Inspector Ismail directly?' Venu studied her intently.

Kaveri's face fell.

'Are you afraid he might refuse?' Venu guessed. 'His constable saw me on the tree and told me to leave. These days, they have started to hold some secret discussions in the station. They close all the doors and windows, and have posted some constables all around, keeping everyone at a distance.'

'That is the reason – well, part of the reason – why I am frustrated,' Kaveri admitted. 'Yesterday, I wanted to get closer to the stage to examine it, but Inspector

Ismail asked me to leave, and Mrs Ismail would not tell me anything either.'

'Why don't you stand somewhere near the station, and wait for the young magician to come out? I'm sure he's still there. He was waiting for a long time. His eyes were red, and he looked like he had been crying,' Venu added, with a sympathetic glance at Kaveri.

Kaveri's face brightened, as an idea started to form in her head. She looked at the large dog, who dropped a stick at her feet, panting with eagerness.

'I will take Putta with me, and head towards the station. Then, I can pretend I've gone out for a walk, and accidentally drop by!' she said, excitement in her voice.

In almost no time, she was on the road, kicking up little puffs of dust, humming under her breath as Putta capered around. Venu normally took him for a walk in the daytime, and Ramu and she took him to the park in the evening. He was especially excited to be out for an extra walk in the afternoon, an additional treat of sorts. The large dog scampered from side to side, tracking the scent of squirrels, cows and donkeys, following Kaveri as she turned away from their home in Basavanagudi, heading right towards the Wilson Gardens police station.

It didn't take long before Kaveri and Putta arrived at the crossroads that led to the station. As she stopped to think, she saw Inspector Ismail walking towards her. The normal smile he reserved for her was absent, and her heart sank.

'Am I supposed to believe that you are here simply because you wanted to take Putta for a walk?' he asked, giving her a stern stare.

She bit her lip. Ismail had told Kaveri many months back that she reminded him of his eldest daughter. He had helped her so much in her previous cases. She couldn't understand why he was being so unapproachable now.

Kaveri shrugged, trying to brazen it out. 'I was walking . . .' she began, then faltered when she saw his brown eyes steady on her face. There was no point in trying to lie – he knew her too well. 'I wanted to know what happened yesterday,' she burst out. 'Why did the magician disappear? Is he dead, or alive?' As she spoke, she saw Ismail scowl.

He drew her aside to stand below the shade of a tree. 'Mrs Murthy, you are meddling in deep waters. Stay away from Anandi – it is not safe for you to be spending time with her just now.' He ignored the indignant gasp that escaped from Kaveri when he used the word 'meddled', continuing to speak over her protests. 'Better still, why don't you go home to Mysore for a few weeks? Visit your family. Come back in February, when things are calmer.' Before Kaveri could respond, he raised his hand in a *salaam*, and turned away, his long legs eating up the ground between him and the station.

Kaveri stood at the side of the road, mouth open most inelegantly. A horsefly, purple and golden, having buzzed around a fresh pile of cow dung, alighted on her hand. She shook it away violently, swatting at the air with her hands, angry and bereft at the same time.

Was she meddling in something that did not concern her? As Kaveri fretted, not quite knowing what to do, she thought of Anandi. Ismail's words seemed to indicate that she was in danger. She could not abandon her now. Deep in thought, Kaveri responded almost automatically to the tug on her leash that Putta gave. Bored of standing in one place, he had decided to keep walking. Kaveri followed, her mind going around in circles as she debated what to do next.

7

A New Client

Kicking stones moodily from her path, Kaveri walked back towards her home, walking past the large park right next to the Bull Temple. Putta tugged at his leash, barking furiously at a monkey on the large fig tree inside. Lost in thought, Kaveri allowed herself to be pulled into the shade of the trees, the wooded grove providing a welcome shelter for her as she grappled with her troubled thoughts. As always when she was disturbed, she ached for Ramu, wanting to fill his ears with the story of her encounter with Ismail. But Ramu was in the hospital and would not be home until later that night.

Kaveri sank down on a bench and picked up a small twig of leaves that had fallen there, and began shredding them to pieces. Oblivious of her dark mood, Putta tugged at the leash, panting in his eagerness to discover the source of the exciting smells all around him. At midday, the sun was high in the sky, and everyone was indoors, sheltering from the sun's heat. She seemed to be the only one foolish enough to be out and about at this hour. She let Putta off the leash, and the dog capered away to a corner.

As she sat, brooding over her reception from Ismail, a volley of excited barks came from the distance. Putta was leaning against a large fig tree that was separated from the road by a wire fence to the right. His gaze was fixed on a branch high above that stretched across the metal fence. A young monkey sat on the fence, chattering mockingly at the large, ungainly dog, and dangling his tail close to Putta's face. As Putta jumped up, trying to grab the tail in his mouth, the monkey hopped sideways across the branch, moving to the other side of the metal fence. Putta's barks grew even more frantic, as the monkey, protected by the wire fence, continued to shake his tail tantalisingly close.

Almost against her will, Kaveri began to smile, watching the monkey make a complete fool of her pup.

She heard a small sound, and stood up, surveying the park. She had not seen anyone nearby, and thought it was empty. She could not see anyone on the road outside. Uncomfortable at the thought of being alone with a stranger in the park, she called Putta back to her side, but the dog, absorbed in his attacks on the will-o-the-wisp monkey tail, paid her no attention. She put her fingers in her mouth and emitted a piercing whistle – Venu had taught her that particular trick. It was not especially ladylike, and she was careful not to do it when she was in Bhargavi's earshot, or in Ramu's hospital – but it was very useful in times like these. Putta came bounding up to her, ear cocked to one side as if to ask 'What happened? Do you need me to help?'

In the nearby corner of the park, on a shaded bench, a solitary figure uncurled itself, sitting up. Peering into the corner, Kaveri realised it was Suman, clad in the same bottle green kurta and pyjama set that she had seen him in the previous evening, though now badly mussed and stained. His forehead was wrapped in a white bandage. The colour of the kurta merged with the dark foliage where he sat – no wonder she hadn't realised he was there before.

Sensing her scrutiny, the young man moved closer to Kaveri, scrubbing at his face to wipe away his tears. Kaveri saw the shadows under his eyes, and the quiver in his hands that betrayed his distress.

'The lady detective, Mrs Murthy! Luck has favoured me.' He hesitated, the bitterness in his tone apparent. 'Perhaps Lady Fortune is mindful of how much of a burden she can continue to place on me, after all. She led me to the famous lady detective of Bangalore, who has solved many difficult cases.'

'How do you know so much about me?' Kaveri demanded, unsettled.

The young man gave her a curiously formal half-bow. She supposed it was habit, borne from years of bowing to the audience on stage.

'Even before the performance yesterday, we had heard much about you. My neighbour's son's brother-in-law told us about the various problems you have resolved, and my father . . .' Suman's voice faltered, and he ran his fingers through his thick curly hair. 'My father was very keen to meet you. He said he had never met a lady detective before. When we lived in Calcutta, my mother used to read Bengali detective novels. She always wanted to write one about a lady detective. She even had a few plots in mind, sketching them onto pieces of paper to entertain me when I was a young child.'

Kaveri's mind raced. At the circus, backstage, she was sure Das had said it was *Suman* who wanted to meet her. Which of them was telling the truth? She could not ask directly.

'Your mother wrote books?' Kaveri asked instead, trying to lead Suman towards a longer discussion of how they came to learn about her.

A shadow came over the young man's face. 'No,' he said briefly. 'But my father wanted to write a play, a play with magic in it. They worked on it together, but she died before they could complete it. Can you help me find my father?' He gazed at her with hope, seeming young and very vulnerable.

Kaveri debated with herself. She still could not see anyone on the road nearby, and was not sure if she could trust Suman. She held Putta's collar, taking strength from his presence, as she thought of the questions she had recorded in her notes. She had suspected that Das's disappearance was planned, connected to the appearance of the masked thieves. But surely he would not have kept such a plan secret from his own son. Looking at Suman's unkempt hair, and the bandage wound around his head, she felt her heart soften.

'Have you received any message from your father since he disappeared from the cage?' she asked, standing a few feet away from him and mentally mapping a path to the nearest side gate in case she needed to make a quick exit. The police station was very close. Surely there could be no danger here. But still, it was better to be safe.

A gust of wind swirled around them, sending her hair flying. A rotten branch fell to the ground with a thud, and she jumped.

Suman clenched his fists. 'Not a word. After the hospital released me last night, I hurried to the police station. I sat on the benches all night, waiting for the Inspector. But when he came in this morning, he refused to help me. He said that there was no proof that anything had happened to my father. Perhaps he just wanted to disappear for some time, the policeman said. As if my father would ever disappear like that without telling me. As if he would ever leave me alone.'

Suman's voice climbed higher. Kaveri could see him swallow, struggling to gain control. He paused for a moment, and then continued. 'I asked him for your address. I thought, maybe you could take the case . . .' He paused. 'As soon as I mentioned your name, the policeman shooed me away. He told me I should stay away from you, if I knew what was good for me.'

Kaveri repressed a hiss of anger. Why was Ismail behaving like this?

Suman spoke nonchalantly, but she noticed his eyes, intently focused on her. 'I did not know your address, and I did not know how to find it. So I came here, planning to take a nap on this bench, under the trees. But it is my fate. I found you in the park instead.' Suman moved forward so suddenly that Kaveri reared back. He fixed her with a pleading gaze. 'You will help me, won't you, *didi*?'

The use of the Bengali word for older sister threw Kaveri off guard.

'Of . . . of course,' she said, hesitating a little as she thought of Ismail's warning. Ignoring the voice of caution in her head, Kaveri stiffened her spine. 'Yes,' she said, more firmly. 'Yes, I will help you.' After all, she had found the man by chance, sitting in the park. That had to mean something. Fortune *wanted* her to take his case.

Then Kaveri shook her head at her own foolishness. 'I mean, I will *try* to help you. I can only do my best. I am not a magician.'

It was better to continue this conversation at home, where she would have people nearby, whom she could shout out to for help in case her conversation with Suman went awry. She bent down to pick up Putta's leash, but the dog was still fixated on the monkey. 'Food, Putta, food . . .' Kaveri called to him softly. '*Rotti*. Bun. Biscuit.' She took a packet of biscuits out from her purse. Losing interest in the monkey, Putta scarpered towards her.

'Come with me,' she told Suman. 'Let us go home, where I can ask you some questions. I don't know how I can help you, or indeed, if I can help at all. But I will try,' she added again.

'When even magicians have failed, I think it is a detective that we are most in need of,' Suman said softly, the soles of his leather shoes making a gentle hissing noise on the leaves as they walked out of the park.

8

Diversion and Deflection

A short while later, Kaveri and Suman were in the shed, flipping through newspaper reports of the magic show which Kaveri had spread across the large wooden desk at the corner of her room. Putta lay on the coir mat outside, contentedly chewing on a large bone-shaped biscuit. Ramu had discovered them on sale at the Anglo-Indian baker's shop on Lavelle Road, and they had met with the pup's unmitigated approval. He was happy to drool on it for hours.

Asking Suman to go ahead to her shed, Kaveri had quickly walked to the side of the house where Rajamma was washing clothes on the large granite slab. Explaining the situation quickly, she asked Rajamma if she could come and water the plants in sight of the open windows where she could keep an eye on Kaveri and Suman. Thankfully, her case notes were safely locked in her bedroom, a precaution she had started taking since the previous month – when she had found a client's nephew, who was stealing from his shop, in her shed

79

searching for the fingerprint evidence she had collected. Swiftly bolting him inside, she had called the police, who had arrested him. Since then, she had begun to lock everything away.

The heat of the midday sun had given Kaveri a headache, and the thought of coffee made her queasy, so they drank glasses of lemon juice flavoured with cardamom while Suman devoured the plate of freshly made *chakkali* that she set before him. He crunched the crisp fried snack, cramming large pieces into his mouth. She sat quietly, watching him demolish the plate, then brought out another plateful from a large steel *dabba* that she kept in her shed for late-morning cravings.

Suman gave her an apologetic glance. 'I was very hungry. Since my father disappeared, I have not eaten. He used to cook for us. Without him, everything tastes like ash. I am a good magician, but a terrible cook. My mother was the same.'

'So your mother was a magician too, then.' Kaveri had read about women acrobats, and she had recently come across the story of a German woman who was a lion tamer – they called her *Sherni*, the she-lion. But she hadn't ever heard of a woman magician before.

'I only meant that my mother was also a bad cook, as bad as me.' Suman shifted in his seat, taking the last *chakkali* from the plate. 'Perhaps I should learn some recipes from you, *didi*. Do you have anything else to eat?'

Kaveri left him with the newspapers and hurried to the kitchen to prepare a quick meal of *nimbehannu chitranna* – lemon rice, her standard recipe for feeding hungry visitors – signalling to Rajamma to stay where she was and keep an eye on Suman.

She hummed as she cooked, her heart lighter. Her day, which had stretched out emptily in front of her, seemed more bearable now. So what if Inspector Ismail and Anandi were not willing to speak to her? Other people, like Suman, still saw value in her skills of detection. Placing a small *bandale* on the stove, she heated some sesame oil with a pinch of asafoetida, and threw in a handful of mustard seeds and curry leaves to the hot oil, waiting for the mustard to splutter before adding a couple of chopped green chillies, roasting peanuts in the spiced oil. She mixed in some cold rice, adding salt, turmeric and chopped coriander, and squeezing in fresh lemon juice, mixing it well together. Placing a fresh banana leaf onto a steel plate, she heaped it with the rice, and returned to her shed.

Suman was crouched on the floor, scratching Putta behind his ears as the dog sprawled out blissfully. Kaveri smiled. She had been a bit uncertain about whether it was safe to bring this young man, whom she barely knew, back to the house with her. But Putta was a good judge of character – if he liked the young man, she felt reassured that she could trust him.

She regaled Suman with stories as he devoured his plate of *chitranna*, telling him how she had not known how to cook when she'd moved to her marital home. Suman laughed as Kaveri described the number of times she had fed Ramu and Venu over-salted lemon rice before she'd learned how to get it right. The lines on his forehead gradually disappeared, leaving him seeming younger, more handsome.

'How old are you?' Kaveri asked.

'Seventeen.' Suman gave her a boyish grin. 'Magicians train early. My father started teaching me as soon as I learned how to speak. It felt like a game, not like professional training. But I didn't start assisting him on stage until much later. After we moved to Belgaum.'

'Did you move from Calcutta to Belgaum?' That seemed like an odd move halfway across the country. What would have taken a Bengali family of magicians all the way to Belgaum? Surely there were enough circuses in Calcutta.

Suman burst into a coughing fit, bent over. He straightened up, clearing his throat. 'My food went down the wrong way. Can I have some water, please?'

He drained the glass of water in a single gulp, and set it down on the table with an audible thump. 'Can you help me find my father?' he demanded, his voice cracking. 'We were so close. He would *never* have left me.'

Kaveri brought out her notepad. 'Tell me everything,' she said.

'There is not much to tell. My father and I are independent performers. We move from circus to circus, city to city, searching for work wherever we can find it. Hearing that the Maximilian Circus was hiring, we made our way from Belgaum to Bangalore. They hired us for two weeks, performing on weekends. The first weekend went by without any problems.'

'Did you perform exactly the same acts last weekend?' Kaveri asked.

His voice filled with pride. 'Yes. They were brand new, invented by my father. Baba hated the fact that Western magicians like Harry Houdini and Howard Thurston came to our lands and stole our tricks – like the basket trick and the mango seed trick – and presented them as though they were their own. They said our illusions were cheap and theatrical, our costumes and stage props crude and inferior, yet they adapted and exploited them. Irked by their double standards, Baba abandoned the traditional attire of the British magician, throwing away his top hat and coat tails and returning to the traditional Indian attire used by *jadoogars*. Even the performance he designed was full of Indian elements. That's why he created an entire act around the story of Krishna and Kamsa.'

Suman paused, seeming embarrassed. 'I am boring you. Sorry.'

'Do I appear bored?' Kaveri scoffed. 'Tell me more. The mango seed trick is the first one you performed, growing a small tree from a mango seed. How did you do that?'

'It's very easy,' Suman said in his earnest voice, beaming at her. 'We are not supposed to share our tricks with outsiders, but you are my friend now. I never thought I would be talking to a famous detective like you one day, teaching you something you did not know.'

He stretched out his hands, holding them a few centimetres apart. 'I showed you a small pot with earth, about this size, into which I placed a mango seed. Then I covered the pot with a tent, made of cloth, and chanted some incantations.' He waited for Kaveri to nod before continuing. 'That was only for effect – to make the audience believe that I was performing magic. The pots rested on a mat of cloth. Between the folds of the cloth, I had hidden mango branches of different lengths. As I removed the cloth, I quickly inserted the smallest set of branches in the mud – that was the "tree". Then I replaced the tent, repeating the process. Each time I took out the cloth, I added branches of greater length, making it seem like the tree was growing.' Suman grinned at Kaveri. 'All you need is a deft hand, and some practice. I can show you how to do it if you like.'

She would be able to do her own magic tricks then, Kaveri thought with delight as she imagined Bhargavi's face!

'But your father – he dipped his fingers in molten lead, drank carbolic acid, and dived into boiling water – escaping unscathed. How did he do that?'

'The molten lead trick requires strong nerves. The key is to keep your fingers perfectly dry, immersing them in sand to remove every last bit of moisture. If you place completely dry hands in hot lead, and pull them out swiftly, the hot lead will roll off your fingers. Without water, done very swiftly, the lead will not have time to cling to your hands and burn them.'

Kaveri thought of her Physics teacher, who used to teach in a monotone so boring that the class often struggled to stay awake. What if her teacher had demonstrated tricks like this? They would have raced through their Physics texts in days instead of months.

'What about the last trick? The cage, and the basket of vipers and cobras?' Kaveri asked.

Suman's face darkened. 'It was a brand new act. Yesterday was the first time he performed it on stage in front of an audience. It was a modification of the standard basket trick, used by many Indian *jadoogars*. I can't tell you what he did with the snakes – that's one of his trade secrets, which even I don't know. But there was a concealed cavity just beneath the cage, separated by a partition made of glass. My father freed himself from his chains, quickly entering the cavity. The first time he made me lock him in and throw away the keys, I was terrified. My hands shook so hard that I couldn't turn the lock. But he was a genius. Our rehearsals went smoothly, and the circus owner was so pleased, he even gave us a bonus.

'Yesterday though . . .' His voice broke again. 'I have no idea what happened yesterday. We could find no trace of my father in the cage. After the performance, when I looked inside the concealed cavity below the stage, where he should have been hiding while we stabbed through the cage – it was empty.' Suman sounded defeated. 'Baba would never have left me. I fear someone may have kidnapped him.'

Kaveri thought back to the last time she had seen Das. Just before Suman had put a hand on his back and pushed him into the tiny cage, the magician had hooked eyes with her, holding her gaze as though he was trying to communicate something to her.

'After your father disappeared, I saw a group of men carrying you on their shoulders, taking you through the room. Men with masks started to spread through the room, trying to snatch jewellery and purses from the people in the front-row seats,' Kaveri said, carefully studying Suman's horrified face. She felt her suspicions shift. Either Das was not hand-in-glove with the thieves, as she thought, or if he was – his son was probably not a part of it.

'Some men rushed onto the stage and picked me up. I have no idea who they were. I begged them to let me down so that I could search for my father, but they acted as though they couldn't hear me. At some point, I think I must have fainted. I have no idea what happened after that. When I opened my eyes, I was on a stretcher, being carried from a horse cart into the hospital.' Suman's voice trailed off in a hoarse rasp.

'I was the one who found you, lying unconscious in the aisle.' Kaveri gently touched the bandage on his head, pointing to the prominent lump at the top of his skull. 'The place where I found you was carpeted, the chairs covered in velvet. You couldn't have got this bump if you fainted, falling off someone's shoulder – you would have landed on soft ground. Someone must have hit you, knocking you out.'

'There is something very strange about what happened yesterday, some larger forces behind this. My father would not have disappeared of his own volition, leaving me alone in a strange city. I hope Baba is alive.' Suman's voice broke.

'I am sure he is,' Kaveri patted his hand, wanting to wipe away the fear she saw in his eyes. 'Did he tell you anything that could explain it? Was he in danger from someone – did he tell you about any threats?' She wondered if he knew about Pawan's murder. If he did not know, she would not tell him – yet. He was already consumed with fear for his father. The news of another killing on the same day would make him suspect the worst.

'I have racked my brains, but I can't think of anything that might help,' Suman said. 'Would you like to come to our room and rummage through his things? Your trained eyes might pick up something that I have missed.'

Kaveri did not immediately respond. The events at the circus last night were still burned into her brain, and Ismail's warning reverberated in her ears.

Seeing her hesitate, Suman shuffled his feet. 'The circus allotted us rooms, just behind the main tent. It is not the best of living quarters – a bit dirty and messy. I should not ask a lady like you to come to a place like that.'

Kaveri stiffened indignantly. 'That doesn't bother me at all. My work takes me all across the city.' She thought of her first visit to Mala's house. How worried she had been then, afraid of venturing into a home that was so different from the places she had been exposed to. She had come a long way since then – and so had her companion, their sheltered neighbour Uma aunty, who went with her everywhere. Uma aunty might like to visit the place where circus performers lived. She had never been to a place like that before, Kaveri was sure of it. And she would ask Venu or one of his army of boys to stay close, just out of sight. That would ensure her safety. Feeling more alive and energetic than she had in a long time, at the thought of investigating a new part of the city, she ruthlessly squashed the voice of caution that reminded her that she needed to be careful.

Suman jumped up from his seat eagerly. 'It's settled then. Can you come tomorrow? At around noon? I will wait for you.' Asking Kaveri for her notepad, he made a rough sketch of the area for her.

As she studied the sketch that Suman had drawn, they heard voices approaching. Putta ran up to the gate, barking out an excited welcome.

'Are you expecting guests?' Suman seemed worried.

'The Bangalore Detectives Club. I forgot that we were meeting today.' Kaveri looked at the large grandfather clock hanging on the wall of her shed.

'Detectives Club? People told me you were the only woman detective in Bangalore.'

'They are good friends. We meet every week to read the newspaper, talk about what is going on in the city – and the world – and sometimes, we also discuss new cases.'

The women were making their way inside the gate, and Suman began to gather his things.

'Come and meet them,' Kaveri urged. But he shook his head.

'I am not in a fit state to meet anyone.' Opening the loose cotton satchel on his shoulder, he took out an oversized cap, placing it low over his forehead so that it hid most of his face. He scurried out of the gate, past the startled women, before Kaveri could ask him any further questions. Kaveri stared at his retreating back, shaken into silence. Her feelings had gone through a 180 degree turn since meeting Suman in the park – from suspecting that he might be complicit in his father's disappearance, she had come around to believing she could trust him. But his sketchy behaviour – the alarm in his voice when

87

he'd heard of the other members of the club, and his quick getaway – had made her uncertain about him all over again.

'Where are the others?' Mala asked as she and Narsamma entered through the front door. 'I thought we would be the last to come. But we seem to be the first.'

'I told you that Mrs Reddy is away for six weeks. Her daughter is pregnant, and she has gone to see her,' Kaveri said, recovering her voice. 'Uma aunty is not at home – her house is locked. Mrs Ismail sent a brief note with Venu to say that she will be busy for the next few weeks and cannot join us. I suspect she may not come for a while.'

'And Anandi?'

'Anandi seems to have abandoned us, along with Mrs Ismail.' Her voice came out sounding more bitter than she intended.

Mala gave her a sympathetic look. 'I recognised that young man who hurried past us, eager to get away. He is the son of Mr Das, isn't he? The famous magician? I saw them last week, at the front of a group of performers who were being taken round the city on open carts to advertise the circus. Why is he here?'

'So much has happened since yesterday that I don't know where to start.'

The three women sat around the dining table, as Kaveri gave them a quick update on the events of the previous day, including Das's disappearance, the attack by the masked men and Pawan's death. Both ladies listened intently, but it was Mala who seemed the most interested, especially in the robbery attempt.

'My brother's former gang keeps me updated on every-thing – I pay them for information. Recently, they told me there is a new gang in town – they target the homes of wealthy people, especially when they are out of the house,' she said. 'We haven't been able to ferret out the details. That is strange – usually, at least one person is willing to speak. This gang is well organised, keeping its secrets close.'

'Have you reported this to the police?' Kaveri asked immediately. 'Inspector Ismail should know.'

'You know what will happen if we tell the police. They will pull us in for questioning, and ask us to reveal the names of our contacts. If we do, we are in for trouble – my brother's friends will turn on us, and make our lives a living hell. And if we don't, the police will toss us in jail.' Mala shuddered. 'I have been there once, tied in chains. I have no plans to go back there again.'

Mala was right. Kaveri could not tell Ismail either. Even if she did not reveal where she had got the information from, he would know that it was from Mala. She was Kaveri's only friend with connections to crime.

'I think Pawan was part of that gang,' Kaveri said. 'He wore a mask, just like the other masked robbers. I wonder if they are the ones who killed him.'

'Whoever killed that rascal deserves an award. Good riddance to bad rubbish.' Narsamma opened the pouch of cloth tucked into her waist, and took out a betel nut leaf, rolling it with a pinch of *sunna* and popping it into her mouth as she spoke. 'I can't believe that Anandi knew that he had returned or joined such a gang and didn't say anything. Especially if she knew you would be at the circus, vulnerable to theft. She would lay her life on the line for you.'

Kaveri swallowed a lump in her throat. 'She *has* put her life at risk for me before,' she reminded them. 'Taking up not just one, but two risky jobs, and almost getting killed in the process.'

She stopped, on the brink of bursting into tears. What was wrong with her? She was unaccustomed to feeling vulnerable in this way.

She heard a small bark behind her, and turned to find Putta, pushing his nose into the folds of her sari. The dog licked her, thumping his tail rhythmically against her shoulder – *thup thup thup.*

9

A Difference of Opinions

Later that night, as Kaveri finished recounting the events of the day to Ramu, she paused. The restlessness that had plagued her all day disappeared as she curled up in his arms, unburdening herself to him.

'There is something of the magician always in Suman, even when he is offstage.'

'What do you mean?' Ramu propped his head up on his elbow, watching his wife as he played with her long hair. 'Did he perform any tricks on you? Try to hypnotise you, or remove and replace something in your possession?'

'No . . .' Kaveri said. 'Nothing quite so obvious. But – do you remember when I went to the Seshadri Iyer Memorial Library last month and picked up a few books on magic?' She tugged her hair with her comb, trying to remove a particularly troublesome knot.

'You experimented on me for days, trying to pull out potatoes from my ear. How could I *not* remember?' Ramu gave her a look of exaggerated shock, catching her hand in his as she tried to poke him in the stomach.

He tugged her hand towards him, planting a soft kiss on her palm.

'None of that now,' Kaveri exclaimed, laughing but also feeling a little flushed as she pulled her hand away from him. 'Focus on the case.'

Ramu folded his palms together in mock penitence. 'Alright. No disturbance henceforth. Explain to me what you meant.'

'There were a couple of times when my questions led to topics he wanted to steer me away from, and he did it so deftly that I didn't realise.' She paused, head tilted to one side as she tried to remember the exact details. 'I asked him if his mother was a magician. He distracted me by eating the last *chakkali*, and asking me for more food. He seems like a very well brought up young man. Polite, courteous. Asking me – a stranger, whom he had just met – for food so directly is not something he would normally do, I think. But it was a good way to distract me. It was only when I was writing down my notes in my casebook later that I realised that he had never answered my question. And again, when I asked him when he had joined his father on stage, he pretended to cough, and asked me for water. It's the classic magician's trick, described in all the books: misdirection, diversion, deflection of attention from the main point.'

'A true magician then,' Ramu agreed. 'He has learned the tricks of the trade young, after all.'

Kaveri gestured with her comb. 'There is something peculiar about his family history – what his mother did, and when they came to Belgaum. He shared the secrets of the magic tricks they performed so freely, yet he did not seem to want to speak about his earlier life at all.'

'What else did he say, Kaveri? Did you agree to take the case?' A small frown had appeared on Ramu's face.

'I couldn't speak to him for much longer. We had a women's club meeting in the evening – he saw the women opening the gate, and quickly made his excuses to me and left.' Kaveri brightened. 'You know, Mala and Narsamma have really progressed in their reading abilities. They brought the children's book I got them from the library and read it to me. They have been practising for the past week.'

'Your club is growing by leaps and bounds – helping solve cases *and* learning how to read and write.'

Kaveri beamed. 'I wish you could have seen them. They had dressed up for the reading, as though they were delivering a performance on stage. They were shy at first, but then picked up confidence as they read. And it was flawless. They had practised so well . . . it was a ten-page book, and they read out alternate pages. I was so proud of them.'

'I'm very proud too – of them, and of you,' Ramu said, gathering his wife into his arms. She snuggled against him, speaking into his shoulder in a muffled voice.

'Before he left, Suman asked me to come to his house tomorrow, at noon. He wants me to see his father's possessions, in case I can uncover a clue.'

She felt Ramu's body stiffen, and raised her chin.

'I don't think that is wise, Kaveri.' Her husband's expression was unreadable in the shadows. 'I don't like the thought of your going to a strange place alone. After all, we don't know anything about this man or his background. Even Ismail doesn't want you to get involved.'

Shocked, she pulled back from his embrace. 'What do you mean?'

'I don't think this is a good idea. His father has disappeared without a trace. These people are magicians. They make a living out of deception – smoke and mirrors, like the fake Swami you encountered, Kaveri. Remember how dangerous that case was?' Ramu shook his head.

Kaveri knew that Ramu was only pointing out what she had already sensed, but she still felt like digging in her heels. 'Suman is not like him at all. Putta likes him. Putta is a good judge of character,' she countered.

'I don't know, Kaveri. Something about this doesn't feel right. Inspector Ismail must have some reason for forbidding you from taking on the case.' Ramu pulled back, cupping her face in his hands. His eyes were serious.

'He can't forbid me,' Kaveri said, her anger growing. But as quickly as it came, her annoyance evaporated, leaving her weary. If even her husband, her biggest supporter on whom she depended unquestioningly for support, was chary of her involvement – should she really take the case?

Kaveri felt torn. It was not just boredom or her desire for validation that drove her on. She also could not just sit by and do nothing as a young man tried to trace his missing father. And try as she might, she could not push the picture of Anandi, being led away in chains, from her mind. As time went by, she was increasingly terrified that the police, unable to find another promising suspect, would arrest her and toss her into a dingy, rat-infested cell. With the Prince expected soon, they would not want to take the risk of leaving a suspected murderer free to move around, as Mala had warned her. The police had already come around to Anandi's old neighbourhood, seeking to speak to their former neighbours, asking them questions about her relationship with Pawan, accounts of their fights, and whether she had a lover.

Leaning in closer, Kaveri tried to explain what she felt, how worried she was about Anandi, and what she wanted to do. Ramu did not speak for a while, remaining quiet as Kaveri spoke volubly, the conversation petering out in the face of his silence. Then he removed her hands from his and patted her on the back, pushing her away from him gently, his voice flat and distant. 'You will always do as you want to, Kaveri. There is no point in trying to convince me. When you have already made up your mind, what is the need for my approval? But please don't go alone to Suman's house. That is the *only* thing I ask of you.'

'I will take Uma aunty with me,' Kaveri promised. Their elderly neighbour from the house behind them was always ready to accompany Kaveri on a bout of sleuthing.

'Uma aunty is hardly going to provide you with security in times of danger,' Ramu said drily. 'And don't tell me you know kalaripayattu, Kaveri. Because this case may be too large to tackle with a few martial arts kicks.'

'I also planned to ask Venu to send one of his boys, keeping him well out of sight,' Kaveri added. 'No one will notice a small milkboy hanging around the street corners. That's what they all do anyway. If there is an emergency, I will scream, and he will run to the police station. It's only a couple of minutes away.'

'You will do as you want to, Kaveri,' Ramu repeated. 'As you always do.' He turned his back to her, facing the wall. 'I can only ask you to be careful.'

Kaveri couldn't help it when her eyes filled with tears – she didn't like to upset Ramu, but her inner core of stubbornness did not allow her to just go along with what he wanted, especially since she also didn't want to let Suman or Anandi down. Disjointed thoughts ran through her mind as she lay staring at the ceiling, which seemed like an upside-down stage.

She fell into an uneasy sleep, waking in the early hours. Ramu had slipped away, leaving her a note to tell her that he had been called to the hospital for an emergency. The dark clouds that had threatened the sky a few hours back had built up into a storm. The wind blew hard outside, throwing small pebbles against the window. The sound of stones rattling on glass made it impossible to sleep, forcing Kaveri to sit up in bed, hugging her knees. She stared at the shadows made by the mango tree branch outside her window. It shook from side to side as the wind blew harder. The shadows capered across the ceiling like a demented magician in a top hat, dancing madly on a stage of horrors.

10

A New Beginning

'I'm not hungry, *athe.*'

Feeling groggy and decidedly not at her best after another rough night, Kaveri waved away the masala dosa that her mother-in-law had just prepared for breakfast. Crisp on the outside, soft and fluffy inside, with a stuffing made of spiced potatoes, this was one of Kaveri's favourite breakfast dishes, and no one made masala dosas like her mother-in-law did. Today, though, her stomach was still roiling, and she struggled to keep the bile down.

She hated sleeping on an argument with Ramu. He had left early this morning, well before she woke – called to the hospital for another emergency surgery. She had not even had a chance to speak to him and make up after their quarrel.

Uma aunty sat next to Kaveri, polishing off the last bite of her dosa. Kaveri had called out over the back wall that separated their homes earlier that morning. She had asked Uma aunty to come over for breakfast so that she could fill her in on the details of the previous couple of days before taking her to visit Suman, as she had promised Ramu the previous night.

Uma aunty shook her head at Kaveri's empty plate. Bhargavi came closer, cupping Kaveri's face in her palms. 'You seem tired, child. Did you not sleep well last night?' She smoothed her palm over Kaveri's hair, affectionately patting her cheek. 'I hope it was not something my son said.'

Kaveri shook her head. Upset though she was, she did not want to say anything about her husband, even if it was to his own mother. It would seem too much like betrayal, especially with Uma aunty listening avidly to their conversation.

'It is about the magician who disappeared from the magic show. His son came to me for help yesterday.'

'And you agreed?' Bhargavi sat down at the table, putting the plate of masala dosa on the side, unheeded. 'You *are* going to help him, aren't you?'

A rush of affection overwhelmed Kaveri as she saw her mother-in-law's eager face. How much had changed in a few months, she thought. Lonely and worried about losing the primary place she occupied in her son's life, Bhargavi had been prickly and judgemental when Kaveri had first moved into their home. But the two women had gradually grown closer, especially since Kaveri had taken on Shanthi's case.

Bhargavi, who had once thought that too much studying made a woman's brains become soft, was now one of her strongest supporters. Kaveri smiled gratefully at her mother-in-law as she settled back into her chair, beginning to recount the events of the previous day to Bhargavi and Uma aunty.

Once she had finished, Bhargavi thumped the table, making the steel plate jerk and rattle on the wooden surface. 'You must take the case, Kaveri.' Uma aunty nodded, placing her wrinkled hand on Kaveri's arm.

'I want to. I was interested in finding out what happened even before Suman spoke to me – for Anandi's sake, if nothing else. But Inspector Ismail's repeated warnings to keep away make me wonder if he has a point,' Kaveri said. 'I think he has also told Mrs Ismail to keep her distance. She didn't join our meeting yesterday, sending a note that she wouldn't be able to come for a few days.'

'It is not like you to lose confidence so quickly.' Bhargavi patted her hand. 'Have some more faith in yourself.'

Kaveri swallowed the lump of sorrow that she felt in her throat each time she thought of Ismail and Ramu's disapproval, thinking gratefully once again of how glad she was that Bhargavi and she had grown closer in the past few months.

'In India, you don't just marry your husband, you also marry your in-laws,' Dr Roberts' prickly wife, Daphne, had commented when Kaveri had first come to Bangalore. At that time, it had seemed to Kaveri like a nightmare. How thankful she was for it now. Ramu was in the hospital most of the time, so it was she and Bhargavi who spent most of their day together. When Bhargavi was away visiting Shanthi, even if it was just for a day or two, the house seemed empty.

She loved the new house she had married into, but it was much too big for three people, even accounting for a dog as massive as Putta. Her natal home at Mysore was a fraction of the size of this house, but Kaveri could not remember a time when it wasn't crammed with people. Her relatives filled every corner of available space, with her grandparents, parents, sisters, brothers *and* sundry cousins and neighbours trooping in and out of the house all day. Kaveri had felt so lonely in the first few weeks when she'd moved to Bangalore, until she had made friends with the women with whom she had later created the Bangalore Detectives Club. She reached out, holding Bhargavi's hand in her right, and Uma aunty's in her left, squeezing tight.

Bhargavi stared at her curiously. 'What do you suspect, Kaveri? Surely you must have some idea of why the Inspector wants you to stay away from the case.'

Kaveri let go of the women, and spread out the newspaper, pointing to the front page. As they had been for the past few days, the pages were filled with photographs of the Prince of Wales and his entourage. Yesterday, they had visited the new Krishnarajasagara Dam, one of the largest in Asia, and the Brindavan Gardens, visiting the wondrous new musical fountains that Dewan Mirza Ismail and his German architect, Krumbiegel, had established. She had pored over the pages, eager to see the dam and the gardens, which had not yet been opened to the public.

'The Crown Prince is visiting Bangalore soon. He will arrive on the eighteenth of January, and then leave for Mysore on the nineteenth. That's just a couple of weeks away. From the manner in which Ismail spoke to me – asking me to leave Bangalore and return only in February, "for my own safety" as he phrased it – I think the disappearance of Mr Das *must* somehow be connected to the Prince's visit.'

'We certainly don't want a repetition of the scenes that accompanied his visit to Bombay. Rioting, stoning British cars, burning shops . . .' A frown spread over Bhargavi's face.

'But that's not the only way to show one's rejection of British occupation of our homeland, *athe*,' Kaveri argued. 'Shanthi *akka* told me that the Congress Party held long debates in 1920 about the best way to proceed, voting in a large majority to follow Gandhiji's approach of non-violence. At the same time, I think not everyone agrees. Ismail probably fears there will be violence.'

'Be careful, Kaveri.' Bhargavi's voice was shrill in alarm. 'It is not good to speak of these things so openly. The police are everywhere these days, and they have planted spies in many places. Practically anyone could be listening in on our conversation – including our neighbour, Subramaniam Swamy. You know what a big supporter he is of the British. He sacked his entire domestic staff last year when they went on strike in response to the non-cooperation call.'

'For that matter, even my son is on the same side as your lawyer neighbour.' Uma aunty's mouth had puckered up. She studied the cold masala dosa as though it contained bitter gourd, and she had just swallowed a plateful of it. 'I don't know how my own son could become such a lickspittle.' She shuddered with distaste. 'My daughter-in-law is no better. She encourages him in all his nonsense.'

'Even Shanthi *akka* has stopped going to the independence meetings these days, because everyone who comes in and leaves is being watched closely, followed, and traced to their homes, their names added to a list of anti-national people to be closely watched.' Kaveri sat back, biting her lip. 'Should I give up investigating the case then? That is what Ramu is also suggesting.'

'Give it up? No!' the two women exclaimed, almost in unison.

'Ramu only wants to protect you, Kaveri.' Uma aunty had a faraway look in her eyes. 'Just like my husband wanted to protect me. I married him when I was only a slip of a girl, just twelve years old. In the forty years that we were married, I never spent a night apart from him. He never let me go anywhere alone, not even to my parents' home. He escorted me everywhere to keep me safe.'

'Your father-in-law – God rest his soul – was exactly the same, Kaveri,' Bhargavi added. 'In their desire to keep us safe and well cared for, they did not realise that they deprived us of independence, making it difficult for us to live our lives alone, with confidence, once they passed away.'

'My son is even worse, Kaveri – you know how much he is opposed to me helping you with your adventures,' Uma aunty added. 'How thankful I am that you came into my life. My son and daughter-in-law want me to sit at home, like a respectable widow, watching over my grandson. They do not expect me to have any interests, or indeed a life of my own.' Her face crumpled. 'Their barbs hurt, but now that you are in my life, I have stopped paying them so much attention. Learning how to read, accompanying you on your investigations – I am having the best time of my life.'

'I am too.' Bhargavi smiled at Kaveri fondly. 'I thought my life was over when my husband died. Spending time with you and Shanthi, helping her take care of the Women's Home, I am beginning to discover myself for the first time.' Her voice was thick with emotion.

Kaveri's heart thumped an irregular beat in her chest, and she impulsively touched their feet for a blessing. 'I am so fortunate to have you in my lives,' she said, her voice coming out a trifle muffled as she found herself squeezed into Uma aunty's bosom, her forehead uncomfortably pressed against her thick gold chain. She extricated herself gently from her neighbour's embrace.

'Ramu has a point, though, Kaveri,' Bhargavi cautioned her, as they all sat down again. 'As does Inspector Ismail.

If, as you suspect, the disappearance of Mr Das is related to the Prince of Wales's visit, and there is violence anticipated, then this is a far more dangerous situation than you have ever confronted before. These are areas bordering on sedition. And you know how seriously the government takes this. Even people as influential as Sarojini Naidu have been thrown in jail for months on end.' Bhargavi's voice had dropped to a whisper.

Kaveri shivered reflexively, remembering Mala's dreadful time in jail. Although political prisoners were treated better than suspected criminals, she could not get the picture of Mala's legs mottled with sores, enclosed in rusty iron shackles, out of her mind. Kaveri picked up her feet and sat cross-legged on the chair, protectively wrapping the folds of her sari around her ankles.

'Are you saying that Kaveri and I should not keep our appointment with Suman at his house?' Uma aunty seemed less perturbed by Bhargavi's comments. The elderly lady had led a sheltered life. She had not seen Mala in jail. She had never even seen the inside of a jail before, and perhaps could not imagine what dangers might await her.

Uma aunty cast a disappointed eye at the ornate cuckoo clock on the wall, which had just struck ten. They were expected at Suman's home at eleven. Kaveri had spoken to Venu earlier that morning, and he had promised to send one of his team of boys to keep watch on them.

'No . . . I am not saying that you should not go,' Bhargavi said slowly. 'Only . . . proceed with absolute caution. Don't discuss these matters with anyone else. Even some of the people who are your friends may be dangerous to confide in – like Mrs Reddy. Mr Reddy is a devout admirer of the British Empire. Have you seen their drawing room? A large photograph of Queen

Victoria adorns their mantelpiece, next to a photograph of our Maharaja.'

'Mrs Reddy is away for a few weeks in any case, *athe*.' Kaveri traced an imaginary line on the wooden table top. 'How strange it feels. We are beginning to create boundaries between our own friends, neighbours, even within our own families. Are these the times we live in? We do not know who might be spying on us, which of our friends may turn out to have values different from those we hold dear to our souls, and who may be willing to sell us out for a bit of official recognition or career advancement.'

'Perhaps it is overdoing it, but I think we can never be too careful,' Uma aunty said. 'Be wary of what you say to Mrs Ismail too.'

Kaveri let out a short, bitter laugh. 'I'm hardly likely to get the chance to say anything to her. I am like a social pariah to her. She has decided to stop coming to our house for the women's club meetings.'

Bhargavi placed a gentle hand on her shoulder. 'She and her husband care for you, Kaveri.'

Kaveri swallowed back tears. 'I know I am probably overreacting. It is just that . . .'

'Inspector Ismail has been one of your biggest supporters, right from the start. He and his wife always say that you remind them of their own daughter. If they are keeping away from you, it must be so that they can keep you safe.' Uma aunty's voice was matter of fact, easing the anxious knot of tension in Kaveri's belly that had made the bile rise up to her throat.

'Thank you, aunty.' Kaveri smiled at her mistily. 'I think . . . I am feeling much better now, *athe*, my appetite has returned after all. I will finish my dosa.' She pulled the cold dosa towards her.

Just as hastily, Bhargavi pulled it back. 'You will do no such thing,' she declared, looking horrified. 'This one is cold and hard, like rubber. I will keep it aside, and feed it to Venu's cow Kasturi later.' She rose from the table, hooking her sari *pallu* into her waist. 'Let me make you a fresh, hot dosa. How can you go out and investigate on an empty stomach, Kaveri?'

11

A Secret Message

The bullock cart dropped them off at the large entrance to the circus grounds in Sampangi. Their surly driver, spitting out a stream of red paan-stained saliva onto the muddy road in front of him, refused to go any further. He pointed to the deep ruts in the clayey soil made by the large vans that transported the tiger and other animals. 'My cart will get stuck in this mud,' he said, taking his hands off the reins and crossing his arms. Kaveri gave him a handful of coins, and then another handful, before he reluctantly agreed to park nearby. He pointed to a shaded spot near the road.

'I will only stay for half an hour,' he grunted, before driving off. 'This is not a safe place for women. Do your husbands know you are out and about like this?'

Kaveri shot him a look of disdain. But Uma aunty tugged at her arm, pointing to the slushy grounds. 'Do you think he's right? Maybe it is unsafe,' she said, her eyes swivelling in every direction.

'I'm sure it is fine,' Kaveri said, disregarding the prickle of fear that seemed to be working its way up her shoulder blades. 'Venu said two of his boys would be around somewhere. We can call them if we are in danger.'

'You are always sure that it is safe, right until we stumble into a situation,' Uma aunty grumbled.

'But you love it as much as I do, aunty,' Kaveri teased, coaxing an unwilling smile out of her. The two women made their way past the empty tents, hitching up their saris to shield them from the muddy soil. They balanced on the slabs of *kadappa* stone laid out to form a rough path that went straight to the makeshift homes at the back where the employees' temporary quarters had been hastily thrown together.

'Suman told me that most of the circus has left, gone to Mysore for a week,' Kaveri told Uma aunty as they navigated their way through the slush. 'The large animals are all there, with their trainers, and the acrobats and clowns. Only a handful of performers have stayed back – mainly the wrestlers, who will guard the circus equipment.'

After the morning showers, the day had turned out fine and clear. The sun shone down, drying out the puddles of water in the slushy mud. Dragonflies hovered around the pools of dirty water, drinking in the salt. Their iridescent wings sparkled in the light, like miniature flying rainbows.

'This entire area used to be a lake, Kaveri. Sampangi Lake. I used to come with my father, to collect fresh milk in the mornings from the buffalo herders. There was a small temple tank here. The steps that led down to the base were decorated with carvings of lions.' Uma aunty stopped. 'Just look at it now. The British built a brewery and bungalows around it, taking away part of the lake. Then they drained the lake so that the regiment could play polo. They threw out the fishermen and farmers who lived here and turned it into this barren ground, rented out for circus performances and cattle shows. How ugly it seems now.' Her voice was loud and agitated.

'Shh,' Kaveri cautioned, pausing. She could not see any of Venu's boys. She had grown to know many of them well. Over the past few months, since Ismail had taken them under his wing, their lives had improved substantially. Shanthi had started to teach some of them to read and write, and they were slowly beginning to bring their sisters with them too.

She willed herself to relax. Even if she could not see any of the boys, she knew at least one of them would be around somewhere. Probably high up in the branches of a tree. If she was in trouble, she could shout for help and he would run straight to the Wilson Gardens police station, where Inspector Ismail sat. It was only a short distance from the circus grounds. Kaveri pushed away the nagging thought in her brain that warned her that Ismail would not be happy if he knew she had ignored his warnings and plunged into the investigation.

She muttered a small prayer under her breath. The women navigated a muddy river of clayey, sticky slush, balancing carefully on the small slabs of stone as they made their way past the semicircular arena that served as the makeshift parking area of the circus, to the ramshackle homes at the back.

What a contrast the circus grounds were from the last time she had been there. The tent stood in a far corner, covering the stage where the performance was held. No longer exciting or magical, as it had seemed at night, its then attractive bright colours now appeared cheap and faded in the sunlight. The parking lot where they had encountered Pawan's body was pitted with car tracks, seeming like it had not been swept in years. A high line of eucalyptus trees enclosed the clearing, pale and tall like eerie silver sentinels. The peeling bark on the trees appeared like distorted faces, watching them as they moved. She could not see people anywhere, though as they neared the wicker gate, she could hear sounds. Metal clanked and water splashed in the distance. Women, cleaning vessels and washing clothes, called to each other as they worked.

They had almost reached the edge of the stone path. Once they were out of the clearing, the women entered an area bounded by a makeshift bamboo fence, ill-constructed shacks with crooked walls and aluminium sheets for roofs standing cheek-by-jowl with each other.

'Strange, that a famous magician like Das would agree to live in such seedy quarters,' Uma aunty said.

Occupied with domestic chores, the circus performers chattered to each other, shouting loudly to be heard above the din. After the silence of the open grounds, the noise seemed deafening.

Muscular grey-haired women squatted next to large stone slabs, taking out heavy bed sheets that had been soaked in large tin buckets. They bundled up the sheets, slapping them against the slabs to loosen the dirt before sluicing them with clean water, squeezing them dry and hanging them out on long clothes lines. Tied to the trees around the edge, the clothes lines dipped drunkenly down to the ground, creating an obstacle course that criss-crossed the clearing. Short and plump, Uma aunty was able to navigate them with ease, but long-limbed Kaveri had to bend and duck to move.

Children capered around playing with cork balls made from the pods of the raintree whose branches shaded them from above, making it even harder for her to get across. Crows cawed, diving down to attack the plates of food that the older children held in their hands as they chased their younger siblings around, trying to feed them. She saw a lot of older people, too, but most of the performers must have left for Mysore.

'Do you know where Suman is?' Kaveri asked an exhausted-looking young woman with a swollen belly, one child on her hip and the other tugging at her hand. But she only stared at her with compressed lips, not saying a word.

Then a man came out from the shack, holding a massive stone dumbbell, gazing at Kaveri and Uma aunty with unfriendly eyes. Kaveri recognised him: it was Harish, who had come to Das's room backstage when Kaveri and Ramu were visiting the magician there. He was bare-chested, his upper body oiled in preparation for exercise. Kaveri's eyes moved from him to an open clearing nearby that held outdoor exercise equipment – metal bars for push-ups, long heavy bamboo *lathis*, stone weights and heavy metal dumbbells. She paused, struck by a memory, then studied him again. When she had last seen him, he'd had a bandage on his forehead. The bandage was now gone, revealing a tattooed snake on his right temple – just like the one Pawan had.

Children surged past Kaveri, chattering noisily as they chased a small dog which held a ball in its mouth. She side-stepped a young beggar who came up to her whining and holding the small of his back as he held his hand out in supplication. She gave him a stern look. She was sure she had seen him a few minutes back, hanging upside down from a tree, plucking fruit. 'Go sell the tamarind you just collected,' she told him.

One of Venu's team of boys, Kaveri realised, as she spotted the orange thread wrapped around his left wrist.

He gave her an unrepentant smile, moving closer and clutching her sari with one hand. 'Venu sent me,' he whispered, leaning close before he skipped away.

Kaveri breathed more freely. Harish's snake tattoo had unnerved her, bringing to mind Pawan's swollen, distorted face. Now that she knew Venu's team was here, she felt safer, knowing they were in calling distance if she needed help. She could not see a second boy, but he could be on top of a tree for all she knew. That was one of their favourite vantage points. Kaveri now moved with renewed energy.

An eagle circling in the sky high above them let out a restless keening call. Uma aunty balanced shakily on the slabs of stone above the sticky mud. Kaveri felt a chill travel down her spine, the unmistakable sense of being watched.

She saw a flash of movement from the corner of her eye. Someone moved amongst the trees, watching them. Who could it be? She slowed, and half-turned back to Uma aunty, pretending that she was waiting for the older woman to catch up to her. Keeping her purse shielded with her sari, she opened it, discreetly removing a small hand-mirror from inside. Palming it in her hand, she raised her fingers to her head as if screening her eyes from the sun, looking into the mirror.

A tall and bulky man stood behind a tree at the edge of the compound wall. She strained, but could not make out his features. Perhaps it was Harish – though this man wore a shirt.

Kaveri slipped the mirror back into her purse as Uma aunty caught up with her. The older lady followed her uncomplainingly, but Kaveri sensed her energy beginning to flag. Where was Suman? No one seemed willing to speak to her here.

Kaveri was just beginning to wonder if they should return home when they saw Suman at last, standing in the doorway of one of the shacks. It was an isolated spot, in a far corner. 'Kaveri *didi*,' he exclaimed, running towards her. 'You came? I was just about to give up hope.'

'Young man, how would you know if we had come or not if you sit inside the house with the door closed?' Uma aunty asked tartly. 'We have been out here looking for you.' She picked up Kaveri's left hand, showing the wristwatch to Suman.

'It is twenty past noon. You said we were to meet at twelve,' Kaveri said, introducing Suman to Uma aunty.

The young man apologised. 'I didn't want to step out and search for you, in case I missed you. You came in one way, but there is another path that enters from the back of the sheds.'

Men and women stood outside their huts, openly staring at them. Kaveri looked around but could not see Venu's beggar boy anywhere. She looked at the trunk of a coconut tree beside the shack, hoping that the other boy was up in the canopy. Trying to get away from the unfriendly stares of the circus folk, she pulled Suman into the hut, towing Uma aunty along with her and closing the door.

It was dark inside. The unhealthy damp fumes made her sneeze and cover her nose with her sari pallu. Uma aunty followed her example, pressing close to her side. Newspapers covered the windowpanes, keeping out the sunlight. Suman lit a petromax lamp, its hissing sound seeming extra loud in the confines of the small room. He dropped his head, staring at his feet when he saw Uma aunty's gaze fall on the room, bare of all furniture. A couple of small straw mats lay rolled up in a corner. In another corner, a torn sheet covered a couple of dusty suitcases.

'When I was out this morning, trying to get a new job, someone ransacked our home,' he said briefly. 'They broke our chairs and table, ripped out our curtains and forced our suitcases open and riffled through our clothes.'

Kaveri's mind immediately jumped to Harish.

'Whoever did this must suspect that your father has hidden something here,' she said, lowering her voice to match his, casting an uneasy eye at the newspaper-covered window. She could not tell if anyone was standing outside, listening to them.

'I came back from the hospital after Baba disappeared, and searched everything in the room. I could not find any message. But I know my father. He would not leave me willingly, without a message for me. That's why I called you here. You might find something I missed.' Suman moved closer, studying her hopefully. He spoke so softly that she had to strain to hear him. At these near quarters, his mouth smelt like cloves and pepper. His voice was muffled by the sound of the noisy lamp.

Uma aunty stood in a corner, surveying the room with pity. Kaveri looked through the pitifully small set of belongings in the room, raising the lamp high. It took very little time, and she could not find anything beyond a set of magic books, and clothes.

He opened one of the suitcases, showing her the interior. 'I was sure my father would have left me a message. He and my mother sometimes left each other messages, inserting them into the side lining. There is nothing here though.'

Kaveri patted the edges of the suitcases. Suman was right – there was nothing hidden here. She riffled through the pages of every book, and shook out the clothes, feeling them with her hands. There was no crackling of paper, no extra thickness of cloth to indicate a hidden message.

She squatted back on her heels, inspecting the room. There was so few places to hide anything. But Das was a magician and all the books she had read on magic said that the first thing a good magician needed to develop expertise on was the art of misdirection. If such a man wanted to hide something, he would do it in the last place anyone would look.

'Where are your costumes?'

'Look at this place. Our costumes are expensive, and we can't keep any valuables here.' Suman's mouth twisted. 'We leave them with the circus owner, who keeps them safe for us. Our neighbours, the wrestlers, are a nasty bunch. They would steal from their own grandmothers.' He gestured towards the straw mats, rolled up in the corner. 'We had mattresses once, but they stole them too.'

Uma aunty's face twisted with shock.

Without conscious thought, Kaveri moved across the room, unrolling the mats, kneeling down on the floor and tracing her fingers across them. Suman and Uma aunty moved closer. Suman held the torch to give Kaveri better lighting as she felt every square inch of one mat, then swept it aside, unrolling the second and resuming her inspection.

She paused when she reached one of the corners. She could feel something in this section, where the flexible material of the mat seemed stiffer. 'Can you shine the light here?'

Suman squatted on his haunches, looking at the section she was pointing at. Holding the light close, he took out a small switchblade from his pocket. Without a word, he handed it to Kaveri.

Moving with care in the dimly lit room, she slit the threads that held the edges of the mat together. Her hands shook with excitement when she pulled out a small envelope that had been hidden in the side binding of the mat. So tiny. What kind of a message could something like this contain?

She handed it to Suman, holding her breath as he opened it, then peered at its contents in confusion. The envelope held three grains of rice.

12

Frightening an Old Woman

Suman grinned, reaching out to hug Kaveri. 'I knew it! My father would never have disappeared willingly without leaving a note for me,' he said, as Uma aunty stared at him.

'A note on rice grains?' Uma aunty's voice was incredulous.

'I will show you.' Suman reached into his pocket again, this time taking out a miniature magnifying glass. 'My father used to document his experiments with new magic tricks, but stopped when one of our rivals broke into our house at night, trying to steal the diaries. My mother suggested he move to miniatures. She had learned the art from her grandfather – she supplemented our income by painting tiny portraits on coins, dice and other objects, selling them to wealthy patrons. She taught us both how to do it.'

Kaveri took the magnifying glass from him, moving closer to the petromax lantern and peering through the glass lens at the rice. She could see a series of numbers, but they did not make any sense to her.

'A code?'

'Yes, they used a secret code, that only the three of us know,' Suman said, squinting at the grains of rice he held in his hand. His mouth moved silently as he counted on his fingers. Kaveri looked on in excitement. She had read about Sherlock Homes deciphering secret codes in some of her favourite books, but even in her wildest dreams, she had never thought that she would find a message written in code in a real-life case.

Suman swallowed convulsively, then looking anxiously at Kaveri as he read her the message: '*If you are reading this, my worst fears have come to life. You are in danger. Flee from this place. Put your trust in the lady detective. Always remember, I love you.*'

The dark walls of the small room seemed to close in on them. Kaveri noticed Uma aunty shudder.

'Your father was a master magician. What do you think he meant by saying "my worst fears have come to life"?' Kaveri asked gently.

'I don't know what to think.' Suman's anguished eyes met hers. 'Could someone have tampered with the concealed partition below the cage, grabbing Baba as he escaped?'

'It could only be someone from the circus. Someone who knew the location of the trapdoor,' Kaveri said, thinking out loud.

'The wrestlers,' Suman said immediately. 'They had a huge argument with my father a few days back, when I had gone out to buy fish for our dinner. When I returned, I saw them huddled under a street lamp, speaking loudly to Baba. As soon as Baba saw me, he said something to them, and they hurried away. He refused to tell me what the quarrel was about.'

'Why didn't you tell me this before?' Kaveri demanded.

'I don't know.' Suman held his head in his hands. 'I have been so worried about Baba that I can't think clearly any longer.'

'Do you know that a man was murdered that same night?' Kaveri studied Suman closely, noting the way his face paled. He sat down heavily on the floor, leaning against the wall.

'Who?' he asked, looking stricken.

'A man called Pawan. Did you know him?'

'Yes.' A look of relief spread across Suman's face. 'I know I shouldn't speak ill of the dead, but he was a terrible man. Pawan is a cousin of the wrestlers. The circus owner hired him recently, on their recommendation. He helps out with odd jobs, loading and unloading, carrying things around. The atmosphere of the circus became much worse after Pawan joined. He was a bully, always harassing the weakest – like the dwarves – for money. Even the women cleaners were afraid of him, especially the younger women, who took care to move around in groups after he joined. He leered at them, forced his attentions on them. Do the police know who killed him?'

'No,' Kaveri said, recalibrating her earlier suspicions as she absorbed these new details. The circus employees whom Pawan had harassed must have held a grudge against him. Perhaps one of them had hated him badly enough to kill him, using the chaos at the circus as a smokescreen to hide the evidence of their involvement?

'Who is Harish, the large man who came to your dressing room backstage that night? The same man followed us here. He is standing outside, there behind the trees,' she said, keeping her voice low.

'That's Pailwan Harish, the older of the wrestlers. They are two brothers – Harish is the leader. His younger brother Ganesh and his cousin Pawan take

– took – their cues from him,' Suman said. 'But why is he following you?'

'I have a suspicion, though I am not certain,' Kaveri said. 'Pawan's wife Anandi is our friend. You remember the young woman who helped you at the circus performance, acting as Putana?' Kaveri waited for Suman's nod of recognition, then continued. 'Pawan used to beat her brutally – once, she was so badly injured that she almost died. Soon after that, he left Bangalore for several months, returning only recently. Anandi told us he had fled Bangalore because he was in debt to moneylenders, for quite a large sum. He had a gambling habit,' she explained.

'The circus pays him very little.' Suman frowned. 'To pay off a debt so large that he fled Bangalore, he must have access to other sources of money.'

'I think he works with the gang of thieves. That night at the circus, he was dressed in expensive clothes – velvet and satin. He must have come into money,' Kaveri said slowly, studying Suman's face. 'Your father's dramatic disappearance helped the gang of thieves by acting as a distraction so that they could fan through the audience. Their plans were foiled only because Major Wilks and Inspector Ismail were there, reacting immediately.'

'Are you suggesting that my father worked with the wrestlers? Baba would never be a part of something like that.'

Suman thumped his fist on the suitcases, making them rattle. Uma aunty jumped at the sound. He apologised, speaking more softly, 'I *know* he would not be a part of something like this. Even when we were in Calcutta, people pressed him to help them with many nefarious tasks. Magicians are much in demand with various types of people. Crooks, charlatans, men of influence – many seek to have us on their side. My parents always refused such offers.' He gestured to the room, bare and empty.

'Does this look like the room of a man who would collaborate with thieves?'

Kaveri exchanged a doubtful look with Uma aunty. Das might not have collaborated with the wrestlers for money, but he could have if they threatened him with harm to his son. It seemed like too much of a coincidence – that thieves would stage a concerted attack on the very day that the magician devised a new and dramatic act. Pawan's death seemed likely to be connected with this in some way. She did not say anything to Suman, though. He was agitated, and would only dig in his heels if she did, defending his father more strongly.

Suman's voice shook. 'If he had any control over it, Baba would never have left me alone in this strange neighbourhood with these unfriendly people.' Suman looked very young, the dark shadows under his eyes standing out starkly against his fair face. 'In the middle of the night, when I was lying in bed, I heard the door handle rattle. I called out, but no one answered. I pushed the cot against the door to keep it closed, but I was so afraid that someone would force their way in that I stayed awake for the rest of the night.'

'You should leave Bangalore immediately. Go to Mysore, with the rest of the circus, for a few days,' Uma aunty urged. 'That's what your father's message urged.'

'How can I?' Suman's jaw was set in a stubborn line. 'I have to stay here so that if my father returns, he can find me.'

Kaveri did not tell him what she was thinking – that perhaps Das was already dead.

'At least move out of this unsafe place,' Uma aunty said again. 'Is there no other home that will take you in?'

'Most of our friends in the circus have gone to Mysore for the week. There are a number of shows going on there. Only a few families are still here.' Suman paused. 'Only the clown and his wife are good to me. They live near the entrance. Perhaps I can stay with them for a few days.' He sounded doubtful.

'Come home with us. You can stay until you decide what to do next,' Kaveri offered. As she spoke, she wondered what she would do if Ramu objected. She knew he was suspicious of Suman. Would Bhargavi support her, convincing Ramu that Suman could stay?

'I know what you can do,' Uma aunty looked eager to help. 'My son has been looking for a gardener for a while now. We have a disused shed at the back of the house, where we store old tools. You can stay there if you don't mind doing some garden work. I will tell my son that I found a man willing to work for the meagre salary he is offering – if we throw in a place to stay, and three meals a day. I will feed you well, don't worry.' She smiled at him. 'I live right behind Kaveri. We share a back wall. You will be close to her in case you need any help.'

'Thank you,' Suman said fervently. 'I will work hard, and repay your faith in me. I'll come to your house this very evening.' He turned to Kaveri. 'You will take on my case, won't you? And find my father?'

'I cannot promise to find him. I can only tell you that I will try my best.'

'How can I pay you?' He took out a battered leather wallet from his pocket. 'I earned some money from the performance in Kolar. It is not much, but I hope it will suffice as an advance. I will take on some more shows and pay you the rest of your fees in instalments. I promise I will not cheat you.'

Before Kaveri could respond, Uma aunty jumped in, placing her hand over his wallet. 'Do you think she does this for money?' she asked. 'She does this for justice.'

'I cannot take your help for free,' Suman said stubbornly.

'Keep your money,' Kaveri responded gently. 'You need it more than me. If you ever have some money to spare, donate it to Shanthi Women's Home, the shelter for abused and abandoned women, where Anandi works. Better still . . .' She turned to him as an idea struck her. 'Teach them some simple magic shows. Tricks that they can perform with ease, that help them increase their confidence.'

'I can do that,' Suman promised. 'Tell me when to go there.'

'I will,' Kaveri said. 'Meanwhile, I want you to promise that you will move to Uma aunty's house. Stay there for a few days. Leave a message for me if you need to tell me anything urgently.'

She turned to her elderly neighbour. 'We must leave now, Aunty.'

Kaveri opened the door, raising her mirror again and holding it in the palm of her hand as she pretended to adjust her hair. At the edge of the trees, she saw another flash of white. Pailwan Harish still watched them.

As they made their way out, she noticed that the chatter that had filled the air when they had arrived had now died down. The women had stopped their washing and cleaning, and were hurrying indoors, keeping a firm grip on their children. The men stood outside, staring at the two women with unfriendly eyes.

Grimy curs with matted hair emerged from the trees, snarling at them. An elderly woman, bent at the waist, her eyes friendlier than the others', shouted at the dogs, hurling a stone at the leader. The pack dispersed, growling as she continued to throw small stones at their feet. Uma aunty let out a frightened squeal as one of the curs veered close to her, fleeing back to its shelter amongst the trees.

122

Kaveri heard a snigger and looked up to see one of the men laughing at Uma aunty, a sneer on his face. White hot rage overwhelmed her, and she forgot to be cautious. She advanced on him, wagging her finger in his face.

'Aren't you ashamed of yourself, frightening an old woman? Pick on someone your own size.'

An ugly look came upon the man's face, and he took a threatening step towards her. Uma aunty pulled at her elbow, quickly drawing her back. 'Kaveri. What is wrong with you?' she hissed.

The older woman with friendly eyes appeared next to them without warning. 'Ganesh.' She glared at the giant of a man. 'Let the women go home undisturbed. They are friends of the police.'

Ganesh? That was Harish's brother, the younger Pailwan. Kaveri studied the large man who loomed in front of them. He did not look as similar to Pawan as his older brother, but she could still see a family resemblance. The young woman with the swollen belly emerged from the hut, pulling Pailwan Ganesh by the elbow, urging him inside. With an oath, he spat on the ground, just missing Kaveri, then turned and flung himself inside the hut, slamming the door which hung crookedly shut on its hinges. The rest of the crowd dispersed, moving away.

The old woman leaned forward, pulling Kaveri close with surprising strength. At this distance, Kaveri could see the grey hair on her scalp, and the browning flowers pinned to her hair. Her lungs filled with the smell of decaying jasmine from the old woman's hair, causing her to cough.

'Go home now,' the woman hissed in her ear. 'Women like you don't belong here.' She gave Kaveri a push, and she lurched forward in the mud, narrowly missing the iron bars on the window of the hut. Through the bars, she saw a glimpse of the huge man holding a large whip in his hands, running his fingers almost lovingly along its length. Before Kaveri could notice anything else, Uma aunty caught hold of her in a tight grip, pulling her away. Together, the women stumbled down the stone path, almost running in their haste to get out of the settlement and onto the road.

13

I Watched Him Watching You

Uma aunty panted and puffed as she ran along the stone steps, and Kaveri held her hand to steady her elderly neighbour. When they reached the gate, Uma aunty collapsed onto a rock, rubbing her sweaty face with her sari pallu. Kaveri leaned against a wall, taking in great gulps of air as she fought for breath.

Spreading out the folds of her sari, Uma aunty shook her head at its muddy hem. 'This will be impossible to clean.'

'I cannot believe you are the same person I met just a few months ago,' Kaveri said slowly. 'You were so worried when I dragged you into the cowherd's colony, saying respectable women should not go to such places. And we were perfectly safe there. Now, when we have just escaped such a scary situation, you are talking about muddy saris.'

After the tense few minutes that they had been through, this suddenly seemed hilarious to them both. The two women collapsed in mirth, breathing freely as they felt the relief coursing through them. Putting hands to their mouths so that no one would hear them, they laughed on, tears running down their cheeks, only stopping when they saw a small boy in ragged shorts climbing down from the branches of a nearby tree.

The orange thread around his arm marked him out as another member of Venu's team of tiny watchdogs. A towel tied on his forehead, screening his head from the sun, the boy held a handful of *jujubes*, coiled fruit pods from the tree above their heads. 'Here, *akka*.' He opened a grimy palm, proffering the peach brown twisted pods to Kaveri and Uma aunty.

'Thank you. What is your name?' Kaveri asked as she opened the pods, sucking the sweet-sour flesh with relish.

'I am Chandru.' The scruffy little boy beamed, puffing out his chest. He reminded Kaveri of a bantam rooster that she had seen in Venu's grandmother's house. 'I was sitting on that tree, watching you. When that large man came out to shake his fist at you, I thought I should run to the police station, to bring Inspector Ismail. But then that *ajji* came and chased him away. Pailwan Harish is a very bad man.'

'How do you know?' Kaveri demanded.

'I know everything about him – and his brother. What they like to eat and drink, how they speak to their mother, what time they go to bed – everything. I have been following them for a week.' Chandru grinned at her.

'A whole week? Tell me everything you know,' Kaveri said eagerly.

'During the day, the brothers mostly rest indoors. After lunch, they start to exercise outside, lifting weights, stretching, and challenging each other. That's when I climb one of those trees over there. They go on for hours and hours.' He turned to point at a large banyan tree. 'I take a nap, and wake up before sunset, but they're still at it. After their exercise they take a hot bath and then settle in for a long drinking session.'

'That's all?' Uma aunty asked, sounding very disappointed. 'Many men are like that.'

'I said this was what they did during the *day*. I didn't tell you what they did at night.' Chandru gave them another cheeky grin. As Kaveri moved towards him, pretending to chase after him, he skipped sideways.

'Alright, alright. Sit down and tell us properly. Leave nothing out.' Kaveri shook her head at him, sitting down next to Uma aunty. Chandru was a handful. He must drive his mother crazy.

Squatting opposite them, Chandru continued. 'At night, I have seen them slip out, going to the mango grove at the back of the circus. Someone else waits for them there.' He met Kaveri's eyes directly. 'I can't see clearly inside – it is too dark, and I am too far from them to hear what they say. The man they meet – his voice sounds strange.' He wrinkled his nose, thinking.

'Strange in what way?' Kaveri asked.

'It just sounds different. Like he has an accent.'

'A Bengali accent?' Kaveri asked, thinking of Das.

'I can't tell,' Chandru said. 'After the wrestlers meet with this man, they go out, carrying large sacks. The sacks are empty when they go out, and full when they return. They put *kappu* on their faces, covering them with black.'

'They moonlight as robbers,' Kaveri breathed, turning to Uma aunty. 'That's why Miss Roberts complained of so many thefts recently in the city.' She stamped her foot in frustration, thinking of the taunting look that Harish had given her earlier. 'Pawan's cousins should be in jail. I wish we could find some evidence, something we could use to hand them over to the police.'

She thought of something. 'When they return, with the sacks – have you seen where they store them?'

'They go to their cousin's house. Do you know that man?'

'Pawan?' Kaveri asked. 'His house is here?'

'It's quite close, *akka*. If you walk around this compound, beyond the end of the mango grove, you will see a small lane. You can't miss it – there is a large banyan tree at the beginning of the lane. There is just one *pakka* house there. That's his house.'

Uma aunty looked very doubtful as she studied his face. 'How do you know so much about these men?'

'When Mala madam found out that Pawan was back in Bangalore, she asked me to follow him and find out everything I could about him. I can take you inside Pawan's house now, if you want,' Chandru offered, shading his eyes from the sun's glare as he squinted at the sky. 'This time of day, the wrestlers will have completed their lunch, and begun their afternoon exercise routine. There is little chance that they will be here. They move out only at night. Pawan's house should be empty.'

Kaveri hesitated. Pawan and his cousins seemed to hold many of the clues to Das's mysterious disappearance, the thefts that plagued the city, and even the question of what had made Anandi so afraid. She itched to explore his house. But she had promised Ramu she would be careful. She gave Uma aunty a questioning look. The older lady nodded gamely, but Kaveri could see she looked tired. If someone came upon them, her neighbour would be trapped, unable to move fast.

Ramu's hospital was close by. She looked at her watch; it was about two p.m., so he would be on his lunch break. With some luck, he might even have a quiet afternoon – on weekdays, most patients came to the Bowring Hospital in the morning. If there were no emergencies, perhaps he could accompany her.

'Let's go closer to the house, Chandru, and find a place where you and Uma aunty can rest and keep watch for me. I will go and get my husband.'

She saw Uma aunty's eyes brighten in approval.

14

A Bloodstained Sari

Leaving Uma aunty sitting on a tree stump in the shade of a large raintree, Kaveri placed Chandru on guard next to her. Then, walking swiftly to the corner, she hailed a bullock cart and directed the driver to the hospital. Fortunately, as she had guessed, the place was largely empty at that time, except for the families of patients who had been already admitted for treatment.

Ramu ran down the stairs as soon as he saw her enter, placing his hands on her shoulders. 'Is everything alright?' he demanded. 'I've been staring at the clock since noon, wondering if you were safe.'

Looking at his worried face, Kaveri's conscience tugged at her. Perhaps she should have stayed home, instead of making him so anxious. But then she thought of everything they had found out – Das's secret message to Suman, and about the gang of wrestlers. If she stayed home all the time, how would they find anything out? Ramu could not accompany her everywhere. He had a hospital ward to run, patients who needed him too.

'Uma aunty is fine, and so am I,' she reassured him. Pulling him closer, and speaking into his ear so that the cart driver couldn't hear, she quickly told him about everything they had discovered, asking if he could accompany her back to the area near the circus, to search Pawan's house. The elderly driver cracked the reins he held in his hand, casting them impatient glances. Not wanting to lose any time, she had promised him a double fare if he waited and took them back. They couldn't afford to drive back in Ramu's car – in Bangalore, where few people owned cars, their Ford was too well known. If the wrestlers saw it near Pawan's house, it would put them on their guard.

Ramu ran up to lock his room, returning quickly and climbing into the cart with Kaveri. They urged the driver on, holding tight as the cart jolted and bounced down the road, and the landscape flew by.

They were there in minutes. A wide grin split the driver's face as Ramu pulled out a handful of coins, dropping them into the man's open palms. As the cart moved off, they hurried to Uma aunty, who stood up eagerly, her face showing her relief as she spotted Ramu.

As Chandru promised, the house was close by. It only took a couple of minutes. They walked swiftly, keeping a lookout for any movement. This time in the afternoon, the streets were empty and quiet. In the heat of the midday sun all they could hear was the buzzing of flies.

When they reached the corner of the road, Kaveri asked Uma aunty and Chandru to stay back, well behind the banyan tree, to keep an eye out for anyone approaching the house. 'I will whistle if I hear anyone,' Chandru promised, taking out a small cord tucked into his grimy *banian* and proudly showing her a small tin whistle tied to it. Uma aunty gripped Kaveri's hand in hers and placed it against her cheek before letting go. Her eyes were frightened, but she gave Kaveri and Ramu a determined nod.

The couple moved swiftly, only stopping to take off their slippers and place them outside the compound wall. Kaveri pushed the gate open gingerly, and despite flecks of black paint peeling away from its rusted surface it opened noiselessly. Someone seemed to have oiled it, keeping it in good condition. Thank goodness, she thought. She followed Ramu's example, squatting on her heels and moving along in an awkward crab-like gait, staying below the level of the front wall so that anyone walking on the road could not see her. Creeping noiselessly on the granite path towards the main door, she took in the dried and withered rose bushes that lined the path on both sides.

A thorn caught in her sari, tugging at her *pallu*. She stopped to untangle the fabric, and then inspected the withered, solitary rose on the bush. A gust of wind shook a dry petal loose and it landed on her peach-coloured sari. The petal stood out like a smear of blood. Kaveri swallowed thickly at the sight but shook it off and crept on. Ahead of her, Ramu was trying cautiously to open the front door. The door was thick and solid, and did not move. They studied the heavy brass mortise lock. They would never be able to force that open, Kaveri thought. They had to find another way inside.

They didn't have much luck at the windows, either – they had been nailed shut with flat planks. Only one plank hung drunkenly askew, high above her, swaying in the wind. Tethered by a single rusty nail, it made a sharp, squealing sound every time it swung, like a pig being slaughtered. Then Ramu waved to get her attention and pointed to her bun, and she pulled out a hairpin, giving it to him. He squatted in front of the locked front door.

One of his first patients, a recovering thief, had taught him how to pick doors with a sharp pin – a skill he had put to good use when he was a medical student, sneaking out of the hostel after curfew with his friends. While he worked on the door, Kaveri searched for another way to sneak in. She took a few cautious steps further, moving around the corner to the side of the house. She inspected the side door, wondering if this lock would be easier for Ramu to open – but this door did not have a lock. It was bolted from the inside. The upper part of the door was made of frosted glass, and one section was broken. Someone had tried to close the gap with a piece of paper but failed.

Reaching cautiously into the gap, Kaveri pulled the paper away from the door, exposing a large, jagged hole. *'Dancing Dolls, Whirligigs and Marionette Show; Peep Show, Jugglers and Nautch Dancers; Fireworks, Balloons and Circular Velocipedes; Performing Monkeys, Goats and Bears; Talking Heads and Tight Rope Dancers'* – the circus poster had a sketch of a man riding a large circular wheel, with a long queue of people lined up behind him, waiting for their turn. Despite the urgency of the situation, Kaveri's mind went to one of the toughest questions in her mathematics textbook, to estimate the distance travelled by a circular wheel from its radius and the size of the tyre. This diagram would make it so much easier to solve the problem correctly! She folded the paper and tucked it into her blouse, then gingerly inserted her hand into the gap, trying to avoid the jagged fragments of glass as she felt around. She suppressed her triumphant shout as she got hold of the door handle, snicking back the bolt that kept it locked.

She went back to Ramu, signalling to him to follow her around the side. He motioned for her to stand aside, and opened the door, cautiously peering inside. The room was dimly lit by the sunlight trickling through the cracked glass in the door pane. After the bright sunlight outside, the sudden change in illumination made it difficult for them to focus on anything. As she blinked furiously in an attempt to adjust her eyes to the gloomy room, Kaveri saw a shadow move from the corner. A loud gasp had her suddenly ducking back against Ramu, her heart thudding so violently in her throat that she was sure the stranger would be able to hear. Ramu held her tightly. She knew he was less sure in the dark than she was. Footsteps sounded from her left, and just as a feminine voice uttered an oath, Kaveri felt a hand push her, hard. She fell, landing on her back.

Kaveri spat dust out of her mouth, coughing violently. As she tried to scramble up, a blurry outline of a figure rushed past her and out through the door. The sound of footsteps faded as the person moved farther and farther away.

Kaveri felt a touch on her arm and jumped back violently, terror washing over her body. Then, squinting into the still dim light, she saw Uma aunty's face frowning down at her. She must have rushed inside immediately. Able to see more clearly with the door open, Ramu came over to her, pulled her up, and ran his hands over her, looking for injuries. She waved him away, letting him know with a touch of her hand that she was fine.

'Wha . . . who was that?' she stammered.

Uma aunty pulled at her arm, pointing to a tiny figure standing on the road, looking across at them. When the woman saw them looking back at her, she turned, running swiftly away.

Kaveri recognised the bright orange sari the woman wore. It was one of Anandi's favourites, one of her best saris.

'*Anandi* pushed me to the ground?' Kaveri turned to Uma aunty, her voice shaking. Ramu gripped her hand.

'I don't think she even knew you were there. She ran past you so fast, like a ghost was on her trail. She did not even see me behind the tree.' Uma aunty stopped speaking, her hand shaking as she pointed a finger at Kaveri's stomach.

Kaveri looked down, placing her hand on her stomach. It came away covered in blood.

Her peach sari, delicately embroidered in gold, was stained with blotches of red. Ramu gasped loudly, pulling her close again and pulling her sari and petticoat away from her stomach. Finding smooth, unmarked skin beneath, he exhaled in relief, pulling her close and burying his face in her hair.

'Kaveri *akka* is hurt.' Chandru rushed up to them, pointing with a shaking hand to the blood on her sari.

'She is okay.' Ramu's voice was gruff as he reassured Chandru and Uma aunty. 'Someone pushed her and ran away.' He pressed Kaveri's arm, signalling to her that they should not reveal Anandi's presence on the scene to Chandru. Kaveri gave him an almost imperceptible nod. Until they knew why Anandi had come to the house, it was best to pretend they had not recognised her.

Kaveri reached for the light switch, then paused, hearing a faint moan. Someone was in the room next to them. She exchanged perturbed glances with Ramu as they heard the sound again, this time sounding like a cry for help.

'Wait here,' Ramu said firmly, putting his hand over hers and switching on the light. He pulled aside the curtain that separated both rooms, going in. Kaveri stood outside, feeling uncertain about what to do. *Should she go in?* She looked at Uma aunty and Chandru. She worried about leaving Ramu alone. It could be dangerous. Only seconds had passed, but she could not hear a sound from within.

Uma aunty and Chandru looked back at her, waiting for her to tell them what to do. Their faith in her bolstered her wavering confidence.

Kaveri made a quick decision.

'Chandru, run to the police station and tell Inspector Ismail that I have asked him to send a constable.' Would that be urgent enough for him to send someone? She thought for a moment.

'Tell him something dangerous is happening,' she amended, hoping that might bring Ismail himself. 'Tell him I asked for help. Quickly.' The boy nodded, then turned and ran, kicking up small clouds of dust on the path outside with his bare feet.

Kaveri's mind raced as she thought of how she could keep Uma aunty safe. She wanted her outside, closer to the road, where she would be away from the danger. But she knew Uma aunty would not leave her – unless she thought she was helping Kaveri.

'Aunty, you stand outside the house. Watch to see if anyone else comes in.' She exhaled, relieved, as she watched her elderly neighbour leave the house, moving towards a position of relative safety outside.

Kaveri took a couple of deep breaths, focusing her mind and making her senses alert to everything in her surroundings before she entered the room. As she stepped through the doorway, she noted every detail, almost automatically. The first room was a kitchen, its shelves bare except for a single plate, spoon and tumbler, empty of furniture except for a pair of dented black dumbbells, tossed carelessly against the wall. A ray of light lit up part of the room, falling through cracks in the boarded-up windows and glinting off the weights. Lying next to the wall, a large man was prone on the floor. Sunlight fell on his body, highlighting the bloodstain that had spread across his shirt. The blade of the large knife buried in his chest glittered, reflecting light into Kaveri's eyes. Ramu was crouched next to him, clad only in his banian, trying to staunch the flow of blood with his shirt.

A roaring noise overwhelmed Kaveri, and she leaned against the doorway, clutching the wall as she fought to remain conscious. The man was motionless, but as she shuffled closer to him, he moaned again. *Not* dead then.

Heedless of the pool of blood surrounding the man, Kaveri hurried over and crouched down to look at him more clearly. It was Pailwan Ganesh, the younger of the two wrestlers who had accosted her on the circus premises before the old woman had pushed him away.

'Water,' Ganesh said weakly. 'Can you get me water?'

Ramu gave her a nod of approval, and she hurried to the tap in the corner of the kitchen, filling the single tumbler she'd seen with water, and handing the glass to Ramu. Ramu asked her to take over from him, and she bent down again, kicking the pair of weights aside to move closer to Ganesh. She pushed down with her palms, increasing the pressure on his chest to staunch the bleeding like she had seen Ramu doing. The acrid metallic smell of fresh blood filled her nostrils, and she gulped in lungfuls of air as she saw her blood-covered hands before her. Sensing her uneasiness, Ramu moved closer to her. She leaned against his shoulder, grateful for the steady support of his warm, solid body.

Ramu dribbled a small thread of water into Ganesh's mouth, watching carefully, but the man was unable to swallow. The water trickled out, flowing down his neck to the ground.

'Gold . . . missing.' Ganesh coughed, grimacing in pain. 'Help me,' he said again. 'Help . . . find gold.' A rattling breath came from his throat. As Kaveri watched, horrified, he gave her a pleading glance and then froze. An unnatural stillness spread across his body and yet, his eyes were still wide open . . . still focused on her.

'Who did this to you?' Kaveri asked urgently. 'Who?'

Her head swam, and she forced herself to stay focused, staring at the white bandage on the right side of his forehead. Just a short while back, Ganesh had been alive, spitting contemptuously at her feet.

Heart racing, hoping against hope, she took off the gold chain Ramu had given her, placing the magnifying glass locket below his nose for a few seconds before looking at it. There was no trace of moisture on the glass.

Ramu placed his fingers on the man's neck to feel his pulse, then shook his head. 'He is dead, Kaveri.' His voice was filled with sadness.

'I can't believe it,' Kaveri whispered. 'The pain on his face . . . however horrible he was, no man should die like that, begging for water but unable to drink, ending his life's journey in a room with strangers.'

Ramu kissed the top of her head gently. They sat on the ground for a long while, as Kaveri closed her eyes, leaning against Ramu. Then he moved her gently aside, getting up and scrubbing his hands at the tap before he returned to examine the body again, gently unbuttoning the man's shirt but trying to leave the dagger undisturbed. 'A doctor will take time to come; at least this way I can give him an informed report,' he said over his shoulder to Kaveri.

Kaveri squatted on her heels, feeling sick to her stomach. He had called to her for help, and she . . . she had failed to help him. Kaveri had seen death before, and the trail of destruction it left behind. However horrible the man might have been, he must have had a family, people who would mourn him. Kaveri remembered the pregnant woman who had pulled him inside – was she his wife? She set her jaw, studying his corpse momentarily. Thoughts of Anandi, running out of the house, overwhelmed her. No, not Anandi – she could not, would not believe that Anandi could be responsible for this. Kaveri looked around the room for anything that might give her a clue to the identity of his murderer, helping silence the voice whispering in her mind – *are you sure Anandi has nothing to do with this?*.

She got up, washing her hands at the tap, and switched on the lamp she had seen in a corner, studying the dimensions of the room, inspecting its walls and ceiling. A few weeks back, after the conclusion of her previous case, she had begun to train herself to sketch, to record the details of a scene or a room in a house so that she could look at it later, to jog her memory. This small room would be easy to draw.

Dusty outlines of rectangles on the floor indicated that boxes had once been stacked here. Chandru had said the thieves carried their stolen goods here. Perhaps they had stored them in crates. Whatever the room may have once held, it was bare now.

The dust was thick on the floor, and she could see the outline of her naked feet, and those of Ramu's. The footprints crisscrossed over marks made by another pair of feet – those had to have been made by Ganesh, she concluded, looking at his feet. But she could also spot two more pairs of footprints. One pair had been made by a very large pair of shoes – a man's. They went all the way across the kitchen floor, and to the room in the back. The man seemed to have moved through the entire house. The second pair of prints were smaller, made by a pair of tiny slippers. Those must be Anandi's – her feet were small and delicate. One trail led from the open window in the last room, going towards the front room. Anandi had walked in, placing her feet flat on the ground. On her return, when she had run out of the side door, she had left partial footprints, outlining just her toes and the upper part of her feet. So she had entered slowly, but come out running. Frightened badly, Kaveri thought. Anandi had to have seen Ganesh's body then. But why had she not stayed to help him? This was the second time Anandi had been close to the scene of a murder. If Ismail knew, he would surely arrest her.

Uma aunty called out urgently, interrupting her thoughts. 'Kaveri. The police are here.'

Kaveri stood, hearing the heavy sound of hobnailed boots clattering on the road, and went to the side door. She saw two figures moving towards them, one large and one small. Chandru ran up to them swiftly. He was followed by Ismail, who covered the ground between them with large strides. The huge inspector was bulky, but could move very quickly when necessary. His face grew more alert when he saw the two women standing near the open door.

'Mrs Murthy?' He moved towards her. 'I thought the boy was pulling a fast one on me.'

Kaveri stood still, not knowing what to say. Her brains felt scrambled, and the stink of blood was heavy in her nostrils. Ramu was still inside, continuing his examination of the corpse.

'There is a man inside, with a knife in his chest,' she said. It came out bluntly, and she flinched, not knowing what else to say.

'Stay here,' Ismail ordered, giving her a hard look.

But Chandru had already darted through the door. 'Dead!' he said, in his thin, shaking voice.

15

She Wouldn't Kill an Ant

'Why didn't you tell him about Anandi?'
'Shh,' Kaveri hissed at Uma aunty as they waited outside. 'If the police come to know that Anandi was in the hut when Ganesh was killed, they will throw her in jail. I want to speak to her, find out what she was doing here. *Then* we can decide whether to tell Inspector Ismail.'

'If she killed Ganesh, she is hardly likely to admit it. She will only lie to you.' Uma aunty's voice was fierce, but she spoke softly, casting worried glances at the closed door as they stood inside the compound. Chandru had been sent to the police station to fetch reinforcements.

'Anandi?' Kaveri scoffed. 'She is incapable of hurting any creature, even an ant or caterpillar. Shanthi *akka* told me that Anandi was transformed when she attended the first meeting of the independence movement, after she read a pamphlet by Gandhiji on non-violence. For her, it represented hope.'

'Hope? Hope for what?'

'For a better society. A different way of life, based on mutual respect. You know, Aunty, Anandi told me that when Pawan beat her daily, her neighbours heard her crying for help but refused to intervene, saying that her husband had a right to do whatever he pleased with his wife. Finally it was Mala – who had been abused herself, by many men, not just one, who eventually saved her. Anandi is attracted to the freedom movement because it represents the hope of a better society based on mutual respect. She reads a lot about leaders like Sarojini Naidu and Ambedkar, who are asking for equal rights for people like her, doubly disadvantaged because they are women and "untouchables", from oppressed castes.'

'Be realistic, Kaveri. We do not know what relationship she had with these wrestlers. Why was she alone with this man in Pawan's house?'

They heard a creaking noise as Ismail threw back the bolts of the door. He would be with them any moment now. Kaveri spoke rapidly. 'Anandi *might* have killed Ganesh by accident . . . if he threatened her, and she pushed him, and he hit his head. She would not take a knife and stab him. I refuse to believe it.'

The women fell silent as Inspector Ismail emerged, Ramu by his side. He looked at Kaveri with stern eyes. '*Another* dead body? I thought I asked you to go to Mysore for a few weeks. If I had my way, I would pack you onto a train and see to it that you did not return till February.'

Kaveri stiffened. What was going on in Bangalore, that Ismail wanted her to leave the city till February?

'She did not have anything to do with it,' Uma aunty spoke hurriedly, eager to help. Ismail held up a large hand. His mustard yellow kurta hung loosely on his bony shoulders. He had bags under his eyes. This close to the Prince's visit, he had to be undergoing a lot of stress.

'I don't want to hear any excuses. Just tell me what happened, in detail. *Leave nothing out.*' Inspector Ismail's voice was hard.

Ramu squeezed Kaveri's hand in silent warning, as she began to speak, quickly summarising the day's events. She left out two pieces of information – the grains of rice they had discovered in Suman's shack, and the fact that she had recognised the woman fleeing from Pawan's house. 'I could not make out who she was,' she said, as Uma aunty nodded vigorously. Ramu remained silent, his face impassive. Inspector Ismail gave them an incredulous glance. He would know it was a woman – the footprints in the dust were a clear giveaway. But Kaveri prayed that he would not realise it was Anandi.

'I have to tell you something else,' she said hastily. Perhaps the other news she had would distract him. 'I need to show you. It is inside the house,' she persisted.

Ismail stared at her hard, then relented. 'Show me quickly, I need to get back to the station.' He opened the door, ushering her inside. Uma aunty hesitated, hovering by the door jamb as Kaveri walked in, stepping around the dead man. She picked up the pair of dumbbells. Ramu looked at her with raised eyebrows. Things had happened so quickly that she had not had a chance to tell him what she had found.

'This is what you wanted to show me?' Ismail asked, frowning. 'Dented dumbbells?'

Kaveri took one of them, holding it up in the sunlight, showing him how the sun's rays sparkled off a section where the paint had peeled off, revealing a glint of yellow within.

'Chandru said that the men went out at night, returning with large empty sacks to this house. I saw the shacks where they live in the circus. There is no privacy there, no place to hide anything of value. I could see outlines of large boxes here, but even the walls are bare. There's no place to hide anything. Except for this. Hiding in plain sight. Pawan was very clever to camouflage gold in such an obvious location, making it seem like something no one would look twice at.'

Ismail's voice was dry. 'He was a clever man. If only he had used his quick mind for good, rather than bad.'

'How did you suspect what it was, Kaveri?' Ramu's voice held an unmistakable tone of pride in his wife's skills of detection.

'I kicked it aside when I bent down to see if Ganesh was still breathing. It was easy to move. That got me thinking, and I looked at it more closely, seeing how dented it was, badly misshapen. Iron is so hard. Even if you pound it with a hammer, it will not lose its shape easily. Then I saw the way that the sunlight glinted off a small section where the paint had flaked off. What other metal is as soft? It had to be gold.'

Ismail gave her a small smile; the first Kaveri had seen from him in days. 'Your skill as a detective is unparalleled, as always.' He picked up the dumbbells, placing them in the large cotton satchel he always carried, slung around his shoulder. 'The men robbed quite a few wealthy homes. Pawan must have melted down the gold, hiding it from his accomplices. You told me that Suman's shack had been torn apart? I wonder if Ganesh thought that Suman and his father were involved in these thefts. From the few words he spoke to you, it seems he had been searching for the gold, suspecting that Pawan had hidden it here. He was correct – but Pawan had been too clever for him, hiding it in a place where he would not think to look.'

'Do you think Ganesh murdered Pawan, then? Because Pawan stole the gold, keeping it for himself?'

Kaveri asked Ismail. 'That makes sense. But it doesn't explain why Ganesh was killed.' She held her breath, trying to block the possibility from her mind that Anandi might have killed Ganesh. She had defended Anandi fiercely when Uma aunty suggested she might be the killer. But now, standing in the dark room where Ganesh's body lay, Kaveri felt less certain. What if Anandi had surprised Ganesh in the house, as he searched for the gold? He might have turned on her, threatening her with the knife. She *could* have killed Ganesh, in self-defence.

Ismail shook his head at Kaveri. 'You helped me find the gold – for this, you have my thanks. Enough now. I will repeat what I said before – you are meddling in matters that are more dangerous than you know. Who killed Pawan and Ganesh, why Das disappeared – leave these things to us. Go home, have a good strong cup of tea, and rest.' He took Kaveri and Ramu by the arm, gently but implacably leading them out of the door along with Uma aunty and closing it behind them.

Kaveri stiffened. She had just discovered something very important, that the police would not have been able to by themselves! Why was Ismail being so pig-headed about refusing her help?

A small smile tugged at the corner of Ismail's lips as he studied her indignant face. 'You look just like Nagma's three-year-old daughter when I scold her,' he said. Kaveri glared at him. She knew his granddaughter was the pride of his eyes. But she was not an infant to be compared with a petulant child – or a precious glass ornament to be wrapped in cotton and put away in a cupboard for fear it might break. Ramu gave her a warning look, signalling to her not to annoy Ismail any further, but she was in no mood to pay heed to him.

She heard the clatter of hooves, and spotted an ornate Victoria carriage trundling slowly down the road. Ismail nodded at it in grim satisfaction. 'I asked Chandru to fetch some transport. Now . . . Please. Listen. To. Me.' He spoke slowly to Kaveri, enunciating each word as though he was speaking to a child with limited intelligence. 'Be careful. Stay out of this mess.'

Kaveri felt Ramu press her arm in warning again. She nodded reluctantly, even though she had no intention of backing down, not now that he had issued her with what amounted to a challenge. Of course she would be more careful, she promised herself. But there was no way she was going to stay away from her case. Not when it was growing in complexity by the day.

'Take these passengers home,' Ismail ordered. The carriage driver looked dubiously at the two bedraggled women and the shirtless dishevelled man standing with them. Ramu had left his bloodied shirt in the house, on the wound that he had attempted to staunch on Ganesh's body. Ismail snapped his fingers again, and the cart driver gestured them in hastily, not daring to demur.

Kaveri wrapped her sari pallu around her shoulders, hastily hiding the bloodstains on her chest from view. Shaking his head at the sight of their muddy feet, the driver took out an old bedsheet and spread it on the floor. They got inside slowly, the two women huddling close together for comfort as the driver climbed back onto his horse. Then the carriage began to move, the horse's hooves clattering noisily on the road.

Kaveri felt the beginnings of a headache coming on. Rubbing her forehead, she leaned back, pressing her cheek against Ramu's arm. She *had* to find Anandi. Anandi held the clues to Ganesh's murder.

16

The Hunt Begins

Kaveri and Ramu directed the carriage to Uma aunty's house, getting off at the corner and walking the last few steps to her house. By the time they entered the gate, Kaveri's incipient headache had intensified. Putta greeted her with a fusillade of barks, and she groaned, holding her head as she entered the welcome coolness of her living room. Hearing them enter, Bhargavi came out of the kitchen with a welcoming smile. When she noticed Ramu in his banian, and Kaveri with blood on her sari, her smile faded. She ran over to Kaveri, holding her by the arms as she inspected the bloodstain.

'What happened to you, Kaveri? Are you hurt?' she demanded, cupping her daughter-in-law's face in her hands.

Seeing that his wife was unable to speak, Ramu patted his mother's shoulder. 'We are both fine, Amma. She is shaken, not hurt.' He made her sit down near the dining table, where the wooden slats on the windows sheltered her from the harsh rays of the sun. 'Can you take care of her, Amma?' Ramu asked, then looked at Kaveri.

'Inspector Ismail asked me to return after I dropped you off to speak to the police doctor and tell him what we observed.' He went upstairs to the bedroom, and came down a minute later wearing a fresh shirt, hastily leaving the house.

Bhargavi studied her intently. 'You are safe?' she demanded. Kaveri nodded. 'Then that is all that matters. You can tell me what happened later.' She guided Kaveri to the small tap out in the garden, poured water on her feet and helped her wash the mud from her legs. Then, placing a hand around her waist, she led her upstairs, helping her to remove her bloodstained clothes and put on a fresh cotton sari. Kaveri felt a small piece of paper fall to the ground as she changed her blouse for a fresh one. *What was that?*

Bhargavi picked up the piece of paper, setting it aside on her bedside table. Then she hurried to the bathroom and returned with a wet washcloth, gently wiping Kaveri's face.

'Why are you holding your head and looking so pale? Headache?' She guided her gently to the bed. 'It is much cooler here than it is downstairs. Rest for some time.'

Kaveri sank down on the mattress, gratefully closing her eyes and stretching out on her back as Bhargavi bustled around the room, pulling the shutters of the wooden blinds down. A couple of minutes later, Kaveri felt a cool, welcome wetness against her eyes as Bhargavi placed a folded wet handkerchief on her eyes and forehead. She groaned with relief.

'Rest now.' Bhargavi smoothed her hair, placing a kiss on her forehead. 'Don't think of anything. I will stay here.'

Feeling comforted and safe, in a way she had not felt even with her own mother, Kaveri closed her eyes.

'Foolish child,' she heard Bhargavi say. But her voice was thick with affection. 'Whatever shall we do with you? I wish you would not take your cases so personally.' Bhargavi leaned back in the easy chair, keeping an eye on Kaveri.

In seconds, she was deeply asleep, her belly softly rising and falling as she collapsed into a dreamless place, drifting along gently. Her tense body, knotted in fear for Anandi, gradually relaxed, the lines in her forehead smoothing out. Bhargavi sighed.

When Kaveri woke a few hours later her headache had eased. Ramu was back home, and she curled up next to him on the sofa. Bhargavi brought her a strong cup of hot coffee, adding a couple of extra spoons of sugar to help her recover some of her energy. After taking a sip, Kaveri unburdened herself to Bhargavi, gratefully leaning against Ramu's shoulder as she told her the details of what had happened after she and Uma aunty had left to go to Suman's house. Ramu gave her a worried glance, but refrained from saying anything, clutching her tightly. When she told Bhargavi of finding the wrestler dead, Kaveri felt a tremor run through her.

'The fact that he was killed, and so was Pawan, cannot be a coincidence. It has to have something to do with the fact that they worked together and with the theft of the gold.' Kaveri slumped back against the cushions. 'Ganesh may have killed Pawan. But who killed Ganesh? Another of the thieves?'

'Relax now, Kaveri. This is not the time to stress yourself further. And the same goes for you, Ramu. After a long day out in the streets of Halasur working on your vaccination campaign, you must be tired too.' Bhargavi gave them both a concerned glance, getting up to prepare tall glasses of *panaka* for them. The unseasonal heat of the afternoon had receded, leaving them dehydrated and on edge. She added a pinch of black salt and a spoon of grated ginger to the jaggery water, garnishing their glasses with sprigs of mint. The drink gave them fresh energy, the sweetness easing the last remnants of Kaveri's headache.

'Shanthi called me this afternoon to tell me that Anandi had disappeared from her room,' Bhargavi said. 'She has taken her clothes, and seems to have fled from the side gate, without leaving a note. Shanthi called Mala and Narsamma, but they did not know where she had gone either.'

'Where could she be?' Kaveri's voice cracked. 'I don't know if she is safe.'

Ramu's arm went around her shoulders. 'Don't fret so much, Kaveri. She will be fine.' But his voice was gruff. He was worried too, she could feel it in the strain in his arm, and in the way he tapped ceaselessly with his fingers on her shoulder. She welcomed his restlessness and the lines of tension on Bhargavi's face. It made her feel she was not alone. How could she be, when they helped shoulder the burden of the worry she carried?

'Enough talking. Now let us eat.' Bhargavi spoke firmly, getting up and moving towards the kitchen. 'Everything always seems better on a full stomach.'

They ate a simple meal of *menthi hittu majjige*, buttermilk mixed with a flour made of roasted fenugreek seeds along with dried salted chillies, which Bhargavi had fried in oil until they were crisp. Their dark brown skins stood out against the pale yellow rice, complementing the green sprigs of coriander that she had used to garnish the rice preparation. They ate it with a side dish of *kosambari*, grated carrots and radishes that Bhargavi had placed in a bowl, with a garnish of roasted mustard seeds and fried curry leaves. Lightly spiced, the food was comforting, filling their bellies without making them heavy and bloated.

After dinner, Bhargavi went upstairs with Putta following close at her heels. Ramu and Kaveri went out on the porch, looking at the stars.

'I don't know what to do next,' Kaveri said, leaning against Ramu's shoulder. 'I've run into dead ends everywhere. I can't go to the police. Ismail doesn't seem to want to speak to me anymore.' Her voice was forlorn. 'Anandi has disappeared, and I don't know how to track her down. Suman is counting on me, but I have no idea how to go about tracing Mr Das. I don't know if I can. I don't even know if Das is alive.'

Kaveri spoke so softly that Ramu could barely hear her.

'Nonsense,' he responded robustly. 'You are forgetting something.'

'What?'

'You are not the same person you were when you first came to Bangalore. You are an experienced detective now. Think about all the different cases you have solved. Not just the murders, but also the smaller cases. The missing goat, the woman who lost her memory, the boy who ran away from home and didn't want to go back – and refused to tell you where his home was. How did you solve those cases?'

Kaveri looked at him.

'You didn't give up.' Ramu took her by the shoulders, and gave her a little shake. 'My Kaveri, the woman I married and fell in love with, never gives up. You realise that, don't you?'

Kaveri squared her shoulders, giving him a small smile. 'I won't give up.'

'That's my girl.' Ramu grinned at her. 'What are you planning to do?'

She jumped up, looking at him. 'I almost forgot.' She rushed upstairs, picking up a piece of creased paper from her bedside table and running down to hand it to Ramu.

'What is this?'

'I found it covering the broken door pane in Pawan's house,' she said. 'I must have absent-mindedly tucked it into my blouse. It fell out when I changed my clothes, but *athe* kept it on my bedside table. I saw it when I woke up, but forgot about it till now.' She smoothed out the creases, handing it to him.

'Dancing Dolls and Whirligigs?' Ramu wrinkled his forehead. 'Why are you asking me to read this? It's an advertisement for the circus. The shows are over. See the dates on this?'

'Turn it over,' Kaveri explained, pointing to the back of the poster. 'See what it says here?' They studied the scribblings in pencil at the back – so faint that they could barely read what was written.

'It's a call for a meeting. See the little diagram at the top? That's a stick of neem leaves – Shanthi told me that's the secret symbol used by members of the independence movement. They say the neem represents Indian culture and knowledge, which is being swept away by the foreign species and practices that the British brought with them.'

'Tomorrow's date, seven p.m., at the "usual place".' Ramu turned the paper over, tapping the poster lightly against his arm. 'We are in deeper waters than we thought, Kaveri.'

'Yes,' Kaveri said, grabbing Ramu's hand. 'From what Chandru said, the wrestlers and Pawan were part of a gang of thieves, working together. Although Suman denies that Das could have been involved, this fits with what we saw the masked men doing at the circus – using Das's disappearance as a distraction to try and

152

rob the audience. If it were not for Ismail's men, they would have got away with a huge haul from a single circus performance. Das may have been a member of the gang. Perhaps his disappearance was part of the plan, to make the act appear more dramatic and keep everyone's attention focused on the stage, helping the thieves enter unnoticed. He may have planned to return the next day, but decided to lie low for a few days after seeing the police break up the robbery.'

'Or, if Suman is correct and his father is indeed innocent. The thieves may have been forcing him to join them, leading him to stage a disappearance to escape them,' Ramu suggested.

Kaveri looked down at their clasped hands. 'There is a third possibility, which I keep trying not to think of,' she said, speaking so softly that Ramu had to strain to hear her. 'If Das refused to help them, he was in a dangerous position. These men are likely to be killers. If what I suspect is true, they have already murdered twice – killing Pawan and Ganesh, searching for the gold that Pawan had hidden in the dumbbells. What if they kidnapped, perhaps even killed Das? Suman says his father would not have left him for so long without a sign, if he was still alive and safe.'

'But this leaflet puts a different complexion on things.' Ramu studied it again. 'It doesn't tell us anything about Das's disappearance, of course. But if it was in Ganesh's house, then Ganesh – and perhaps Pawan as well – must have attended these secret meetings.'

'We need Shanthi *akka*'s help to proceed now,' Kaveri said decisively. 'She is the one person we know who can tell us more about the meetings. She may know something that she does not realise is important. Perhaps she has even seen them there before.'

'We can't wait until tomorrow, Kaveri. Call her now,' Ramu insisted.

Kaveri nodded, going inside and picking up the telephone. After a few rings, she heard Shanthi's voice at the other end of the line. 'I will come immediately,' she told Kaveri.

Kaveri and Ramu waited impatiently, making their way to the gate to greet her as soon they heard her car approach. A few minutes later, they sat in their drawing room, studying the crumpled leaflet together.

'Where did you say you found this, Kaveri?' Shanthi demanded.

'Stuffed into a gap in a broken window in Pailwan Ganesh's house. I thought he was trying to cover the hole with paper.'

Shanthi shook her head. 'This is how the movement communicates news about its meetings without attracting suspicion from the police. A piece of used paper, stuffed into a broken window, or used to paper over a crack in the wall – what could seem more innocuous?'

Kaveri and Ramu exchanged glances. 'Clever indeed. Anyone walking past the house could take the pamphlet, read it and put it back – for the next person to find,' Ramu said softly.

'I can't figure out why thieves like these two men would be part of the independence movement, helping to transmit secret information like this,' Kaveri exclaimed. 'These men are crooks. They have no values.'

Shanthi looked troubled. 'As I told you, there are rumours that Bangalore might witness violent protests during Prince Edward's visit. Perhaps the men planning the protest enrolled men like Ganesh, experienced in violence, to help with their plans. In fact, from the way you describe Ganesh, I think he could be one of the two men I saw attend the last couple of meetings. Their tone was harsh, provoking, so different from the others at the meetings.'

'Who was the other man?' Kaveri demanded.

'No one reveals their real names – people use aliases. It is best if each of us knows as little as possible about the others. This way, if one person is captured, there is not much they can tell the police about the others,' Shanthi said soberly. 'But I can tell you that both men who were at the meeting were large and muscular, with a very strong family resemblance to each other – and to Pawan, whom I had seen some time back, when he came looking for Anandi soon after she started working for me.'

'Did they have tattoos on their right temple? Tattoos of snakes?' Kaveri asked eagerly.

Ramu gave her a confused look, and she slapped her forehead, realising that she had forgotten to share this detail with him.

'Do you remember that Pawan had a snake tattooed on his right temple? His cousin, Pailwan Harish, had the same tattoo on his forehead too,' she explained. 'He had covered it with a piece of sticking tape when we saw him backstage at the circus, but when I saw him near his home earlier today, the tape was gone, and the tattoo visible.'

'Ganesh had a small bandage on the right side of his head.' Ramu nodded slowly. 'Now that I know what you're getting at, I'm sure his bandage hid a tattoo too. But why do they all carry such a visible, strange image on their body?'

'The men I saw didn't have visible tattoos, but they wore loose caps, which they tugged low, keeping their foreheads hidden,' Shanthi said.

'They probably didn't want to be recognised easily,' Kaveri said with excitement. 'I think they must have been Ganesh and his older brother, Pailwan Harish.'

'Harish seemed like the leader. He kept interrupting our discussions, arguing that we should disrupt the Prince's welcome by setting buildings on fire, or with bomb blasts, like they did in Bombay and Calcutta,' Shanthi said.

'That would be disastrous.' Ramu drummed his fingers on the wooden table in front of him. 'If there was even a hint of violence, the British police would be on them in an instant in Bangalore.'

'It would set the movement back years.' Shanthi met his eyes. 'The jails in the other cities are crammed with political prisoners and there are rumours that they will soon arrest Gandhiji too. With all the leaders in jail, the movement might falter.'

'Look at the force the English have on their side – armies, police officers, weapons. We can't defeat them with violence – we will be crushed. Just like we were in 1857,' Ramu agreed. 'I don't like the approach the Maharaja is taking. Inviting the Prince here, escorting him on hunts, hosting a pageant for him. I can understand why he does it, though. He is in such a difficult position.'

'Why?' Kaveri asked, leaning forward.

'During the Rendition, the British snatched away the power of the Maharaja. Krishnaraja Wadiyar got back his throne only in 1883, and not completely at that. Under the Rendition Act, he only holds the kingdom as a subsidiary of the British. He pays a huge privy tax – money that comes out of the pockets of his subjects. But at least this lets him have some control over what happens to his people. Like implementing famine relief measures, building dams, promoting industries and education.'

'If it wasn't for the Maharani's Girls' School in Mysore, I would never have been able to complete my school studies, or dream of attending college,' Kaveri agreed.

'My husband would not have been able to build up a business like his in another city, without interference from the British,' Shanthi added. 'Look at what the British did to the cotton industry in Dhaka. It was prized across the world for its fine cotton. Entire saris could fit into matchboxes, the weaving was so delicate. They destroyed it, forcing farmers to export their cotton to Manchester. Now they make us re-import the finished products, paying huge taxes for inferior goods. All to keep their blessed Empire afloat.' Her voice was bitter.

Ramu nodded. 'The Maharaja can't openly challenge the Prince of Wales. He seeks to appease him with pageants and hunts. At the same time, he doesn't stand in the way of people like Gandhiji, or Sarojini Naidu, visiting Bangalore. He buys time for us, and time is more precious than gold. Only time can convince the British that it is in their better interest to leave us.'

'I can't believe that men as vicious as Pawan or Ganesh can have any interest in a larger cause such as the country's independence. If Pawan had a pamphlet in his house, there must be some nefarious reason for it.' Kaveri turned to Shanthi. 'I will attend tomorrow's meeting. Perhaps it will help me figure out who killed Pawan and Ganesh. Where is the "usual place" they mention?'

17

A Most Becoming Disguise

The corner of the attic was piled high with tin trunks painted green, and SS – Shanthi's initials – painted on them in bold white letters. Shanthi opened the trunk on the top, pulling out silk scarves and stoles, saris and dupattas, brocade cushion covers and lace curtains, tossing them to one side as she rummaged in the pile.

'Did you know Gandhiji suffers from high blood pressure?' Shanthi's voice echoed in the small room. She pulled out an old newspaper from the trunk, tossing it to Kaveri. 'It's in the newspaper coverage of his visit to Bangalore in 1920. I saved every paper I could find.'

'Inspector Ismail helped to arrange his address at Idgah Maidan in the Cantonment,' Kaveri said. 'He told me there were forty thousand people there.' She spread the dusty newspaper on her lap. 'He told me so much about the visit that I felt as though I had been there myself. That was in the past, though. When we were friends.'

Her voice was wistful. Sitting on another trunk, Suman gave her a sympathetic look.

Shanthi dived into the trunk again, pulling out a series of saris with appliqué work in shimmery sequins. The delicate georgette fabric shimmered, casting patterns of light and shade onto the khadi bed sheet she had spread onto the floor for protection. 'Where *is* that beard and moustache set? I know we had it somewhere. Last month, the women put on a show for the Rajkumari when she visited. The princess loved it. We kept the costumes in the trunk. . . Aha!'

She emerged from the depths of the trunk with a triumphant shout, holding a white beard aloft in her hand. Then her face fell as clumps of fibre came off in her hands, leaving bedraggled remains that looked like a party of rats had gnawed at the fake beard with gusto.

Holding the beard by the tips of her fingers, Shanthi gave Kaveri a crestfallen look. 'What do we do now?'

Suman jumped up. 'The circus has a set of costumes, and I think they left a few behind when they went to Mysore. I know where they are kept – on stage, below the alcove where the musicians sit. They will have it all – turbans, beards, moustaches, even cheek pads to change the shape of our faces, stomach pads to make us look fatter, and false heels to raise our height.'

Seeing the two women nod in approval, he ran towards the stairs. Kaveri listened to his light footsteps making a *rat-a-tat* sound as he ran. 'I used to run like that,' she said. 'But these past few days I have been feeling sluggish. Did you see how slowly I climbed the stairs?'

Wiping her dusty hands with a rag, Shanthi tossed the costumes back into the chest. 'It isn't like you to be so downcast. And you look tired.' She sat down next to Kaveri, taking her hot hand in her cool palm and placing her fingers on her wrist. 'Your pulse is racing.'

'Maybe I should follow a natural diet too, like Gandhiji. It says here that he went to Nandi Hills to recover, eating a light diet of fruit and boiled vegetables.' Kaveri pulled a face. 'I don't think I could do that. No *dosa, bisi bele hulianna* or *kootu*? I would rather be tired all the time.'

'Nothing is wrong with your health. You just need to stop fretting yourself sick about Anandi, Kaveri. She will take care of herself,' Shanthi remonstrated gently.

'How?' Kaveri questioned. 'She doesn't know anyone else in the city, apart from us, and Mala and Narsamma. Nobody knows where she is.' She took a deep breath, trying to rein in her rising panic. 'Let's speak of something else. Tell me more about today's meeting.'

Despite the oppressive heat, Shanthi closed the window. 'That's better,' she declared, returning to sit next to Kaveri. 'One cannot be too careful these days.' She took a glass of water from the clay pot on the windowsill and poured some of it onto her hands, splashing it onto her face before offering the water to Kaveri, who did the same, closing her eyes as the cool water trickled down her forehead, easing some of the tightness around her temples.

'The meeting is in Cubbonpet, as I told you yesterday. You know the area? A maze of narrow lanes, with small homes and shops on either side. There are goldsmiths, watchmakers, cloth and rice merchants, and small printing shops.' Shanthi cast a meaningful glance at Kaveri. 'The shops print pamphlets advertising various services – a sale on handloom saris, or a special discount on silver plates – two for the price of one. No one, seeing a stack of these placed on a table, being handed out to customers, would suspect anything. All of them look identical – but a few are reserved for special customers. If you open them, you will find a flyer inside – with details of the next campaign or protest meeting.' The older woman grinned, her white teeth flashing in the sun's rays that filtered through the window.

'That's very clever,' Kaveri breathed, her eyes shining with excitement. 'And the British do not suspect anything?'

'They don't go much to this part of town.' Shanthi flashed her another wicked smile. 'Cubbonpet is too crowded, too messy. Cows wander the streets, and there are animals everywhere – the British call this a metropolis of monkeys, and a malarial cesspool teeming with mosquitoes. We don't have to do a thing to keep it secret from them – filled with prejudice, they warn each other to stay away. It is the best place for us to meet, hidden in plain sight in the most congested part of town.'

'Are we are meeting in one of these shops?' Kaveri persisted.

'Of course not. Those shops only distribute information. The owners do not know any other details. If anyone asks, they can plead innocence, and say that they did not know who placed the pamphlets inside. It is safer for them to stay ignorant. We meet in one of the coffee shops. No one raises an eyebrow when they see strange people going in and out. That is the type of clientele a coffee shop is supposed to cater to.'

'How do we know when the meeting is underway?' Kaveri asked.

'We use signals. A pile of neem twigs at the beginning of the street indicates that a meeting will be held that day. The police pay no heed to such signals – they are used by all the houses around, to signal the presence of chicken pox.' She waited for Kaveri to nod, before continuing. 'A small pile of wet cow dung in front of the door indicates that the meeting is in progress. If the cow dung is dry, or has been swept away, the meeting is over.'

'Then do we need to wear disguises?' Kaveri asked.

Shanthi nodded. 'I think Ramu is right when he says the Prince's visit is making the police extra careful. If they are patrolling nearby, I don't want them to recognise you.'

Kaveri thought back to the previous night. When she had said she wanted to go to the meeting herself, Ramu had shaken his head. 'It is too dangerous, Kaveri.' Then he sighed, looking at Kaveri's eager face. 'I can see that you have made up your mind. If you love me, listen to one condition of mine.'

'I will do anything you want,' Kaveri had promised, bringing his hand to her cheek.

'Don't go alone. I will come with you.'

'Not you,' Shanthi had exclaimed. 'No matter how carefully you disguise yourself, someone will recognise you.'

They had all had a heated discussion after that. Shanthi was dead against Ramu accompanying Kaveri. As one of the few local doctors, he was too well known, she argued. No matter how well he disguised himself, someone would recognise him. Shanthi could not go with Kaveri either. She suspected that the police had her name on a list, keeping a watch on her. If she went to the meeting, she might put others at risk. Uma aunty was too old – she would not be able to run away if there was a police raid. And Anandi was nowhere to be found.

At her wit's end, Kaveri had suggested Suman.

'Maybe it is better to have him with you. You can keep an eye on him, see if he knows anyone who attends the meeting – and watch how he reacts,' Shanthi had responded.

Ramu had not liked it – but he agreed with Kaveri that Suman seemed to be the only possibility remaining.

'Disguise yourselves,' Ramu had said. 'Wear men's

clothes, like you did before, but add some additional elements. Put on a beard, or a turban. I don't want anyone to know who you are. The police will be keeping watch. You need to find a way to slip in and out without anyone knowing who you are.'

The memory of those discussions faded a little as Suman came rushing back in, but Kaveri still felt a frisson of fear run up her spine. She squeezed her eyes, dispelling her worries. When she had married Ramu, she had vowed that she would not become one of those women content to sit at home all day, busying herself in the kitchen or with a pile of darning to complete. Strange to think that before her marriage and her move to Mysore, she had looked forward to weekends, when she could stay at home all day, reading a pile of books while lying down on the bed, with a bowl of raw mango slices dipped in chilli powder and salt. Those days seemed like a distant memory now.

Kaveri focused her attention on Suman with renewed determination, mustering a smile for him. He smiled back at her eagerly before opening the satchel on his shoulder and exposing a cornucopia of costumes.

Oh, but these costumes were splendid – suits and trousers, tall turbans and luxuriant beards that she itched to try on! Kaveri eyed the pile in his hands with delight. The worries that had consumed her seemed to melt away, and she felt her pulse quicken at the prospect of following another promising trail. Was it just yesterday evening when all had seemed lost? Now things were looking up.

She had dressed in men's clothes a couple of times previously, when she was out sleuthing with Ramu. But back then they had borrowed Rajamma's husband's old clothes, which had reeked of stale tobacco and alcohol.

Kaveri and Suman rummaged through the bag, selecting costumes for themselves. Kaveri chose a brown suit that she liked, placing it against herself. Her face fell when she realised how large it was. The suit would fit two of her and still have extra cloth remaining.

Suman selected a turban for himself, along with a moustache and beard, placing large cheek pads inside.

'You look completely different.' Kaveri eyed him in astonishment.

'You will too, when we are done.' Suman flashed her a confident smile. 'Try this.' He handed her another Sikh turban, pulling out another beard and moustache for her as well as shoulder pads, a pair of shoes with false heels, and a padded stomach.

'Perfect.' Shanthi clapped her hands. 'You can wear these and walk all the way through Cubbonpet with ease. No one will look at you twice.'

'And what will you wear, Shanthi *akka*?' Suman turned to her.

Shanthi shook her head. 'I am too well known there. You can put me in any disguise you wish – make me six feet tall, or give me the stomach of a woman who is nine months pregnant.' She nodded at a fake stomach, three bands of cloth attached to it, lying amongst the other materials. 'Whatever I wear, people will know it is me. Much as I want to, the Home is my first priority. If I am discovered and questioned, the government may stop giving me funds for the women. I can't abandon them now.' She spoke sadly, her voice tinged with resignation.

'But how will we know where to go, what to do?' Suman asked.

Shanthi went to the door, closing it and shooting the bolt. Placing a hand on Suman's shoulder and putting her other arm around Kaveri's waist, she pulled them close.

'Here is what you must do. At the stroke of seven . . .'

18

We Have to Stop Meeting Like This

A little before seven p.m., a group of small boys sauntered into Cubbonpet. Dressed in dirty shorts with torn banians, grimy towels slung across their shoulders, they attracted little attention. They looked like any of the other small scruffy boys that were dispersed across the city. They moved casually, confidently, as though they belonged to the area. Two of them took up position in a small alley near the gate of a famous local coffee house, kicking a ball across the road to each other. A third boy held a rope in his hand, tied to a cow with dangerously curved horns – a cow that Kaveri knew very well. Her name was Kasturi, and she was a wicked kicker. Kaveri had narrowly avoided being hit by her a couple of times. Only Venu, who had hand-reared her when she was a baby, could deal with her.

Venu took Kasturi over to an empty plot, tying her to a nearby tree and leaving her to graze on the weeds that grew in abundance there. A white cattle egret flew down to perch on her back, adjusting its long-legged stance to pick flies and insects off her back with its sharp beak, as the cow ambled around the plot. Venu leaned against a tree, propping himself against its trunk, blending into the surroundings. The two old men playing a game of Indian ludo below the peepal tree across from him paid no attention to him. Neither did the woman across the road, intent on taking her washing from the clothes line.

From his vantage point, he could see the entire road. The boys in the alley could keep watch on the back entrance. His team of watchers were in place, and there were no police in sight. Yet. He whistled a tune, a Kannada folk song about a boy who fell in love with the moon.

Standing at the corner of the road, just out of sight behind a clump of trees, two young Sikh men wearing large turbans looked at each other. One was slim and short, while the other seemed taller, with a protruding paunch. They wore large kurtas with baggy *patiala* salwars. The bottom half of their faces was obscured by large hairy moustaches and full, long beards.

Hearing Venu whistling, Kaveri tugged at her kurta, which felt uncomfortably snug around her bulging false stomach, and said, 'That's Venu's "all clear" signal. Let's go. It's almost seven.'

Suman patted his beard, making sure it was in place. Then he followed Kaveri as she led the way down the narrow alley. The clack-clack sound of typewriters filled the air as they passed a printing press, a set of pamphlets piled high on the table advertising jobs available for school graduates. Kaveri's fingers itched to pick one up and look inside to see if it contained any articles by Indian leaders from the movement. She reined in her curiosity. They had come there for a different purpose.

Shanthi had drawn her a little map that proved very accurate – even though Kaveri had never visited Cubbonpet before, she knew exactly where to go. Striding confidently, so that she did not look out of place, she moved towards the end of the lane, alongside Suman. The roads looked different to her as she walked along, the built-up heels of her shoes adding extra inches to her height.

She paused as they passed a small eatery with a board in Kannada letters – *Rao's Military Hotel*. Despite her urgency to get to the coffee shop, she stopped to peer in. Growing up in a vegetarian home, Kaveri had never seen the inside of a 'military' hotel, which served meat. She saw a number of people sitting on the ground, eating from large sal leaves. Waiters carrying copper buckets filled with rice stopped in front of them, ladling biriyani onto already heaped leaves.

A waiter peered out. 'Can I help you?' he asked, looking hopefully at a prospective customer. Kaveri shook her head, backing out of the eatery hastily.

Suman coughed, pointing discreetly to a building at the end of the lane.

There it was.

The yellow and white building had a little wooden sign hanging over the front door. A cup of coffee was painted on the sign. The painter had added touches of artistic flourish – white puffs of steam seemed to rise from the top of the cup. A plate of *vadas* was painted next to it. Even someone who did not know how to read would be able to recognise it for a coffee shop. Who would think that such an innocuous location might host a gathering to discuss matters far more serious than coffee and light gossip?

Kaveri passed the empty plot where Venu stood with his cow. She carefully avoided looking at him. They had a prearranged signal – he would imitate the screech-cry of a barn owl if he saw danger or anything that seemed out of place. It was comforting to know that he was there.

Suman stopped in front of the wooden double doors, pushing them open and stepping inside. Kaveri followed him closely.

The room was dingy, with one yellow light illuminating a small alcove. There was only a faded red carpet and a couple of bent metal chairs placed against the wall covering the space.

The man behind the counter spoke up in his hoarse, cracked voice. 'Table for two?' His rheumy watery brown eyes peered out at them from thick soda-glass lenses.

Kaveri cleared her throat, deepening her voice. 'I want a quiet table, for vegetarians only. No meat.'

'What do you want to drink?'

Kaveri looked at Suman. 'Green mango sherbet, if you have any.'

She kept her face impassive, but inwardly she quaked as she waited for his response. While Shanthi had given them the secret code, she had warned them that she had not attended meetings for the past few weeks. If the code had changed in the intervening time, they would be refused admittance, and marked out as suspicious, prevented from attending future meetings.

The man stared at them. Kaveri felt Suman fidgeting next to her. She squared her shoulders, trying to appear confident as she met the man's eyes.

It seemed to work, for he moved out from behind the counter and pulled back a curtain to expose a small doorway.

When they went inside, they found themselves in a men's bathroom. Shanthi had prepared them for this, but Kaveri still felt herself flush in embarrassment at the sight of the public urinal, stained with use.

Suman poked her in the side, gesturing towards her eyes. Collecting herself, she reached into her pocket, pulling out a pair of dark glasses. Between the glasses and her beard, her features would be completely obscured. No one would recognise her. Kaveri pulled a face, remembering how strange she looked in the mirror. But Shanthi had assured her that there would be others in the room adorned with false beards, moustaches, glasses, hats and other kinds of disguise. Many in the movement were on the run, escaping from the British police who hunted for them in Calcutta, Bombay and other parts of British India. Labelled as terrorists, their lives were in danger. Even those who protested peacefully and non-violently were being pursued, moving from place to place, rarely spending more than a night in one location.

They pushed open another door, emerging from the quiet into a hubbub of noise.

Even more dimly lit than the reception area, the room had no furniture, and the walls were bare. It looked so different from the interior of the coffee shop, shown in the photographs hanging on the wall near the entrance. Here there were no scruffy wooden tables, no white china cups, no plush velvet chairs or fake Persian carpets. No liveried waiters in white, with red sashes and turbans, bearing silver platters with flasks of coffee and plates of snacks. This room had plain lime-washed masonry walls. People sat cross-legged on *chaapes*, straw mats, spread on the rough plastered flooring. Kaveri looked at the narrow windows, secured with heavy iron grilles. The glass had been covered with brown paper to prevent light shining through from outside. A mirror on the left wall reflected the dim light from the overhead bulb, providing a bit of additional illumination.

'Be careful. Keep your wits about you,' she spoke into Suman's ear.

They chose a quiet spot near the back entrance so that they could leave in a hurry if they needed to. As they sat down by the wall, Kaveri watched Suman pull his legs into *vajrasana*, and marvelled at his flexibility. If she sat like that for an hour, her knees would be frozen. As a magician, flexibility must be one of his key assets, she supposed. Not bothering to even mirror his efforts, she pulled her knees up, propped her arms on them and looked around. Shanthi *akka* was right, most people *were* in disguise, she thought.

A man stepped into the middle of the room, holding a little silver bell in his hand. He rang the bell, making a musical tinkling sound. Everyone stopped talking.

He looked down at the expectant faces. 'Friends. You know we don't use our real names here, but you can call me Manoj. We have gathered here today to hear from a comrade from Calcutta, Kalyan, who joined us recently. He participated in the protests against the Prince's visit on Christmas.'

A murmur went up around the room and Kaveri quickly exchanged glances with Suman. Many of Calcutta's freedom fighters were known to hold opposite views to Gandhiji, even though they respected him highly. After their last discussion, Shanthi had shown her an essay written by a young Bengali nationalist, Subhas Chandra Bose. Kaveri had found it very thought-provoking. Bose wrote openly about his difference of opinion with Gandhiji, stating that India's path to independence would have to be purchased with whatever means lay at hand, including the possibility of armed rebellion.

'Let us learn more about what you plan for the Prince's visit to Bangalore. It is just a few days away,' a voice interrupted. 'Manoj' turned in surprise, staring at the person who had spoken. He was a stout, short man with a slightly hooked nose.

'There is nothing to speak about there. We have discussed it at previous meetings,' Manoj responded in a firm voice.

'But we have not reached a conclusion,' the portly little man persisted. The pleats of his baggy pants fell around him comically, like the folds of a sari, but Kaveri noticed that the audience listened to him attentively. 'What are the plans for his visit? Surely we cannot let the Prince come and leave unharmed. The Maharaja plans to hold a special performance at Bellandur Lake just for him.' He appealed to the people sitting in front of him, waving his hands in the air. 'Think of the indignity. Bombay threw the white prince out, welcoming him with a barrage of stones and firecrackers. But us? We will welcome him with floats, dancing girls and a pageant with stalls for the public. Where is our pride, our belief in ourselves?'

Manoj rapped his stick on the bell again, motioning for silence. 'We have debated this before,' he repeated, raising his voice. 'We decided that we would follow Bapuji's call for peaceful protests.'

He stepped back, giving way to the man from Calcutta, 'Kalyan'. Kalyan stepped into the middle of the room, looking around at everyone. 'My comrade is correct. I participated in the protests in Calcutta. But your situation in Mysore is very different. You must stay steady on the path you have already chosen. This is not the time for you to resort to violence.'

Kaveri felt a gaze boring into her back. She turned. On one side, a tall burly man stood near the single table and chair in the room, one hand on the back of the chair. It was the man who had accosted her at the circus when she had gone to visit Suman – Pailwan Harish.

How stupid they had been! Kaveri felt like slapping her forehead. He must have recognised their costumes. It had been a mistake to take them from the circus. They were too recognisable, especially to other circus members.

Kaveri looked across at Suman. He was staring at the man from Calcutta, hanging on his words with focused attention. Shielding her actions with her bulky bag, she reached into her pocket, scribbling in the small notepad she always carried with her. She folded the note in her hand and surreptitiously pushed it into Suman's hand. He palmed the note, cupping it in his hands and keeping it hidden with his satchel while he read. He glanced sideways, giving the wrestler a quick look, then looked away immediately.

Kalyan continued, 'Your Maharaja will be forced to turn against his own people, implementing harsh restrictions that make it difficult for us to gather in groups to spread the word across the country. We are in the early stages of our struggle, and must be tactical.'

People turned to each other, speaking in small groups as the leader tinkled his small bell in vain, trying to quieten them. The portly man and Pailwan argued with Kalyan.

The volume of conversations grew louder and louder as tempers rose in the room. Finally, taking control, Manoj stepped back into the centre, ringing his bell loudly. Once everyone had fallen silent, he spoke slowly and clearly.

'Friends, beware. We have a spy in our midst.'

19

Unmasking a Traitor

Suman's horrified eyes met Kaveri's.

'What are you saying?' Kalyan glared at him. 'Are you accusing me – *me*? – of being a traitor?' His voice was savage.

'Not you,' Manoj replied. He turned towards the portly man, who stepped back.

'Him.' He spat in his direction.

'Nonsense,' the short man blustered. 'What do you mean, I am a spy?'

'I mean,' Manoj spoke slowly, deliberately, 'I mean that I have not seen you here before.'

'So what? It is my first time here. I admit it freely. But I am not a traitor. There are many others who must be new too.' The man looked around the room, his shrill voice calming a little, looking at the nodding faces. 'There are always new people at these meetings.'

'There are some new people,' the man in the centre of the room said, in a mocking tone. 'You are very clever to say so. But then,' his voice grew louder, 'why did you say that we have not yet reached a conclusion? How do you know what we decided on in previous meetings? I have not seen you before, and I have not heard of you before. I say that you are a spy, trying to egg us on to violence, so that you can then have a reason to arrest us.'

The crowd looked around in alarm. A group of men stood up, moving threateningly towards the portly man.

He took a few assured steps away from the crowd before bending down and taking a gun from a concealed holster tied to his calf. Hidden in his baggy pants, no one had realised he carried a weapon. The people sitting closest to him screeched, moving back to get out of the line of fire. With surprising agility, he manoeuvred himself to the centre of the room, grabbing hold of Kalyan. Before Kalyan could react, the man had shoved his arms behind his back, snapping handcuffs on him with his right hand while holding the revolver against his forehead with his left. 'I'm from the government. And you – you are under arrest.'

The portly man pulled Kalyan, waving his revolver wildly. Just then an owl hooted, three times.

'Venu's signal. The police are here,' Suman hissed into her ear. 'Run.'

Loud thuds told them that someone was trying to break down the door, which must have been bolted after the meeting began. The man with the silver bell rushed towards the wall at one side of the room, pushing back a wooden bookcase to reveal another door. Throwing the bell aside, he fumbled at his belt until he'd detached an ornate iron key from it and quickly unlocked the door, ushering people through. They formed an orderly queue, placing the women and older people at the head, urging them to move out first as the able-bodied younger men took up the rear.

Kaveri saw the portly man still trying to pull Kalyan towards the entrance as he dug his feet into the floor, resisting the man's grip. People streamed past them, heedless of their fight in their eagerness to escape. Pailwan Harish scrambled to the front of the line, pushing an old man with a walking stick aside to reach the door. *Coward.*

Only Suman stopped, staring at the two struggling men. 'I wish we could free him,' he shouted, as Kaveri tried to urge him towards the exit. 'If only I had my throwing knives with me.'

A small figure appeared at their side, thrusting two ornately carved daggers at Suman. 'Will these do?'

'Anandi?' Kaveri's mouth fell open in shock. Clad in a pinstripe suit, with a thin pencil moustache on her upper lip, Anandi looked almost unrecognisable. 'What . . . what . . .?' she stuttered.

'There's no time to waste. Take them.' Anandi's voice was sharp, impatient, as she pushed the daggers towards Suman again.

Suman took them hurriedly. Taking aim, he threw the daggers, one after another. The first hit the revolver, knocking it from the portly man's hand. He turned in surprise, but before he could do anything, the second one hit the centre of his hand, turning it into a bloody mess. He screamed, releasing Kalyan.

Suman moved swiftly, towing Kalyan, still in handcuffs, towards him. They rushed towards the door. Kaveri ran after them, the sight seared in her brain – the portly man screaming as he stared with glazed eyes at the dagger with a peacock head buried in his flesh, the blood from his hand dripping to the floor.

'Hurry!' Manoj urged them, his voice frantic. 'The police will break down the other door soon. They cannot not find us here.' As soon as they had exited, he closed the door behind them and locked it. 'That will hold them off for a while.' He mopped the sweat dripping from his forehead with a grimy handkerchief.

'Wait. Where is Anandi?' Kaveri stopped, looking around frantically. They were in a long corridor. She took a step towards the now locked door. 'Did we leave her inside?'

'The young woman who was with both of you? She ran in that direction.' Sweat ran down Kalyan's face too, but his voice was calm. He jerked his head in the direction of the road.

A piercing police whistle cut through the air as they ran along the corridor towards a back entrance. *Their pursuers were getting closer.*

'Thank you, friend,' Kalyan finally said as they emerged into the alley behind the coffee house. Kaveri looked at him in surprise as he moved close to Suman, holding him by the shoulders and looking deep into his eyes before kissing him lightly on the forehead. 'I will not forget your help.'

Manoj took hold of the handcuffed visitor, guiding him into a narrow alley. 'We must part ways here. Small groups will be easier to hide. Godspeed.'

With a hurried farewell, the two men disappeared. As the whistles sounded again, nearer this time, Suman looked around frantically. 'We can't be caught here. What do we do now?'

'*Akka. Pssst. Here.*' An urgent whisper came from above, and they looked up as a rope ladder dropped down a wall at the end of a lane. Venu peered at them through an open window on the top floor of the building. 'Quickly.'

Pounding footsteps were now coming closer. They moved quickly – Kaveri climbing up first, Suman following close by. As soon as they reached the top, and squeezed through the open window, Venu drew up the ladder before closing it quickly. They were on the top floor of a massive warehouse, surrounded by crates.

'This way,' Venu urged them again. They followed him through the warehouse to the back window, from which they climbed out onto the roof. This roof overlooked another small alley, parallel to the first one from which they had escaped. Kaveri could hear running feet, the sound of *lathis* pounding on doors below them. She saw bright torchlights being flashed on the road, and heard loud angry voices. 'I hope everyone escaped,' she said, in a small voice.

'Come, *akka*, we have to move quickly. We are not yet safe.'

Venu's voice was urgent. A thread of fear coiled around Kaveri's throat. If the police were to find them, she knew even Ismail could not save them now. Suman had wounded a policeman, possibly someone in the secret service, someone powerful. He would be thrown in jail, and she would be too, taken for his accomplice. Inspector Ismail would not be able to save her. Not even Ramu could.

Kaveri squeezed her eyes, horribly afraid. Her husband had been right all along. What possessed her to take such risks?

Numbly, she followed Venu, responding to his instructions almost automatically.

The sound of sirens began to cut through the air. Kaveri heard the sound of boots reverberating on the streets as police continued to move through the area, breaking open doors and shouting into bullhorns. The streets were not safe for them anymore. She felt like she was moving through treacle, her brain paralysed with fear. Then Suman gripped her hand hard. 'Buck up, *didi*.

It's alright. We will make it out of here.' He gave her a reassuring smile, though he could not hide the quaver of nervousness in his voice.

'We will have to avoid the streets,' Venu said.

Kaveri lost track of the direction in which they moved as Venu guided them through a maze of connected rooftops, jumping nimbly from one terrace to another. In a couple of places, people looked at them with astonishment, but before they could shout to stop them, they had disappeared.

Finally, when Kaveri thought she could go no further, Venu stopped. Panting for breath, she gasped out, 'Where. Are. We?'

'We are back in Halasur, near my house,' Venu responded airily. 'Now we are safe.' His white teeth shone in the moonlight as he grinned at them. 'Wasn't it good that I scoped out an escape route for us? I had a sense it would come in handy.'

He looked startled for a brief instant as Kaveri pulled him close, planting a kiss on the top of his grimy head. Then he hugged her back, burying his face in her waist.

'I could not bear it if anything happened to you, *akka*.' His voice was gruff. 'That's why I follow you everywhere you go. Even if you don't realise it, I or one of my boys is always close by. Ramu *anna* told me to keep you safe, and I will always guard you. With my life,' he added fiercely.

20

Too Healthy to Be One of Us

'I will give you one of my saris.'

Venu had taken Suman and Kaveri home, and they were now sitting in his hut, sipping hot tea from a clay mug. Her frazzled nerves slowly relaxing as she took huge gulps of the tea, liberally sweetened with lumps of jaggery, Kaveri looked around.

'This is our new roof.' Venu pointed, showing them the new terracotta tiles.

'Our roof used to leak,' his sister-in-law, Muniamma, explained, smiling at Suman. She looked happy and relaxed, her young son drawing circles with a stick on the mud floor next to her, while her baby slept in her lap. So very different from when Kaveri had first met her, when she was mostly skin and bones with a distended belly, pregnant and half starved. 'Venu helped me set up a home business. I make snacks and tea for the policemen working on the night shift, and the street vendors and security guards who also stay up at night. He takes it in, and they pay us well for hot food.'

'My *athige* makes the best *bajjis* and *uddina vadas*,' Venu pronounced. 'And Shanthi *akka* took me to the bank, to open an account. We put all the money in the bank. That way, *anna* can't come home and demand the money from us. We don't have any to give him.' His face darkened before he left the room to take fresh bedding for the cow.

Venu's brother Manju used to be an attendant in the Bowring Hospital, where Ramu worked. He was a reformed drunkard and gambler who used to beat his wife – until Ismail had intervened, putting the fear of God in him. He had not dared to raise a hand against Muniamma since then. He no longer worked at the hospital; instead he had been doing odd jobs for money. He was now sober most of the time, Ramu had told Kaveri, but he still went on an occasional drinking binge. And when he did, he lost all sense, coming home and shouting, demanding money.

Muniamma placed her sleeping baby into a makeshift cloth cradle fashioned from a torn sari tied to a rafter in the roof, and picked up her son, placing him on her hip.

'What will you do now?' Kaveri asked Suman. But before he could answer, Venu returned, bearing armfuls of straw. 'My neighbour says that the police have announced a curfew.' They listened to the sirens, sounding in the distance. 'Until tomorrow, no one is supposed to be outside their homes. The police are combing the streets. I will make up a bed for Suman *anna* here, in the corner.'

He moved across the room and pulled out a clean gunny sack, draping it over the straw. 'Will this be alright for you?' Venu's voice was doubtful. 'We don't have mattresses, like you rich people do.'

'This looks very comfortable.' Suman gave the boy a grateful nod. 'We go to all kinds of places in the circus.

I have slept on rooftops, on the top of the train, in bullock carts, even standing up. I can sleep anywhere.' He turned to Kaveri. 'What will you do? You can't spend the entire night here. Your husband will be very worried.'

'I will give you one of my saris,' Muniamma repeated. 'Our neighbour has a bullock cart. We will ask him to take you home. Venu will sit in the cart with you. If the police are inspecting vehicles on the road, they may stop you, to look inside, but all they will see is a cart owner returning home with his wife and son after a long day's work.'

'She is too young to be Venu's mother,' Suman objected.

'So many women are married when they are ten, eleven.' Muniamma's voice was even. She gave Suman a small smile at his look of astonishment. As the import of what she had said dawned on him, he looked down at his feet, shaking his head. 'It's not right,' Kaveri heard him mutter.

Muniamma turned to Kaveri again, taking her chin in her hands. 'But Suman is right. You look too healthy to be one of us. Shining teeth, clear skin . . . Keep your pallu over your face, and they will not find out.'

There was no trace of recrimination in her voice. Yet Kaveri felt a sharp twinge of guilt, thinking of the elaborate beauty routine she performed at night. She cleaned her face with a flour made of *hesarbele*, and used a face pack made of *mosaru* and *kadalehittu* with a little honey. Once a week, she used a herbal oil that her mother made and sent from Mysore, with gooseberry juice to keep her hair thick and long, drying her wet hair over *sambrani* placed on hot coals, with a couple of drops of jasmine oil for fragrance. Time was a luxury that she and women like her had but Muniamma could never dream of. Even Venu, who was so young, worked all the time. The only break he had was when he sat with Kaveri and the Bangalore Detectives Club members to learn how to read.

Venu glared at Muniamma. 'Now you've made *akka* feel bad,' he said. 'She does so much for us. Before we met her, we all went hungry, every day. So what if she looks healthy?'

Kaveri placed a placating hand on his shoulders. 'Don't shout at your *athige*. She is not saying anything untruthful to me. She is only trying to take care of me.' She turned to Muniamma, her voice gentle. 'I will keep my pallu over my head so hopefully they will not see my face or question me too closely.'

21
At an Impasse

Kaveri's face dripped sweat as she sat huddled up on herself in the musty bullock cart. She swiped at it with her hands ineffectively. She did not want to wipe her face on Muniamma's sari. The woman had precious few clothes as it was.

They had been fortunate on the journey so far. Though they had seen police on the streets, the cart kept to the smaller lanes, avoiding the brightly lit roads. A couple of times, when they crossed an intersection with a wider road, Kaveri had held her breath in fear. Even more so when a policeman had rapped out a warning, stopping them and peering inside. But as Muniamma predicted, he did not search the cart, only asking them if they had seen anything suspicious. He shone a torch into the cart and then waved them on, ignoring Kaveri completely, as she lay huddled in a corner, covering her body with the faded sari, quivering in fright.

As soon as the cart neared their home, Kaveri braved a peek out of the window and saw Ramu's face peering out anxiously from the gate. The cart slowed down as they approached the gate. Not willing to take further risks, Kaveri immediately jumped out. Ramu pulled her in and closed the gate noiselessly, gathering her into his arms. He looked at her in the light of the street lamp, taking in the old sari she wore. 'I asked you to wear men's clothes,' he said.

'I disguised myself as a Sikh man. But I had to change. The police were after us,' she whispered in his ear, clutching him tightly. She could finally breathe again now that she was safe in his arms. 'I went to Venu's house. Suman and I left our disguises there along with our boots. He said he would bundle it all up in an old bed sheet, weigh it down with stones, and drop it in the middle of Ulsoor Lake. No one will think of looking for them there.'

Ramu's face was set in worried lines as he hugged Kaveri tightly to him.

When she went inside, she saw Bhargavi and Shanthi sitting on the sofa. They sprang up as soon as she entered, rushing towards her and pulling her into a hug. 'We were so worried,' Shanthi exclaimed, at the same time her mother-in-law fretted over her, muttering about her appearance. Both women fell silent as the cuckoo clock chimed. It was midnight. *How did it get so late?*

As the women untangled themselves from one another, the questions began. 'What happened to you? Why are you so late, and where did you get that torn sari from?'

'From Muniamma.' Kaveri sank down onto the sofa opposite them, her knees weak as she breathed deeply, the tension in her body evaporating for the first time in many hours. Ramu closed the door and bolted it with an audible sigh of relief. He sat down next to her, putting his arm around her shoulders as if he, too, could not believe that his wife had returned to him safely.

'I just made some fresh decoction.' Bhargavi disappeared into the kitchen, returning with a steaming cup of coffee, to which she added generously heaped teaspoons of sugar. Shanthi opened a tin of biscuits, placing them on the table next to Kaveri. The smell of roasted coconut filled the air, and Kaveri realised how ravenous she was. She drained the coffee cup in gigantic gulps, stuffing two coconut biscuits in her mouth at the same time. She coughed, as a crumb went down the wrong way.

Ramu patted her back, slipping a biscuit to Putta, who lay next to Kaveri. He had not left her side since she had come downstairs, sensing her distress.

'You are very lucky to be sitting at home, sipping coffee in your husband's arms, instead of being locked up in jail.' Shanthi broke the silence. 'We heard about Suman's knife attack on the spy. Mala and Narsamma came home around eight-thirty to pass on a message from Anandi. She told them there had been a police raid on the meeting, but you had escaped safely. I left immediately, to tell Ramu and Bhargavi *akka* so they wouldn't worry.'

'But I was still tense,' Ramu said, his voice cracking. 'It was hardly a calming piece of information, to be informed that your wife was on the run with a young magician and a milk boy after they had stabbed a police spy with a dagger.' He looked at Kaveri and reached for her hand. 'I wanted to leave immediately, take the car out to look for you on the streets, heading towards Venu's house. But the police imposed a curfew on the city. They switched off the sirens only an hour back.'

'Venu's idea of putting you in a cart was good.' Bhargavi gave her an approving nod. 'Anyone listening would think it was just another cart driver heading back home with turnips or carrots after a long day at the local market.'

'Especially our ever-curious neighbour, Subramaniam Swamy.' Ramu grimaced, his arm tensing on her shoulder. 'You have a lot of explaining to do, Kaveri.'

Kaveri looked at Ramu's tired face, and melted. Her husband had warned her of danger, and yet she had insisted on going. She rubbed his palm with her thumb, his hand still resting in hers.

Bhargavi and Shanthi pulled their chairs closer to the table as Kaveri launched into her story, sipping refills of hot coffee when her throat dried up. The clock ticked on as she spoke, her hands waving in the air as she described the room, the people there, and the events of the meeting in detail.

When she had finished, leaning down to scratch Putta's ears, Shanthi spoke up. 'The man you described, the one in the centre of the room, holding the silver bell – the one who called himself Manoj – that is Mr Guruswamy. He is the local leader of the movement in Bangalore. I think I also know who the man from Calcutta is. The newspapers reported last week that there was a raid on the police station. Two people, pretending to be a husband and wife quarrelling, distracted the police. When they were trying to settle the domestic fight, another gang entered the station from the back and took away a safe containing a lot of money, and a huge cache of guns and bombs.'

She rose from the table and began searching through the pile of old newspapers lying in a corner. 'You said he called himself Kalyan. His real name is Kailash. Here is a sketch, drawn by a police artist.'

'It's the same man,' Kaveri nodded. 'The entire journey home in the cart, I was trying to understand why Suman took such a huge risk, throwing knives at a government agent, for a stranger. Do you think he and Kailash knew each other from before?'

'It is one more of the things we need to find out, in addition to the question of why Anandi came armed to the meeting.' Ramu, who had been sitting silently, now spoke. 'This is the third time now that she has been found at a scene of violence. First when Pawan was killed with a knife, then Ganesh – and now we find her carrying a set of daggers to an independence meeting. It is too much to be passed off as a mere coincidence.'

Kaveri nodded reluctantly. 'I still don't want to believe Anandi had any role to play in the murders – apart from being an innocent bystander. But even I agree that the evidence is mounting against her.'

'Do you think Anandi is involved?' Shanthi stared at her incredulously. 'I cannot believe it.'

'If she is as innocent as we believe, why would she not confide in us, tell us the truth – whatever it is – so that we can help her?' Kaveri pointed out. 'She knows she can trust us completely. We have helped her before. She is one of us.'

'I find it very strange that you found her in Pawan's house,' Ramu said soberly. 'Anandi hated Pawan, was terrified of him. Why would she go to his house alone, especially after he was violently murdered – unless she wanted to recover something from there, like the gold dumbbells, or, meet someone in secret, like Ganesh? Either way, it's very suspicious.'

'I will go to Mala's house tomorrow morning to see if I can find Anandi.' Kaveri stifled a yawn. She was exhausted, her body aching in every pore. The desperate escape over rooftops, the tension she had felt at Venu's house, the terror-filled ride in the bullock cart home through roads filled with police – now that the adrenaline of the past few hours had faded, fatigue was catching up with her. She could feel her eyelids growing heavy, speech becoming more difficult as tiredness overcame her.

Dimly, she heard Shanthi dissent. 'She is not with Mala. She refused to stay with her, or to tell her where she was going. All she wanted Mala to do was to send a message to your home, to tell your family that you were safe.'

Putta jumped up next to Kaveri, comforting her with the warmth of his heavy body. 'I can't believe we lost Anandi again. Where could she be now?' Kaveri muttered, before falling asleep on the sofa.

22

More Messages

They all slept in the next morning, waking up at ten a.m. Halfway through their breakfast of *uthappam* and tomato chutney, Kaveri and Ramu heard a furious fusillade of knocks on the main door. Stopping their breakfast, Kaveri opened the door, and Suman came rushing in.

'Kaveri *didi*.' His words came out in fits and starts as he struggled for breath, visibly winded. 'I have a new message from Baba.'

'What kind of message?' Ramu asked sharply.

'I left Venu's house early, as soon as dawn broke, and returned to Uma aunty's garden hut. Her son scolded me, saying that I had left for the night without permission, and immediately put me to work – without any breakfast.' Suman pulled a face. 'A couple of hours later, as I was pulling weeds, a small boy came running to the gate and motioned me over. He handed me a *dabba* saying my cousin has sent me some food. That is, of course, impossible. Apart from my father, I have no other relatives.' Suman's voice was flat. 'When I opened the *dabba*,' he continued, 'I found this note.'

He took out a tiny steel vessel from his pocket, opening it and displaying it to Kaveri and Ramu. Inside, there was a small piece of paper, folded and refolded several times.

'What does it say?'

'I didn't stop to read it. I brought it here, so that I can read it with you.' Suman beamed at Kaveri, his face transformed by happiness. 'It is written in the same code as last time. You know what this means, don't you? It means that my father is alive.' He did a little jig around the room. 'My. Father. Is. Alive.'

Kaveri exchanged glances with Ramu, her spirits lifting for the first time since the dreadful incident at yesterday's meeting. They had worried that Das might be dead, killed by the thieves for not cooperating with them. Finding out that he was alive came as a welcome piece of information after all the bad news of the past few days.

Why had he disappeared then? Was he in cahoots with the thieves after all? Kaveri cast covetous glances at the code, eager to try to decipher it and find out what he had written. Sherlock Holmes was a master at cracking codes, and she had always wanted to give it a try.

'How did the boy know that you were at Uma aunty's house?' Ramu asked Suman.

Kaveri looked at him, surprised at the sharp tone of his voice. He still did not trust Suman completely, especially after the previous night's incident.

Suman did not appear to have noticed, responding normally, 'I have no idea.'

'Sit,' Kaveri commanded, bustling over to the desk in the drawing room where she kept a notepad and some sharpened pencils ready for use. She brought them to him, and pulled up a chair. 'How can I help you?'

190

Suman pointed to the paper. It was divided into small boxes by lines running from top to bottom and left to right. Each box contained a set of dots, small and close together, clustered into two groups separated by a small space. 'This is the code my parents used to note down their magic tricks. The number of dots is related to letters. Count the number of dots on the right side – that's the number, in tens. The number of dots on the left side corresponds to the number in units.'

'It's transposed?' Kaveri deduced. She looked at Suman's uncomprehending stare. 'I mean, it's the opposite of the way in which we normally write numbers down. If we normally write 58 as 5 followed by 8, in this code you will write it as eight dots on the left, followed by five dots on the right.'

'That's correct,' Suman said. 'Except that you won't find any numbers greater than 50 – that's the maximum number of letters in the Bengali alphabet. Each number corresponds to a letter or a vowel, but the order is jumbled up. I know it by heart – my father used it to write down all his tricks in a diary. If you read out the numbers to me, I will write down the letter it represents.'

As Kaveri began to read out the numbers, Suman started to scribble them down. Pushing aside his breakfast as he looked at the clock, Ramu left them to their work, going upstairs to get ready.

A few moments later, Kaveri came rushing into the bedroom. Panting for breath, she thrust her notepad at Ramu. 'We have deciphered the message. Suman is in grave danger. I sent him to Uma aunty's house to collect his clothes. We have to get him out of here.'

Ramu started reading the deciphered message. *Dearest child – I am safe, hiding from the Pailwans. They blackmailed me, wanting me to join their gang of thieves.'*

He looked at Kaveri. 'Blackmail? So you were right.

I wonder what information they had on him that was so serious that they could use it to blackmail him.'

She nodded, pointing to the note.

He continued reading. *'Pailwan Harish saw you at the meeting yesterday. He knows where you are staying now. He plans to hand you to the police. Run and hide. I will send for you soon.'*

'How does Das know what happened at the meeting?' Ramu asked.

'I have no idea – the man seems like a true magician. He seems to know more than he should.' Kaveri turned frantic eyes on Ramu. 'Many people saw Suman. He was in disguise, but his fingerprints will be on the blades of the daggers. It could be a hanging offence.'

'Do you have a safe place where he can hide?'

'I can't think of anywhere,' Kaveri said, pulling out a map of the city from the desk drawer and scanning it frantically. 'Except the Women's Home. But he can't hide there. It will put the women in danger.'

'I know where Suman can hide,' Ramu said, speaking rapidly. 'The hospital has an animal facility that lies disused now. We used to breed rabbits there, and collect their blood to use to make the anti-cholera vaccine. With cholera under control, the facility has nothing but rusty cages. We don't even station a guard there now. It is not the best of accommodations, but he can spend a few nights there until we figure this out.'

They heard the back door bang open, and hurried down-stairs. Suman carried a small cloth bag with a few clothes. He looked haunted, the joy of hearing his father was alive overshadowed by the shock of finding out that he was being hunted – fighting off the danger of being imprisoned, even hanged. Seeing the pitifully few possessions that he owned, Kaveri felt a pang of sorrow for him. After the loss of his father, the young man had become reduced to living like a fugitive, moving from place to place.

'How do you think they found me?' Suman choked out, his mouth tipped downwards in a frown.

'Someone must have followed you back from Venu's house,' Ramu said, pulling on his socks and tying his shoes. 'Perhaps you and Kaveri were not as unobserved as you believed. Come with me.'

Suman's eyes grew wet as he looked between Kaveri and Ramu. 'I don't know how to thank both of you for your help. I hope, when all this is over, that Baba and I can be back together again, and live life like a normal father and child. He is all I have in the world.'

Ramu put an arm around the young man. 'You will get him back. But first, you need to hide until this furore subsides. Come, let us leave. There is not much time.'

The two men rushed out to the car, followed by Kaveri. She rushed to open the gate. Ramu opened the dicky at the back of the car and asked Suman to get in. Picking up a stone, he placed it in a corner and then closed the lid, creating a tiny opening through which air could enter.

'Can you breathe inside?' On Suman's affirmative grunt, Ramu dropped a quick kiss onto Kaveri's forehead, then got in and drove quickly away.

Kaveri stared after them, her heart heavy with a mix of emotions – fear for Suman, worry for herself, questions about Anandi. As she closed the gate and went in, Bhargavi and Shanthi, who had stayed the night, came downstairs, followed by Putta padding noiselessly at their heels.

'Where did Ramu go?' Shanthi demanded, looking around at the evidence of their hasty, interrupted breakfast – the plates still on the table, the drying chutney congealing on their plates. And then, seeing Kaveri's face, she asked, 'What did we miss?'

23

A Tale of Two Cities

'I don't know what to do now,' Kaveri said as she completed her update. The three women sat around the table while Putta thumped his tail on the floor, standing next to Bhargavi as she fed him the dosa left on Ramu's plate. 'There are still too many unsolved mysteries.'

'I don't understand,' Bhargavi complained. 'Explain it to me in full, Kaveri.'

'There were three possible reasons behind Das's disappearance,' Kaveri explained, holding three fingers up. 'First, we thought he had been killed by the gang. Thanks to the note, we now know that isn't true. Das and Suman are the only ones alive who know the code. So, Das must be alive.'

She folded one of her fingers. 'That leaves us with two possibilities. First, Das is part of the gang of thieves. If so, he could have staged his disappearance to hide from the police, after he saw Wilks and Ismail at the circus, worried that they might arrest him for creating a diversion to help them steal from the audience. Second, he is not part of the gang – he disappeared because they were forcing him to join them.'

'Doesn't his note confirm your second possibility?' Bhargavi asked.

'Perhaps, but I am still not one hundred per cent sure. Das is a magician, an expert at creating smokescreens. What if all of this is part of an elaborate trick, aimed at deceiving us?' Kaveri sketched a series of clouds on her notepad, shading them in with her pencil. 'I can't figure out how his note ties into the murder of Pawan and Ganesh, or the secret that Anandi is undoubtedly hiding from us. A part of the note rings true to me. Harish recognised us at the meeting. He must have tracked him after we escaped, and found out that Suman had moved to Uma aunty's house. But Das could have made up the part about being blackmailed by the thieves. What if he is collaborating with them on the robberies, without Suman's knowledge – but trying to save his son, keep him out of the situation to protect him?'

Kaveri pushed her notepad away, throwing her pencil down at the table. 'This is getting us nowhere. Let's try another tack.' She looked at Shanthi. 'Yesterday, at the meeting, both Harish and the government agent were pushing the group to plan something big and disruptive, an act of violence at the welcome pageant that the Mysore Maharaja plans to hold for Prince Edward. When people start to flee, they will exploit the confusion to make their move. Just like they tried to at the circus, except the police foiled their plans.'

'It's the perfect opportunity,' Shanthi said drily. 'All those English people, dressed in their best finery, along with our own wealthy residents? It's like laying out a banquet of bananas for a monkey.'

195

'The police will be there in full force, Kaveri,' Bhargavi objected. 'Inspector Ismail will never let them get away with this. He knows your tendency to get involved in everything. He must have heard the same rumours, and wants you to stay out of it to keep you safe.'

'It is too late for her to stay out of it now,' Shanthi pointed out. 'Let us think of what to do. We have to foil the gang's plans. If they succeed, people will think that the freedom movement has descended into sordid crime and burglary, and its reputation will be destroyed.'

Kaveri nodded. 'Perhaps the police will be at the site, to foil the burglary once it's set into motion, but we – we have to stop it from taking place at all.' She ground her teeth. 'This is still so murky. There is much we do not know. Das could just have refused to cooperate with them. What hold do they have on Das that is so damaging that he needs to stay hidden? I wonder who else is part of the gang now, too. With Pawan and Ganesh dead, Harish must have someone else still helping him. He doesn't seem sufficiently intelligent to plan and execute something of this complexity. I wish I had asked Suman more questions about the wrestlers and their connections before he got into the car, but we were in such a hurry to get him to a safe place.'

'Don't forget another central part of the mystery here – who killed Pawan, and Pailwan Ganesh,' Shanthi pointed out. 'I wonder if it was Harish. He could have killed Pawan because he stole their gold, hiding it in the dumbbells. But why would he kill his own brother, Ganesh?'

Kaveri let out a heartfelt groan. 'Anandi holds the key to this mess. I wish Mala and Narsamma had kept hold of her last night, when she came to give them a message.'

'She is a grown woman. How can you keep hold of her by force? If they did try anything like that, then they would be no better than Pawan, who kept her virtually imprisoned at home,' Bhargavi pointed out.

The women stopped talking as the telephone bell rang. Kaveri rushed to pick it up, hearing Ramu's voice. 'Did you—?' she asked, wanting to ask if he had dropped Suman off safely.

He interrupted her. 'We will speak of that later. Can you come to my office now? Dr Roberts wants to speak to us. I will send you his car, be ready – it will be there in twenty minutes.'

Why did Roberts want to speak to her? Shaking her head in confusion, Kaveri rushed upstairs to get dressed.

When she arrived at the hospital, she saw Ramu waiting for her at the gate. He got into the car, speaking rapidly, anticipating her questions.

'I don't know why Roberts wants to meet us either. He sent a note to my office asking us to be at his house at noon.' He pointed at the driver, raising his eyebrows at Kaveri. She nodded. They could not speak freely in front of this man.

They spoke of minor domestic challenges as the car drove on towards Roberts' home. Kaveri looked around as they entered. The house was familiar to her, but she had not visited for a while. A guard opened the gate, looking miserably hot in his starched white shirt and crisp white pants. They saw a man on the left side of the entrance scraping moss off the walls with a blunt knife, a pot of plaster next to him. Again, the British passion for keeping things neat and tidy in the tropics. Their roof had moss too, but there was no point in employing a person to scrape it off each year and re-plastering the building. When it rained, plants would grow – that was just the way of life. Why did the English want to dominate everything around them, she wondered.

There was no time for further wool-gathering. Ramu had rung the bell, and Roberts himself opened the door for them, giving her his usual genial smile.

'Come in, my dear, come in.' He clasped her hands warmly in his. 'My thanks to you for coming so swiftly in response to my message.' He gave Ramu a brisk handshake, and urged them to follow him in. 'Right here, towards the back of the house. Into my study.'

They followed him down a long corridor carpeted with a Kashmiri carpet. Kaveri admired the emerald and amethyst jewel colours. It seemed like a museum piece, not something to be trod on with shoes. It was a strange practice the English had to bring dirty footwear into the house with them, she thought as she followed Roberts down the corridor, her hand on Ramu's arm. So unlike the Indian habit of keeping their shoes and slippers outside the house, and walking barefoot inside the home. She wouldn't like to have carpets everywhere inside her house either. Think of the dust they would gather.

As they reached the end of the corridor and arrived at his study, Roberts turned to them, keeping his hand on the door knob. 'I have asked you here to meet a special visitor,' he said softly. 'He has some very important questions to ask of you.'

Who could that be? Kaveri exchanged a puzzled look with Ramu as Roberts opened the door.

She stared, feeling her jaw drop open.

Major Wilks stood up from the desk where he had been seated, looking down at them from his considerable height. She had not realised the man was so tall when she had seen him at the circus. He must be well over six feet.

'Thank you, Dr Roberts. If you can wait in the drawing room? We will send for you when we are done.' The note of dismissal was clear in Wilks' voice.

Dr Roberts did not seem to mind at all. He nodded at Ramu and Kaveri, and went back down the long corridor as Kaveri stared after him. Ramu pressed her fingers, warning her to stay silent as Wilks pointedly cleared his throat.

'Please come in, sit down.' He waited for Kaveri to take a seat on the chaise longue before turning to Ramu. 'Close the door behind you please.'

As the two men shook hands, Kaveri realised she had forgotten to thank Major Wilks. 'I wanted to let you know how much we appreciate your thinking of us,' she said. 'For sending us three tickets to the circus that day.'

She could see his eyes on her, perplexed as he studied her face. 'Tickets? I'm afraid you must be mistaken. I did not send you tickets to the circus.'

Kaveri looked at Ramu, surprised. 'They were in an envelope, on my table in the hospital, Sir. Mr Roberts and I thought that maybe you had left them for me,' Ramu said.

'Not at all. It must be someone else. Perhaps one of your clients?' Wilks turned to Kaveri. 'I know you have many admirers.'

He perched on the edge of his desk, idly flipping through a leaflet for Carlsbad Natural Mineral Waters. Another pamphlet on his desk caught Kaveri's attention – *Improved Gelatine Capsules for Hot Climates by John Richardson and Co., Winner of Eleven Gold Medals*, the pamphlet proclaimed. Kaveri stifled a giggle at the pomposity of the advertisement, hastily composing herself as Wilks looked at her.

She stiffened, moving closer to Ramu. Wilks caught her slight movement, staring down at her with his penetrating eyes. His long bent nose gave him the look of a fierce eagle.

'You must be wondering why I called you. Let me get straight to the point. The magician who disappeared – Mr Das. We have reason to believe that he is a traitor to the Empire.'

Kaveri schooled her face into impassiveness, not wanting him to notice her disagreement. Das might be in cahoots with the thieves, but how proudly he had spoken of Indian traditions of jadoo, developing Indian acts to showcase on stage, discarding the magician's top hat and tails in favour of native costumes. He could not be a traitor to the Indian cause. Wilks must be trying to discredit him – a standard British tactic, just like the government agent at the meeting trying to discredit the freedom fighters. She supposed she could not blame Wilks, who was only doing his job, working for *his* homeland. But how different he was from Dr Roberts, who believed in the good of all mankind, thus bringing out the best in each person he met and treated.

'I know that Das's son, Suman, asked you to help him find his father.' After a pause, Wilks resumed speaking, looking at Kaveri and Ramu in turn.

How did he know?

He smiled, seemingly reading her thoughts. 'You look shocked, Mrs Murthy. I have my people in place. We must prevent a repeat of what transpired in Bombay and Calcutta.' Wilks studied her closely. 'I assume you are aware of the events to which I am referring?'

Mutely, she nodded.

'And have you made any progress?' Wilks asked.

Kaveri squirmed. She felt like a butterfly that she had seen her biology teacher bring in for them once, pinned to a piece of cork as it struggled to break free.

'Not yet.' How could she tell him that she and Suman had attended an independence meeting the previous night? Ramu slid his hand under hers, enfolding her palm in his.

Wilks gave her a thin smile. 'You should also know that Das's brother-in-law, a traitor called Kailash, is on the run from the police. He blew up a police station in Calcutta. Our latest evidence indicates that the man is in Bangalore. He narrowly escaped from the police last night.'

Kailash was Das's brother-in-law? Suman's uncle?

Kaveri felt her jaw drop, staring foolishly at Wilks. Was this true? It explained much that had previously confused her. She had wondered why Suman would take such a risk, attacking a powerful government agent to free a stranger. But if Kailash was his uncle, of course he would want to save him at any cost. Chilled to her bones with dread, Kaveri slipped off her slippers, surreptitiously burying her feet in the wool of the Kashmiri carpet. Its warmth brought her strength.

Wilks peered at her for a long time. Apparently satisfied with what he saw, he nodded. 'If you find any news of Das, please let me know at once.' He stood up, and they stood up as well. 'We have some news filtering in from several sources that Das is planning an attack at the time of the Prince of Wales's visit. I hope I do not need to impress upon you the disaster that would ensue as a consequence. Please let me know as soon as you hear anything about Das. And be careful. The man is very dangerous, as are his accomplices, the wrestlers. I have it on good authority that the Pailwans and their associates have made death threats against you. They know where you live. I have suggested to Inspector Ismail that he station a guard at your gate, to protect you from further harm.'

He opened the door of Roberts' study, ushering them out, ignoring the startled gasp Kaveri had let out when she'd heard his high-handed pronouncement. Kaveri's back pricked as they walked down the corridor. Her thoughts were tangled, like a ball of wool that a cat had played with. Watched by Ismail's men, what could she do now?

24

The Beauty of a Pneumatic Duster

Kaveri and Ramu did not say a word to each other. Aware of the driver in front, they sat silently in the car, getting out when he dropped them off at the hospital. As soon as the man had driven away, Kaveri turned to Ramu, raising worried eyes to his face. 'Do you think Wilks knows?'

'About last night?' Ramu shook his head. 'If he did, you would be in jail, being questioned.' For a moment, his jaw clenched. She could see a pulse beating violently at the corner of his throat. 'I think he only wants to find Das.'

'Why didn't Suman tell us that Kailash was his uncle?' Kaveri closed her eyes, recalling how Kailash had moved towards Suman, kissing him on his forehead. It had seemed odd to her then, but her attention had been focused on fleeing the place safely, and the incident had gone out of her mind. Now, when she thought back to it, Wilks's revelation helped her make sense of that oddly gentle gesture, almost paternal in its affection.

'We need to find out more about Das, and his past relationship with Kailash,' Kaveri said. 'This may hold the answer to many of the questions puzzling us. Should I go speak to Suman now?'

'No, Kaveri.' Ramu's voice was urgent. 'It is far too dangerous now. I don't know who is watching us, tracking where we go, whom we meet. I will go there tomorrow, early in the morning, on my way to the hospital. I can ask him whatever you want at that time.'

Kaveri nodded reluctantly. 'Do you really think Das is a terrorist?' she whispered.

'From the perspective of the Empire, he must be. From our perspective – I don't know what to make of the man. We are groping too much in the dark,' Ramu observed.

Kaveri looked at Ramu. 'Suman said that he and his father moved from Calcutta to Belgaum six years back. He is seventeen now – he must have been about eleven then. Perhaps there will be something in the newspapers from those times. Something that can help me.'

Ramu held her by the shoulders, gently tipping up her chin with one hand. 'You are going to the library then – your usual haunt when you are stuck.'

She nodded.

A few minutes later, she was on the road, walking briskly towards the library. The sun was shining and now that she had a goal in mind, she felt better, more positive than she had felt in a few days. This was a more complex case than anything she had worked on previously, and Kaveri hated to be in the dark like this. Hated that she had to wait patiently to question people she seemed to be unable to reach, like Das, Anandi and now even Suman. At least in the library, there would be no newspapers mysteriously hiding out of her reach.

Kaveri reached the library, and quickly ran up the steps to enter. She walked in past the studious college students immersed in their textbooks and the old men reading newspapers and magazines. The head librarian knew her well now and came up to her, smiling. 'New case, Mrs Murthy?' He had become a good friend, always interested in news on her cases.

'I want to look at older newspapers – I am looking for past announcements of mathematics programmes in other cities,' Kaveri said carefully. There were too many curious ears in the room, and she did not want them to know what she was looking for exactly.

He beckoned her forward, pointing to a wooden crate behind the counter where he stood, his eyes shining. 'I was hoping you would come today. I have something to show you.'

She went behind the counter, peering at the machine inside the open crate. It had a set of leather bellows attached to a long handle, mounted on two wheels, much like a harmonium on wheels – minus the musical keys.

'That's a pneumatic dusting machine.' The librarian ran his hands over its polished handle, as gently as if it were a precious necklace or a newborn baby. 'By the inventor Charles Harvey. It sucks out the dust, sending it to this cloth bag, here.' He showed her the calico bag on the side. 'We employ six people, full time, to dust all our books. Their wiping cloths get dirty, and no matter how much I scold them, they weaken the bound covers by banging them to shake out the dust, so we also have to employ two full-time book binders who sit in one of the side rooms here with a supply of glue and thread. And by the time we finish dusting and repairing all the books, it is time to begin all over again.'

Kaveri raised her eyebrows. She had no idea that it took so much work to keep a library clean!

'This machine was expensive, but thanks to the generosity of the Maharaja, we finally managed to purchase it.' The librarian was rubbing his hands with satisfaction. 'I saw it in the British Library ten years ago, when I went on a study trip, and have desired one ever since. I knew you would appreciate it. Few do, you know. Most are scared that a machine will destroy the books.' He looked incredulous at the thought.

Kaveri bent double, leaning into the crate to inspect the machine. Her school physics textbook had included a paragraph on pneumatics, relating it to the human lungs, and Ramu's medical books contained a fuller explanation, but she had never dreamt of seeing a real live machine in action. How beautiful it looked. Ramu had bought her a milk steriliser when she had moved to Bangalore, which she prized more than rubies or diamonds – she wished she could show him this machine. Kaveri promised to return with Ramu to the library in a week, to be there when a technician from Madras was going to start up the machine for the first time.

With a spring in her step, she followed the librarian into the inner room. 'We have newspapers from Calcutta, Bombay and Delhi. Will that do?' He opened the door with a massive iron key, and unlocked the heavy wooden chest of drawers which contained bundles of old newspapers, neatly arranged by date.

Kaveri thought for a moment. If Suman was correct, and they had left Calcutta six years ago, she needed to look at newspapers from that time. Perhaps a couple of years back as well.

'Can you show me where the newspapers are for 1914 to 1916?'

An hour later, Kaveri massaged the small of her back, stiff from bending over and studying the fine print for so long. It would have been nice if the library carried copies of *Young India*, the weekly magazine that Gandhiji wrote. What a writer he was! Kaveri had read a few articles of his in Shanthi's house, admiring the clarity with which he wrote, spelling out the country's path towards complete non-cooperation. The magazine was shared in secret, from one person to another, but Kaveri longed for the day when a public library could freely display Gandhiji's writings. Would things change in her lifetime?

Flipping through reports of miraculous electric healers and descriptions of horse races, skipping past advertisements for half-price Japanese screens and English toilet soaps with increasing frustration, she had failed to spot a single mention of a magician named Das. If he was that famous, surely there ought to be at least one news article that mentioned him?

She tapped her pencil against her teeth. What if she was on the wrong track? Perhaps the man had assumed a false name. She picked up the newspapers from Calcutta again, starting in December 1916 and going backwards. Instead of rapidly scanning the papers, she forced herself to read them in detail, ignoring her stomach's increasing protests of hunger. A few minutes later, she had spotted what she was looking for.

'Famous magician Chatterjee to perform in the Maidan tomorrow. Come and see the unique performance, where the magician traps his beautiful wife, the amazing acrobat Mansee, in a cage – and saws her in two. Will she get out alive?'

It was a small advertisement in the Sunday section of advertisements. No wonder she had missed it before. It contained a small, cyclostyled photograph of Das and his wife, inserted below the text.

Blurry though it was, she recognised Das instantly. The man's real name had to be Chatterjee. His hooked nose and hooded eyes stood out even in the black and white print, though he was clean-shaven in this image.

She studied his wife. Suman looked nothing like his father, but he looked so much like his mother. She was a beauty, with her long nose, chiselled cheekbones and expressive oval eyes. In the photograph, she stood proudly wearing a cap decorated with a plume of peacock feathers, her hand possessively resting on her husband's shoulder. Kaveri felt a lump of sorrow form in her throat as she remembered how matter-of-factly Suman had said 'I have no family left, apart from my father.'

Only the previous month, Kaveri had borrowed a book from the library on famous circuses of the world, with profiles of women acrobats from Russia and London, but none from India. His mother must have been quite unique. She wished she could have met her.

Swallowing a lump in her throat at the thought of Suman's loss, Kaveri went through the newspapers again, standing up to get a better view of the newspaper as she searched for Chatterjee's name. When she found the papers from December 1915, she collapsed heavily onto the chair.

The article was on the front page of the newspaper, taking up several inches of newsprint at the bottom.

Mrs Chatterjee's body had been found in her room. She had been stabbed, just like Pawan and Ganesh. That could not be a coincidence. Could Wilks be right in labelling Das as a vicious criminal – had he murdered his wife in Calcutta, and his criminal associates in Bangalore? Kaveri swallowed a nasty burp, once again nauseous with tension.

She riffled through the pages of the newspapers of the next few days, searching for updates.

Chatterjee had been arrested a couple of days later. According to the newspapers, which carried interviews with other circus employees, Mr and Mrs Chatterjee had been quarrelling – they even said he was a jealous and possessive man who abused his terrified wife. The police claimed that she was planning to leave him, but he had found out and killed her, stabbing her in a fit of rage.

Kaveri closed the newspaper and leaned back in her chair. Suman must have only been about ten or eleven years old then. No wonder he had been so reluctant to say anything when she had asked him about his mother. He would have been shattered when his mother had been murdered.

Could Das really have murdered his wife? Surely Suman would not have been so attached to his father if Das had murdered his mother. She thought back to the first time she had seen Das, backstage, telling her that his wife had loved to read detective novels. That didn't sound like a man who had hated his wife so much that he had killed her. He had spoken of her with love, nostalgically. Nor did the confident woman in the photograph, standing with her hand on her husband's shoulder, look like a terrified, abused wife.

Appearances could be deceptive, and Das was a magician, Kaveri reminded herself again. She could not trust her usually reliable instincts where he was concerned. Her head whirling, she picked up the next set of newspapers. After a day's gap, she found another short piece. Chatterjee had escaped from prison, fleeing from the city itself.

Though the police had searched for him at the city's exits, they had not been able to find him anywhere. She paged through the newspapers for the next few months, inspecting every inch of newsprint. After Chatterjee's escape, she could not find any news of him in the papers.

Kaveri made furious notes in her notepad, copying down as much as she could verbatim and summarising the rest. She had spent hours in the library. Her nauseous stomach reminded her that it was well past lunchtime, and she had skipped her lunch. She looked into her purse, taking out a small box of *Bhavna Shunti* to suck on the salted pieces of dry ginger. Mrs Reddy had given it to Kaveri last month, saying it helped to ward off pangs of hunger. Her older friend was on a perpetual diet but loved to eat, so it never took her very far. The dry ginger, made by the celebrated ayurvedic practitioner B.V. Pandit's factory, eased her nausea and cleared her head.

Returning the keys to the librarian, she left the library, walking swiftly towards the circle outside to hail a Victoria carriage. She had solved one mystery – finding out Das's real identity. But once again, answering one question had only led to another set of questions. Was Das responsible for Mansee's death? She wished she had a pneumatic machine that would help her dust off old mysteries, revealing the truth within.

25

Eyes and Spies

Kaveri walked back to the hospital and collected the car keys from Ramu, who was working late again that night. She kept her foot on the accelerator all the way as she drove home, impatiently tapping on the steering wheel as she drove. Her mind whirled with the questions she wanted to ask Suman. As soon as she reached the entrance of her house, she pulled up and jumped out, running towards the gate in her eagerness to park the car. But as she strode towards the gate, she heard an unearthly screech. A barn owl, which normally slept in the morning hours, calling in the middle of the day? Her stomach turned. Too many strange things seemed to be happening these days, keeping her constantly on edge.

Kaveri kept moving, opening the gate to hurry inside while she listened. *There it was.* The owl hooted again, and then again. Three times in total. She recognised the signal. It was the same one that Venu had used to signal when she and Suman had gone to the meeting in Cubbonpet. Danger!

Kaveri breathed a sigh of relief when she saw a young policeman sitting in a comfortable chair inside her compound, below the neem tree. His eyes were shut, and he snored loudly, but she felt safer knowing he was there. Wilks must have moved fast, to send a guard to her house in such a short time.

What could the danger signal be warning her about, then? She walked back to her car, humming a song and moving casually so that an onlooker would not sense she was on the watch. Only her eyes swivelled from side to side, watching for anything that seemed out of place. Just as she bent down to get into her car, she saw what it was. A massive figure was crouching in the shadows, wedged uncomfortably between the wide trunk of a banyan tree and a muddy ditch just below.

From this distance, she recognised him instantly. Pailwan Harish had picked a good spot, she thought. Thanks to Wilks's warning about the wrestlers and Venu's signal, the man was on her mind. Even so, if she had not looked across the road at the right time, just when she bent down to get into the car, she would never have spotted him. He had hidden himself well.

Once she turned into their front yard, she closed the gate, restraining herself from looking at the corner where she knew Harish stood. If she woke the sleeping constable and told him about her watcher, his gang might just replace him with another man, whom she could not identify as easily. Best that Harish stayed in that uncomfortable ditch, where Venu could keep an eye on him.

Shielding her eyes from the midday sun, Kaveri looked up and saw a black kite making swooping circles above her. She pursed her lips and imitated its keening call, repeating it three times. There. Venu would know that she had received his message.

Pushing away the thought of the man standing guard outside, Kaveri thought with satisfaction that she was really getting quite good at these bird calls now, picking up quite the repertoire from Venu. She could place two fingers to her lips and produce a piercing whistle; reproduce the distress call of a squirrel; screech like an owl, trill like a bulbul and imitate the keening of a kite. None of her school classmates would be able to do this, she thought in satisfaction. Not even Priya, who had been her biggest competitor when it came to swimming *and* mathematics.

Priya's parents were very progressive – the last time Kaveri had heard of her, Priya was in Madras, studying to be a doctor. Kaveri's smile dimmed when she remembered how fervently she had pleaded with her mother to let her continue to study, and postpone her marriage. Her father had been supportive, but her mother had insisted that they accept the proposal that had come from Ramu's home – a doctor son-in-law, from such a wealthy house too, was too good a catch to turn down.

She did love her husband very much, Kaveri thought. She was very grateful to her patron saint, Raghavendra Swami, for her good fortune in arranging her marriage to such a supportive partner. Yet there were still so many things she could not do as a married woman. Occasionally, she thought of how her life might have turned out if she too could have gone to Madras, stayed alone in a working woman's hostel, and studied further. Free and independent, without anyone to tell her all the things that she could not do.

Well, there was no point in moping about things she could not change. Shrugging off her nostalgia, she called out for her mother-in-law and Shanthi. 'Bhargavi *athe*? Shanthi *akka*?' Hearing no response, she hurried upstairs, looking into her mother-in-law's bedroom. The room was empty. She peered into her room, and saw a note, folded and neatly placed on the bed.

Kaveri, the note read. *We are going out to the Women's Home, and then to Chick Pete for some shopping – we need to buy more silk material, thread and sequins for the women to embroider cushions for the charity sale. We will be back only in the evening. Putta looked so sad to see us go that we decided to take him with us.*

In the *evening*? That was several hours away. What was she supposed to do in the meanwhile? Kaveri went back down to the drawing room, picked up the cushions lying in an untidy pile on the table, hitting them against each other to plump them up and placing them back on the sofa with more force than necessary.

She heard a small cough. Rajamma was standing in the doorway, staring pointedly at her.

'You need something, and are not able to get it done.' Rajamma looked at her shrewdly, but there was kindness in her voice. 'Kaveri. You will not be able to solve all of the world's problems in one go. You must learn to be patient.'

'I know, Rajamma, but it is so hard at times.' Kaveri caught her bottom lip between her teeth. 'Did you know there is someone outside our gate, keeping a watch on us? I wanted to go visit Uma aunty, but how can I now?'

'That huge man?' Rajamma snorted. 'I saw him from the upstairs window when I was dusting. If they wanted to send a spy, they should have sent someone skinny and short.' She shook her head at the policeman snoring softly. 'He asked me for food, ate three plates of rice, and then slept. I guess he is of some use though, as a deterrent for this man outside.'

She looked at Kaveri. 'Why don't you do what you usually do? Hop over the wall to Uma aunty's house, and then disappear from that lane? You just came in. He will think you are taking a nap. Meanwhile, you can go do whatever you . . .' She stopped, her voice muffled as Kaveri squeezed her in delight and did a little jig around her.

'Take some buttermilk before you go,' Rajamma called, as Kaveri rushed down the stairs. 'I left some in an earthen pot on the dining table, to keep it cool.' She looked down the stairs, giving a satisfied nod as she watched Kaveri take a metal dipper out of the pot and pour herself a tall glass of freshly churned salted buttermilk, garnished with ginger, sprigs of coriander and fried curry leaves.

26

My Life Was a Waste Until I Met You

Kaveri had climbed over the wall that separated the back of their two homes, hopping onto the stool that Uma aunty had placed strategically below her wall for her to cross over. She tapped lightly on the kitchen door, not wanting Harish to hear the sound. 'Don't tell me she is not at home too,' Kaveri muttered, not hearing a response. She stopped, as an even worse thought struck her. 'What if her son is at home and she is not?'

'He is not at home, but I am, Kaveri. Why are you always in such a hurry?' Uma aunty's voice scolded her, but Kaveri didn't mind. She heard the wealth of affection that the scolding concealed, and smiled at the elderly woman as she came out of her back door, wiping her hands on a towel.

'I was just washing up, cleaning the lunch dishes.'

Kaveri's stomach heard the word 'lunch' and emitted a loud gurgle. She put up her hand to her mouth, embarrassed. Uma aunty clucked at her like a concerned brooding hen. 'Haven't you eaten?' She came closer and peered at Kaveri. 'What's that around your lips?'

'I drank a glass of *majjige*,' Kaveri admitted.

'This is no way to look after yourself, Kaveri. If your mother-in-law were at home, she would have scolded you, and made you eat. Come, eat with me. I have still not put away the food.' Drawing her into the cool darkness of her house, Uma aunty pulled Kaveri into the kitchen, unrolling the straw mat she kept rolled up in a corner.

'Sit, child. What can I get you?' Uma aunty placed a heaped spoonful of *heerekayi* chutney and a small mound of rice before her, over which she poured a generous tablespoon of fresh ghee. She added a few spoons of beans *paliya*, finely chopped beans cooked with mustard and grated coconut, and poured hot pumpkin *huli* onto the rice. Kaveri folded her legs and sat cross-legged on the mat, relaxing into the comfort of being cosseted and looked after as she tucked into the meal. Uma aunty sat next to her, urging more food on her, and fanning her with a small bamboo *beesanike*, the handmade fan keeping her cool as she devoured the food with small sighs of satisfaction.

When she could not eat a single additional grain of rice, Kaveri held her hand over the plate. She helped Uma aunty put the food away and wash the dirty dishes outside in the backyard with a coconut husk and some sand. The two women stood watching the water drain away towards the banana plants at the back of the garden.

'See how well my bananas are growing?' Uma aunty pointed to the plant, bent double with fruit. 'Suman was here only for a couple of days, but he transformed my garden, and had this idea of digging a channel here so that the kitchen waste could flow directly to the plants and provide them with more nutrition.' She turned towards

Kaveri. 'Where *is* Suman, though? I saw him early in the morning, but I didn't see him after that. His clothes are not in the shed either. Is he alright?'

Kaveri stared at her for a long moment, as she thought of where to begin. Then, pulling Uma aunty down with her, she sat on the back steps, playing with a strand of banana fibre as she spoke. 'I went to the library, and found out something quite disturbing.' Quickly, she brought Uma aunty up to date, telling her everything she had read in the library.

'So Suman's father, Das, is actually Mr Chatterjee, the famous magician of Calcutta?' Uma aunty rested her chin on her hands. 'My husband saw him perform once. He worked in the sales department of a Mysore silk sari company – remember, I told you?' Kaveri nodded. 'He went to Calcutta for a meeting – it must be about twenty years back.'

Uma aunty stared off into the distance, deep in memories of the past. Kaveri fidgeted on the steps as she sat next to her. She knew the older woman missed her husband, especially in recent years when her son had taken control of the household. But she wished Uma aunty would speed up her story. She winced, and looked down at her finger in surprise. She had wound the string of fibre so tightly around her finger that it had cut off her blood supply. She hastily unwound it.

Uma aunty was still lost in her reverie. 'Aunty? What did your husband say about Mr Chatterjee?'

'Oh, nothing much.' Uma aunty turned to regard her with mild surprise. 'Chatterjee was very good at getting out of tight spots. I believe he was heavily inspired by Harry Houdini, the famous American magician who made so many daring escapes. But my husband was even more impressed with his wife.'

'The incredible acrobat Mansee?' Kaveri sat up straight. She had never seen a woman circus performer before, and was very eager to learn more about this woman. 'I asked Suman about his mother a couple of times, but he changed the subject.'

'I don't remember what her name was. But she was very agile. I remember one stunt that my husband described to me, where she rode a cycle in vertical circles, and then jumped off right when she was at the top, being caught by her partner.' Uma aunty gave a wistful sigh. 'The things that some women can do. I wish I had a skill that I could be proud of. All I have done, all my life, is to cook, clean and keep my house running. Every woman does that. My son says my entire life is a waste. That *I* am a waste.'

Kaveri leant across to give the older woman a fierce embrace. 'You are *not* a waste, Aunty. If it were not for your help, I would never have gone to Halasur – and if it were not for that trip, we would have never been able to solve Ponnuswamy's murder. Later, if you had not taken me to meet Lakamma, we would never have been able to find out who murdered Mr Sharma.'

Uma aunty's face brightened. 'That is true. Since you moved in, my life has certainly become far more interesting.' She got up briskly. 'So. What do we do now, Kaveri?'

'I wish I could speak to Anandi.' Kaveri banged her fist on her thigh. 'I thought earlier that the independence meeting would be the key to everything. Now, I find it has revealed a further set of questions. I am sure that Anandi holds the answers to many of the unsolved mysteries. And . . . I am really worried about her. Where could she be hiding? She knows so few people in Bangalore, Aunty. She is not with Shanthi *akka*, or in the Women's Home. Where else could she be?'

'What about Mala and Narsamma, Kaveri? They were her neighbours, when she lived there with Pawan. Did you ask them?'

'They don't know where she is. Neither Venu nor his team of boys have seen her either.'

'Maybe there was something in her appearance that can give you a clue.' Uma aunty looked at Kaveri eagerly. 'The book you gave me, about that detective. What was his name, Sherwin Home?'

'Sherlock Holmes,' Kaveri corrected her with a smile. She had taught Uma aunty to read just a few months ago, but her neighbour was quick to pick up, absorbing her learning like a sponge. At first, Kaveri had taken her to the library, getting her a membership and selecting simple, easy to read children's books for her, but now she had progressed to more complex books. Her favourites were the kind Kaveri loved to read, the ones with mysteries in them.

'Yes, yes, that man only.' Uma aunty nodded her head vigorously, her bun working itself loose from its confines. 'He looked at everything the person wore and brought with them, and then deduced their background, age, where they were staying – everything. Can't you do the same?'

'I couldn't tell anything from seeing her at the meeting. We only saw her at the end, when she appeared out of the blue, handing two daggers to Suman. There was so much confusion that I couldn't focus on anything clearly.'

'What did the daggers look like?'

'Small, sharp. The hilt though . . . there was something strange about the hilt.' Kaveri closed her eyes, trying to recreate the scene in her mind. 'It had a parrot head at the end.'

As Kaveri spoke, Uma aunty's eyes widened. 'That's it!' She clapped her hands in delight. Kaveri stared at her.

'The knife you saw was a Kodaga knife. All Kodaga men, from Coorg, own a knife like that. With a flat blade and a wide hilt, often decorated with the head of a parrot in silver. It is mostly ceremonial, used in weddings and other celebrations, but they also use it for ritual sacrifices, and always keep it sharpened.' She grinned at Kaveri. 'Can you think of any Kodaga person we know, and whom Anandi knows too?'

Kaveri racked her mind, but could only come up with one name – the tiny yet formidable coffee entrepreneur whom Uma aunty had introduced her to a few months back: 'Coffeepudi Lakamma?'

'It has to be her, Kaveri. Who else do we know who has a house big enough that Anandi can hide out there safely? Lakamma has the courage of a lioness. Only she can give Anandi sanctuary at a time like this, without fear.'

'She can't hide Anandi in her home for days on end,' Kaveri objected. 'A house of that size must have a number of servants. Someone would tell someone, and the word would spread.'

Uma aunty shook her head. 'I have known Lakamma for years. She is very independent. She does not like to have servants at home. She told me once that she has people underfoot all day at the coffee factory. When she comes home, she just wants to be by herself. It is the perfect place for Anandi to hide.'

'Aunty, you are a wonder,' Kaveri said, hugging her tightly. 'Just a few minutes ago, you told me you had never been of use to anyone. Never done anything of value. But you've proven yourself wrong.'

Uma aunty wrinkled her nose at Kaveri. 'Don't flatter me so much. I will get a swollen head.' But she looked very pleased with herself, nevertheless. 'I will leave a note for my son and daughter-in-law, so they will not wonder where I am. Let's go beard the lioness in her den.'

Kaveri followed behind Uma aunty, marvelling at the energy that her elderly neighbour seemed to have. Coffeepudi Lakamma was about the same age as Uma aunty. Widowed when she was younger than Kaveri, she had taken on her husband's coffee empire and expanded it, setting up a factory in Bangalore and supplying specialty coffee to the Maharaja himself. She was a firebrand, and Uma aunty a deeply conventional house-bound woman – yet they had become firm friends. It was Aunty who had introduced Lakamma to Kaveri a few months back, when she was investigating Mr Sharma's murder.

Lakamma may have been tiny in height – but she was as formidable as a small army. On her own, Kaveri did not know if she would have been comfortable going up to her house and demanding that she speak to Anandi, that too without proof, only speculation, and connecting the dots. But with Uma aunty at her side, Kaveri felt that she could achieve anything.

27

Conversations Over Coffee

T he women walked fast, eager to reach their destination. The road was hot and dusty, and the vendor selling tender coconut water on the pavement called out to them as they passed. Uma aunty forged ahead with long, determined strides, barely glancing at him. Eager to press Anandi for answers, Kaveri kept pace with her.

When they reached Lakamma's house, Uma aunty picked up the heavy brass knocker, in the shape of a parrot head and gave Kaveri a significant look. She pounded on the door.

'Coming, coming. Where's the fire!' an irritated voice spoke from behind the door.

Kaveri saw the shutter behind the lens in the door move aside, and heard the sound of a stool being pulled across the floor. Lakamma was short, and needed to climb on something to see who her visitors were, she suspected.

There was a long pause. Then a grunt, an accepting sort of grunt. Kaveri heard the sound of a bolt being snicked back. The door slowly opened a few inches, and stopped, held by a chain. Lakamma peered out from below, looking up at them. Her expression was forbidding.

'Well?' she demanded. Before they could speak, she raised her hand. 'I suppose you've come for that special coffee I sent you a message about.' She raised her voice so that the sound carried outside. 'I have kept it for you. It's been here for a few days. I expected you to be here sooner.' She took the chain off the hook, letting them in.

As soon as they entered, Lakamma closed the door and bolted it firmly. She led them into her drawing room. The two women sat on the sofa. Lakamma moved to a wooden swing hanging from two hooks at the side of the room. She sat down, and pulled up her legs, sitting cross-legged on the slab of rosewood, swaying gently.

'You have a visitor whom we would like to speak to,' Kaveri began, then paused. She was not sure if Anandi had told Lakamma about the secret visit to the independence meetings.

Lakamma let out a short bark of laughter. 'When Anandi told me she saw you at the independence meeting, I thought to myself – the girl is smart, she will think about the knives that Anandi used, and turn up at my doorstep.'

'Actually, it was Uma aunty who helped me,' Kaveri interrupted.

Lakamma turned and gave Uma aunty a long approving stare. 'I should have realised. She is quiet, but my friend here notices everything.'

Uma aunty reddened, beaming at her.

'I gave her my late husband's clothes – his pinstriped suit, and his ceremonial knife, to carry for safety. If she got caught, I warned her, I would report the clothes and the knife stolen.' She waggled her eyebrows at Kaveri. 'Don't look so shocked. I have my personal beliefs, but

I am also a businesswoman. The Maharaja is one of my biggest clients. If he knows where my real support lies, then my factories will be out of work. And what happens to all the people who depend on me?'

Kaveri bit her lip. She knew Lakamma employed a number of people who would otherwise be starving and homeless – widowed women with young children, ex-soldiers who had returned from the war with injuries – she found jobs for those who would not be employed by anyone else. Lakamma paid for their medical treatment, their children's education – insisting that they educate their girls and their boys. And they repaid her in spades, throwing their hearts and souls into working for this woman who took care of them and their families so generously.

'Your personal beliefs?' she asked hesitantly.

Lakamma wagged her finger at Kaveri. 'Even the walls have ears. Let us just say that I think you and I, we share the same feelings about many things. But I am careful, that is all. I keep an eye on what goes on in town. The winds of change are blowing, and when the change arrives, I will be ready for it. That is all I will say at this time.'

She got up from the swing. 'I assume you want to speak to her?' Without waiting for a response, she led the way upstairs. When they arrived at the top of the steps, Lakamma pointed to a bedroom at the far end of the corridor, the door to which was closed. 'She is inside.'

Kaveri moved towards the door, stopping when she saw Uma aunty pause.

'You speak to her, Kaveri,' the older lady said softly. 'She will speak more freely if I am not there. Lakamma and I will drink some coffee and catch up on the news.'

Kaveri gave the two women a heartfelt look of thanks, then opened the door to the room softly.

Inside, Anandi lay sleeping, her body curled into a ball. Huddled close to the wall, she looked tiny and defence-less – far from the determined woman that Kaveri had seen holding a pair of knives at the secret independence meeting.

'Anandi? Wake up, Anandi,' Kaveri whispered as she shook her shoulder gently.

Anandi got up with a jerk. 'Kaveri *akka!*' Her eyes were wide and fearful. 'How did you find me?'

'Uma aunty traced you, not me,' Kaveri admitted, sitting down on the edge of the bed. 'She heard me describe the knives you carried, and the disguise you wore, and deduced that you were here.'

Anandi would not meet Kaveri's eyes. She looked down at her feet as she spoke. 'What must you be thinking of me, *akka*. You must feel I have betrayed you.'

'None of us blame you, Anandi. I know you feel you are in trouble. But help us understand, so that we can help you.' Kaveri took both of Anandi's hands in hers, gripping them tightly as the young woman looked away from her. 'Please, Anandi, you have to tell me what is going on.'

'There is no one I trust more than you, and Ramu *anna*. You both rescued me from my wretch of a husband. But I . . . I betrayed your trust.' Anandi broke down into an agony of sobs. Kaveri gathered Anandi into her arms, drawing soothing circles on her back with her hand as she attempted to comfort her.

Anandi sat up, wiping her face with the edge of her sari. Hearing the sounds of her sobs die away, Lakamma entered the room, followed by Uma aunty carrying a tray of coffee.

Lakamma took four tumblers of coffee from the silver tray that Uma aunty carried, handing them around. 'Has she told you yet?' she demanded. When Kaveri shook her head, Lakamma stood at the edge of the bed. Scarcely taller standing than Anandi was when she sat, the older woman nevertheless loomed over the younger one. 'Don't be a weakling. No one can help you unless you first help yourself.'

Lakamma's imperious tone seemed to have an effect on Anandi, as she bobbed her head, clearing her throat. Lakamma gave her a satisfied nod, perching at the edge of the bed. Uma aunty followed suit, as Anandi spoke, her voice quivering.

'I did not tell you before. I *could* not tell you. I am a thief.'

The coffee cup in Uma aunty's hand trembled. Lakamma put a steadying hand on her arm.

'A thief?' Kaveri looked at her in disbelief. Anandi held the keys to the money safe in the Women's Home, and Shanthi had never found a paisa missing. Kaveri could not believe her.

'Pawan made me do it.' Anandi's words were bitter. 'He wore expensive clothes, and jewellery – a thick gold chain and rings on every finger. Simpleton that I was, I did not wonder how a driver could afford such things. Then I found out that he was part of a gang of criminals that burgled rich homes.' She looked up, meeting Kaveri's eyes. 'You know how we met. I was a maid in the same house where he worked.'

Kaveri nodded, as Anandi continued.

'Our employer had a lot of wealthy friends. He took Pawan with him when he went to their homes. While he visited them, Pawan struck up a friendship with their servants, finding out details of their daily patterns, and getting to know little details such as when they went to sleep. A few days later, he would return to the same place with his friends and burgle it. When I found out what he did, I was horrified. I threatened to leave him, to tell the police.' Anandi reflexively put up a hand to her throat. 'He beat me so badly that night, I was sure I would die. It would have been better if I had.' She spat the words out, her voice filled with bitterness.

'But you were not responsible for his thefts,' Kaveri argued.

'You have not heard the worst of it. He forced me to accompany him. I was to be the decoy. A couple of times, the police came by on the road. He made me pretend to be a prostitute waiting for a man. The police would shout at me and make me move on. He and his friends would hear the noise, and quickly hide.'

Uma aunty looked horrified. 'That must have been very unsafe. What if the police . . .' Her voice trailed off.

Anandi's face crumpled. 'Some policemen were good. They only shouted at me and made me move. Others thought . . .' Her voice trailed off into a whisper. 'They thought I should give them free samples.'

Lakamma's face was grim, but unsurprised. Clearly, she had heard this story before.

'It became more and more difficult for me,' Anandi continued. 'One day, I escaped with difficulty from a policeman who was pulling me away with him. I refused to join Pawan again. He beat me brutally that day. Thanks to Mala, and to you and Ramu *anna*, I could recover, and escape. You gave me a chance at a new life.'

Kaveri looked at Anandi's face, pinched with worry. She hated to press her, but this was important. 'When you saw Pawan at the circus, was that the first time you knew he was back?'

She waited for Anandi's nod of confirmation before continuing. 'I saw him speak to you, at the circus, after

228

Das disappeared. You pushed him away, but then he said something to you which shook your confidence.'

'He told me that he had joined his cousins, who had formed a new gang. They were on to big things now. He wanted me to act as their decoy. I refused, and told him I was free from him now. He laughed, and said in a sneering tone "You mean that Women's Home? The walls are flimsy, like eggshells. With a blunt knife, I have snapped your window clasp, entered your room at night and watched you sleep. I stole your silk handkerchief – a nice, elegant one with your fine embroidery of a butterfly on it – and kept it with me." He pulled it from his pocket and showed it to me. "It has your fingerprints on it. If you do not come back to me, I will be sure to leave this at the site of my next burglary. The police will throw you in jail. Your employer, that fancy lady who acts so proud – her reputation will be in shreds, all because of you.'"

Kaveri stared at Anandi. 'That was what scared you so much? Oh Anandi. You should have come to me right away. I would have told you not to be afraid.'

Anandi stared at her, slowly looking doubtful.

Kaveri pulled Anandi into a hug. 'Handkerchiefs are made of cloth. Cloth can't hold fingerprints. It is too rough – fingerprints can only be retrieved from smooth surfaces. Like doorknobs, or windowpanes. You didn't accompany Pawan on any of their burglaries *this* time, did you?'

Anandi shook her head.

'Then he couldn't have trapped you. Not by taking your handkerchief with him,' Kaveri assured her. 'You embroider dozens of these – no, scores – for sale for charity. Anyone could have taken your kerchief.'

Tears came into Anandi's eyes. 'He fooled me. And I – like a dummy, I fell for it.' She sounded defeated.

'When you ran away from him, did he follow you?' Kaveri asked.

'No . . .' Anandi sounded horrified. 'I ran outside, but then I saw his cousins Ganesh and Harish. They were masked, but I recognised them. They were directing other men inside, issuing instructions to them to go to the front seats and rob people of their possessions. I was terrified that they would grab hold of me and force me to join them. I couldn't think clearly, I was so scared after what Pawan told me. I ran away and hid behind one of the parked cars. When the couple who owned the car rushed out to the car, I had to move away. I looked around for another car to hide behind, but all the people had begun to exit from the tent, moving towards their vehicles. So I returned to the entrance, standing near a policeman for safety. That's when you saw me.' She pressed Kaveri's hands. 'Believe me, *akka*. I didn't know that Pawan was dead until I saw him near the car.'

'Then why did you go to Pawan's house that day? When Pailwan Ganesh was killed?' Kaveri demanded.

The haunted look reappeared in Anandi's eyes, and Kaveri cursed herself. But she needed to get some answers from Anandi. If she did not press her now, they might never get at the truth.

'I thought Pawan's death had set me free. But Pailwan Ganesh followed me that morning, when I had gone to the market. He cornered me, forcing me against a wall.' Anandi shook violently. 'He placed his hand on my throat, almost throttling me as he repeated one question, over and over. "Where did you hide the gold?" I struggled to breathe, begging him to stop. I said I didn't understand. He shook me like an eagle shakes a snake in its beak, insisting I knew. "You killed Pawan for it. Is it in your room? Tell me, or I will tear the Women's Home apart."'

She looked at Kaveri with tear-filled eyes. 'I swear to you, *akka*. I don't know what he was talking about.'

'I do,' Kaveri said. 'Pawan double-crossed his cousins, taking the gold they had stolen and melting it down into a pair of dumbbells. Some of the black paint he had used to disguise it flaked away, and I realised it was gold. I gave it to Inspector Ismail. He must have returned the gold to its rightful owners.'

'I wish I was clever like you, *akka*.' Anandi sounded crestfallen. 'I should have come to you before, but I was so terrified that I could not think clearly. Ganesh told me that he would give me a week. If I did not find the gold, he said he would contact the police and turn me in. I returned home, shutting myself in my room. The walls pressed in on me, and I felt suffocated, scared. Then I got angry. Angry with myself for being so scared. I determined that I would go to Pawan's house and search for the handkerchief he'd stolen from me. If I found it, I thought I would be free. Without evidence, Ganesh would not be able to turn me in.' Anandi's voice broke. 'I was a fool. I will never be free of Pawan or Ganesh.'

'What happened when you went in?' Kaveri demanded.

'The front door was open, so I went in, closing it behind me. It locked automatically, startling me. I knew something was wrong as soon as I stepped inside and the smell of blood hit my nostrils. I thought of running, but my curiosity got the better of me. I tiptoed into the front room, staying close to the wall. And then I saw Ganesh.' She closed her eyes, shuddering violently. 'His eyes were open, fixed on me. Oh God, I will never forget that stare. Every time I close my eyes, I see his face. "Water . . . give me water," he begged me, his face twisted in agony. I crouched down, and put my hand on the knife, trying to see if I could pull it out, and help him. My hands were covered in blood. Before I could do anything, Ganesh looked down at his chest. "He's killed me," he said, sounding surprised. "I'm dead."'

Anandi uttered a keening sound, rocking from side to side. 'And then . . . I heard a sound. Someone was coming in from the side door. I was so scared that I simply pushed open the door, knocked down the person and ran.' She looked up at Kaveri, the tears spilling down her cheeks. 'I only stopped to look back when I reached the road. That's when I realised it was you that I had knocked down. I wanted to return, to explain to you what had happened. I stood behind a tree but just as I plucked up the courage to approach you, I saw Inspector Ismail coming down the road. I was covered in blood. I was terrified that he would lock me in jail.'

There was a long silence in the room. Lakamma broke it. 'And so, this silly child ran away. She picked up a towel from a clothes line hanging behind one of the homes she passed, and wrapped it around herself like a shawl, hiding her bloodstains. That was how she landed on my doorstep.'

'Just the previous day, I had come to *ammavare's* house to pick up a special batch of coffee for Shanthi *akka*. We spent a long time chatting. *Ammavare* told me she does not keep servants at home,' Anandi broke in. 'I was terrified of the police. I couldn't go back to the shelter and put Shanthi *akka* at risk. I didn't know what to do. I came here and asked her to shelter me.'

28

Dribs and Drabs

After telling her side of the story, Anandi fell into an exhausted sleep. Leaving Lakamma to watch over her, Kaveri and Uma aunty tiptoed out of the room, closing the door gently.

The two women left the house swiftly after, carrying a bag of coffee powder with them. An inquisitive neighbour watching the house would think they had come to collect an order. They walked back equally silently, each lost in thought. When they reached Uma aunty's house, Kaveri went to the back wall and climbed over to her house, slipping in through the back door. Rajamma was waiting for her.

'Where is the policeman? And the man outside?' Kaveri whispered to her.

She snorted, speaking softly too. 'The policeman is awake, reading a newspaper. He drank two cups of coffee already. I told him we can't provide him dinner so he has asked his wife to bring him a *dabba*. The man outside is still in the ditch. I hope he gets tired of staying hungry and goes home,' she added with a wicked smile, before continuing in a normal voice.

'Bhargavi *ammavare* called to leave a message for you. She is staying with Shanthi *akka* for a couple of days. Putta is with them. Ramu *anna* also called. He will be back soon.'

Exhausted by the day's events, Kaveri sank down onto the carpet, aching for Ramu to return. Was it safe to leave Rajamma alone at home if the wrestlers had made death threats against her family? Again, she felt thankful that there was a policeman outside her house. However ineffectual he might seem, he was certainly large and stolid, a most obvious deterrent to any criminal with evil designs on her loved ones.

Lost in her own thoughts, she barely heard Rajamma tell her that she was leaving. She lay flat on her back, watching the second hand on the cuckoo clock move as the seconds ticked by, waiting for her husband to come.

She did not realise she had fallen asleep until she awoke to Ramu standing over and her gently shaking her shoulder. 'Why are you sleeping on the carpet?' he asked, the concern evident in his voice. He switched on the light and Kaveri blinked, her eyes gradually growing accustomed to the brightness. Her tongue felt thick and fuzzy, and the full feeling from all the food she had eaten for lunch was long gone. She slowly rose up from the carpet and asked Ramu, 'Are you hungry? Shall I make some dosas?' She felt like she could eat a table full of food.

After Kaveri had pulled together something to eat, they sat in their favourite place on the back steps, balancing plates of dosa and chutney on their knees. Venu had dropped by the hospital on his way home to tell Ramu about Pailwan Harish, and they discussed the situation in soft whispers, deciding to do nothing for the time being.

The policeman outside the house should be enough to keep him at bay.

They drank the filter coffee Ramu had brewed and munched on food as they looked at the stars. Kaveri leaned against Ramu as the cool evening wind blew, and he took off his jacket and placed it around her shoulders. She relaxed, feeling warm and safe, refusing to spoil the moment by thinking of the policeman keeping watch in their front yard, or the wrestler watching the house from the ditch outside.

As they ate, Ramu told her about his exhausting morning at the Infantry Line, trying to enforce the sanitation guidelines of the municipality, who had levied a compulsory conservancy fee to keep the toilets clean and to employ a sweeper. His face dark with anger, he told them of a wealthy man whom he had fined that morning for employing and housing a labour colony of hundreds of men without providing them with a single toilet.

'But enough about my day. What have you learned so far?' he asked.

'Dribs and drabs which I am trying to string together into a story, with a few conjectures and many leaps of faith,' Kaveri said. 'I don't even know where to start.'

'The further we proceed, the more my distrust of Das increases,' Ramu said. 'Thanks to Wilks, we now know that Kailash is Das's brother-in-law. What if he and Kailash are working with the wrestlers, instead of against them, towards a common goal – of disrupting the Prince's visit? Suman may also be part of this elaborate scheme.'

'I agree that we can't trust Das,' Kaveri said. 'He might be a killer too – at least of his wife, if what the newspapers say is true. Pawan, Pailwan Ganesh and Suman's mother were all killed in the same way – stabbed in the chest. That makes me believe that the same person killed all three.

But I cannot believe that Kailash would be involved in the murder of his own sister. He robbed a police station, but not for personal gain – he would not participate in something as sordid as petty theft. It would tarnish the reputation of the very independence movement for which he risks his life, fleeing from city to city.'

Picking up their plates, she went inside and left them in the kitchen, returning with her notebook. She tapped her pencil on the diagram she had made on one of the pages, showing Ramu the little circles she had drawn, each with the name of the people involved, with arrows connecting them.

'I cannot believe that Suman is lying to misguide us either. He saved us all at the independence meeting. Anandi had the knife, but neither she nor I would have been able to free Kailash. Suman acted with such courage.'

'I'm not as sure about Suman as you are,' Ramu said. 'Why did he not tell us that his father was really Chatterjee?'

'I wish you could go and ask him now,' Kaveri said. 'I want to know if his mother's death is connected to the murders of Pawan and Ganesh. Ganesh asked me for help. I can't get that out of my mind.'

Ramu riffled through the pages of her notebook. 'This is one of your most complex cases so far. Every time we think we have pieced together one part of the truth, something turns up that contradicts everything we believed.'

'Like today's meeting with Anandi,' Kaveri agreed. 'I thought that Pawan may have been killed by Ganesh, over the stolen money. But that can't be. Anandi says he kept asking her why she killed Pawan, and where she had hidden the money. If Ganesh didn't kill Pawan, who did?'

'Perhaps it was his brother. Pailwan Harish,' Ramu offered.

Kaveri looked doubtful.

'You are too tired to think clearly, Kaveri. Come to bed. A good night's sleep will refresh you. I will leave early tomorrow, and go meet Suman. I'll give you a call as soon as I get to the hospital after speaking to him. You can come to my room there, and we can talk more.'

Kaveri tossed and turned all night, falling into an uneasy sleep in the early hours of the morning. She was fast asleep when Ramu slipped out of bed, only waking to the shrill sound of the telephone ringing some time later.

'Kaveri? There's no point in coming to the hospital today.' Ramu's voice was guarded. 'The rabbits escaped from their hutch.' He put down the phone.

Suman was not in the animal home! Kaveri sank down against the wall, her head spinning again, her legs unable to hold her up. Did he leave on his own, like Das – or had someone kidnapped him, taking him away forcibly? Worried about him, and frustrated that she could not ask him the questions plaguing her, she pounded her fists on the ground. The sounds of her bangles clanging noisily on the red oxide floor caused Rajamma to poke her head around the kitchen door.

'At a dead end again? The Club meets in an hour. Perhaps you will get some ideas then.'

Feeling a spark of hope, Kaveri hurried to her room to get ready for the meeting. She was ready in a jiffy, but her visitors were late. Just as she had given up on their arrival, Mala hurried out of breath and apologising.

'We got caught up in the *jatre* of the Gavi Gangadhareshwara cave temple,' she explained. 'They were distributing cartloads of coconuts and bananas at the chariot festival. The crowds! You should have seen them.

It took us an hour to travel the remaining few yards to your home.'

She sat down with Narsamma, looking hot and bothered, quaffing down glasses of water from the earthern pitcher.

'It is very hard,' Kaveri was complaining a short while later, as they sat down with slates and chalk, going over the alphabet. 'Life used to be so simple, a few months back. Now, Mrs Ismail is avoiding us, and Anandi is in hiding. I cannot speak to Mrs Reddy freely, because her husband is such a strong British sympathiser.'

'Wait for the Prince to leave, and things will return to normal,' Narsamma advised. The older woman seemed inured to worry, after all the hardship she had endured in her long life.

Mala gripped her hand. 'In times of crisis, it is not friendship, but our values, that hold us together. The building that holds us together looks well constructed, but the foundation is rotten – laid with a mix of bricks and pebbles. Prince Edward's visit has exposed cracks below the surface. Differences can be a strength, but not in this instance. Once the Prince leaves, we will resume our normal lives. In time, we may even forget that we had once stopped seeing each other so often. We will pretend to forget. But the cracks in our relationship will remain. And as the days and years progress, as they will, the rumbles of discontent will grow, and everyone will have to take a side. Either they are with the fight for freedom, or against it.'

A silence fell on the room as everyone thought about what she had said. 'The real challenge . . . well, at least for now,' Kaveri amended, 'is the clash between the two ways of fighting for freedom. The non-violent way, that Gandhiji asks us all to adopt, and the second way, which others are advocating for. The approach that people like

Subhas Chandra Bose advocate.' Kaveri hurried up to her bedroom, returning with the essay written by Bose that Shanthi had given her, which she kept hidden between her saris. Returning downstairs, she read the essay to the women.

'I think that this man, Bose, is right,' Mala said. 'Violence cannot be combated by turning the other cheek. It may have worked for Gandhiji, but then he is a man, and a well-born one at that. Look at us.' She gestured to Narsamma and herself. 'It is only because we now control the purse strings that men listen to us. If we spoke to them gently, and pleaded with them to reform themselves, do you think they would? Fat chance.'

'But this is a bit different,' Kaveri argued. 'Look at the resources the British have. If we want independence from them, we cannot rise up against them in violence. We know how the 1857 mutiny turned out. And Jallianwala Bagh? They raised their rifles and shot at us mercilessly. Elders, children, mothers . . . they did not spare anyone. We need to find a different way to oust these foreigners from our land, through legal and peaceful means. Otherwise, we will all die.'

'Enough of this gloomy talk,' Mala said, setting her slate aside. 'Now, tell us – how can we help you?'

'I wish I knew, Mala. I feel like I am at a dead end. Only Suman can give us some more answers.'

'For that, you need to wait for Suman.' Mala's voice was kind, but practical. 'There must be something we can help you with. Where is that notepad in which you write down everything?'

Kaveri pulled it out of her reticule and opened it. 'I have a gut feeling that once we find out what plan the gang of thieves have in mind for the Prince's visit, we will have the answer to what is going on. I wish that meeting had not broken up so soon. If the informer had not infiltrated the meeting, if the police had not broken it up, I am sure I would have learned more.'

'Well, you cannot go to any more meetings. It is too unsafe,' Mala advised. 'I have asked around and people are unwilling to talk about the gang. As I told you earlier, it consists of a number of thieves . . . the wrestlers are only a small part of it, though they seem to be the masterminds. People seem terrified of the leader, unwilling to speak about him or their plans to anyone. Especially after the two murders that have taken place. Still, let me see what I can do. I will ask my brother's friends to try again. We can offer them money in exchange for information. Money loosens many lips.' She stood up. 'There is a lot to be done.'

'Be careful of Pailwan Harish. He seems to be the leader. Pawan and Ganesh took their cues from him. He has a team of men,' Kaveri warned. 'There were a number of masked men at the circus that day and if Wilks and Ismail had not foiled their plans, they would have succeeded in making a huge haul.'

Mala scoffed. 'My men were doing this kind of work when Harish was a babe in his mother's lap. They will take care of me, and make sure no one ventures close. I will send Venu if I get any news.'

She gave Kaveri a quick embrace before turning towards the door. Narsamma gave Kaveri her characteristic toothless grin, departing with her mistress.

Uma aunty stood with Kaveri, watching the guests depart.

'We are back at an impasse, just like yesterday.' Kaveri's voice was wobbly.

'I feel as though the winds are changing. Tomorrow will bring us fresh hope.' Uma aunty spoke firmly, as though she were willing the future to change.

29

In Coles Park

Ramu came home early that day, entering just as the clock struck four p.m.

'We have been invited to Coles Park for a concert, Kaveri.' He gulped down the cup of tea she handed him, thirstily accepting a refill. 'I thought it would be a nice change for you.'

She started to protest, but then he stood up, putting his hands in the back pockets of his trousers and rocking back and forth on his heels. 'Ah, but you haven't guessed the real reason. So much for being a famous lady detective who can read minds.' He put out a hand to protect his teacup from the cushion that Kaveri tossed his way, laughing. 'Dr Roberts will be there with Major Wilks. I thought we might get some more details on the plans for the pageant, so that we can learn the schedule and get a sense of when the gang might be planning their attack.'

Kaveri hurried to the calendar on the wall. 'It's the fourteenth already, and the Prince's visit is on the eighteenth. We need to know so much more than we do.'

Ramu put his arm around her shoulders, giving her a little nudge towards the stairs. 'Go put on your fanciest sari and be at your charming best. We will inveigle as much information as we can.'

In a short while, Kaveri was in the car with Ramu, dressed in one of her favourite saris, in rust orange with a dark grey border and pallu, with a border of elephants embroidered in gold. She wore a choker of Burmese blood-red rubies, with a matching bracelet, taken from her mother-in-law's collection. Stealing sidelong glances at her husband – handsome in his formal suit and bow tie, but with dark circles under his eyes evidencing the sleepless nights they had had lately – Kaveri decided to enjoy herself for the rest of the evening. Of course she would be on alert, trying to pump everyone for information, but the tension of the last few days had got to them. They could not sustain this indefinitely, and being on edge would not help her find Suman or Das, or free Anandi from suspicion.

'I don't think I've been to Coles Park before,' she said, enjoying the feeling of the cool breeze on her cheeks. Ramu gave her a distracted nod as he spun the wheel to the right. They drove past a row of kadamba trees, and Kaveri put her head out of the window, admiring the round fruit hanging heavy on the branches. Ramu parked under one of the trees, next to a line of carts with coloured balloons, cut guavas with chilli powder and salt, and roasting corn on the cob. Kaveri's mouth watered.

'The park is one of the largest in Bangalore, after Cubbon Park,' Ramu said. 'Cole was the British Resident of Mysore about a hundred years ago, but the park is only eight years old, built in 1914.' He pointed out the Wesleyan Mission School on their left. 'It's one of the oldest schools for Indian girls in Bangalore. They teach them in Tamil.' Noting her questioning expression, he added, 'But no science or mathematics. They learn history and geography, catechism and scripture.'

'All that is standardly believed to be improving for women,' Kaveri said, a trifle bitterly, as Ramu squeezed her arm.

The sound of a band playing grew nearer as they approached the gate, fending off requests to purchase balloons and keychains, or to eat cotton candy and peanuts. 'And that's the Bangalore Battalion – until recently, they were called the Bangalore Rifle Volunteers,' Ramu added. 'They play military tunes on special occasions. Roberts told me this is a prequel to the Prince's visit, a practice session of sorts for them.'

They stood at the entrance for a couple of minutes, admiring the band in their crisp khaki uniforms. Kaveri stood transfixed – she had never heard anything like a bagpipe before. They saw Miss Roberts, wearing a large fascinator with what looked distinctly like a bowl of tropical fruit stuck onto it. The brightly coloured fruit clashed with her frock, with its vivid prints of scarlet and purple flowers. The fascinator bobbed and quivered precariously as she spoke to Major Wilks, whom she had cornered next to the dessert table. Wilks looked bored, but kept a wary eye on the fake fruit, stepping back as Miss Roberts moved forward, in full flow.

They walked towards Dr Roberts, whom they had spotted in the opposite direction, settling into the wicker seats on the grass to enjoy a performance by Mr and Mrs Nunn, who proceeded to enact scenes from *The Merchant of Venice* and *Romeo and Juliet*, concluding with a hilarious scene from Sheridan Knowles' *The Hunchback*. Ramu and Roberts became absorbed in the drama, but Kaveri could not focus on what she saw on stage. Her mind was on Suman, and her gaze kept darting around the gathering.

The balloon seller outside the compound moved back, shaking his fist at the badminton ball tree. Ripe fruits had fallen on his balloons, puncturing a few of them. Kaveri thought of their car. Had fruits fallen across the bonnet? It would be impossible to clean without water, and difficult to drive back with sticky fruit sap spread across the glass, blurring their vision. She squinted at the tree near to where they had parked, trying to guess how ripe its fruit was.

Then she blinked. And looked again.

In the tree, between its branches, she saw a face appear and disappear. It was Harish – what was he doing there? Kaveri tugged at Ramu's arm, speaking rapidly into his ear.

'He followed us here,' she said in rising panic. 'What if he does something to the car?'

Ramu looked pleased with himself. 'He can't. After your last accident, when your car was tampered with, I know we can't be too careful. I told Venu to make sure our car was under observation at all times. The balloon seller is Chandru's uncle. He's keeping an eye on the Ford for us.'

'But why *is* Harish here? What does he want?' Kaveri asked. The performance ended just then, and she had to speak louder than she had intended. A couple of seats ahead of her, Wilks turned around and frowned. Kaveri winced.

People got up, making a beeline for the makeshift stage to congratulate Mr and Mrs Nunn. Asking Ramu to stay and engage Major Wilks and Dr Roberts in conversation, Kaveri slipped out of sight, sidling around the wall towards the tree where she had last seen Harish. With any luck, they would think she had gone to ease herself – though Major Wilks was probably far too sharp to fall for such a trick.

She searched fruitlessly for Harish, but could not spot him anywhere. On her way back, she paused to look at the different stalls. A stout Anglo-Indian man beckoned her close.

'This way, young lady. Sign up for a stall at the pageant. Just ten rupees for a counter.'

'What kind of counter? And for what pageant?' A thrill of surprise ran through Kaveri.

The man looked distinctly taken aback, drawing his bushy eyebrows together. 'What world are you living in, m'dear? The pageant for the Prince of Wales, of course. See the list, here.' He pointed with pride to a long list of names next to descriptions of stalls.

Kaveri took out her purse, pulling out ten rupees, and watched his face brighten as he caught sight of the notes in her hand.

'What can I put myself down for?' she enquired in an artless voice, remembering Ramu's injunction to be 'charming'. 'I'd love to do something unique. How about embroidery?'

As she expected, the man shook his head, looking regretful. 'We have three embroidery stalls, four water-colours, four oil pastels, two displays of crochet and knitting, and five of jams, jellies and confectionery.'

'What about magic tricks?' Kaveri held her breath.

'That's available.' He gave her an intrigued glance. 'What sort of magic tricks do you do?'

So Das hadn't booked a stall then! Kaveri's face fell, but then she composed herself. 'Oh no, it's not for me,' she said. 'It's for a friend. He's here, filling his plate with cakes at the dessert stall. I'll send him your way.'

She cast a longing look at the list in front of the man, partially hidden by his plump forearm. Waving the notes in front of him again, she leaned forward, giving him what she hoped was an enchanting smile. He moved back, watching her uncertainly, and she realised she had bared her teeth.

'Can I see the list? I want to know what else I could sign up for,' she demanded.

To her surprise, the man handed it over to her. She read it as fast as she could. Embroidery, oil paints, watercolours, embroidery, watercolours, watercolours, painting on rice, more watercolours . . . wait, what was that? She paused and went back over the list, running her finger across the words she had noticed.

Seeing Miss Roberts approaching, she hastily pushed the list back to the man, murmuring something about leaving to look for her magician friend, and fled.

30

A Surfeit of Bananas

Kaveri opened the door the next morning to find Venu outside, squatting down and milking Kasturi. She moved closer to him, standing at a strategic distance from the cow. She was a serious kicker with a wicked temper, as Kaveri had learned when she'd tried to approach her in the past.

Venu crooked a finger, beckoning Kaveri closer. His face bent, he took a stick and sketched the outline of a tree, giving the policeman under the tree a quick sideways glance. Then he drew the outline of a ditch below the tree, a stick figure in the ditch, and erased the figure.

'The wrestler has gone away,' Kaveri guessed, speaking in a low voice. Venu nodded. Still looking down, he whispered, 'Shanthi *akka* asked me to give you a message. Anandi is back.'

'What?' Kaveri burst out. Venu shot her a furious sideways glance. She saw the policeman look up from his newspaper, and tried to make amends for her outburst. 'What do you mean, you cannot give me two *serus* of milk?' she demanded loudly. Seeing nothing of interest, the young constable picked up his paper again, paying no more attention to them.

Venu raised his voice too. 'Kasturi is not feeling well today. There is not much milk. I am sorry.' In a lower voice, he added, 'Mala *akka* spoke to her. She told Anandi she cannot sit and cry all day, Pawan is dead, and she is free. Anandi agreed to return, and be of some use to you. The Maharaja is hiring part-time workers to help put together the stage and arrangements at the lake for the Prince's pageant. Mala took Anandi there and got her a job.'

Kaveri felt a knot of worry worm itself into her throat. 'Is that safe?' she wanted to ask Venu. But he would not be able to answer.

'Did Mala say anything else?' she asked.

'She is still looking for information. After Pawan's death, no one is willing to speak to anyone.'

The milking was done. 'I have to go now, or it will look suspicious,' Venu whispered.

She clenched her fingers into fists, watching Venu leave.

It was breakfast time but she was not hungry. The nausea that seemed to be an ever present companion to the pit of tension in her stomach had returned. She picked up a bottle of Wilkinson's Sarsaparilla, giving the brown bottle a dubious look as she read the label. Claiming to deal with all kinds of ailments – from a torpid liver to lassitude – by cleansing the blood of vicious humours, it had come as a free sample with a leaflet that proclaimed its efficacy since 1829. She opened it and took a sniff, recoiling from the strange smell and setting it down with a shudder before preparing a glass of fresh, sweet milk for herself with *arasina* instead. She drank it down, hastily wiping away her turmeric milk moustache.

*

The next two days passed at a crawling pace. Feeling doubly confined by the possibility the wrestler had returned to the ditch outside and the policeman outside her front door, Kaveri fretted about not making progress on the case. She pestered Venu for news every time he came to the house, so much that the boy began to look hunted, quickly milking Kasturi as soon as he entered, hanging his head as she pelted him with whispered questions. The young policeman – whom Kaveri thought must be one of Ismail's most useless recruits – barely noticed anything was awry. But Ramu noticed. 'Stop bothering the poor boy, Kaveri,' he chided her. 'Can't you see? He fidgets as soon as he enters the gate, afraid that you will accost him again.'

'It's so *hard* to do nothing,' Kaveri wailed.

'I know, Kaveri,' Ramu pulled her close, rubbing her back in small circles. 'Believe me, I understand.'

She pulled away and sniffed. 'I don't think you *can* understand.' At his puzzled look, she reached up and took his hand. 'You men, you go to the office every day. You have a routine, something to do. I have . . . nothing. One day I have a lot of work, the next I have nothing to do. I try to keep myself occupied, I swim, read, or play the veena. But it is so *hard*.' She added bitterly, 'In Great Britain, women can vote. But here, in British India, I can't even study beyond matriculation!'

Ramu looked stricken. 'I wish you could register for a Junior Intermediate, but those obstreperous men on the education board have not yet decided whether to allow women to study science. I know the Maharani is trying to change the policies and open a science college for women in Bangalore and Mysore. But the Superintendent of Education is a hard man. He is a friend of our neighbour, Subramaniam Swamy. And I fear both men are cut from the same cloth. I pity Mrs Swamy.'

'And I thank my stars daily that I married you, and not Mr Swamy,' Kaveri responded, giving Ramu a peck on the cheek. It was not his fault that she was feeling isolated. She needed to learn how to wait with patience – never one of her strengths.

Without warning, Venu burst into the room. Seeing them embracing, he placed his hands over his eyes. '*Ayyo.*'

'So much drama,' Ramu said drily, removing his arm from Kaveri and strolling towards the boy. He tapped him lightly on the head. 'What is it?'

'And why are you making so much noise and running in like that?' Kaveri chided him. 'Aren't you afraid the policeman in the compound will hear you shout and follow you inside?'

'That's just it.' Venu gave her his characteristic gappy-toothed grin. 'There's no one outside the house now. Inspector Ismail sent someone to get him back to the police station.'

'That's because Prince Edward's visit is imminent,' Kaveri said bitterly. 'And we are no closer to finding out the truth of what happened at the circus that night – or what the gang has in mind for the pageant. It's the sixteenth – the pageant is two days away.'

'Suman *anna* can tell you,' Venu said airily. He beamed in satisfaction as he saw Kaveri's jaw drop. 'I found him. That's what I came running to tell you. When he disappeared again, I was sure that he had gone to join his father. I was so annoyed that we could not find a trace of them. We looked everywhere. In the *pete*, where the traders live – in the grassy fields where itinerant herders set up temporary camps, and in the fishermen's shacks near the lakes. But we couldn't find them anywhere. And then I got my brainwave.' He did a little jig in front of her. 'If we have looked at all the obvious places, and those which are unusual, where is left?' He paused, surveying them, looking so obviously pleased with himself that Kaveri's heart melted.

'What *is* left?' Ramu shook his head. 'I can't think of any place you haven't looked.'

Kaveri snapped her fingers. 'I think I've got it. Did you find them in the circus?'

Venu nodded encouragingly.

'In the stage,' she guessed. 'Don't tell me, let me think. You said they were hiding in the last place that anyone would have thought of searching. There must be a hidden partition of some kind there, which Das used to stage his disappearances. Am I right?' She gave Venu a delighted smile. 'What a brainwave you had, Venu. You have become a good detective.'

Venu puffed up his small chest, standing like a proud bantam rooster. 'I have learned well from you, *akka*.'

A worrying thought struck Kaveri. 'What if they realised you found them, and have already left again?'

'They could not have found us out,' Venu said firmly. 'We did what we usually do – climbed a high tree, and looked at them from a distance. We did not even venture within a few hundred feet of them. Suman *anna* had stepped out to buy some bananas from a street vendor at night. It was midnight, and I had almost fallen asleep in the tree. But then I heard a sound, and looked down. No wonder we haven't been able to find them, if they only go out in the middle of the night.' He made a face. 'They must be hungry. I would be *sick* of eating bananas by now.'

31

A Proper Bat and Ball

'Should we call Ismail?' Kaveri asked Ramu.

'No, Kaveri. What he if arrests Suman and puts him in jail? We are not sure of where the Inspector stands in this entire situation.'

Kaveri and Ramu were in their car, speeding towards the circus. About a kilometre away, following instructions from Venu, who was sitting in the back seat, Ramu turned left, stopping the car next to a small children's park. A couple of grimy looking urchins played cricket, using a makeshift bat – two planks held together with a piece of twisted metal and some rusty nails. A massive raintree shaded the grounds, its pods scattered across the ground. Kaveri saw that the boys had fashioned a misshapen ball from the pulp of the raintree pods. Her heart ached for them. They could not even afford proper cricket equipment. They still played with passion, however, shouting with joy as one boy scored a boundary off another.

Venu hailed the boys, introducing his friends to Kaveri and Ramu with pride. 'Look after this car for me,' he ordered them.

'We will buy you a proper bat and a cricket ball after we return,' Kaveri said impulsively, and was rewarded with a piercing whistle of approval from the smaller of the two boys. His khaki shorts, tied with a piece of string around his skinny waist, hung below his knees. She exchanged a glance with Ramu.

'Later. Later, we will feed them,' he whispered in her ear as they followed Venu.

Their young milkboy-turned-spy led them down a series of winding, interconnected lanes that had so many twists and turns that Kaveri lost all her sense of direction. She passed a man taking a succession of goats for their morning breakfast, keeping them moving with a stick. A tiny child squatted in a corner, making mud cakes, while her older sister kept a vigilant eye on her. Her chubby cheeks wobbled as she giggled, singing a song of gibberish.

'She's adorable.' Kaveri pointed her out to Ramu, seeing his lips curve up in a smile as he saw the little child's dimpling face, intent on her masterpiece.

As they passed the children, Kaveri saw the older girl swat her sister's hand when she tried to pick up a worm and place it in her mouth. The infant let out an ear-splitting wail. Lately, whenever she saw babies, she felt an intense urge to pick them up and squeeze them tightly, holding on and never letting go. Strange, for someone like her who had never really played with dolls as a child. She was always happiest with her nose in a book, and had never really cared much for babies. Her thoughts turned to a discussion that she and Ramu had had several months back. It was soon after she had moved to Bangalore, and she realised Bhargavi was very keen for she and Ramu to have children as soon as possible. After her mother-in-law had dropped an especially heavy-handed hint about the possibility of Kaveri being pregnant, she had confronted Ramu, telling him that she had no intention of having a child before she completed her studies. Ramu had comforted her, agreeing that they would do whatever she wanted. He had spoken to his mother in private, and Bhargavi had stopped raising the topic of grandchildren with her.

But now . . . Kaveri wondered if she had been too hasty. If she waited until she completed first her Intermediate, then her BSc, it would take at least five years. Now that she and Bhargavi were closer, she felt sure that her mother-in-law would help her raise a child, as she helped her run her household. Could she balance motherhood with mathematics?

Lost in her thoughts, Kaveri realised she had no idea where she was. She stopped as Venu drew up at the dead end of a dusty alley. On one side, a rickety wooden fence separated them from a marshy wetland. On the other side, a high brick wall blocked their view of what lay behind. Venu pulled them closer and whispered, 'This is the wall that leads to the back entrance of the tent in which you watched the circus show.'

'How do we get in?' Kaveri looked around. The wall was tightly fitted with bricks, all the way to the top. It had once been painted white, but was now a grimy brown, with layers of accumulated mud and filth.

'We can climb that tree.' Venu pointed to an old banyan tree at the far end of the wall. Kaveri could not see its trunk, but one of its branches protruded over the wall, just beyond her reach.

'How . . .?' She looked around helplessly.

'Ramu *anna*. Can you hoist me onto your back?' Venu requested.

When Ramu nodded reluctantly, Venu scarpered up his back, and stood on his shoulders, his fingers straining towards the branch just out of his reach. Ramu lifted himself onto his tiptoes, giving Venu a boost with his hands. Finally, Venu grabbed the branch, and swung up onto it, breathing heavily. He pulled up his shirt, revealing a rope wrapped around his waist. After unwinding it, he tied one end to the branch and dropped the other down to the ground by their feet.

'Climb up,' he said.

Kaveri needed no further urging. Kicking off her slippers and tucking them into the waist of her sari petticoat, she started to climb up. Ramu remained below, waiting until she was safely up before following her. From there, it was surprisingly easy. Venu untied the rope, and they made their way from branch to branch before easing themselves down onto the ground on the other side of the wall.

'Be very quiet now,' Venu hissed.

They followed him as he led them to a set of stairs made from wooden crates nailed together. Taking off their footwear, they climbed up, entering a dark, dimly lit cavernous space. As Kaveri's eyes slowly grew accustomed to the darkness, she realised they were backstage, behind the curtains – they had been on the other side of the same space when they had watched the circus performance. She smelt the pungent odour of rat droppings and heard the sound of scurrying feet, looking down quickly to see several small furry bodies dart past them, running towards the exit. She covered her mouth, fighting the urge to retch.

Slowly, taking tiny breaths and walking on tiptoe, they groped their way through the pitch-dark space, not daring to switch on the torch that Ramu carried in his pocket for fear they might be spotted by Das and Suman. With the lights off, and no place for the sunlight to penetrate, the back of the stage looked deserted – like a haunted house, inhabited only by ghosts. An involuntary shudder ran down Kaveri's spine. If it were not for Ramu's solid form, following her close behind, with one hand on her waist so that they were not separated in the dark, she would have stopped, unable to proceed. Even now, the weight of dread pressed down on her, the dark seeming to get heavier with every step they took.

'Here.' Kaveri could barely hear Venu's faint whisper. He tugged at her hand, and she tugged at Ramu's, as they all stopped. He bent and opened a trapdoor set into the floor. 'Now, we can get them. There is no other way out.' Even in a whisper, Venu's voice sounded triumphant.

'Stand back,' Ramu warned. Picking up a thick iron rod that he had seen lying in the passage, he raised it high above his head, handing the torch to Kaveri. She switched it on, shining it into the small hidden room below.

'Come out. We have you surrounded,' she called, her voice reverberating, the echoes dying slowly away: '. . . surrounded . . . rounded . . . ded. . . dead . . . dead.'

32

Clever Enough to Solve
Any Puzzle

A shout of laughter came from the room below. 'The lady detective. I told you, Suman. She is clever enough to solve any puzzle, even one as complex as ours.'

Das's face appeared in the trapdoor. He looked gaunt, practically emaciated. In a crumpled white kurta and pyjama, with his overgrown beard and unkempt moustache, the man before them was a far cry from the immaculately dressed magician whom Kaveri had seen on stage. She recoiled from the stench that emanated from him.

The magician gave her a cheerful smile. 'I apologise for my lack of personal hygiene, madam detective. I am afraid the facilities are somewhat lacking in my current quarters. I have had to make do with what was available.' He made a courteous bow, and then climbed out, looking quizzically at the metal rod that Ramu still brandished, holding it high in the air like a club.

'My dear young man,' he murmured, in an impeccably clipped English accent. 'My *dear* young man. Surely there is no need for such violence.' He placed a gentle hand on the bar, and Ramu lowered it, looking apologetic.

Kaveri's heart fluttered in her chest. The man was so charismatic, he seemed to have cast a spell over Ramu. She could feel the tug he exerted too. It was easy to forget that the newspapers had marked him out as a killer. He sounded so charming, so likeable.

Das smiled at her, dropping the British accent. Now he sounded very Bengali. 'Do not be frightened of me, child. I am just an old man, nearing the end of my life. Harmless, seeking shelter – and justice. Will you not help me?' He stretched out a hand to her. Kaveri took a step back, gripping the torch. She tried to speak, but her tongue seemed glued to the roof of her mouth. She had been so worried about Das, hoping against hope that he was alive, especially for Suman's sake. She thought of all the trouble she had gone through to find him – and looked at his sanguine countenance. She felt anger building inside her.

'Baba.' Suman's face appeared in the frame of the trapdoor. The young man climbed out, looking rather worse for wear since Kaveri had last seen him. His clothes were grimy and streaked with stains, his expression annoyed. 'Do not stage a performance here. We can trust her. We should tell her the truth.'

'But that is just what I am trying to do.' Das cast an injured look at Kaveri, spreading his arms dramatically wide. 'Am I not, madam detective?'

Kaveri opened her mouth to say something – she had no idea what she planned to say, only that she needed to speak, to break the dreadful spell of fascination that this man had cast over them all. Ramu stood, frozen, in the circle of light cast by the torch, staring at Das. Venu had retreated a few steps, and was standing with his back to the curtains that separated backstage from the area where the audience sat. His eyes darted as he looked first at the magician, then at Suman, then back at the magician.

To Kaveri's horror, only a squeak came out of her mouth. Das beamed encouragingly at her, completely in control, as though egging on a favourite child to perform a trick that they were not so good at. Kaveri curled her fingers into fists, willing herself to speak. She cleared her throat.

'I think . . .' she began firmly.

Just as she was about to continue, an explosive sound echoed around the room. Kaveri jumped back as a bullet whizzed past, out of nowhere, narrowly missing Kaveri and Das.

The torch fell to one side, the light going off and leaving them in the dark. Kaveri's body jerked with fear as Ramu pulled her down, placing himself on top of her to shield her and sliding forward with her in his arms towards the trapdoor. More bullets whizzed past them as they shrank against the floor, huddling behind the open trapdoor. One – two – three – four – no, *five* more bullets.

The person holding the gun cursed violently, flinging it aside. There was something about his accent, something unfamiliar. What was it?

They heard the sound of footsteps running and then a scuffle as one huge body hit another. Kaveri recognised Das's voice, the theatrics gone from it. He was swearing in Bengali, though she could not understand the words. The other man was quiet, grimly quiet, as they grappled with each other, rolling on the floor. She strained to see what was happening, but it was too dark. She could not make out any details.

'Ah!' Das let out a satisfied exclamation. Kaveri tried again to see what was happening, but Ramu kept hold of her firmly. 'Wait, Kaveri,' he hissed into her ear. 'It is not safe to get up yet. What if the man lying in wait has another gun? Or an armed accomplice?'

They heard more footsteps, clattering down the makeshift staircase from which they had entered. Das's voice called out, 'Suman? Suman . . . I am safe, *beta*. I will take shelter. Do not follow me.'

Ramu reached for his torch and switched it on. But it must have broken when it fell to the floor, for only a faint light now came from it, in which they suddenly saw the silhouette of a tall figure crumpled against the wall. A guttural sound of suppressed anger and violence came from the figure. He got up, dragged himself across the stage with a scraping of shoes on the floor, then made off, running with a loping, limping stride, as though injured. Kaveri squinted, trying to see if she could recognise him, but it was too dark, and she could not see him clearly enough.

The sound of his footsteps faded away as he disappeared into the darkness beyond and down the stairs – leaving only silence. Ramu rolled off her, pulling Kaveri to her feet. Blinking in the near-darkness, Kaveri stood still, unable to see anyone apart from Ramu.

'Venu?' Kaveri screamed in fear. 'Venu!'

'I am here,' a small voice called out from below. 'I fell through the trapdoor. But it is alright,' he added. 'I landed on a pile of hay. It stinks here.' A small hand grappled with the entrance to the trapdoor, and Venu heaved himself up.

With an audible grunt of satisfaction, Ramu got his torch working properly again. Immediately, they were able to make out a trail of blood across the stage. Ramu moved the light, following it. A few feet away, prone on the dusty floor, Suman's body lay motionless. Only the slight breathing as his chest moved up and down, and the trickle of blood from the flesh wound on his scalp, indicated that he was alive.

33

Answers to a Few Questions

Ramu carried Suman to the steps, Kaveri leading the way in the faint light of the torch. Venu followed behind, bringing up the rear. They looked around nervously as they went, fearing that the man with the gun might return at any point. But there was no sign of him. As they reached the entrance, the torch flickered, then went out completely.

'Thank god, we made it out,' Kaveri said, relieved.

Ramu placed Suman gently on the ground. 'I'll go get the car,' he said, setting off at a run, leaving Kaveri and Venu to watch over Suman. Kaveri squatted down, wiping the dust off Suman's face with her sari tenderly, as Venu sat cross-legged on the ground, looking anxiously first at Suman, then at her. They watched as his chest heaved up and down with each breath, too tense to speak to each other.

In a few minutes, Ramu was back. 'How is Suman? Will he be alright?' Kaveri asked.

'It's just a flesh wound. It looks worse than it is,' Ramu reassured her.

She felt lightheaded with relief. They lifted Suman into the back seat, and Ramu got in with him. His scalp wound was still bleeding freely, and Ramu placed Suman's head in his lap, holding down on the wound with his kerchief to staunch the flow.

Kaveri hurried into the driver's seat, and Venu got in on the other side. 'Where do we take him?' she asked her husband.

'Not to the hospital. Dr Roberts will see him, and word might get to Inspector Ismail. Let's take him to Mala's house.'

She drove quickly, keeping to the smaller lanes, trying to stay away from places where the police might spot them. Her heart pounded as she drove, making an irregular rat-tat-tat sound as it beat against her breastbone. Now that the worst of the imminent danger was over, she felt lightheaded. She dug the nails of her free hand deep into her palm, welcoming the pain, and the growing clarity of thought that came with it.

Mala had built a new house at the edge of the city, protected by a high hedge that shielded them from curious eyes. They drove in, and Venu hopped out to warn Narsamma of their arrival. Ramu carried Suman inside, placing him on the diwan in the drawing room. He blinked his eyes, slowly returning to consciousness. The blood at his temple had congealed, and Ramu sponged it with a cloth dipped in hot water, cleaning a scratch on his neck.

'Baba? Where is my father?' Suman pushed Ramu's hand away from his body, looking around him wildly.

'Your father is safe,' Ramu reassured him. 'He escaped. He called after you, saying he was fine, and would take shelter. You should not follow him.' He leaned forward, inspecting Suman for injuries, placing a hand on his kurta sleeve.

Suman flushed, sitting up abruptly and dislodging Ramu's hand. 'I am fine,' he muttered, looking nervously at Mala and Kaveri. 'I don't need any help.' He dabbed at his neck with his sleeve, trying to mop a trickle of water. Noticing him shiver, Mala handed him a shawl, and he wrapped himself in its folds, hunching his shoulders slightly.

Ramu stepped back from his patient, raising his eyebrows at Kaveri. Kaveri sat down in front of Suman, holding him by the chin and forcing him to meet her eyes. 'We need some answers from you. And this time, the real ones.' Looking at the dejected slight form of the young man lying in front of her, she suppressed a feeling of pity. Mala stood by her side, staring at her in surprise. But time was running out. She wished she could wait until he was feeling better, but they needed to find Das, and understand what was going on quickly. The pageant was just a day away.

Ramu slipped an arm around Suman's shoulders, helping him to sit up and sip from a glass of hot tea with extra sugar that Mala slipped into his hands. As he drank, the colour came back to his pale face. He scrubbed his eyes. 'Ask me anything, Kaveri *didi*.'

'Promise you will answer me with the truth, first.' Kaveri's voice was tinged with bitterness, as she thought of all the ways in which Suman had stonewalled her, refusing to tell her they had fled from Bengal, that his father's name was Chatterjee, or anything about his mother's death. He had even hidden the fact that Kailash was his uncle. Her brief encounter with his father, the master magician, had shaken her. Das was an expert at manipulating people. Suman had seemed so different from him – straightforward and likeable. But even Suman had kept so many secrets from them. How could she trust him now?

Stung by thoughts of how Das had seemed to have a hold on her in just a few minutes, her words came out more harshly than she'd intended. 'Why did you lie to me?'

'Lie about what?' His voice was wary.

'So at least you do not deny you lied.'

She saw him recoil. Even Mala looked at her askance.

'If you knew what forces we were up against, how desperate we were . . .'

'How will we know, unless you help us understand?' she demanded, as Ramu sat down next to her, placing a calming arm around her shoulders. 'Help us get the complete picture. Only then can we help you.'

Suman sat still for a long time. Then he let out a defeated sigh. 'I don't know where to start.'

'We know some of the story,' Kaveri said. 'We know that your father's real name is Chatterjee. He fled from Calcutta with you after your . . .' She hesitated, not knowing how to finish her sentence. 'After your mother was killed,' she said quietly.

'How did you find out?' Suman demanded, turning his astonished gaze to Ramu and Kaveri in turn. 'Everyone told us you are a most excellent detective. But I did not think you would be able to see into the past.'

Ramu pressed her shoulder gently with his hand in warning, and she pressed her foot against his, in silent acknowledgement. They did not know how much they could trust Suman. It was better not to tell him about the newspaper article, Kaveri decided. Let him think she was a master detective with extraordinary powers – he would be less inclined to hide things from her in the future.

'Never mind how I found out. Tell me what happened in Calcutta. Why did you flee to Bangalore?'

'My mother was a famous acrobat,' Suman began. Kaveri looked around the room. Mala and Narsamma had settled down on the floor, leaning against the wall. Venu squatted next to them. Suman paid them no attention. His eyes were intent on Kaveri and Ramu.

'She had a star act in the circus – a serpentine dance, on horseback, which she was famous for.' Suman's voice was filled with pride. 'She trained her dog Percy to accompany her – the only somersault dog in the world, they called him.' He paused to clear his throat, before continuing, 'Ma met Baba when she was only fifteen, and he was eighteen. They eloped a year later, marrying against the wishes of their families. It was an inter-caste marriage, but they didn't care. My parents were so in love, you should have seen them. Always whispering together, laughing, giggling like children.'

Kaveri reached out and grasped Ramu's hand, still resting on her shoulder. She saw his face twist with sympathy.

'Everything was fine for a few years. Then, they were approached by a group of circus performers. They told my parents that they were being cheated by the owner – they both performed such dangerous acts, putting their life in daily peril – and earned a pittance for it.' Suman's voice was bleak. 'They were right, of course. Well-dressed men and women visit the circus daily, dressed in silk and brocade, dripping with diamonds and rubies. When they like a performance, they show their appreciation by tossing coins or notes to us. We smile and pick them up, like well-trained dogs, picking up a thrown ball or a bone.'

Kaveri winced, remembering the turbaned gentleman who had sat near them in the first-class seats that night at the circus, throwing rupee notes onto the stage for the performers to pick up.

'Owners always keep most of the profits.' Suman gave Kaveri a wry smile. 'My parents didn't really care about money. Baba wanted to move to a smaller town with my mother, leaving the circus to perform on their own. He didn't like cities too much. My mother was a follower of Gandhiji. The only jewellery she ever had was a gold chain which she gave away when she was twelve – after she heard him make an appeal to all Indians to donate their gold for the independence movement. Her father beat her severely, but she didn't care. She decided that she would never buy or accumulate any jewellery.' Suman pointed at his own bare neck. 'My father followed her example when they got married, and I did the same.'

'What did the circus performers ask your parents to do?' Venu asked.

'To join them. They planned to steal from the audience. Using my father's and mother's show as distractions. My parents refused to join them, but what could they do to prevent them? Their shows were the centrepieces of the circus. They were so good that the audience did not pay any attention to their surroundings when either of my parents was on stage, focusing only on their acts. The circus performers began to target the wealthy circusgoers in the expensive front-row seats. When the seating area was dark and the audience's attention fixed on the spotlit stage, they moved silently through the tent, snipping chains and stealing purses. They mocked my parents for refusing to share in the spoils.'

'But didn't the circus owner realise what was going on?' Venu looked confused. 'He couldn't have been so stupid, not if they were doing this in every performance.'

'He realised.' Suman nodded. 'After one or two instances of this, he asked the police to station extra guards in plainclothes, spread across the circus. The gang saw this, and blamed my parents. They had nothing to do with it. But by then, my father said they should have realised the dangers of staying there. He blames himself for not foreseeing what would happen, and taking the decision to leave the circus.'

'Why didn't he?' Kaveri asked. Das seemed like a genius to her. She couldn't believe he did not have the basic common sense to escape what seemed like a dangerous situation – even to her, hearing about it third-hand.

Suman looked weary. 'My parents had started to quarrel by then, and were consumed by their own differences. My mother was obsessed by the desire for an independent India. She started to spend most of her free time working for the movement.' Suman looked up at Kaveri. 'The man you saw in handcuffs at the meeting in Bangalore? That is my mother's brother, Kailash. He started attending the meetings first, then convinced her to join him. My father was very worried about her safety, and mine. He warned her that she was playing with fire, but she refused to listen.'

Kaveri blinked in relief. When Wilks had told her that Kailash was Das's brother-in-law, she had been shocked, her faith in Suman shattered. Now that he had revealed this to her of his own volition, she felt her trust in him beginning to return.

'What happened then?' Venu asked.

'Then the circus gang started burgling homes,' Suman said. 'They noted the names and addresses of people who had booked tickets for the circus, targeting Indian shopkeepers and businessmen. Many of them were supporters of the movement. They didn't declare their profits so that they could avoid paying taxes to the British. The money they had saved was kept in cash, at home, to be used for the movement. The circus thieves exploited this. The wealthy men they robbed would not report the thefts. They did not want too much attention focused on their homes, or their assets – how they earned their money, and where they spent it.'

'This sounds too complicated and well-planned for a group of amateur thieves,' Ramu said.

Suman returned his gaze, his eyes serious. 'We think so too. Some of it is quite hazy to me. I was only about eleven then. My father filled in some of the missing details. He suspected that there was someone else masterminding the thefts. He never found out if his suspicions were correct, though. Perhaps he never will.' Sweat trickled down from his forehead to his neck, and he swiped at it with his sleeve. 'The word started to spread within the business community, and they began to secure their homes with grilles and bars. This was when the gang approached my mother. She had a body like rubber and they knew Ma would be able to squeeze through the grilles and gain entrance while others would not.'

Suman's voice trailed off. Kaveri reached out and smoothed his sweaty hair away from his forehead tenderly, fighting a pang of guilt for keeping him talking when he looked so tired and strained. She brought him a glass of water, and they waited while he took a series of thirsty gulps, draining the glass.

'Ma refused, but she did not tell my father at first – by then, they were barely speaking to each other. She wanted to leave the circus and work for the movement full-time. He resisted, as he feared it would place the two of us in danger. Eventually, one day when they had cornered her, she told my father what was going on. He was alarmed and tried to convince her that they needed to flee Calcutta, to lie low for a while. She didn't want to leave the movement but when he pointed out that her stubbornness was putting me at risk, she reluctantly agreed. They planned to leave that night. My father took me out to purchase a few things we would need to take, while my mother stayed back to pack. That afternoon, while my father and I were at the market, someone entered our room and attacked my mother. She fought back, but in the struggle her attacker killed her. Whoever it was, they escaped.' His voice was thick with tears.

'That's when your father was arrested,' Kaveri guessed gently.

'The circus performers pinned the blame on Baba. They told the police my parents fought a lot, that my father was a jealous man who murdered my mother because he believed she was in love with someone else. Fortunately, my father had admirers in influential positions. One of them helped him escape.' Suman rubbed his tired eyes. 'We fled Calcutta in the middle of the night, without a word to anyone. We didn't even tell my uncle Kailash. He knew my father was innocent. But Baba was very bitter. He hated the fact that my mother had chosen to confide in her brother, but not in him.'

34

A Fantastic Tale

'You should have told us about this right at the start,
yet you kept it concealed. How do we know you are
telling us the truth now?' Ramu demanded.

'At first, I didn't know if I could trust you to believe me,'
Suman said, reaching out a hand in appeal. 'I was scared.
My father is still in hiding from the police, accused of my
mother's murder. At my mother's funeral, my father had
made me promise never to share this information with
anyone else. It was only now, when I met my father again
and asked him, that he gave me permission to tell you.'

'Why did you not tell the police the truth, instead of
running from them in Calcutta?' Ramu still sounded
doubtful.

'Do you think people like us can tell the police anything, once they have made up their minds?' Mala scoffed.
'You are a high born, well-respected doctor. I'm sure the
police would believe anything you tell them. Das is a circus
performer. He must have told them, but they probably did
not listen to a word he said.'

Suman shot her a grateful glance. 'Exactly.'

'Did you resume contact with your uncle after that?' Kaveri asked.

Suman shook his head. 'My father wanted to leave *everything* behind. We never spoke of the world we once inhabited. He worked his way up from the bottom, once again making his way into smaller circuses, where he gained a name for himself. He grew a beard and a moustache, and stayed away from the big cities, worried that someone would recognise him. A month back, he got an invitation to come to Bangalore and Mysore for a special set of performances, timed around the Prince's visit. After all these years, he felt it would be safe to accept, especially since it was only for a few performances.' Suman's voice trailed off.

'Go on,' Ramu urged Suman. 'What happened next?'

'The rest of the story is only what I learned secondhand, from my father – when we reunited again.' Suman looked shamefaced. 'I didn't reveal all of the secret message my father sent on the paper, Kaveri *didi*. It was in Bengali, so you didn't realise. My father also told me where he was hiding but I was scared that the word would spread – Uma aunty told me how close you are to the other women in the Bangalore Detectives Club. I know you trust all of them' – he gave Mala and Narsamma an apologetic look – 'but secrets can spread, even if nobody intends to let out the news, and I didn't want the police to get to know where my father was. After Ramu *dada* dropped me off in the rabbit house, I made my way there on foot, sneaking back into the circus.'

Kaveri nodded at him. It still stung that he had not confided in her completely. Still, if it had been *her* father in hiding, his life threatened, would she have done anything differently? She thought of the many secrets she had kept from Ismail, whom she considered one of her closest friends – and kept quiet.

'Baba said that Pailwan Harish called my father to his room on the very first day. We don't know how he had found out, but he knew everything about my father. He threatened to reveal my father's real name to the police. Baba said he didn't know what to do. If he refused, they would have him thrown behind bars – and he was worried about leaving me alone. So he decided to trick them, making them believe he would fall in with their plans.'

'What *did* they want him to do?' Kaveri asked.

'The police in Bangalore are far better than the police in Calcutta, it seems. Far less corrupt. Your friend Inspector Ismail had started to investigate the thefts, and quickly realised there was a single connecting thread. Everyone whose home had been burgled was out at the circus. It was so simple and obvious, but the police in Calcutta had never figured it out.' Suman shrugged. 'The thieves must have paid off someone very senior in the police department there.'

Kaveri felt a surge of pride as she thought of dear, upright, incorruptible Inspector Ismail.

'The police began to station plainclothes men at every empty house and the thieves realised they could not continue for long in Bangalore. They decided to make two big, final hauls. They told my father to announce a grand new performance, the likes of which had never been seen before, to help the thieves gain entry into the circus tent, and grab the audience's valuables. After that, they said they had one last job for him to do – at the pageant for Prince Edward. That was going to be their last haul. They wanted him to perform for the Prince, and while the attention of the Prince and his entourage was focused on Baba's performance, they planned to explode a series of small bombs and firecrackers. In the ensuing smoke and confusion, they would make their final haul and then escape. Baba knew he could not afford to agree. The police would be sure to arrest him, assuming he was complicit in the plan.'

'So that's why there were so many masked men in the circus! So that no one would see their faces, and be able to recognise them at their second, and bigger, attempt at the pageant,' Kaveri burst out. 'Was Anandi's husband Pawan part of the gang?'

'He was. That man was pure evil.' Suman shuddered. 'My father convinced them that he had agreed. They did not trust him though, keeping a close eye on him from that moment on, following us during the day and locking us into our rooms at night so that we could not escape. No locked door can stop him, but he had me to think of. If he was alone he would have managed to disappear before the night of the circus. He toyed with the idea of approaching Inspector Ismail, but after his experiences in Calcutta, he was worried about placing his trust in the police.

'Baba was at his wits' end; he didn't know what to do. Then while visiting Raja Market to buy some props for the show, he spotted my uncle Kailash on the street. He felt that providence had sent Kailash *mama* to him, to show him a way out of his predicament. My father had grown a long flowing beard, and changed his hairstyle, but he could not deceive Kailash *mama*, who knew him so well. My uncle had been searching for us ever since we left Calcutta. He and I were very close, and he knew that my father would never have killed my mother, no matter how much they fought. Someone had told him about a new magician in Belgaum who was garnering quite a reputation for himself. Hoping it might be Baba, my uncle had made his way there – but found we had left for Bangalore. He had followed, and started loitering near the clothes markets, hoping he might see one of us there, coming to order costumes for the show.

'As soon as Kailash *mama* had spotted Baba, he wrote him a message informing him where they could safely meet then pretended to bump into him by accident, slipping the note into his pocket. Baba pretended to go to the bathroom, then climbed out of a back window, giving the man who had been following him the slip. He and Kailash *mama* met on the roof of a factory, an isolated spot where they could speak privately without fear of interruption. Kailash *mama* helped Baba hatch a plan in the next half an hour. After that, Baba returned to the circus.'

'What was the plan?' Venu was bouncing up and down on his toes with curiosity.

'My uncle had heard of you.' Suman turned and looked at Kaveri. 'Even in distant Calcutta, people have heard of the famous lady detective who takes up the cause of justice and truth. Baba wanted to attract the attention of someone who would investigate the case, and expose the thieves – but be immune to political influence or corruption. Kailash *mama* told my father that we needed to get you interested. You would find out the truth, and then you would let everyone know. They knew that Inspector Ismail was your friend, and thought he would listen to you.'

'Why not simply *tell* me the truth?' Kaveri burst out. 'Wouldn't that have been easier than all of this rigmarole?'

'Baba did not think that you would believe such a fantastic tale,' Suman said. 'You did not know him, had no proof that he was telling you the truth. Everyone told him that you were not a normal detective, taking cases for hire, for payment. You took up the cases you were interested in, to see justice done, deciding on your own. He wanted you to witness his disappearance and want to solve the mystery yourself. That was why he sent you the front-row tickets, dropping them off to Ramu *dada*'s office.'

'So *your father* sent us the tickets,' Kaveri said as she reached for her diary, crossing out a line from one of her lists. 'That clears up one more of our unanswered questions. Why did your father keep this a secret even from you, though?'

Suman gave her a sheepish look. 'I am a very bad liar. From childhood, I have always been incapable of bluffing. Baba knew that he had only one hope of convincing you to take up the case. If I really didn't know what had become of him, he knew I would be frantic with worry.' He held her gaze, his eyes large and earnest as they fixed on her face. 'I wouldn't blame you if you turned away from me now and refused to help us. But it was Baba who held the truth back from you, not me. I know it seems like he manipulated you – and perhaps he did. But I beg of you, before you decide, put yourself in his shoes. What else could he have done?'

'You are right.' Kaveri's voice held a tinge of bitterness, however. 'Your father has made it difficult for me to trust you completely now. But I will not step back from the case. For your sake.'

Suman knelt at her feet, holding her hands. 'I owe you my life, *didi*. Please trust me now. I need your help to save my father.'

'Where is he now?' Ramu leaned forward.

Suman looked uncomfortable. 'He must be in hiding, but even I don't know where. Kailash *mama* has fled to another city, but said it would be better for us that we don't know where he is. He charged my father with the task of foiling the gang's plans for the Prince's visit.' He turned to Kaveri. 'Pailwan Harish's gang doesn't want to get arrested, so they will create a false trail, leaving fake evidence to implicate the freedom fighters in the theft. Pamphlets with independence slogans and speeches, and fake identity cards with my father's photograph. My father stole into their shack one night, and saw the material they had collected. If they are allowed to proceed, the independence movement will lose its reputation, and many of its most ardent supporters. The businessmen who contribute funds for the movement will stop, believing them to be common criminals. People like my uncle conduct raids to support the movement, but they are not common thieves.'

He turned to Kaveri, pleading. 'Help me. My father had a plan in mind to find the thieves and unmask them at the time of the crime. But he didn't tell me what it was, fearing that we might be captured by the police at any time. Now that Baba is gone, I don't know what he plans to do, or how we can help him. But I can't sit around and do nothing, allowing Pailwan Harish's gang to get away with their plans. If they do, I will never be able to prove the innocence of my father.'

'Or the integrity of the movement,' Kaveri said soberly. She thought of the rice painting stall that she had seen on the list, but something prevented her from telling Suman. She was not sure if that was Das's doing, but she did not want to risk news of her plans getting back to the magician.

'We must do something,' she agreed, looking around the room. 'But what?'

35

A Sudden Attack

'What can we do now?' Venu sounded frantic in the back seat of the car.

Kaveri and Ramu had left Suman with Mala and Narsamma, who promised to keep him well hidden while they searched for Das.

'Let's go to the Women's Home and find Anandi. She must have started to work at the float by now. Perhaps she has seen or heard something,' Ramu suggested.

'Tomorrow evening, the Prince will be at the gala. By then, it will be too late to do anything.' Venu's voice sounded thin with worry.

'It won't be too late. Even if we let Das get captured, we will not let the reputation of the independence movement be compromised,' Kaveri said firmly, squashing her doubt.

'At least we now know why Inspector Ismail has been so distant from all of us,' Venu said, poking her with a bony finger.

'*All* of us?' Kaveri craned her neck to the back seat, giving him an incredulous look.

'Did you think it was just you? He has stopped giving any jobs to me and the other boys too. He shoos us away when we come close to the police station. I think he is caught in a hard place. He is looking out for us. He knows something very bad is going to happen, and wants to keep us safe.'

Kaveri sat back, mulling this over. Venu was right. She had been so oblivious to everything else around her that she had not realised that her favourite policeman was not just blocking her, but everyone else from speaking with him. He was not rejecting them – he was only trying to protect them. She felt much lighter, as though an enormous boulder had slowly been rolled off her chest.

In a few short minutes, they had arrived at the Women's Home. Shanthi stood at the entrance, watering the plants.

'Anandi? She is at the lake, working at the float. Why do y—'

Before Shanthi could complete her sentence, they were back in the car, heading towards the lake.

The site of the pageant was a hubbub of activity. A makeshift stage had been built with wooden logs, over which a tent in white, red and gold had been erected to provide shelter from the sun and wind. The sides were open, and the rear of the tent looked onto the calm waters of Bellandur Lake. Upon the lake, a number of coracle boats, *theppa*, floated in formation, each decorated with clay lamps. In the evening gloom, the lights glistened on the water like coruscating diamonds, shining like radiant stars onto the stage where women were lined up wearing Bharatanatyam costumes. The pleats of their blue and gold silk saris fanned out from their waists like peacock feathers. An elderly lady, bent almost double, held a thick bamboo stick in her hand, inspecting the dancers as they got into formation, whacking their hands and legs to make them hold the precise positions she wanted.

'Ouch,' Venu said in sympathy. 'We need to tell this *ajji* not to hit all the *akkas*. They are trying their best.'

'Shhh,' Kaveri hissed back. 'Focus, Venu. We need to find Anandi.'

They could not see her anywhere on stage.

'Let's split up,' Kaveri suggested.

'I'll look near the lake. You and Venu go together on the other side,' Ramu agreed. 'We'll meet back here in fifteen minutes.'

Kaveri and Venu hurried down the stage, looking for Anandi. On one side, they saw two bullock carts laden high with provisions. Men and women lined up to carry bundles of firewood, sacks of rice and dal, and tins of ghee, taking them from the cart to a building in the distance.

Venu's eagle eyes spotted Anandi first. 'There, *akka*.' He pointed to a figure in a nondescript green sari. Anandi carried two hens upside down, holding them by their feet as they squawked, struggling to free themselves.

'There are too many people around. I'll follow her. Maybe she will go to a quieter place where we can tell her everything we learned from Suman. You go and get Ramu *anna*,' Kaveri urged. She watched Venu run off, then followed Anandi.

Anandi entered a room and handed the chickens to a man, who stuffed them into a cage. 'I need at least ten more to make enough chicken cutlets for tomorrow,' he shouted to her above the din. 'Go to the back of the compound, towards the godown. Ask Lokesh to put them in a box for you.'

Keeping behind the line of trees on the side of the compound, Kaveri followed her at a distance. How would

Ramu and Venu find them now? But if she went back to fetch them, she might lose Anandi. She decided to keep moving.

In her second of hesitation, she had lost sight of Anandi. She sped up, rounding the corner, then pulled up short.

Anandi was standing against the wall, shrinking away from Pailwan Harish. He reached out and grabbed her by the throat, raising her above the ground. She thrashed her heels, extending her hands into claws and trying to grab at his eyes, but he fended her off with ease.

'Thieving bitch,' he swore at her viciously. 'Give me the gold!' He released the pressure on her throat for an instant.

'Let me go. I don't know what you're talking about,' Anandi gasped, trying to pull his hands away from her throat.

'Liar!' Harish screamed. 'You killed Pawan for it, and then my brother. Give me back what you stole from us.'

Kaveri started to run towards him, but slipped on a decayed pile of leaves, going down with a thud. She spat out the mud she had swallowed, scrabbling for purchase on the slippery pile of compost, trying to regain her footing so that she could save Anandi.

'I didn't kill anyone. Let me go. I can't breathe,' Anandi pleaded, shaking her head from side to side.

'All the gold is gone. Everything we collected from our last haul. I know you have it. It's not in Pawan's hut. I sent my brother to search for it, and he ended up dead too. Why did you kill him?' He shook Anandi like a rag doll. 'Tell me where the gold is, or I'll kill you now.'

Kaveri recovered her balance and ran towards them, watching in terror as Anandi's cries for help became weaker, her struggling less vigorous. She looked around for help, but no one was in sight. She was still yards away. She would not reach them in time.

As Anandi's body went limp and her eyes rolled to the back of her head, a slim, athletic figure swung over the wall. Suman? Kaveri blinked her eyes rapidly. It couldn't be. He had promised to stay safely hidden in Mala's house.

Suman advanced towards the weightlifter. Focused on Anandi, Harish paid no attention to him. The man was huge and burly, and Suman slight of build. Kaveri held her breath, worried. But Suman must have had years of practice training with his parents in the circus. He raised his legs, kicking the weightlifter in the head with one swift move. The hefty man went down, collapsing heavily onto the mud. Anandi fell too, but Suman grabbed her by the arms and pulled her up. 'Quickly, run.'

Kaveri finally reached them, looking at Anandi in worry. She was trying to stand, holding one hand pressed to her side as she gasped for breath, taking huge gulps of air. Her throat was mottled in red and brown, the marks of Harish's hand clearly visible.

'We must hide. The whole gang will be here soon,' Suman urged.

'Let's go to the car. I can drive us away.' Kaveri led them around the building, drawing them into the line of shelter provided by the tall Ashoka trees lining the compound wall. Anandi stumbled as she ran, heaving for breath, leaning on Kaveri and Suman, who half-supported and half-carried her.

Where was Ramu? Kaveri looked around frantically for him as they neared the car. She eyed the few feet of open space between them and the Ford. Could they reach it in time without being accosted by the wrestler and his friends?

But when they reached the car, it was not the wrestlers who met them, but the police. Kaveri barely noticed as Suman slipped away, melting into the shadow of the trees. If the police had seen him, they gave no sign of it. All their attention was focused on the two women walking towards them, one supporting the other.

Kaveri fell back, holding Anandi tightly as she looked at the implacable face of Inspector Ismail. The man whom she thought was one of her dearest friends stepping forward to arrest another of her friends?

'Anandi Pawan. I arrest you in the name of the law, for murdering your husband Pawan by stabbing him with a knife.' Ismail moved towards Anandi, holding out handcuffs.

'Noo . . .' Kaveri shielded Anandi with her body. 'How can you arrest her? You *know* she is not guilty. She was with us at the circus. She couldn't have killed Pawan.'

Ismail ignored her, his eyes intent on Anandi. He held out the handcuffs towards her. Tears ran down Kaveri's cheeks as Anandi stepped out from behind her, holding out her hands to the inspector. 'Don't worry about me, *akka*. You take care of yourself,' she whispered. 'Find the man who murdered my husband, and Pailwan Ganesh. That is the only way to set me free.'

Just as Ismail fitted the handcuffs onto Anandi, Ramu found them. Venu stood beside him, eyes wide with terror as he watched the police take Anandi away. A constable placed a heavy hand on her back, forcing her into the police car. Two burly constables sat on either side of her, hemming her in. She looked tiny and defenceless, and Kaveri's stomach churned with bile as she leant against Ramu's shoulders. Ramu's gaze was filled with sorrow as he stroked Kaveri's hair.

'Surely Ismail can see the marks on Anandi's throat where Harish tried to strangle her,' Kaveri whispered to herself. 'Why is he doing this?' Taking control of her tangled emotions, she straightened up and stepped away from Ramu's side, moving towards the inspector.

But Ismail only stepped away from her, getting into the vehicle and closing the door in her face.

36

An Explanation
Is Forthcoming

Kaveri collapsed into tears, sobbing as Ramu held her tightly. He helped her into the car and drove them back to the Women's Home. He drove as fast as he could, keeping one hand on Kaveri's and casting worried glances at her as he navigated the streets. Fortunately, at this time of day there was little traffic, so they arrived at the Home after no time at all.

'Where is Anandi?' Bhargavi and Shanthi asked, hurrying forward. Shanthi stopped when she saw Kaveri's stricken face. 'Is she dead?'

'Inspector Ismail arrested her and took her away, charged with Pawan's murder,' Kaveri said bitterly. 'How can he arrest her without any proof?'

Her legs felt like rubber. Ramu guided her to a chair, keeping a supportive arm around her waist. 'Why would Ismail be acting so strangely, Kaveri?' he said. 'He helped the hungry young urchins with the rat-catching exercise, helped Anandi before . . . why would he now turn against her – and us? I wonder if we are being too quick to jump to judgement.'

Shanthi's practical voice cut through Kaveri's tangled emotions as she processed what Ramu had said. 'If you get so involved in a case that you feel ill, how is it going to help Anandi?' she said. 'Come. Let us go to the kitchen. Wash your face and have something to eat. Then we can talk.'

'No, I will take her home,' Ramu interrupted. 'She is weak, and needs to sleep.' When Kaveri started to object, he stopped her with a sympathetic look. 'When did you last have a good night's rest, Kaveri? You are so tired that you cannot think straight. We will go home for food, then sleep. Tomorrow, you can go to the police station and try to see Anandi.'

'I will come with you, Ramu. You cannot manage her alone.' Bhargavi cast a worried glance at Kaveri, and bustled out of the house behind them, after a hasty farewell to Shanthi.

Kaveri slept in the back seat on the way home. She barely registered eating dinner, as Bhargavi mixed rice, dal and curd into small balls, feeding her like a child. The hot food comforted her, reminding her of the *kai thutthus* that her grandmother had given her when she was a child. Ramu led her upstairs and tucked her into bed, singing one of her favourite Kannada songs to her in his husky baritone. The rumble in his voice soothed her, and she drifted off to sleep as he ran his fingers through her scalp, giving her a head massage. His fingers worked magic, pulling the tangled thoughts from her mind, and leaving it free from worry.

She slept through the night without waking, getting up only when she heard Rajamma standing at the door, calling her. 'Kaveri? A messenger has come from

Coffeepudi Lakamma's house. He says your special delivery of coffee is ready.'

'Special delivery?' Kaveri looked at the tiny alarm clock in her room. 'Nine o clock already. Why didn't you wake me?'

'Ramu and Bhargavi *ammavare* left strict instructions for me not to wake you. Ramu has gone to the hospital. He said he will be back at noon. *Ammavare* went to the Women's Home. But what do we do about this messenger? He is very insistent that you pick up the delivery immediately. He says the coffee will get spoilt.'

Kaveri looked at Rajamma blankly. She was still woolly-headed. 'Why would coffee powder get spoilt?'

'How would I know?' Rajamma tossed over her shoulder, going down the stairs. 'Oh, and Venu is also here. He took Putta for a walk, but they are now back. I gave him breakfast. You should also eat.'

Kaveri hurried downstairs, but the messenger from Lakamma had left. As she drank the hot cup of filter coffee that Rajamma placed in her hands, her brain cells, asleep until then, slowly began to awaken. 'Coffee powder? How stupid I have been.' She jumped up, waving away the plate of *uppittu* that Rajamma carried. 'Venu, wait here for me. I will return soon.'

She hurried to the car, driving as quickly as she could to Lakamma's house. When she rang the bell, Lakamma opened the door.

'Hmph. You took your own time, didn't you?' Lakamma said, ushering Kaveri inside.

Kaveri pulled up short. Mrs Ismail sat on the diwan, flipping through a magazine. Lakamma patted Kaveri reassuringly. 'I know the two of you have much to catch up on,' she said. 'I will be in the kitchen when you have finished.'

Kaveri stared blankly at Mrs Ismail. The older lady, whom she had always considered like another aunt, got up and came over to her, studying her gravely.

'My husband sent me here, Kaveri. He wanted to convey a message to you. One that he cannot risk anyone else overhearing. With the Prince of Wales visiting today, there are eyes on us all, and we need to be very careful. But Lakamma's house? Everyone comes to a coffee store to purchase coffee. And Lakamma is discreet.'

'He arrested Anandi yesterday, and threw her into jail,' Kaveri said. 'How could he do that? Doesn't he know what kinds of things can happen to innocent women in jail?' Kaveri's voice broke, and she stared accusingly at Mrs Ismail. 'I saw the conditions in the central jail when Mala was incarcerated there. The rusting iron fetters they put on her ate into her flesh, and left her with festering wounds. There were maggots in another prisoner's wounds. Anandi is so young, so vulnerable. How can she survive an experience like this?'

'My husband knew you would fret yourself sick, Kaveri. That is why he asked me to speak to you.' Mrs Ismail's voice was kind. 'He is keeping Anandi in a safe place. In a high security jail, where she has a cell to herself, and a constable standing guard over her. There is something very dangerous going on.'

'What?' Kaveri demanded.

'I can't tell you all the details. I don't even know all of it myself. But something big is being planned today. If it goes through, Ismail says it will be devastating for the future of Bangalore. The city will change. Armed police will be everywhere, interrogating innocent citizens, invading homes and searching for evidence. After the Prince's visit, Bombay has become a powder keg. My husband wants to keep Bangalore from going the same way. But if events turn ugly today, then no one will be able to stop the change. Even our Maharaja will be on the back foot, unable to stave off the brutal suppression that is underway in Bombay.'

'I went to a meeting three days ago,' Kaveri began, wanting to share the details with Mrs Ismail, but her friend leaned forward, placing a finger on Kaveri's lips to stop her.

'It is better if I am not aware of everything, Kaveri. I am only a bearer of a message. Two messages, to be exact.'

Kaveri took a deep breath and nodded, castigating herself for being too open. 'Tell me.'

'First, Anandi. She is safe. You know that Pailwan Harish suspects that Pawan made away with the gold that they stole together. They think that Anandi killed him and Pailwan Ganesh, and stole the gold. She is in danger from him – he has told everyone that he plans to kill her. My husband has arrested Anandi as that is the only way to keep her safe.' She smiled at Kaveri's astonished face. 'Yes. In times like this, when danger is all around us, the safest place to seek shelter is with other criminals. I told you that he has kept Anandi in a separate cell in the main station, where high security prisoners are kept. He has also ensured it is reasonably comfortable. Anandi will be released once the Prince leaves. By tomorrow morning, she should be back home with you.'

'What will change between now and tomorrow?' Kaveri asked.

'By tomorrow, my husband thinks that Pailwan Harish and all of his associates will also be rounded up, and in jail.' Mrs Ismail gave Kaveri a wicked smile. 'And their quarters will not be anywhere near as comfortable as Anandi's.'

Kaveri laughed, then sobered abruptly. 'What is the second message?' she asked.

'I can only tell you what I know. But there are rumours swirling in the underworld. A new man has come from outside Bangalore, the leader of the gang. He is reputed to be vicious, and will stop at nothing. His men are terrified of him, and he represents a threat to the security arrangements for the Prince's visit.'

'Can we do anything to help?' Kaveri asked.

'You should stay home. That is what my husband asks you to do. He wants to ensure that there is not a whiff of suspicion in anyone's mind that can connect you, Ramu, or anyone else in your circle to the events that take place tomorrow.'

Mrs Ismail rose, collecting her reticule and shawl. 'I have spent too much time here already. Let me leave first, from the back door. You can wait half an hour and then leave from the front, the way you came. Make sure you carry a packet of coffee powder prominently in your hands, and leave it on the dashboard of the car. And remember: stay home. Danger is everywhere.'

37

Meddlesome Woman

'I will not stay home with my embroidery while danger is rampant at the pageant today.' Kaveri's face was fierce as she looked at Ramu.

'I didn't expect you to.' Ramu's face was calm, but his fingers drummed restlessly on the chair.

Kaveri's heart melted. 'Are you worried about me? Do you want me to stay home?' She held her breath, worried what he might say.

'No, Kaveri, you will only fret and make yourself ill with worry if I ask you to stay home today. But this time, no disappearing anywhere without me. You and I – we will stick together like the strongest glue on earth.'

'I will not leave your side, even for a minute,' Kaveri promised. Her heart swelled with love for her husband. Despite her earlier wistful thoughts about being free to study in Chennai, *this* marriage was everything she had desired – and more. With Ramu at her side, she would always be free to fly – he would be beside her, always ready to give her a boost.

Before she could give him a fierce hug, Venu came running in, another small boy behind him. 'Kaveri *akka*, some of my friends have taken up odd jobs, helping to get the float ready for the Prince's visit. Here is one of them, Krishna. I thought you might have some questions for him.'

'Indeed I do.' Kaveri took the small boy by the shoulders. 'Tell me about the arrangements for today. What are the various stalls that will be there?'

'There will be so much to see, *akka*.' The little boy's eyes lit up. 'Beautiful women, like apsaras, will dance to songs from the Ramayana. There will be coracle boats with lit lamps.'

Kaveri nodded. 'We saw all this yesterday. Anything else?'

The boy blinked. 'There are bangle sellers and old ladies who will apply *goranti*, henna, to your hands. There is a stall to display English flowers and fruits. A man who paints portraits of you as you stand in front of me, on grains of rice. A woman who spells your name out in jewels. A . . .'

'A man who paints on rice?'

'Yes, *akka*, he was such a nice man. He painted a portrait of me. For free. See?' The boy reached into his shorts and pulled out a small box, showing it to Kaveri.

'How old was he?' she asked. Das could disguise his height, weight and face, but he couldn't make himself look younger than he was.

'He was old, like a *thaatha*. Why?'

'That could be Das.' Kaveri turned to Ramu. 'Let's find him and speak to him, and ask him to leave before the police find him. It is too dangerous for him to be there.'

'But how do we get in?' Ramu held out a hand. 'We need tickets. Entry to the gala is by invitation only. Even if we manage to get our hands on some tickets, by a miracle, Inspector Ismail and his men will see us, and send us back.'

'I can get you in,' Krishna piped up. 'They are short-staffed and need some people to help them clean and carry things around. They asked me to bring someone. I was just going home to fetch my brother and sister-in-law. I can take you instead.'

Venu let out an excited whoop, doing an impromptu dance as he hopped on one foot, then another. Krishna looked startled for a second, then grinned, joining him as the two boys danced around the verandah. Putta joined the excitement, contributing his barks to make a deafening noise, and Kaveri held her hands over her ears, trying to scold them, but failing to bring enough annoyance into her voice. She saw Ramu fighting a smile, and she couldn't help but wonder what he would be like with their own children.

They all stopped when they heard Suman's voice. 'What's happened?' He looked at them in astonishment. Kaveri hesitated, then decided to tell him about the stall. It was too late to keep anything from him now.

Half an hour later, after giving Suman a rapid summary, the three of them were at the venue. Ramu, Kaveri and Suman had changed into old, well-worn clothes that Rajamma had brought them.

Krishna spoke to the supervisor, introducing the four of them as his relatives, willing to take up temporary jobs. Kaveri had been worried that the supervisor might interview them and find something suspicious. She need not have, she thought. The supervisor looked stressed. His scarlet trousers and overcoat were creased, and his curly hair stood out wildly from under the brim of his scarlet cap, trimmed with gold lace. He studied them for a second, then waved them in.

'I hope you can clean well, and don't mind the police. That's all I ask for,' he muttered. 'These fools, they hired me to take charge of the event but did not tell me how many policemen there would be at the venue. So many of my staff just ran away and refused to come, they are so scared. I told the fools, "The police are here to keep you safe". But do they listen? No. Fools.' He squinted at them. 'Are you scared of the police?'

'No, sir,' Ramu exclaimed hurriedly, dragging out his words with a broad accent and looking down at his feet. 'We will work hard, sir. We are good workers, my wife and I. That is my wife's brother' – he pointed to Suman – 'and our son.' Venu came forward, folding his hands in a *namaskara*.

The supervisor exhaled heavily. 'You can't wear these awful clothes,' he said, looking them over with a critical eye. 'Everything needs to be spic and span for the Prince's visit. It's not every day that a royal from foreign lands visits us, you know.'

And thank God for that, Kaveri thought rebelliously. She kept her mouth shut, for fear she would say something that revealed her identity. She was not as good with accents as Ramu was. She shuffled her feet, trying to move further into the background, but the man barely gave her a second glance, speaking only to Ramu.

After negotiating terms and conditions, he took them into a room and handed them uniforms. Kaveri changed into a scarlet sari with gold trimming and *pallu*, while Venu, Suman and Ramu pulled on white pants, crisply starched and ironed, with white shirts. They adjusted the wide scarlet sashes they had been given, wearing them diagonally over one shoulder; Kaveri helped them secure the sashes with silver pins. As she did so she admired the pins, which featured the *gandabairunda* – the two-headed mythological bird that was the symbol of the Mysore king. 'Keep them carefully,' the supervisor had warned. 'Steal them or lose them, and you will not be paid for today's work.'

They were ready just in time, as the first sets of visitors began to arrive. Kaveri draped her pallu over her head. Ramu and Venu pulled the caps that came with their uniforms down low, obscuring their faces. They need not have worried. Invisible in the attire of waiting staff, no one gave them a second look. Richly dressed in silks and georgette, the English visitors mingled with the Indians as the crows cawed and croaked amongst the trees, occasionally trying to swoop in and grab the food. Small boys in livery stood at the edges of the tent, fending away the birds with bamboo sticks.

Ramu and Venu moved around carrying drinks on trays and stacking and removing plates of food from tables covered in white and scarlet satin. Kaveri kept her head down, mop in hand, pretending to wipe up spills. Her head swivelled from side to side as she tried to see if she could spot Das anywhere. The supervisor had placed them in the tent where food and drink were being served. The sides of the tent were open, and from there she could see another pavilion, a few feet away, where stalls were being readied for the Prince's visit later in the evening. The stalls held a variety of arts and crafts – paintings, embroidery, crochet and knitting, Indian handicrafts, and a separate section for agricultural products: English roses, apples and prodigiously sized pumpkins.

She strained her neck, but could not see anyone who looked like Das. Would she even recognise him, she wondered? He was a master of disguise, after all. She saw

Suman step back, surreptitiously surveying the pavilion. His face fell and he looked away in disappointment. Perhaps better sense had prevailed, and Das had decided not to attend after all? Kaveri thought it was unlikely. Das did not seem like a man to back away from dangerous tasks.

She froze for a second when she saw a bulky man in the uniform of a watchman on the far side of the pavilion. Harish! He looked in her direction as though he had heard her thoughts, and she stepped back into the shadows, holding her breath. His gaze moved over her as he surveyed the room before slowly moving through the crowd. Kaveri exhaled a sigh of relief – he had not recognised her.

Ramu was nowhere in sight, but she signalled to Venu and Suman with a jerk of her head. As they carefully made their way over to her, she kept an eye on the wrestler. Suman had seen him too. His eyes were intent on Harish as the wrestler made his way out of the tent.

'Hey, you. Where do you think you're going?'

Kaveri looked up and saw the supervisor advancing towards Suman and Venu, who had both been making their way towards her.

'We are out of plates, sir. Going to get new ones.' Venu pointed to a rapidly diminishing stack of white plates, each decorated with a scarlet band around the edge.

'Go, but return quickly.' The man pointed to the godown they could see behind the pavilion. 'That's where the plates are being washed and kept. Don't break anything, mind!'

'Go and fetch my husband,' Kaveri whispered to Venu. 'Come to the godown. We will find you there.'

Picking up a tray each, Suman and Kaveri made their way out of the tent. The guests were talking and laughing as they made their way around the edge of the crowd, trying to blend into the background and keep an eye on Harish. Kaveri walked past Miss Roberts, giving her a sideways glance as she did so, hoping that she would not notice her disguised as a cleaning woman. But the Englishwoman was in full flow, her attention fixed on a handsome gentleman in a topcoat with tails.

'I hope you are planning to go to Cole's Park tomorrow, sir,' she said, placing a flirtatious hand on his arm. 'I hear that the band of the Bangalore Rifle Volunteers will be playing some tunes for us there.'

The man took a hasty step back, but she followed him, holding tightly to his arm. Miss Roberts was so focused on her quarry that she did not even blink as Kaveri slipped past her.

Where was Ramu? Kaveri fretted, worrying that Venu would not find him in time.

They kept among the trees, following Harish at a safe distance. He was taking the same path that their supervisor had just pointed out to them, towards the godown. As they neared it, they saw a stack of clean plates on a table in front. Setting down their trays in a corner, they looked around for the wrestler. Where had the man disappeared to?

As she looked around, Kaveri caught sight of Ramu arriving. She took his elbow and rapidly explained the situation to him. 'Let's go around to the back of the godown.'

Ramu nodded, pulling Suman and Venu with them.

They stayed out of sight, fanning out to look for Harish. After a few minutes of fruitless searching, Kaveri saw Suman running back to them, swift and noiseless on bare feet. He pointed in the direction from which he had come, gesturing to them to follow him. After a few yards, they saw Harish. He was standing behind a wide pillar in the godown, talking softly to another man, who was short and stocky. The short man handed him a parcel wrapped in newspaper.

'What is that?' Ramu mouthed to Kaveri, moving his lips silently.

'Wait here,' Kaveri mouthed back, sliding past Suman and Venu, and edging closer to the men. They were involved in an animated conversation, and did not look up. She kept her head down, concentrating on the grass. It had rained earlier in the day and the ground was wet. She sent up a silent thanks to the weather gods. The ground she walked on was covered with twigs and leaves. If it was drier, a snap of a twig or a crackle of a leaf would have given her away.

Kaveri sniffed the air, edging closer to the men. It carried a smell she recognised from a school field trip she'd taken with her chemistry class to a factory producing festival crackers. *Gunpowder.*

She made her way back to the others, whispering rapidly to Venu, 'There are explosives in those boxes. Run, find Inspector Ismail quickly. Send him to arrest these men. They should not leave with the explosives in their hands.'

Kaveri watched Venu run off, hoping that the police would return before the men disappeared. Then she felt a hand tugging at her sari. She looked up.

'I think it is better for me to disappear,' Suman said softly. 'I don't want the police to see me, to arrest me like Anandi. You will never find Baba if I am not there.'

Kaveri nodded, pushing him with her hand as she heard a set of piercing whistles cut through the air. Suman moved swiftly, merging into the trees. She looked up, grateful to see three policemen heading their way, guns in hand. Ismail led them, and once again, Kaveri found herself marvelling at how light-footed the bulky policeman could be.

As soon as they heard the whistles, the wrestler and his accomplice froze. After a second of indecision, Harish stowed the parcel wrapped in paper behind a box and turned to run. Kaveri and Ramu looked at each other in horror. The police were too far away. The men would easily escape.

Nodding to each other in unspoken accord, Kaveri and Ramu stepped into the path of the two men. Harish's accomplice tried to move around Ramu. Ramu tripped him, jumping onto his back and holding him down as the sound of pounding footsteps grew louder.

Harish stepped closer to Kaveri. 'I should have known we would find you here. Move out of my path, or I will break your bones.'

Despite her *kalari* training, Kaveri knew she could not tackle someone of Harish's size. One quick glance at Ramu told her that he could not help – his hands were full trying to restrain the short man, who bucked under his arms, screaming insults at him. The police were a few feet away – unless she did something, Harish would escape.

As Harish advanced upon her, Kaveri looked around, spying a stack of ghee tins nearby. She lunged towards the pile, swiftly twisting off the lids from a couple of tins and toppling them on the ground. The sticky ghee poured out, mixing with the wet leaves and twigs, forming a slick mess that spread across the slippery ground. Kaveri stepped aside, watching as the weightlifter, feeling his feet slide beneath him, fell with a crash to the ground, knocking his head against a pillar as he did so. His head slumped down to his chest; he'd knocked himself out cold.

In seconds, the police had arrived, surrounding Harish and his accomplice, giving Ramu a helping hand as they placed the two men in handcuffs.

Ismail raised an eyebrow at Kaveri. 'I did not expect to find you here,' he said drily. 'Though I should have known. You are not very good at following instructions.'

Kaveri felt the pressure of Ramu's hand pushing on her back in warning. She held her tongue, only pointing to show Ismail where the parcels that the men had been holding had been hidden. One policeman moved forward, opening the parcels carefully as Ismail waved the others back for their own safety. Kaveri held onto Ramu's shoulder for support, standing on her tiptoes to peer at the open boxes. She ignored Inspector Ismail, who was shaking his head at her. Inside the boxes were a number of roundish objects with long pieces of thread sticking out of them.

'Handmade bombs.' One of the constables emitted a relieved whistle. 'There must be dozens of them here. Enough to blow up this entire place.'

'Mrs Murthy, once again, we must offer you our gratitude,' Ismail said gravely. 'And you, Dr Murthy. We have been on the trail of these men for a long while. But the police are obvious, easy to spot, and they kept themselves well hidden from us. As usual, you have been successful where we have been less able.' He gave her a long look. 'However, you placed yourself in danger. Again. I am less pleased about that.'

Kaveri nodded, stepping back from his displeasure as Ramu pulled her against him. She knew that she had openly disobeyed the policeman's instructions. But if she had not done so, the men might have got away with their plans to detonate the bombs.

Ismail's men hauled the handcuffed wrestlers away, while Venu was deputed to fetch pails of water from the well outside to douse the bombs and render them harmless. As Ismail moved away from Kaveri and Ramu to direct his men, he looked over his shoulder. With an unmistakable jerk of his neck, he asked them to leave.

'We still have to find Das,' Kaveri whispered to Ramu as she pulled him away, back towards the tent. 'Now that the gang has been arrested, surely he will have the sense to leave?'

38

A Missing Piece

Ramu patted down his uniform, removing fragments of leaves and sticks from it. Kaveri helped him spruce himself up, speaking to him urgently now that they were out of sight of the police. 'Something still does not make sense. I don't think we have all the pieces of the puzzle in place.'

'I agree,' Ramu said soberly. 'This seems far too easy. Such a simple plot – two men and a sack of explosives. Can this be all? The scene we saw in the circus, everything we have heard about the conspirators – they seem like intelligent men, people with a complex strategy deploying many moving pieces. Harish is a bully, with limited capacity for thought.'

'Let's find another place where we can talk without being overheard,' she breathed into his ear, as they moved further into the grove of trees. A small distance away, they spotted a small hut. The door was locked, but there was no one in sight. There, next to the wall, a cut tree stump provided a perfect spot for two people to sit. Heads close together, Kaveri and Ramu spoke in quiet voices.

'The police have been tricked – and so have we. Harish is only the sacrificial goat. It seems so stupid of him to have been standing around at the edge of the tent – almost as though someone wanted us to spot him. While we caught the small fry, the bigger fish will get away.' Ramu's foot swung restlessly.

'Some things just don't add up,' Kaveri agreed, pulling her notepad out of her sari blouse, where she had tucked it for safekeeping. 'Das said that Harish tried to blackmail him into working with them. I can't understand how Harish knew that Das was a fugitive, hiding from the police, suspected of murdering his wife in Calcutta seven years back. Someone who knew him before, someone from Calcutta, must have told him.'

She ticked off one finger, continuing. 'Second, Mala said repeatedly that she was unable to find out anything about the leader of the gang. We saw several masked men at the circus. But we found only four so far – Pawan, Ganesh, Harish and the fourth man who was just with him. Where is the leader, and the rest of the men? Are they somewhere else, planning another attack, leaving Harish and his short accomplice to be unwitting decoys? The way we captured them . . . it was surprisingly easy.'

Ramu nodded. 'And third, most important,' he interjected, 'we still don't know who killed Pawan and Pailwan Ganesh. We thought it was Harish, but now we know that's not true. You said that Harish assaulted Anandi, claiming she had murdered his brother and Pawan for the gold. If he didn't kill his brother and cousin, and doesn't know who did, then who could it be?'

Once, when she was a child, Kaveri had gone swimming in a muddy stream near her uncle's farm. Her foot had got caught in a plant growing on the side of the banks. Trapped in the muddy water, she had struggled to free herself. Before any damage was done, her uncle had pulled her out. Old memories came back to her in a flood, bringing a sense of breathlessness and unease. She hated it, this feeling of being unable to see the landscape in front of her with clarity.

'There is the clear signature of a mastermind plotter behind this,' Ramu said. 'Someone who knew Das in Calcutta, knew that he was Chatterjee. This may be the gang leader, the fearsome man Mrs Ismail said is the leader of this gang of thieves, who has recently come to Bangalore. A man who is intelligent enough to orchestrate a complex plot, using the Indian independence movement as a front to pull off a robbery.'

They heard the sound of trumpets heralding an announcement, followed by a loud voice booming over the megaphone announcing the arrival of the Prince in half an hour.

'Strange as it seems, I am beginning to think that our only hope lies in Das – the man we suspected of being involved in this trickery at first,' Ramu added. 'If he has set up a booth at the pageant, he must have something in mind. I'm sure he knows who the ringleader is.'

Kaveri riffled furiously through her notebook. 'Here is the page where I wrote down all that didn't make sense to me. Maybe that will offer us some clues.'

They studied it together. 'Why was Harish working with the government agent at the independence meeting?' Kaveri asked, pointing to one of the items on her list. 'The two men spoke in tandem, both trying to push the people at the meeting towards violence. That collaboration puzzled me. Why would a petty thief like Harish have spent time attending these meetings, exposing himself to risk, when he and his men could have worked alone to create chaos at the pageant? Why would Pawan's house have a flyer for the Congress meeting on the window? They did not have an iota of interest in the movement, or the fate of the country. They were only concerned with themselves and their profit.'

Kaveri stared at Ramu, her mind churning furiously. With every step they took, every leap of deduction, they seemed to be heading deeper into the morass.

'Unless . . .' Ramu tapped a rhythm on his knee. 'Harish's real motivation was not theft, but to sully the reputation of the independence movement. That is the only reason why a government agent would collaborate with a man like him.'

Kaveri gripped Ramu's leg, her heart pounding with the sheer thrill of working with her husband, her quick mind matching his as they laid the foundations of their case, argument by argument.

'And who else would want the Indian independence movement discredited, if not the British?' Kaveri said in a soft hiss. 'How easily fooled we were. We thought the motive behind all of this was theft, petty profit. It's far more dangerous. It's the death of the movement itself! The leader of the gang has to be Wilks!' She spoke rapidly, words tripping off her tongue as her mind churned with furious thoughts. 'Wilks came from Calcutta. He could have been connected to Das's past life. He even tried to warn us about Das, because he didn't want us getting too close to the magician – in case Das told us about him. Also, Chandru said he saw the wrestlers speaking to a tall man at night – a man who spoke with an accent. That fits – it could be Wilks.'

39

An Exposé

'Congratulations, Mrs Murthy. You are every bit as intelligent as my reports indicate.'

Kaveri jumped up as she heard a mocking voice behind them. She gripped Ramu's hand tightly as they turned to confront Wilks. Speaking in his characteristic clipped accent, the man strolled towards them, wearing his full regimental uniform. Ramu tightened his hold on Kaveri as Wilks revealed the pistol in his hand.

'Follow me inside.' Wilks waved the pistol at them, keeping a few steps behind as he directed them into the hut that had previously been locked. Inside, Kaveri shrank against the wall, eyes filled with dread as she saw a row of crates. The smell of gunpowder was strong in the confines of the small room.

Wilks smiled at her shocked face. 'Your reputation preceded you, but I see that you are not as clever as they make you out to be. You fell for a simple sleight of hand – thinking that Harish was the mastermind. Foolish fellow. He had his uses; muscle men usually do. But they can't think, you see.' He tapped his head with the gun. 'No brain cells here, only brawn. I told him to take one sack of explosives and stand in public view, talking to an associate. He didn't even question why.'

'What I can't understand is why you did it,' Kaveri asked.

Ramu looked at her in surprise. Her voice seemed respectful, admiring. She moved her foot slightly, pressing it against Ramu's in hidden warning, seeing him relax as he recognised the plan she had in mind. *Keep Wilks talking.*

She cast a surreptitious glance at Wilks' wristwatch. When Wilks had been facing them, holding the gun, over his shoulder she had caught a glimpse of a small boy stopping, taking in the sight of them, then running quickly away. Focused on them, with his back to Venu, Wilks had not seen him run for help. At least, Kaveri hoped that was what Venu had been doing. It felt like at least five minutes had passed since she had seen him go. If she kept Wilks talking, surely she could stretch the time out, keep him in the room until Venu arrived with help in the form of Inspector Ismail?

Wilks stared at her suspiciously, but Kaveri kept her eyes wide and naïve. 'We had no idea you were the man behind it until now. Meeting us to warn us of Das's connection to Kailash was a masterstroke. We thought that you had come to the circus to stop the thefts. In reality, you intervened only when you saw Ismail had already got his constables in place, didn't you? You distracted him with added instructions, slowing him down so that your men could get away.'

Slowly, Wilks nodded. 'It is a delight to talk this through with someone who has the intelligence to appreciate my planning. Why did I do it? To kill two birds with one stone. Destroy the petty little efforts of your countrymen for freedom – and line my pockets simultaneously. I did the same in Calcutta, several years ago. The circus performers had a simple racket going, cutting purses in the audience. I spotted their game as soon as I saw them, and realised they had potential. Men and women, each with unique skills – strength, power, flexibility, prestidigitation. They were an unruly mob, a mess. I formed them into a coherent, well-orchestrated team. Through my network of spies at work, I knew the homes of the wealthy businessmen who supported the independence movement. I trained them to attack those homes and steal the money meant for the so-called 'movement'. My superior officers did not know the details, of course. But they could see the results of my efforts – see the movement beginning to weaken as it was starved of funds – and they promoted me.

'Only that man – Chatterjee – and his wife frustrated me. She was intelligent, just like you. Her brother was involved with the movement. He told her about the homes that were being targeted. She became suspicious, asking the circus members who were part of my team questions about me. I had to kill her, otherwise word would have spread.'

Wilks studied Kaveri, his gaze cold and assessing. 'I am afraid I will have to finish you both, too. There is very little time remaining, as my men will be here soon.' He studied his wristwatch. 'In fifteen minutes, the Prince of Wales will be here. This room is packed with crates full of explosives. Ten minutes after he arrives, when we take him to the side of the lake, to see the women dance – there will be a series of explosions. No one will die – except for a few dancers, people like that. No one important. But my men will be there, ready to exploit the chaos.' For a second, his face contorted with emotion, as he snarled, 'This time, I will make sure the gold doesn't leave my sight.'

His face cleared, looking calm again. He raised his weapon slowly. Kaveri looked at him, blinking as a flash of sunlight came through the high window. She saw Venu's face, slowly peering into the room. He waved his hand in a spiral, as though he was cranking a record playing one of his favourite music songs on a gramophone. *Keep him talking.*

'Wait,' Kaveri said hastily. *Where was Ismail?* 'I understand now why you killed Mansee. And I figured out why you killed Pawan too. Pawan double-crossed you and stole everything. But why kill Ganesh?'

Wilks looked annoyed but lowered the gun. 'I wanted to search Pawan's house for the gold. When I entered, I found him also looking for it, planning to keep it for himself no doubt. I couldn't permit that. We exchanged words, and the man had the temerity to try to attack me. He got what he deserved.' Wilks raised his pistol again.

'One last question,' Kaveri spoke again. 'Why did you send a policeman to guard our house?'

'You're not as clever as you think, are you?' Wilks jeered. 'I wanted the policeman to keep an eye on you, so that you wouldn't go off and search for Das. I stationed Harish in front of your house as a backup. But then I realised my mistake – I needed to find and eliminate Das, and for that, I needed to let you roam free. So I asked Ismail to withdraw the policeman, and told Harish to leave. But I came in his stead, keeping a watch on your home from a distance. I told your neighbour, Mr Swamy, that I needed his house for a day for some official work. Stupid man, didn't even ask why, just handed over his home to me. I saw you leave in the car, and followed you in Swamy's vehicle, staying at a safe distance.'

He gave her a sharp look. 'And that's the last question you'll get to ask, Kaveri Murthy. I know exactly what you're doing – trying to distract me, hoping the police will come looking for you. Your flat-footed policeman friend won't be able to save you, you know. He's thick-headed, like all native policemen. It won't even occur to him that a British officer like me could be the man behind all of this.' Wilks aimed his gun at her, cocking back the trigger as he squinted down the barrel.

Was this the end, then? Kaveri moved closer to Ramu, placing her shoulder against his arm. If they died, they would go together. Her nostalgia about a different life melted like salt in water, her desires to go to Madras and study by herself seeming petty, insignificant. She would not have exchanged this life, with Ramu, for any other.

Ramu stepped in front of her, trying to cover her with his body. Refusing to let him risk his life for her, she pulled him back, standing side by side with him, fingers tightly clasped in his. Bracing to take the force of the bullet, Kaveri gulped in relief as she saw Ismail's face appear at the window. Ismail held up his fingers, imitating a gun, then raised his other hand, knocking the imaginary gun down.

Kaveri looked across at Ramu, noting his almost imperceptible nod. If Ismail and his men burst in, they would be risking Ramu and Kaveri's lives. The gun was pointed directly at them. They needed to disarm Wilks first.

'You aren't as clever as you believe, you know,' she informed Wilks, raising her chin. 'You didn't find the gold. Pawan hid it in plain sight. Even *he* was cleverer than you.'

Wilks' face contorted with rage. 'You're lying. Where did he hide it?' He advanced on her, waving the gun in the air. 'There was nothing in that house. Not even a chair to sit on, or a rug. Even the windows were boarded up with planks, not curtains.'

'There were a pair of dumbbells,' Kaveri reminded him, keeping an eye on the gun. He had taken a step closer to her now, his face incandescent with anger. She sent up a quick prayer to Raghavendra Swami, asking him to keep them safe. A couple of inches closer and she could—

Yes! Wilks was in range. He held the gun steady, squinting as he stabilised it in both hands, aiming it directly at her. She pretended to faint in fear. Wilks grinned in satisfaction, moving close to her. Kaveri reversed direction, catching Wilks off guard as she took a quick step toward him. She raised her foot in a high kick, as her elderly *kalari* teacher had taught her, giving a high war cry – *aieee* – and hit his wrist with her foot, sending the gun spinning through the air. Ramu dived at it, picking it up and turning to Wilks, his chest heaving as he held it high, aimed directly at him.

Wilks screamed, a high-pitched keening as he cradled his right hand with his left. 'My wrist! You've broken my wrist, you she-devil.'

His face contorted with fury, Wilks moved forward, heedless of the gun that Ramu held steady before him. Just as Ramu braced himself to fire, the police burst through the door, Venu at their heels. 'Major Wilks – you are under arrest,' Ismail intoned in his most official voice. A burly constable placed a handcuff around the Englishman's left hand, chaining him to his own wrist as he pulled him away. He went, still screaming in pain as he held his fractured right hand, volubly protesting as he was dragged away, unable to believe that the Indian police would dare arrest a British officer like him.

40

The Last Step

'Wilks said his men would be here in five minutes,' Kaveri exclaimed. 'What if they see he's been arrested, and escape?'

'We have captured them already,' Ismail reassured her. 'On the way to get me, Venu saw Wilks' men standing in a group by the side of the lake. When he told me, I sent my men to round them up. When we realised that the gang uses tattoos to signal their membership, it became easy – all we had to do was to seal the exits and inspect the faces of each person in the pavilion carefully. The whole gang is in our custody now, and the Prince is safe.'

Kaveri took Ramu aside, watching as Ismail ordered his men to seize the crates of explosives in the room. 'Soak them in water from the lake,' she heard him tell the men. 'Make sure they cannot be used by anyone.' She saw Venu running alongside the constables, showing them where the cans of water were stored.

'The Prince may be safe, but we still don't know what Das has in mind. While the Inspector is busy, we have to find him. We don't have much time,' she hissed into Ramu's ear, pulling him with her. They ran to the main pavilion, where Das's stall had been set up.

Steadying themselves as they ran over the slippery leaves, they arrived at the pavilion. Just as they reached the entrance, British officers appeared in front of them. 'Clear the way,' an Englishman ordered, roughly shouldering them aside.

'They think we are just the cleaners,' Kaveri whispered to Ramu as the officers pushed past them into the tent. 'We have to tell Das that the gang has been captured and it is safe for him to leave. He has to get away before the police find him.'

Ramu looked around helplessly. British policemen were everywhere, slapping their batons on their palms, making the cleaners line up along the wall. Nearby, they saw the expensively clad guests standing in a queue, waiting to receive their royal visitor.

Kaveri felt Ramu press her hand again, warning her to stay quiet. There was no point in trying to speak to the officers. They were dressed as cleaners, and the British would not believe them. Kaveri looked around frantically. She saw Suman standing against the opposite side of the pavilion. Dropping his arm to his side, he subtly pointed with his finger, nudging Kaveri's attention towards one particular stall.

She would never have recognised the stall's owner as Das if Suman had not pointed him out, Kaveri thought, tugging at Ramu's hand and nodding in his direction. The man appeared completely different – taller, thicker, more heavyset. He wore a turban and had shaved off his moustache and beard. He was sitting on a bench, looking unconcerned as he bent over a magnifying glass, painting something onto a tiny grain of rice affixed to a small piece of paperboard.

Kaveri and Ramu looked at each other helplessly. Surrounded by uniformed police, they could not move.

To the sound of trumpets, the Prince of Wales entered.

'We cannot do anything now, Kaveri,' Ramu whispered to her, tugging his cap lower to obscure his face, then stepping back and pulling Kaveri with him. 'Ismail shouldn't see us now. Let's wait. Our only hope now is for Das to realise that the gang have been captured and keep a low profile.'

Kaveri stared at the Prince. He looked as handsome as the newspapers had described. He was also as much of a ladies' man as they said he was, she thought, wrinkling her nose as she saw him take the hand of a pretty young woman showing him a swathe of embroidered silk. The fair-haired woman flushed and giggled as the Prince raised her hands towards his lips. Kaveri reflexively rubbed her hand against her sari. How did these foreign people tolerate such permissiveness? She would not like to have her hand kissed by an unfamiliar man, even if he was the Prince of Wales himself.

She saw Suman stare at his father with anxious eyes as the Prince and his entourage ambled through the exhibition, stopping at the stalls that caught his fancy. Time crawled, agonisingly slowly, as the procession kept stopping for its members to appreciate the fine embroidery and lace crochet. The Prince seemed to avoid all the stalls with men, making a beeline for the younger women.

When they reached the stall with the rice grains, Das stood up and bowed deeply to the Prince of Wales. The Prince stopped and looked at him curiously. Kaveri felt Ramu gripping her hand tightly. Dread soaked her every pore as she tried to get closer, to hear what Das was saying. She saw Suman inching past the servants lined up on the other side of the tent, trying to reach his father too.

Das handed the Prince a grain of rice in a velvet box with a deep bow, saying, 'A gift from a humble man to a great Prince.'

The Prince took the box, opening it and examining the grain of rice with interest. He took out the tiny magnifying glass inside the box and peered at the grain. Then his face darkened. With a muttered oath, he threw the box down. It landed violently on the floor, skittering away to rest near a pillar a few feet from Kaveri and Ramu.

'Arrest the man!' he said, turning away curtly.

Das pulled off his fake beard and turban as the police surrounded him, raising their guns. He raised both hands in the air in surrender. As they moved close to him, he quickly lowered one hand, pulling a sign from his pocket. Before the police could react, he unfurled the sign, holding it high for all to read. 'Quit India'. The words were printed on the sign in bold letters. The people in the room all looked at each other, exchanging shocked murmurs. Kaveri saw Suman's eyes filling with tears of pride.

The British police, with guns drawn, were everywhere now. Ramu moved protectively closer to Kaveri as the police fanned out close to them. Handcuffing Das, a policeman jerked at his cuffs, pulling him roughly so that he stumbled after them. They passed Suman, who was now sobbing. Suman reached out a hand to his father, but Das looked away from him, not wanting to implicate his son. 'Long live the Indian Motherland,' he said loudly, before being dragged out of the pavilion. Kaveri and Ramu stood silently as the Prince marched on, his back stiff with annoyance.

Holding their brooms, they moved around the corner of the tent, pretending to clean up. Rushing from the tent, the crowd passed them without a second glance.

In a short while, the tent was completely empty. Kaveri and Ramu made their way towards the box with the rice grain, now lying forgotten in a corner.

Suman got up, wiping his eyes, and joined them. He picked up the grain of rice, inspecting it closely. Kaveri went to the stall where she had seen Das, returning with the magnifying glass that he had left behind. On the grain of rice, Das had painted the *charkha*, the spinning wheel that symbolised the independence movement.

'That's the flag that the Provisional Government of Free India adopted in 1921,' Ramu said to Kaveri and Venu, who had just come up behind them. 'No wonder the Prince was so angry. Das managed to do what no one else was able to, in Bombay or Calcutta. To hand the heir to the throne a symbol of Indian independence!'

'What a brave man,' Kaveri responded softly. Suman did not respond, but his eyes, shining with intermingled sorrow and pride, spoke for themselves.

41

Odds and Ends

A week later, the room resounded with laughter, as the members of the Bangalore Detectives Club got together over afternoon tea and snacks. Putta was in food heaven, wagging his tail furiously as he went from seat to seat, cajoling the club out of bits of *bendekaayi bajji* and *alugedde bonda*.

Absently scratching Putta's ears as he spoke, Suman looked at Kaveri, tears shimmering at the corners of his eyes. 'Everyone has a plan. I am the only one who doesn't know what to do, now that my father is in jail.'

'You should revert to being a girl,' Kaveri responded. 'It suits you better.'

Suman jerked back, pushing his chair away and standing up abruptly. Startled, Putta moved back, giving a small bark as he looked up at Suman.

'How did you know?' Suman demanded, turning to Kaveri.

'Both Ramu and I realised it when you were in Mala's house, recovering from your injuries. You pushed him away when he tried to examine your injuries, and the wet neck of your kurta clung to your body – we both realised at the same time.' Kaveri looked directly at Suman. 'How many secrets will you hide from us?'

'No more secrets. I will tell you everything.' Suman spoke up. 'My real name is Tamanna. When we left Calcutta, my father took me to smaller villages and towns. We moved from place to place, hiding our identities. My father often left me alone for hours, looking for new jobs, scouting out safe places to stay. It was not safe for a young girl to be alone, in strange places. He made me disguise myself as a boy. It helped us if we changed our identities further. I was learning to be an acrobat in Calcutta, but after my mother died, I began to train with my father. No one connected Mr Chatterjee of Bombay, a magician with a daughter who was an acrobat, with Mr Das of Bangalore, with a son who was also a magician.'

'You should embrace your identity as a woman. Change your name again. With your father in jail, it is best for you to take on a new identity, so that the police will not bother you.' Mala pursed her lips. 'They are still searching for the man who threw the daggers, attacking an agent of the government. If they see you visit your father, they will start investigating your past too, and eventually find out what you did. Word gets around.'

'I can take you with me,' Lakamma offered. 'I live alone at home. It gets lonely sometimes. I will be happy to take you, and sponsor your launch as a new discovery. Women magicians are a rarity, and I can easily help you gain some prominence.'

'Lakamma aunty, thank you so much, I will take up your offer for now, and change my identity. But I will never abandon my father.' Suman's voice rang out loud and clear. 'Wilks went mad as the Indian police dragged him away. He could not believe they had the audacity to arrest a British officer. He was even more horrified to find that the British administration, shocked by his deeds, essentially disowned him, disclaiming knowledge of his shenanigans aimed at discrediting the movement. Trying to explain his past doings, Wilks tied himself in knots, confessing to my mother's murder but trying to claim he had killed her to protect the British Raj. Thanks to his statement, my father is finally free of the charge of murder – though he is now arrested for what he painted on the grain of rice he handed Prince Edward, for supporting the cause of independence.' Suman looked weary, but his voice rang with pride. 'One day, my father will be released without a stain on his name. That day may come one, five or ten years from now. I will be ready and waiting when he is freed, to assume a new life with him.'

'If they release your father, you will have to escape with him again, to a new place, and change your identity,' Kaveri warned.

'We have done it twice already. A third time will not be difficult,' Suman said, shrugging her shoulders.

Kaveri clapped her hands, waiting for everyone to stop talking. 'I have one more piece of good news for you,' she said, calling Anandi over.

Anandi made her way to the front of the room. Her face was still pale, and the mottled bruises around her neck marred her delicate beauty. But she was strong and resilient, Kaveri thought, surveying her fondly. Like most women of Kaveri's acquaintance, Anandi would bend, but not break.

'Anandi, this belongs to you now.' Kaveri handed an envelope to her. 'Inspector Ismail gave this cheque to me. It is a reward given by the wealthy families whom Pawan stole from, for recovering some of their wealth.

It rightfully belongs to you. I found the gold in the dumbbells – but you were the one who almost lost your life because of the stolen gold.'

'I don't want any of it,' Anandi said fiercely. 'It is blood money, from an act of evil. I will give it to you, Shanthi *akka*. You can use it to train more women, rescue them from abusive homes – like mine was – and educate them, so they can go on to save more women. Just like Kaveri *akka* is doing.' She looked at Kaveri. 'I did not wish Pawan dead. It is not good to wish *anyone* dead. But with his passing, for the first time in many years, I feel finally free. I can live my life in peace, without forever looking over my shoulder, worried that he may return.'

A chorus of agreement came from all the women in the room. They crowded around Kaveri, congratulating her.

She smiled weakly at them, but they were too close. She felt suffocated as they came to hug her, her breathing shallow as she struggled to take in fresh air. She turned from them abruptly, running to the back of the shed, where she threw up.

Bhargavi brought her a cloth, and sponged her face, all the while smiling.

'I have thought for some time . . . when you were dizzy, and then nauseous, but then you did not say anything, and I did not know if I was right or wrong. But maybe you just did not realise,' Bhargavi said, while Kaveri looked at her blankly. Uma aunty joined them, also smiling. But Kaveri felt like she had before she had confronted Wilks – as though she was swimming sluggishly through a murky pond.

Bhargavi supported her, bringing her back to sit on the sofa and handing her a delicate handkerchief soaked in camphor. Kaveri pressed it to her nose, inhaling deeply as she felt her stomach beginning to settle.

'Have you been nauseous for some days, my dear? Tired, sluggish? As though your brain doesn't function clearly?'

'Yes,' Kaveri said, surprised that Bhargavi knew all of this. 'It's the stress of this case. It's been much worse than the past two cases. Like a lump in my stomach.'

Bhargavi shook her head, grinning. Even Anandi was beaming now. Why did they have such foolish grins on their faces?

'When did you get your last period?' Mala asked.

Kaveri looked at her, surprised. 'I can't remember,' she said slowly. 'I think . . . sometime back . . . in November, just after Deepawali?'

'It is not the stress of the case that's making your stomach heave. It's your child. You have a baby growing in there.' Bhargavi leaned across, patting Kaveri's belly gently.

Kaveri looked at her, mouth agape. A foolish grin swept over her own face. Her close brush with death had spooked her more than she liked to admit. Confronted with her own mortality, she had started to think more intensely about whether she really wanted to postpone motherhood for several years while she focused on studying further. How strange this week had been. She had almost lost her life, along with her husband's, and now – she had found she carried another, miraculous life within her.

'So that's what it is,' she murmured. 'The best gift of all.'

42

Epilogue

A month later, Kaveri's nausea had receded. Ravenously hungry all the time, she was tucking into a plate of food – her second breakfast of the day, even though it was just 9 a.m. Licking her plate clean, she looked with greed at the bowl of *shavige payasa* that Bhargavi had placed in front of her along with a piece of mango pickle. Ramu made a face, and she ignored him. She would have found the combination of pickle and sweet inedible too, just a few weeks back – but now it was a combination she craved. Bhargavi made a fresh bottle of pickle for her each week, but it was never enough.

Venu burst into the room. 'Akka! I have big news. Das has escaped.'

'What?' Kaveri leaped up.

'It was a daring midnight escape, last night. I just heard about it. He was being held with other prisoners in a low security prison, and he created an illusion of some sort – made the jailers think the bars were being bent open, and snakes coming out to attack them. They fled, leaving the

321

keys behind, and Das made his escape with the rest of the non-violent protestors. Some were caught and retaken, but Das was not found.'

'Can you run to Suman – to Tamanna – and see if she knows? Ask her if she needs any help from us,' Kaveri said. But just as she spoke, she heard the telephone ring.

'Lakamma?' Kaveri knew what she would say before the older woman spoke.

'My tenant has left for quarters unknown,' she said. 'I just thought you should know.' With that, she placed the phone down.

'So Tamanna has joined her father after all.' A foolish grin spread across Kaveri's face. 'The British police must be furious, to have the man who cheeked the Prince of Wales himself disappear from jail.' She tucked into her plate with relish. 'Maybe Ismail had a role in it,' she murmured to herself. 'Perhaps he and his men turned a blind eye to Das's plans.' She knew Ismail would never tell her the truth.

A few weeks later, Kaveri was reading the newspaper and trying to decide if she had the space in her stomach to begin on her third meal of the day – though it was only 10 a.m., Bhargavi had just placed a bowl of freshly cut guavas in front of her. Chewing on a piece of the fruit, Kaveri jumped up with a grin, calling out for Ramu and Bhargavi to join her. 'A young woman magician has appeared in Ahmedabad,' she read out from the paper slowly. 'She calls herself Menaka, after the celestial being known for her beauty and intelligence. She claims to have come from Nepal and has captivated the entire city.'

'That is all? No mention of a father?' Bhargavi asked.

'He must be with her, but lying low.' Kaveri looked at Ramu. 'What must the father-daughter duo be planning next?'

'Perhaps they will join the groups congregating at Gandhiji's *ashram* in the city, on the Sabarmati River,' Ramu said.

'I wonder what news we might hear from them in the years to come.'

They heard the doorbell ring. The mailman stood at the door, holding an envelope.

Kaveri brought it in, opening it as soon as she had closed the door. Then she looked at Ramu, puzzled. The envelope was empty.

'Look inside carefully,' Ramu said.

Kaveri slit the envelope open, but there was nothing inside. She ran her fingers across the paper, stopping when she felt a small bump in one corner. Ramu, watching intently, passed her his penknife. She inserted the narrow blade of the knife into the bumpy corner, opening it and shaking it over the wooden table. A grain of rice fell out.

Kaveri picked up the magnifying glass she always kept close by, and peered through it, studying the single grain. Painted with a delicate hand, the grain depicted a woman in a sari – her, she realised -- with a magnifying glass, a typewriter, and a dog at her heels. On top of the scene, in flowing script, a painted scroll contained the words 'The Bangalore Detectives Club'.

Kaveri's eyes filled with tears as she looked at the grain, sending Das her silent thanks. Bhargavi and Ramu clustered around Kaveri, looking through the magnifying glass at her side, holding her close.

Kaveri's Dictionary

ajji – grandmother

akka – older sister, honorific used to address an older woman

almirah – cupboard

ammaavare – mother, honorific used to address an older woman

anna – older brother, honorific used to address an older man

annas – unit of currency – in British India, 16 annas equaled one rupee

appa – father

apsara – celestial Indian spirits famed for their beauty

ashram – hermitage

avallaki – parboiled, flattened rice

athe – mother-in-law

ayyo – flexible exclamation used to express shock, grief, disapproval, pity or allied emotions

barfi – solid, dense Indian sweet, usually served in rectangular or diamond shapes

bhayandanguli – colloquial, someone who is easily scared

bidi – hand rolled cigarette

chee – expression of disgust

dharma – duty

grahana – eclipse

hundi – money box for cash offered by devotees, usually found in temples

idli – savoury steamed cake made from a batter of fermented rice and lentils, traditionally eaten for breakfast

jamkhana – hand woven cotton rug used as a carpet

kamblihula – small bristly caterpillar that, when touched, causes intense itching

kalarippayattu – ancient Indian martial art from Kerala, believed to be thousands of years old

laddu – round sweet

lathi – large, heavy stick

lungi – loose piece of unstitched cloth worn around the waist by men

namaskara – respectful greeting

paan – betel nut leaf, with various additions, commonly eaten after meals

pallu – the loose end of a sari, usually draped over the shoulder

panchanga – Indian calendar which follows Indian systems of timekeeping. Used by many households to ascertain dates and times and dates of religious significance to Hindus

payasa – Indian sweet

pranayama – Indian breathing technique used in yoga

purdah – head covering for women, seclusion of women

prasada – sacred offering given to devotees

pravachna – religious exposition

pudi – powder

puja – Hindu rituals of worship

rangoli – a common household art, in which geometric patterns are drawn on the floor in front of a house every morning, using rice powder or chalk – considered auspicious, bringing good luck to the home

rava – semolina, coarsely ground wheat

sambhar – sour and spicy lentil dish with vegetables

saaru – sour and spicy watery dish made with lentils

swami – honorific title of a holy man or woman

thumba – extremely

tiffin – light meal of snacks

uppittu – savoury breakfast dish made from semolina – broken wheat

vada – savoury fried snack

yakshagana – traditional street theatre art form of south India, with performers wearing colourful costumes with masks and elaborate face make-up

Kaveri's Beauty Routine

Face scrub – hesarbele hittu (moong dal flour) – Uma aunty's recipe

Take 250 grams or half a pound of moong dal, split or whole, preferably with the green skin still intact (you can also use red lentils, or masoor dal, as a substitute). Grind it into a coarse powder. Once it cools (the powder will heat up slightly in the grinder), mix with a tablespoon of organic turmeric, and store it in an airtight jar. Bhargavi prepares a fresh batch of this scrub for Kaveri every month.

Before sleeping at night, Kaveri takes a tablespoon of *hittu* and mixes it with a spoon of milk to make a thick paste. She massages the paste into her face and neck with her fingers for a couple of minutes, making small circular movements to lightly scrub her skin - then washes it off with cold water, gently patting her face dry with a thin cotton towel. Afterwards, Kaveri rubs a teaspoon of fresh cream onto her face and neck, leaving it overnight.

Hesarbele exfoliates and brightens the skin: like many lentils, it is rich in vitamins that are good for the skin. Turmeric evens out skin tone, reduces inflammation, and tackles pimples and acne, while yoghurt softens and moisturises the skin. The cream acts as a moisturiser, keeping her skin soft and smooth. Kaveri skims the cream from the top of the unhomogenized milk that they get from Venu's cow, Kasturi, but you can use cream purchased from the market.

Face pack – Badami hittu (almond powder) – Mala's recipe

Soak 8-10 almonds in a small amount of water overnight. Next morning, grind them into a fine paste with a tablespoon of milk. Add a pinch of cinnamon powder and a tablespoon of honey. Apply over your face and leave it to dry, then wash it off with cold water.

Mala once recommended this to Kaveri after she spent the day outdoors in the hot sun when working on a case, and got an allergic skin rash. The combination of almond and cinnamon soothes the skin and acts as an antiseptic to prevent infections, while honey and milk hydrate the skin. Mala uses the skin pack twice a week. Kaveri lacks patience – she only applies the face mask on Sundays, when she is not working on a case, and if she remembers!

Nellikai-karubevu hair oil – Kaveri's mother's recipe

Take 250 ml of cold pressed sesame oil, and heat it on medium flame in a large heavy bottomed vessel. When the oil becomes smoking hot, add half a cup of deseeded, crushed Indian gooseberries (these are not the same as American gooseberries), and continue to cook on medium flame for five to ten minutes until the juice of the gooseberry dries up, and the residue begins to shrink and turn brown. Then add half a cup of coarsely chopped fresh curry leaves, and one teaspoon of fenugreek seeds, and cook for another five to ten minutes until the curry leaves start to crisp up and turn brown. Turn off the flame, and let it cool – then filter the oil using a thin cloth towel (you can also use a strainer with a very fine mesh).

Kaveri's mother makes this for the entire family in Mysore, and sends a few bottles at a time to her daughter's home in Bangalore. Once a week, Kaveri decants a few tablespoons of oil into a bowl and heats it with a couple of peppercorns. She applies the warm oil to her scalp and throughout her hair, massaging it in and leaving it on for an hour, and then washes it off. Sesame oil acts like a conditioner, while curry leaves keep her hair black and free from dandruff, and the fenugreek and Indian gooseberry promote hair growth. It is also extremely relaxing – when Kaveri needs to relax after a tough case, Ramu insists she applies hair oil and has a 'head bath' – she is sure to sleep very well that night, waking up stress-free and refreshed the next morning.

Rose water: Bhargavi's recipe

Take a couple of roses (ideally home grown – but definitely organic, and pesticide-free) and remove and wash the petals. In a small steel vessel, take a glass of water, add the rose petals, and cook on medium flame for about twenty minutes until the water reduces to half the original volume. Let it cool, and remove the petals with a clean spoon.

Rose water is excellent at soothing the eyes and reducing eye strain. When Kaveri returns from an afternoon at the Sir Sheshadri Memorial Library in Bangalore, after poring through bundles of old newspapers, Bhargavi insists that she lies down in a cool dark room, placing a thin piece of cotton soaked in rose water on her eyes. This eye mask makes her feel better almost instantly, reducing puffiness. Rose water can also be used on the face and skin to soothe inflamed, itching skin. You can also purchase it from the market – but it is most effective when made at home and used fresh, soon after preparation. It can be stored in an air tight vessel for a day in the fridge, but not for longer.

Detoxifying lemon water – Rajamma's recipe

Squeeze half a lemon into one large glass of water, and add a couple of slices of fresh ginger root, a pinch of salt, a pinch of pepper, a tablespoon of honey, and a sprig of fresh mint (optional). Leave it to sit for a few minutes so that the flavours can meld, and then - enjoy.

Kaveri drinks this delicious detoxifying juice after applying her face mask and hair oil. It refreshes her, and gives her something to do while she's waiting. She recognizes the importance of beauty routines, and the need to take care of her skin and hair – but she also tends to get impatient with them. She wants to be done with everything quickly, so that she can go to her studio and open her maths book, or start work on a new case that has grabbed her attention!

Note: Do remember that what works for Kaveri need not work for everyone else – do check for allergies and test this out on a small scale to see that it suits you before going ahead with any of these. And please avoid these beauty recipes if you are allergic to specific ingredients (like almonds).

Historical note

The historical setting of Bangalore in January 1922 is largely accurate, with a few exceptions. The Krishnarajasagara dam, which the Prince of Wales visits in this book, was indeed one of the largest dams in Asia – but it was still being constructed in January 1922. Work on the Brindavan Gardens, which housed the musical fountain, was only initiated in 1927. The violence at Chaura Chauri, to which Shanthi refers in the book, took place a few weeks *after* the Prince's visit to Bangalore, on 4th February 1922. British police aimed their guns at Indian protestors, who retaliated by setting fire to a police station, and 25 people lost their lives, including several policemen. The ensuing violence deeply affected Gandhi and the Indian National Congress, who halted the non-cooperation movement – this decision agitated Subhas Chandra Bose, who disagreed with Gandhi, feeling that India should adopt a more aggressive path of nationalism. I have taken authorial liberties in advancing some of these timelines.

Prince Edward visited Bangalore on 18 January 1922, and inspected his troops, seizing the chance to play a game of polo. He was welcomed by a Municipal address at Cubbon Park and a grand reception at the Residency. But he did not visit a lake. It was another visiting prince, Albert Victor, who came to Bangalore in November 1889, and was welcomed by a pageant on the Dharmambudhi lake, in front of the railway station. The Kannada writer and poet D V Gundappa described the pageant in lyrical language, talking of the beauty of the Bharatnatyam dancers who welcomed the Prince, and the floating coracle boats with lamps that lit up the lake. It was such a picturesque setting for a murder attempt – I had to move it into this book!

The Shanthi Womens' Home is fictional, but loosely based on the Seva Sadan Society in Mumbai. Established for 'oppressed women' in Bombay in 1908, the shelter trained women to become independent, teaching them sports (table tennis was popular with many of the women), equipping them with skills in embroidery and cooking, and running a teacher training school for women.

Coffeepudi Lakamma is modelled after D. Sakamma, an inspiring woman who lived in Bangalore in the 1920s and ran a famous coffee industry. Married at sixteen, she was the third wife of a rich coffee planter in Coorg. When Sakamma's son was just a year old, her husband died of a sudden illness, with his other two wives. Barely eighteen, she was left in sole charge of a large plantation. She took over the plantation and moved to Bangalore, setting up a coffee shop and processing unit which supplied the rich and famous of the city.

Kaveri is fascinated by machines, so I had to include a few here. Harvey's Pneumatic Dusting Machine first made its way to the India Office Library in August 1904. Libraries expended a great deal of time, effort and money in dusting their books. It took two years for twelve men to dust all the books in the British Library, after which they had to begin all over again. Given the time it took for some of these technologies to make their way to India on ship, it is quite possible that the Sheshadri Iyer Memorial Library in Bangalore acquired such a machine only in 1922. Pencil sharpeners, on the other hand, were invented in 1822 – a whole century before Ramu ordered them from a catalogue for his wife. But they were not in common use in India even as late as the 1970s, when I went to school. Most people still used an old razor blade to sharpen their pencils – I did too, and had nicks and cuts all over my fingers to show for it!

India's freedom fighters deployed a number of innovative ways to signal to each other – including the practice of leaving moist cowdung pats outside a building where a meeting was in place, and placing small piles of twigs on the ground. I am indebted to P. Sainath's book of interviews, The Last Heroes: Foot Soldiers of Indian Freedom, for insights into these lived experiences.

Jadoo, the Indian art of magic, was fascinating to read about too. Western magicians were obsessed with the exotic 'oriental' practice of *jadoo,* hungry to learn these acts. Performing at the Chicago World Fair in 1893, a young Harry Houdini blackened his face and dressed as a 'Hindu fakir'. At the same time, many western magicians also sought to discredit their practitioners, labelling them as fraudulent tricksters, trying to expose their supposed charlatanry by proffering rational explanations for their acts of magic. (Wilkie Collins' *The Moonstone* is a perfect example of this kind of description.) One can only speculate, but there must have been many magicians like Das, irritated by this simultaneous appropriation and dismissal of their heritage.

Finally, it is unlikely that Kaveri would have been able to openly learn and practice *kalaripayattu* in the 1920s. A martial art used in Wayanad for a revolt against the British, it was banned by the British government in the early nineteenth century – though it continued to survive as a form of covert resistance, encouraged by the Swadeshi movement against British colonial rule, passed on from teacher to student in secrecy. It is a wonderful martial art, one that Kaveri enjoys – and finds very useful in her line of work.

Acknowledgements

This book would not be what it is without Venkatachalam Suri and Dhwani Nagendra Suri, my husband and daughter, who have brainstormed ideas with me, and read, edited and commented on multiple drafts of the book. Dhwani was not yet born when I started writing the Bangalore Detectives Club – it has been so lovely to watch the series come to life as she grew, started to read and added her strong feminist perspective. And without Chalam, who has been my support, inspiration and sounding board for ideas for thirty years, none of this would have been possible. Their love and support makes it all possible.

This book is also for my grandmother Thungabai, who tied knots into her sari to remind herself of the many things she needed to do – her early version of the digital calendars we now find so indispensable! And for my most beloved father, CV Nagendra, who hooked me onto mysteries early. I know he's burning the telephone lines up in the sky, calling up his friends to tell them his daughter wrote this series!

This book is a tribute to all the remarkable women who lived in times past, including my great grandmothers Ammanithai Ammalu and Padmavati Bai, the real-life women who inspired characters in the book such as Coffeepudi Sakamma and Kalyanamma, and many others. Defying societal restrictions to forge their own path, they blazed the way for generations to follow – as Kaveri, Anandi, Bhargavi, Mala, Mrs. Ismail, Shanthi, Uma aunty, and the other women of the Bangalore Detectives Club are doing.

Family stories, reminiscences and recipes shared by my mother Manjula gave me an intimate view into the lives of women and men who lived more than a century ago, impossible to get from books and maps alone. Since Bangalore's history is an area of professional research for me (as part of my day job as an ecologist), I also benefited from a treasure trove of information on colonial Bangalore. I am indebted to a number of archives, including the Karnataka State Archives, the Mythic Society, the Indian Institute of World Culture, and the British Library.

Priya Doraswamy, childhood friend and incomparable agent, has been the best advocate for the book that I could ever wish for. And I truly lucked out with a dream team of publishers, with editorial inputs from Rebekah West and Krystyna Green at Little, Brown, Tom Feltham's insightful copyedits, and the terrific support provided by Claiborne Hancock, Jessica Case and Meghan Jusczak at Pegasus Books in the US, as well as Thomas Abraham, Riti Jagoorie, Naina Tripathi and Raghu Nandan at Hachette in India.

Above all, I am deeply thankful to the number of readers who have reached out to me over the past two years to share their love for Kaveri, Ramu and the rest of the Bangalore Detectives Club crew, exchanging so many of their own stories in turn. I have made so many friends in different continents thanks to these books – your support and enthusiasm keeps me afloat!

Harini Nagendra is a Professor of Sustainability at Azim Premji University, Bangalore, India, and the author of *Nature in the City: Bengaluru in the Past, Present and Future*. She received a 2013 Elinor Ostrom Senior Scholar award for her research and practice on issues of the urban commons, and a 2007 Cozzarelli Prize with Elinor Ostrom from the Proceedings of the US National Academy of Sciences for research on sustainability. *The Bangalore Detectives Club*, the first book in the Detective Kaveri mysteries, is her first fiction novel.